I0762169

THE BRIDE OF ATLANTIS

MAYA GRYFFIN

FIRST EDITION

For Pavol

One

A fire warms my back as I look out over the icy land.

Winter.

We weren't supposed to still be here by now.

"Shut the door," my husband says behind me. "You'll let the cold in."

It's barely first light outside. I close the door, and turn. The fire crackles behind him, lighting him up in its golden glow—but he'd glow anyway, fire or no fire. My husband may be a fallen god with waning powers, but he still looks every bit the part. Any mortal would know by looking at him that he's a creature of some other realm.

At least, they would know it for a moment or two, before the sight scrambled their brains and drove them crazy. Humans aren't supposed to look at gods, and especially not *this* god. It is some special curse he was born under: all the gods are born beautiful, but not like this. Not the kind of beauty that destroys the senses. As to why I can look upon him when other mortals can't, well, it's a mystery. I don't know why I'm the exception to the rule. I'd like to say it's the work of the Fates, allowing us some special kindness, only I know the Fates don't deal much in free favors.

Besides, it's not the only thing about me that's not quite ordinary.

"You're daydreaming again," he says, teasing me or chastising me, I can't tell.

"I'm thinking of Atlantis."

He nods.

"Soon," he says.

*

Atlantis is where we have been bound these many months, though it has been a slow journey, and halted completely when winter fell. If we weren't hiding from all the gods of Mount Olympus, it would have been a different story. But to hide from their gaze we must journey as mortals do, slow and steady. And this winter was much harsher than any I have known before. We began our journey to Atlantis before the leaves started to turn—I thought then we'd arrive before the last leaves had fallen from the trees. But a journey that, even for mortal travelers, should have taken no more than a short season, has taken us two long ones.

The snows were so heavy that many of the roads became impassable, and the blizzards too harsh for a mortal like me to travel in. Not to mention the rivers froze solid and ice cracked the trees in droves, throwing them across the mountain paths. When it thawed, the ice melts flooded many towns. Everyone says they've never known a season like this one, not even in the north do they have such weather. The gods are angry, they say. And well they may be. The world is in uproar—in its weather, in its peace among men, or lack thereof. Sometimes I even wonder if we're the cause of it. That sounds arrogant, no doubt, but since Aphrodite's son tricked his mother in order to take me as his bride, the unthinkable has happened more than once. Since then, Eros has been exiled from the Pantheon, and his brother, Deimos, was almost killed at my hand.

Eros says he doesn't blame me for what happened with his brother, back on Olympus, and indeed I had no choice; what I did was only to save him. But still, it was my hand that threw the blade. That maimed a son of Aphrodite for eternity, that left him flightless and deformed.

That is one of the reasons we are pursued: for vengeance. Eros's brothers, Deimos and Phobos, will not rest without it.

But there's also the question of the knife, that blade that severed Deimos's wing. No ordinary knife can do such a thing. Silver or iron or bronze: a god is infallible to all of them. But somehow, the blade I carry with me, the only inheritance I have of my dead mother's, turned out to be an adamantine blade.

How she came to possess such a thing, I cannot fathom. But it has made every god distrust me, and turned them all against us. They want us found so that they can wrest my mother's blade from my hands—and whether those hands are warm with life or cold with death, I suspect is all the same to them.

*

"Are you ready?" Eros says.

I nod, and he hoists me up onto Ajax's back. This horse and I have known each other for some time now. He is a horse of the gods, quicker and more sure-footed than any I have known. I wrap my feet firmly around his broad back, and Eros leaps up behind me, finding his seat with one bound. His arrows rattle in the quiver on his back.

My husband's arrows are not like human arrows. They come in two kinds, and the tips of each contain a potion: one, a toxin that brings death to any mortal creature; the other, a potion that makes them fall in love with whoever they next lay eyes on. I used to think the first kind of arrow was the dangerous one, but now I'm not sure. After what I've seen, I wonder if love isn't the most dangerous curse of all.

Some would say it's the curse I live under.

After all, a year ago I had a home, a family, a peaceful life. I was engaged to the best discus thrower in Sikyon town. I thought I was happy. And then there was Eros, and my old life disappeared.

But though my life is infinitely harder now, and we live from day to day in uncertainty, I know I would give up nothing. Every time I look in his eyes, I know it. Every time his fingers touch my skin. I used to think it was some witchery of his, some enchantment, that stirred such feelings in me, the flush of rapid heat that sparks through me at his touch. But now I know it is the most natural thing there is. That is what the gods are, after all: they are nature itself.

*

The dawn sky is one such as I have never seen. Flame colors in the east, and the color of a plum in the west, the colors fusing in the center like wine mixed with blood.

Whether it's a good or bad omen, I can't say.

The snow around us has started to melt, but there is still enough of it to create a strange reflection of the sky overhead, mirroring its unnatural colors. Below us is the village, and below that, the path that leads down, out of these mountains.

Now we are in the last mountains of the Argolic, one of the three great peninsulas that mark the end of the southern lands. There is nothing after this but islands. Any ships of note in these parts set sail from Skala, the great southern bay ruled by Sparta, and carve around the peninsula to the east. By coming overland to the coast here, we hope to keep a lower profile. These are rugged mountains, and beyond them, Eros has warned me, are only small towns. They will not have anything larger than some small fishing-craft, but that will suit our needs well enough.

Eros nudges the horse's flank, and we make our way carefully over the crest, and onto the narrow path that zigzags down the first portion of the mountainside before disappearing around a high pass. I take a breath and feel the cold air in my lungs.

We step carefully, little by little. The sky grows thick with clouds again, and I wonder if there is one more snowfall left in this season after all. That would not serve us well.

Eros jumps down.

"You ride. I will walk alongside you a while. I need to stretch my legs."

Often he makes this excuse, but I think it's just to protect me and Ajax. Now he walks in front, acting as our sentinel, lest any white wolves of these snowy lands or other dangers befall us. Then again, maybe he does need to be in motion. He is a restless god, full of energy despite his weakened state. Here and there, pockets of his followers still exist, but since the great split with Olympus—since his mother ostracized him—his temples have been outlawed here in mortal lands. Without them, without mortal worship, his powers grow weak. But not his *ischys*, his life force. That is what keeps a god immortal, what keeps him alive. And *that* sill flows through him like golden fire. I feel it whenever I touch him.

The hours pass slowly, painfully. Ajax must tread carefully, and we walk in silence, listening for the creak of snow ahead or behind. Listening for danger.

Until something sounds above us.

"Watch out!" Eros shouts, and Ajax bolts forward. A heavy snow-slide comes tumbling off the ledge above us, smashing into the ground where we were a moment ago, before rolling forward, down into the abyss, shuddering. I watch it gather momentum, rolling away from us until it explodes in a final blast of white, far below.

The ice is cracking and the snows are melting; the world is changing and shifting again. I should be afraid, but I cannot find it in me, not today. It would have been wiser to stay in our wooden home some weeks longer, to let the new season settle, but I was eager to be on the way. We have been held back long enough already.

"Are you all right?"

His tone is rough with concern; with anger, perhaps, that I insisted on this early departure. But I have been impatient to reach Atlantis for a long time now. So has Eros, come to that. There have been rumors of war on the island—it is a rich island, often fought over—so Eros has hopes of finding his father Ares, the god of war, there. He thinks Ares might take our part, and defend us against the other Olympians.

"If we have one god on our side," he says, "others will follow." But I think finding that one may be harder than he thinks.

As for me, Atlantis is my mother's ancestral home, and a place I have long wanted to see. But there is another, more urgent, reason for me to be there, and soon.

Months ago, in a small hamlet outside Kalavryta, we heard tell of two travelers who'd journeyed that way before us—travelers bound for Atlantis, whose description was exactly that of my sister and father. Eros warns me not to hope too much, and yet I feel an inner conviction that my family is alive, and that I will see them again. Somehow.

But it is a long way from Kalavryta to Atlantis, and much could have happened between now and then. And even if they reached it, that would have been three seasons ago by now. The longer we delay here, the less likely it seems that I will find them.

"Psyche," Eros asks again, his voice growing taut now. "Are you all right?"

I answer without turning around, my gaze still locked on the foot of the valley floor where the avalanche tumbled.

"Fine."

But Ajax loses his footing after that, and skids on a sheet of frozen ice below. I lose my balance, tumbling from his back onto the ice-layer. Eros grasps me by the wrist, stopping the momentum from carrying me further towards the edge.

"This is madness." He breathes through his nose. "Psyche, you risk too much. We cannot continue like this."

But we can't turn back now. Besides…

"Listen," I say. "Gulls."

I can hear them on the wind, and not, I think, so far away. Gulls mean water.

Just ahead, the path curves around the side of the mountain, beckoning. Before Eros can stop me I step forward, my tread firm and stubborn on the icy ground. I round the bend, and exhale.

There, below us, is the sea.

*

The final descent is neither quick nor easy. In some ways, now that our destination is in view, it teases all the more cruelly, and as the light begins to dim, the path only grows more treacherous. But as evening falls, we are riding into the village, a sleepy seaside place, and excitement overtakes exhaustion.

We cannot see Atlantis from here, not yet, but I know it's out there. We'll be there in a few hours—or, if there's no one to take us tonight, by morning at the latest. If only morning didn't seem so far away! Small stone houses gather in the lee of the mountain, and here and there a battered fishing craft is tied against the rocky coast. The wooden hulls are weathered, drifting in the still-icy waters of an early spring. Down here, though, the snow-covered world already seems a lifetime ago. Even now, after sunset, the air is cool, but not icy. And yet I wonder why it all feels so quiet.

Eros rides behind me again, his warm weight cushioning me as I lean back into his grip. His hood is down now, as it must be, whenever we are among my people, to shield them from the dangers of his face.

We pass through what must be their central agora. The large square is empty but for a few men clustered together, talking.

"*Khaire*," Eros hails them. He jumps down, leading Ajax behind him. The men are clearly surprised to see us. Not many travelers here, I'll warrant, certainly not the kind that walk here through the mountain passes.

"We seek transport. Have you a craft that will bring us to the isle of Atlantis?"

The men look at each other. They don't trust a man with a hooded face; why should they? Little do they know it's for their benefit.

"Aye, we have the craft right enough." One of them looks from Eros to me. "But I'll be damned if you make it to Atlantis. Been living under a rock, have you?" The man laughs harshly, probes some wax from his ear and wipes it on his robes.

Eros looks at me.

"It's not safe to travel, then? The war rages?"

I know what he's thinking. News of war doesn't trouble him—quite the contrary. If war rages in Atlantis, the chances are good that the war-god is to be found there. But I'm not sure I share Eros's optimism that Ares will help our cause—and besides, if my father and sister *did* somehow make it to Atlantis, it only gives me reason to fear for them.

But the man frowns at us, shakes his head.

"The uprising? That's over these many months. The old king was killed in his bed. The man who killed him is king now. And no one"—he eyes us, glowering—"*no one* gets on or off the island except according to the new king's will."

Two

He explains that soldiers line the battlements day and night, to be sure no illegal craft lands on the island's shores.

"The new king says Atlantis must not share its riches. He says Atlantis is for Atlanteans alone, now." He shakes his head, and one of the others spits on the ground.

"We used to trade freely with the Atlanteans." He glares out towards the sea. "Our land is poor, not much to farm, but we are fine craftspeople and healers. Our potion-makers can cure most any ailment, and they say our midwives never lose a babe. We have made our way as a town of trades—besides the healers, we have woodworkers and metal workers, clay-fashioners and smiths." He shrugs darkly. "But now such free exchange is over. And we are to starve with the next harvest, I suppose."

"Aye," his friend chips in. "The seeds that die in our earth, sprout green in theirs. The fish that elude us, leap into *their* nets. Not that they ever did much to deserve such bounty."

I look at Eros.

This is dark news indeed.

A dead king is nothing special in these lands—those who rule tend to pay with their heads, sooner or later. But how are we to reach Atlantis, now? And if my fancies are real, if my father and sister *are* there, how do they fare under such a regime? *No one gets in or out,* the man said. In other words, while the people of this town fear for their livelihoods, the people of Atlantis are all the king's prisoners.

But Eros has a different thought.

"If the war is over," he says slowly, "if the blood has dried on the battlefields, Ares will not have lingered here."

The circle of men snicker.

"The gods will forsake this place altogether, if they have

not already. King Kostas does not bother to maintain their shrines. He prides himself on being a self-made man. They say he won his battles without ever once calling on the gods." He lowers his voice. "Though perhaps he called on worse things."

"And yet, what could be worse than the gods?" Eros says dryly. One of the men raises an eyebrow. Another chimes in.

"Well, the old king was devout enough—but it seems the gods didn't care to save *him*."

"Questioning the gods now, are we, Isidoros? Do you want to be struck down where you stand?"

While the men bicker, Eros takes me aside, lowers his voice. The sun is lost behind the horizon now, the evening growing colder.

"I fear Atlantis is not the destination for us after all. The gods have abandoned this place."

I look at him.

"But my family—they could be in there." I hesitate. "I believe it. I believe that they are inside those walls." I can't say why, but I do.

Eros puts a hand over mine.

"They could be anywhere, Psyche. You know this. They could be-" He stops himself from saying the word.

Dead.

"You could fly us," I point out. "You still have the strength to do that, do you not?"

It has failed, like all his powers have, in the months since Aphrodite ordered his temples boarded up, and his followers disbanded. But I do not think it has failed completely. And Atlantis is not so very far away.

"It is too dangerous," is all he says. Perhaps he means his wings will give out and he will fall from the sky and drown me, or perhaps only that it will draw the gods' attention to our whereabouts. Either way, I know that voice of his. It's the one that brooks no argument.

"What is it you seek on Atlantis, anyway?" One of the men—he speaks like the leader of their small group—calls over to us. He scoffs. "You want to see if the legends are true?"

"My wife has been separated from her family," Eros says coolly. "We received word that they might have traveled here."

"Atlantis has had its share of refugees, all right, but no longer." The man shrugs. "Give it up—you will starve before the king changes his mind."

I glance at Eros. I can tell he thinks the man is right. He wants me to see sense. He wants us to focus on finding Ares, in the hopes that he will help us. He wants to focus on getting his powers back.

And how can I persuade him otherwise, when I have no answer, no plan? *Patience*, the sea itself seems to whisper to me, between its sighs and rock-tossed shudders. I glance over at the men. It is almost fully dark now, and soon they must be getting home to their families.

"Surely, sirs, you are right," I say. "But it is late, too late for us to take to the road tonight. Might we presume upon one of you for some lodging?"

They look at me, as though surprised to hear a woman speak.

Then they glance at each other. No doubt they are imagining what their wives will say if they turn up with two odd strangers, appeared as if by magic out of the mountain passes.

"Come with me, then," the eldest says. "We'll find you a place at the table."

*

The sea's thrashing has died now. Instead a hushed lapping, irregular.

Inside the hut we've been given for the night, the wooden walls seem to exude a salty breath, the briny air sharp in my lungs. The coverings are coarsely woven blankets, itching at my skin. I do not bother asking Eros if he's awake. He's always awake. Sleep for him is a kind of meditation, a trance state where he floats as one with the universe. But his eyes are closed, and he seems far away from me.

The walls of the little hut are hung with fishing-nets, strangely luminous in the dark. My eyes drift over them: the *kitharis*, the small hand-nets, and the bigger ones, drag-nets and seines that will be used to drive whole schools of fish to shore, pushing them towards their death. Depending on what's to be caught, the men will knot their mesh in different sizes: large enough to let the little fish swim free, and only catch the big ones left behind.

I always used to feel like a little fish, wanting to be big. Now I think perhaps it would have been better after all to stay small; to stay narrow enough to slip unnoticed through the holes.

I reach for the amulet I wear around my neck, touching the cool stone for reassurance. The Shroud—Eros gave it to me many moons ago. It conceals me from the eyes of the gods, if they should search for me in the mortal lands—Eros needs no such thing, of course. He can conceal his whereabouts at will, as can all the gods. I have not taken the amulet off, not for an instant, since the night he gave it to me. But sometimes it feels like scanty protection against what's out there. Against more than one god who must wish me dead.

I sigh and turn over.

I don't care what those men said. I have not come all this way only to be turned back at the last. I've waited through the many months of winter, snowbound and hungry, for Atlantis, for my family. They have to be there. Because if they're not, it's like Eros said. I have no other clue of their whereabouts. They might as well be dead.

*

I bolt up from our bed in the darkness, ears ringing. A klaxon is sounding, and there's confusion everywhere.

"Eros? Eros!" But he's awake too, already out of bed, and standing at the door of our tent.

"What is it?" I say, and he turns.

"A boat rowed in—a messenger, by the looks of it." He

grabs the arm of a man going by. It's a moonless night, and his face is still in the shadows of the tent; they're safe enough from glimpsing him.

"Tell us what's happening, man!"

The fellow shrugs off his arm, annoyed.

"In Atlantis the new queen delivers a child, but they say it is a bad birth. They say she is fit to die. The king seeks one of our midwives."

And he's gone.

We glance at each other, pull our robes to a hasty decency, and make our way as quickly as we can from the tent, to find a crowd gathered down by the waterfront. A brazier has been lit, its orange light illuminating the clusters of villagers, and beyond them, two men who stand apart, tall and severe, helmeted and armored.

The king's men.

"Why rush to his aid," one of the men nearer to us is saying, with a tone of disgust. "He will let us starve, and the Kytherans, and everybody else, no doubt. What do we care about his heir?"

"You *will* care," a woman, perhaps his wife, hisses. "You'll care when he comes to take his vengeance on us because we did not do as he asked. You'll care when he sends his ships to come and burn what we've stored until harvest."

The tide is growing higher, the night seems more alive. The village is larger than I had thought: from here, I can see the bobbing of small lights, torches flickering many houses away as people run about the streets.

"They are looking for Ekaterini, the birthing-woman," one of the men we met earlier tells us, his voice gruff. He's watching the torches bob throughout the village, too.

"She is well known in these parts. No infant nor its mother has died in this village in many years. She has the true gift of Eileiythia."

Eileiythia, daughter of Zeus, goddess of childbirth. To have her gift would certainly be a happy thing—but it is just as likely that this midwife has only been lucky. I don't hold with the favor of the gods the way I used to.

The king's guards stand in their bright armor, arms folded. They speak to no one, not even each other, only now and then barking at one of the villagers, telling them to hurry. But it seems the birthing-woman, Ekaterini, is not in her cottage tonight.

"The witch is probably out gathering her night-herbs," one of the men grunts. But a woman approaches, breathless.

"She's been at Leontia's house, did you not hear? Her baby came at last."

The guards turn, the bigger one cuffs a youth that stands nearby.

"What are you waiting for, fool? Do you know this house? Then go and get her!"

There is a battering on doors, a chorus of voices, and it seems the woman has been roused from her bed then, for they are making their way back through the streets, not so fast now as before but with urgency. The woman Ekaterini is elderly, perhaps.

Once they can tell she's been found, people start to move on the waterfront. One of the men is wading into the water, hauling his boat in over the rocks, as though readying it for a journey. Aren't the guards ferrying the midwife to Atlantis themselves, then? I turn to our host and ask. He shrugs.

"It will save them the trip of bringing her back."

True enough. And an idea comes to me. A plan, or half a plan—a crumb of a plan—is forming.

"Eros," I whisper. "This is our chance."

He looks at me, sees where my thoughts have traveled, and he does not like it. But I take his arms in the darkness, and stare up at his shadowed eyes. When I speak, my voice has all the conviction I know how to muster.

"We have to be on that boat."

Three

The ferryman will not hear of it.

"I'll be run through, if the king's men find out. It's not worth the risk to me," he shakes his head. "And it shouldn't be to you."

"It's dark," I plead with the boatman. "His men won't see us. And if they do, you'll say we stowed away. That you knew nothing about it." The boat's transom is piled with gear and nets, and a blanket. We could hide in there. And the little skiff is covered—just a piece of canvas knotted to a few posts, enough to give shelter from the sun during a hot day. But in the shadows, it cloaks the back of the boat well enough.

Behind us, the klaxon sounds again. The whole place seems to be in pandemonium now, everyone asking panicked questions, babies crying.

"It will be chaos over there, too," I point out. "The king's guard will be hell-bent on escorting your birthing-woman to the palace in time. That's all they'll be thinking of. They won't have time to think about searching your boat."

He's silent for a moment.

"You're asking me to risk my life," he says at last, and I don't have anything to say to that. I suppose it's true, and wrong of me. It's nothing to him, whether I remain sisterless, fatherless.

"What'll you give me for it?" he says.

I look at Eros.

"We have coin," I say, and show him, but he shakes his head.

"Not enough. For what I'm risking, not nearly enough."

I stare at the coin in my hand, wondering what else I can offer. My mother's knife? Eros carries it now, sheathed at his hip. But even if I could bring myself to part with it, Eros has said it himself—an item so powerful, so dangerous, cannot be left in the wrong hands.

"You can have my horse," Eros says, and I turn and stare.

Ajax?

"Eros, you can't-"

To part with him, to sell him...Ajax is not a horse that deserves to be bought and sold.

"My horse," Eros repeats firmly, speaking only to the boatman.

*

He leads us quietly to where his small skiff bobs in the darkness. The water is black as squid-ink.

"Get in the back," the boatman—his name is Herodotos—mutters. "I'll cover you with blankets."

He does, foul-smelling ones. I suspect they've been used to mop fish-guts with, and more than once.

His orders are to row after the king's guards' boat, and tie up under their watch. Another guard will wait with him while they take the birthing-woman to the queen's chambers. When Ekaterini has done her job—nobody dares suggest that she might fail—then he will row her back.

I watch through a tear in the blanket as the woman is bundled unceremoniously onto Herodotus's boat. I feel the dip as her new weight is added to ours, and the boat sinks lower in the water. I hear her breathing, quick and shuddering. The small crowd by the dock are wishing her well, exchanging looks with one another. They know—we all know—that Ekaterini's life hangs in the balance too, should she fail—should the queen die, or worse, the child. Especially if the child is a boy: kings do not lose their sons lightly.

The guards' gold-edged robes catch the moonlight as they board their craft, moored a little way ahead of ours.

"Make haste!" the guards call back, and push off into the night.

My heart hums in my throat as Herodotos follows suit.

The oars creak in their locks. Ekaterini is humming to

herself, but the sound is more like a prayer than a song. She is afraid—of course she is. Would she betray us, if she knew we were here?

"Faster, you simpleton," one of the guards, standing on the stern of his boat, shouts back. But Herodotos is ferrying three people's weight, not one.

The night smells of the sea, the clean, sharp scent of salt. I can almost taste it on my lips. I try to inhale it as deep as I can, blocking out the stench of the blanket draped over us. It is quiet; the sea-birds are all sleeping. Only the plash of water against the hull, of the oars turning, of Herodotos's grunts and the woman's anxious humming.

I feel Eros's body against my back, the safety of his presence. None of these guards' arrows could wound him; with one look, he could undo their minds, scrambling all their senses like a whisked egg.

But any of those arrows could kill *me*.

*

The little skiff heaves to starboard; I feel us swing around. I put my eye to the peephole again—and there it is, an island small enough to fit in the palm of my hand, all lit by moonlight.

Atlantis.

As we get closer I can make out the great shape of a castle—the palace, it must be—looming up from the walls that rim the island's edge. There is a great bay here, too, and what looks to be a shipyard. A small fleet bobs in the darkness: triremes, war-ships. On the other side of the shipyard is another great edifice, rearing up into the night. A grand flights of stone steps leads up from the landing towards it. This is a city meant to be approached from the water: made to awe, but also to welcome.

It is not welcoming now. As we draw closer, I see the small black shapes of men stationed in the castle battlements. Braziers mounted along the walls barely illuminate their shadows.

There are no guarantees that Herodotos will stick to his promise, it occurs to me. He already has the horse; he could hand us over to the king's men and pocket some reward as well.

I think once more of Ajax, with a pang. I reason we could not have taken him with us, not across these waters. But we will go back for him, I tell myself. Once we have what we need. Once *I* have what I need.

The thrashing water slows against the hull; the oars pull a different, slower rhythm, as Herodotos turns the skiff towards shore.

"Do not worry," I hear him mumble to Ekaterini. "You have the gift. You will succeed."

"May it please the gods," the woman answers. I hear the anxiety in her voice.

Herodotos gets up, makes to escort her from the skiff.

"Get back in your boat," the guards shout at him, already tying up their own. "Only the woman sets foot on this island."

Herodotos acts as though he doesn't hear them, knotting his boat tight to the mooring-post and stretching a long leg out to make the leap ashore.

"Did you hear me, simpleton?" The guards call out to one of their own: "Perikles! Come down here and keep watch over this fool. He's to wait in his boat until we bring the birthing-woman back. Come on, you." And he marches Ekaterini up the landing as another robed guard walks down.

This, we had not anticipated. The one called Perikles boards the boat, seats himself where Ekaterini sat—the comfortable, padded side—and takes his dagger out, motioning to the boatman to sit back down. The other guards march Ekaterini up some stone steps, and they all disappear through a gateway.

"Now—any more nonsense," Perikles says, still handling the dagger, "and you'll feel the wrong end of this." He stretches, takes off his helmet, and sets it down beside him. The bit of uniform is for show; Atlantis faces no invasion tonight.

Except our very small one.

Eros moves as silently as the night. The blankets are cast

off; he brings down the heavy hilt of my mother's blade on the soldier's bare head, and with a soft moan, the man keels over.

"He's out."

Quickly, Eros strips the guard of his gold-edged chiton and dons it, then takes the helmet from the bench and tilts it low over his face. It will disguise him, and more than that, it will protect whomever we might meet. Who knows who else we will pass on our way into the citadel, or on the other side.

Now Perikles, the guard, lies unconscious in the bottom of the boat, dressed in Eros's shabby cloak.

"You can't leave him here!" Herodotos hisses. "Take him with you, damn you!"

It is a good thing he speaks low. Although men are stationed above us, looking out from the battlements, we're right at the base of the rock. There's no way for them to see us, unless they were to lean out over the battlements and crane their heads down. But loud voices may travel on a night like this, even over the thrashing of the waves.

Eros rips off a piece of the old cloak and gags the soldier's mouth. He tugs the cloak low over the man's face. I take a breath, not daring to think too hard about what we're doing, what we've already done, and follow Eros in his soldier's garb up the steps in the rock. I pull my robe over my hair too: the more nondescript I look, the better, for I am to play the part of a guard's prisoner, and soldiers often like to share a pretty woman.

But I need not have worried. The guard waiting at the top of the stairs is sleepy, unconcerned. But his eyebrows raise all the same at the sight of this guard and a couple of peasants, one of them thrown over Eros's broad shoulder.

"I found these two on my patrol," Eros says. "A drunk and his whore."

"Degenerates," the guard sniffs. "Well, go ahead then."

I steal a glance back as we walk out the other side, but the guard has leaned back against the wall. When I turn around again, my pace slows involuntarily as I take everything in. This place—the castle behind us, the crashing sea to our right, a great open square before us, with that towering building I saw from the water. And beyond, to the left, the island rolls away from us—dark fields, dark forests, all under moonlight. In the distance, a single mountain peak cuts into the sky, a steep black cone against the night. *My mother's homeland.* The thought runs through me, a shiver in my mind.

"Quickly, Psyche," murmurs Eros. He's right; this is no time for dreaming.

I can see roads fanning out from the far end of the great square, sloping down away from the citadel into whatever towns and villages lie below. Which one to choose? Either way, we will have to rid ourselves of this comatose soldier, but he will spread the word when he wakes—whichever route we take, we will have to move fast.

We have made it only fifty feet or so when his bundled form begins to move. His foot twitches; he aims a kick, and misses. Through the gag, his muted, angry cries pierce the night.

I glance at Eros, who keeps walking—faster, now. I do the same, until a voice calls out from behind us.

"Halt! *Stamatíste!*"

Four

Eros doesn't break stride.

"I said, halt!"

An arrow whizzes through the air. I cry out; it's pierced the edge of my cloak, pinning the fabric to the hard ground. At that, Eros stops short, as though he were the one struck. He curses.

"Get behind me," he murmurs.

We turn around slowly, only to see the same guard from before—the sleepy-looking one, but not so sleepy now. Bow in hand, he's walking across the agora towards us. A flicker of fear runs through me, but whether it's fear for myself or for the guard, I don't know. Eros still carries my mother's knife; his quiver of gods' arrows still rests on his back. It would be just a moment's work to deal with this one guard. But my husband has made promises. He will not inflict such harm except for in the direst necessity. Is now such a moment?

I feel him hesitate…and in that moment, my heart sinks further. Two more guards emerge, then another, and then still more. Eight in all. I feel Eros's dismay—he cannot take eight innocent lives.

"We will not harm them," he says quietly, "unless they try to harm us." By which of course he means, harm *you*.

He drops our writhing hostage on the ground and takes a step back, with me in his wake.

"What have we here?" One of the approaching guards, sharper-looking than the rest, steps up to the cloaked bundle on the ground and throws the hood back from his face. Recognizing one of his own, he scoffs, then looks back at us.

"You will not deal with us as easily as you did with that oaf, Perikles."

The men fan out in a semi-circle around us, bows high,

arrows notched.

"Show your faces," the sharp-faced man says. He doesn't understand what a dangerous command that is. I glance at Eros, then pull back my hood. But Eros can't—not unless he wants to destroy these men.

"I swear to you, I mean no trickery," he says slowly. "My face bears a curse. Any who see it can know no peace."

The soldiers look at each other. The leader, the one standing before us, gives a snort.

"Don't toy with me, stranger," he says in a low, harsh voice.

"Aye, show us your ugly mug!" another guard jeers, and the others laugh along.

"I cannot," Eros says, unmoved.

"*Will* not, you mean." The sharp-faced one draws a sword from his belt. "Well—and what say you now?"

Eros spreads his palms, his meaning clear: his answer is unchanged.

With an angry grunt the guard lunges. His sword-hand is quick and unhesitating, but with the smallest flick of my mother's knife, Eros sends the weapon out of the other man's grip and clattering to the ground. It takes the guard a half-second to register that he's been bested, and when it does, his eyes flash; he doesn't like being embarrassed in front of his men.

"A swordsman, are we?" he says. "Very well. But even a great swordsman cannot hope to defend himself from seven archers." He gestures at the men around him.

This is all going too far, too fast. I step forward.

"There is no reason it need come to that. Please, we mean no harm. We have acted rashly in trying to gain entry to your land, but we have no ill intent. I seek my family, that is all—my father and sister, who came to this island many months ago. Until now I thought them dead. I seek only to find them." I give him my most earnest look. "We have plenty of coin. Let us slip into the night, and you need see no more of us—and go home rich to your wives tonight."

The narrow-eyed one doesn't miss a beat.

"Train your arrows on her," he says, and in a second, they have.

I curse myself for imagining I could appeal to them in common cause. Not when a man has his wounded pride to restore.

Eros turns his head towards me, and though I can't see his face, I can see what he's feeling. Achilles had only one weakness: one patch of skin that was fully mortal, vulnerable to all harm. Eros's weak spot is me.

"You'll both come with us," the man says. He turns to Eros. "And not a step out of line, or we'll put a hole in your lady's pretty neck. Now take off that helmet, it doesn't belong to you."

Eros looks at our new captors.

"I will do all that you say. Only allow me to keep my face shielded."

"Perhaps we ought to let him keep his face hidden, sir," one of the soldiers blurts. He sounds younger than the rest, anxious. "My gran said there was a woman in her village who-"

"Myths, you cretin. Myths." The leader cuts him off, and yet there is a touch of hesitation where there was not before.

"Keep your face hidden, then. We'll give you your mangy cloak back soon enough." He throws a dirty look at the one called Perikles, still wearing Eros's old robe. "Then you may wrap yourself in it as you like."

*

The room they put us in is not a proper cell: by the looks of it, it's used by the guards for breaks, or a few minutes' shut-eye while their colleague takes the watch. There is a small, hard bench for a bed, and a table with two chairs. A game of *petteia* is set up on the table, half-played. *Petteia* is a game of strategy, much favored in our lands. My father used to play it with our neighbor, Kirios Demou, the man whose son I was once engaged to marry. And yet it seems all their strategy did not help very much in the end:

Demou is dead, most likely, and my father…if he is not lost to me completely, then he is a refugee on a tyrant's island.

The door slams behind us and we're left in the dark, but Eros summons the sconces to light and we sit looking at each other in the flames. Everything smells damp, of bilge water and seaweed. Although I would wish us somewhere else—most anywhere else—I am glad to be alone with Eros again: that he can drop his hood, and that I can see his face. It is a face that strikes me even now with its beauty, its majesty; those eyes. Golden as a lion's, eyes that hold galaxies inside them.

"You could break us free of here," I say. Heavy as the door is, and guarded at the other side, he could break it down in a moment.

He gives me a silent look. We would face the same problem as before, only with the power to do greater harm, and bring still greater attention on ourselves. And too much attention risks alerting gods as well as men.

"I'm sorry," I sigh. "I shouldn't have tried to bargain with them like that."

"Men are greedy," Eros concedes. "But not all men are greedy for coin."

I lean back against the stone wall, my eyes drifting over the *petteia* board, its carved pieces paused in their half-fought battle. Is it only my people that are so obsessed with war; with conquering, and victory? Or are people everywhere like this?

Outside the window, I notice Herodotus's skiff is gone. He wasn't fool enough to wait, then. Just as well. No doubt one of the king's ships will bring the birthing-woman home, if she survives.

I look back at Eros.

"So what do we do now?"

"Perhaps," Eros says slowly, "it would be wise to do as they say."

I stare at him. I've accused him of arrogance often enough in the past, for the high-handed way he deals with mortals. He has never yet entertained the idea of taking direction from one of them.

"They intend to bring us before the king," he says. I don't argue with that; we heard as much from the captain when they threw us in here.

"Yet that is hardly a warming prospect," I point out. Nothing I've heard about the king makes me want to be in the same room as him for a moment.

Eros cocks his head at me.

"He may be a ruthless man, but even a godless king respects power; he sees where his advantage lies. I will prove to him what I am. No doubt he will be more…amenable, then."

My skin prickles. Eros has warned me about what may come, if we expose his true identity.

"But then he'll know. He'll know what you are. He could tell anyone."

Eros shakes his head. "Kings do not gossip; they trade." He looks towards the door, as if he can see through it to the guards keeping watch outside.

"Those men, if they were to know the truth—word would spread like wildfire. Soldiers are worse gossips than fishermen's wives." He looks at me. "But the king...I think we may find him a shrewder man than that."

I stare. "You mean to bargain with him."

Eros shrugs.

"I'm sure it will not be hard for me to offer him something he likes."

My eyes drift back towards the game of *petteia.* I have only known one king before, and he is the man who had me chained to a rock. I have no great desire to meet another.

And yet, it seems, meet him we must.

*

I toss and turn throughout the night, but I must fall asleep at some point: when the door slams open, it's no longer first light.

"You two. Up and follow me." There's a small phalanx of guards here now. The watch must have changed, as I don't recognize any of their faces, but the first of them has a spear pointed at my throat.

I get to my feet, and Eros follows.

"That's right, Champion," one of the men sneers. I feel Eros's irritation, but he doesn't allow it the upper hand. It must be a struggle for him: he does not suffer insults lightly, certainly not from those he deems beneath him.

"The king wasn't planning to hear any trials today—but you two, he wants to see." The guard leers. "He likes to make an example of folks like you. But you're lucky, nonetheless. An heir was born last night, a son. He might spare your lives yet."

A successful birth. A boy-child. That's good news for Ekaterini, at least.

"And the queen?" I say. "She lives?" The woman is only a stranger, nothing to me. But my own mother died on the birthing-bed, and I know what it is for a child to grow up with such a loss.

The soldier gives me a contemptuous look.

"None of your business, wench."

Of course: why should anyone care for news of the queen? She is just a woman, while the babe will grow to be a man.

"Take them to the throne room," the guard says. "The king can dispense his justice there."

They march us out into the agora, and I get a quick glance of Atlantis in daylight. The towering castle, and across from it the other tremendous building, which by daylight I recognize as a great temple. In the distance, the mountain I saw last night is still more striking, its sides sheer and steep, its peak fringed with pink-hued clouds. And in the long sweep of land between here and there, fields of lush green and clusters of villages. But a glimpse is all I get—there are spears at my back.

The great doors of the palace swing open to a massive staircase, with more guards waiting in formation. They lead us up the stairs, then push us through a set of wide doors, aiming a strong kick at our backs so that we stumble, kneeling, as we hit the floor. I know enough not to look up: I keep my eyes on the glistening marble beneath us, away from the king's dais I glimpsed at the far end of the room. I feel Eros's quickened breath beside me—short with anger, I suspect, not fear.

And then I hear a gasp from across the room. A gasp that sounds…familiar.

Fool that I am, I look up, straight at the dais. Beside the king, a beautiful woman sits: her dark hair, straight as an arrow, fanned beneath her gold diadem. Her face is pale with shock. As I'm sure mine must be too.

Because the woman I'm looking at is my sister.

Five

"Dimitra?"

I stand staring. My feet are frozen to the floor. The world seems to spin. The last time I saw her I was standing on a cliff, waiting for death. Hers was the last face I saw: she was the only one to turn back, her dark eyes fixed on mine as the king's carriage took her away.

And now here she is…on a throne.

"I don't understand," I stumble over the words. "How—how is this possible?"

"Wife," a strong voice says, and as if for the first time I notice the man sitting next to her, on a throne twice the height of hers. Tall, bearded, with dark eyes like my sister's, and a soldier's build. He's draped in purple robes—Tyrian purple, the most expensive dye in all the Hellenic lands.

His voice is calm but carries an undercurrent.

"You know this woman?"

I feel Eros beside me, startled too by the turn of events. Yet he has seen the twisted hand of fate at work before. He understands the games it can play. But as for me, I'm still reeling.

"Dimitra…Didi…" The room dazzles, literally dazzles: the walls are lined with mirrors, reflecting all the points of light, the guards' bright metal spears, their helmets; the gold decorations all about the room.

I take a step closer to the throne. Two guards step forward, spears at the ready.

My sister's face is ashen, her eyes wide. But then something in her face shuts down, the look of shock covered over like a wound, and her jaw tightens. I've seen this expression before, I've known it since my youth. The hardening of the eyes, the jutting of the chin. But this time it is no tantrum with our tutor; this time, it is not to insist Father take us to the market, or let her wear expensive jewels.

"Some trickery," she says. "Some illusion." She turns to the king.

"I do not know her." Her gaze moves towards me again. "The sister I once had is dead."

The words slice into an old wound. Does she really not know me? Or is her heart so hardened against hope? I stare at her, so familiar and yet so foreign. Her finery, her diadem, her regal throne. Even her face seems different. Thinner, more hollowed.

"Dimitra, this is no trickery. It's me. You know it is!"

Her eyes flash with that old pride. My sister does not like to be contradicted.

The king's eyes travel over me, taking me in in a way that I remember: the men of Sikyon used to look at me this way. Unhurried, shameless; as though I did not see them looking. No, not even: as though it didn't matter that I saw. Because they had power and I had none.

I recall the things I've heard about this new king of Atlantis. Every story has its bias. But I do not have much reason to trust this man.

"You were—" Dimitra stops, corrects herself. "*She*, my sister, was taken by a monster. The gods destroyed her. Everybody knows it."

Eros steps forward. Until now he's been quiet. But when he speaks his voice hushes the room.

"Your sister is very much alive, and stands before you. She was taken to safety by me, against the wishes of the goddess Aphrodite."

"And who, sir, are you?" The king's teeth flash as he speaks. His politeness is silky, dangerous. The *sir* slipped from his teeth too smoothly.

"I will tell you who I am," Eros says calmly, "if you tell your men to leave us."

The king gives a short laugh.

"You wish me to dismiss my guards? Those sworn to

defend me? To leave me alone with a stranger; a criminal?"

"You are a mighty warrior, I hear," Eros says evenly. "And your guards have taken my bow and arrows."

They failed to discover my mother's blade, which lies sheathed under my chiton, between my breasts—but that is no matter now.

"Besides, I give you my word I mean you no harm."

The king's eyes narrow. He does not want to concede anything, but his pride is piqued by the challenge; he is not the type to hide behind his men.

"Your identity is a close-guarded secret, then?"

"It is," Eros says simply.

The king assess us coolly a moment longer.

"Very well." He flicks a hand at the guards. "Go."

"Your highness-" One with a crested helmet finer than the rest protests.

"Go, Dareios," the king says. "You may wait outside the door."

Watching them, it is clear they are a well-trained army. Their movements are sharp, flawlessly aligned. I have heard only the Spartans show such discipline. Their spear-tips dance in the light as they file out, and the mirrored room, its many points of light, seems to spin for a moment. Perhaps that is its purpose, a space designed to dazzle, to stupefy. It's hard to think straight in here.

"Well?" the king says when they are gone, the stomping of feet and the clanking of iron giving way to a strange hush. "You will let us in on this great secret of yours now."

Eros doesn't hesitate.

"I am a son of the goddess Aphrodite," he says, and if the room could hush even further, it does. I think perhaps there will be laughter and disbelief, but there is only silence. The king licks his lips: in other men I would take it as a sign of nerves, but not in him.

"So: you would have me believe we have a god-child in our midst." His voice is slow, neither believing nor disbelieving. The half-mortal children of the gods are spoken of in myth. But today, for the most part, they are considered creatures of the past.

"Not a god-child," Eros corrects, his voice calm and quiet. He must be the only one in the room to possess such calm.

"I have no mortal blood. I am the third of Aphrodite's true-born sons: I am the god Eros."

There's silence then, and in it, Dimitra's eyes meet mine. I feel the burn of her stare, her furious intelligence at work. Trying to parse truth from lies; to decide what she can believe and what is out to deceive her. Father always said she had a mind like a steel trap.

Father.

Does he live, too?

"And this woman by my side," Eros glances at me, "is none other than who she claims to be. She is Psycheandra, daughter of Andros of Sikyon. By Aphrodite's decree she was brought to a sacrificial rock, and chained there by Sikyon's king. But I intervened before my mother's wish was fulfilled." He turns to Dimitra. "Your sister is now my wife; she has been under my protection since that day."

My sister looks pale and dazed, but not the king. He looks intrigued, yet casually so, as if this is a play staged for his amusement. I cannot say if he is skeptical, but certainly he is not afraid.

"It would be an honor indeed, if the god Eros stood in our midst. And yet"—a smirk is at his lip—"all I see before me is a man in a dirty cloak."

"My claim is easily proven," Eros says. "Look in your mirrors, king."

And he turns to the wall, away from us, and removes his hood. My heart jumps for a second at the thought of his uncovered face, at what it might do to Dimitra and her husband, but then I remember the nature of mirrors. They dull the effect, lessen the power. It is an old trick. It is how Perseus managed to slay the creature whose face turned men to stone: by looking only at her reflection, not the face itself.

I turn with the others, to see what they see. The room of

mirrors bounces the image back to us, multiplied. The mirror may shield them from the effects of looking upon his face, but it does not mask any of his glory. You cannot look at a face like that without feeling some urge to bow your head or fall to your knees. Do they see what I see? The way the air around him seems to shimmer; the way light radiates from his face.

I remember the first time I saw him. It was like looking at the sun.

I hear the short intake of breath from my sister. The king says nothing at all. But when I look at him I see the jolt it has given him, and how quick thoughts are starting to move over his face.

There is no way not to believe my husband's words now.

"It's true then," Dimitra breathes. Her eyes move to me, staring. Letting herself believe what surely her bones and blood have known from the moment I walked in the room. "It's really you, Psyche."

Her voice is strangled; by what emotion, I can't say. Her eyes flick back to Eros, straining to understand, to absorb the wonder of it all.

"And—and my Lord—" she stumbles over the words. Eros slips the hood back, shielding us all from his face again, and turns to face the throne. It is as though a thousand lights have been extinguished; for an instant the room seems dark.

"My face bears a curse to mortals," he says. "None can afford to look on it directly. But more than that," he goes on, "I sent your men from the room because I have need of your discretion." He looks to Dimitra. "I doubt I need to remind you of the fate my mother intended for your sister."

Dimitra stiffens. How could she forget?

"My mother has forgiven nothing," Eros explains. "Indeed, my disloyalty has only roused her fury further. Besides which, my two brothers, her first-born…" he trails off. There is no need to overwhelm my sister and her husband with stories of Eros' brothers and all the many ways they would like to see us harmed. Nor, I think, does he want to disclose the reasons behind that hatred, or the fact of the adamantine blade we carry.

"There has been a great rift," he says simply. "For all our sakes, it is crucial that my god-kin do not find me here. Your people must not speak my name."

I have rarely seen my sister stunned—perhaps even a small bit afraid. It is a point of pride that she guards herself well, and such vulnerable emotions are not in the habit of showing on her face. But even she cannot entirely conceal her feelings, now.

"I don't understand," she says, shaking her head, as though to clear a humming from her ears.

I step closer to the throne, and take her hand. Her skin is cold; she touches mine as though still half-expecting to find me a ghost. Closer, I can see her eyes are blood-shot, and her skin beaded with sweat, though her touch is icy.

"We came here in search of you," I say. "By some fated luck we took shelter in the north, at a cottage where you had stayed. The lady of the house described you. I knew it was of you she spoke. She said you sought the isle of Atlantis."

Dimitra's gaze travels over my hair, my features, my clothes, taking in the last details.

"Well, well," the king clasps his hands. "An extraordinary day." His voice is slow, his thoughts arranging themselves carefully, like bricks in a wall.

"An auspicious day indeed," he says again. But with a jolt his words remind me. Just as my sister's icy hands, her bloodshot eyes, remind me. The uproar in the village, the klaxons.

The queen gives birth tonight, and they say she is like to die.

"You have a son," I murmur.

Yet here my sister sits, by the king's side, as though the ordeal had been nothing at all. Not for the first time, Dimitra's fortitude astounds me.

"I will summon my men back into the room, if I may," the king continues smoothly, and I sense that even though he's in the presence of a god, the *if I may* is only for show.

"But on my honor, my lord, your identity will not be spoken by me. Meanwhile—" he looks over at my sister.

"It seems to me there is a reunion to be had."

My throat closes over.

"Father?" I whisper.

Dimitra blinks at me, those dark, familiar eyes. Then she grips the arm-rest of her throne and, wincing, drags herself to stand. This is a woman who gave birth not a day ago. She is as fierce as I remember; steel runs in her blood. She adjusts her fine robes, touches the diadem on her head. It catches the light, blazing gold.

"Come," she says. "I will take you to him."

Six

He's sitting on a long couch by the window. At the sound of the door, he shakes his head, as though he knows who approaches.

"No more wine," he says. "You may take it away."

My voice all but disappears. But, "It's me, Father," I manage to say, and he freezes at the sound. His head turns slowly, like a blind man's. Does he fear what he will see?

Does he, too, expect a ghost?

The wine glass falls from his hand, spreading red across the floor.

"Great God of all the lands," he whispers. "*Psyche.*"

He stares at me as though he were Odysseus himself: an old and sightless wanderer, staring blindly towards the sound of my voice. He blinks, as though coming back from some distant place.

"Is it real?" He looks to Dimitra, and then behind her, to the king, whose large, robed figure stands in the doorway, watching us all.

"It is her, Father, it's Psyche," Dimitra says, and I cross the room, wordless, and take his hand. He stares at me, then gets to his feet, the better to assess the truth for himself. He takes both hands in mine, holds me away from him a moment, then touches a hand to my face.

"You are no sorceress? No teasing dream, come to make a fool of an old man?"

"No, Father," I smile, tears pricking the backs of my eyes. "And you are no old man."

But if he is not quite old, he is certainly no longer young. This one year has worn hard on him. They say old soldiers age faster than other men, their bodies taxed by old wars. And yet my father, despite his limp, was always the sturdiest of men, his military bearing uncompromised, his strength, even in middle age, quickly apparent. When I last saw him, red hair was still visible through the grey, and on the short beard that softened his strong jaw. Now all trace of red is gone. His hair is grey throughout, and softer, wispier, like a duckling's first coat.

*

"I went to Delphi," I say, my hands still warmed by my father's. His eyes are watery, red-rimmed, the wrinkles around them deep. His hands feel lighter than before, as though his bones no longer weigh what they once did.

"The oracle told me..." But I stop myself. Perhaps her strange riddle isn't one I need to confess right now. I thought I knew what she meant, until Eros put a different meaning into my head. But those are not stories for this moment: for my father's wide and staring eyes, or the king's watchful ones.

"I did not think I would see you again," I say simply.

Father squeezes my hands, his eyes never leaving mine.

His breath smells of wine—a lot of it. Before, my father was always sparing with his drink.

"I did hope," he says. "I always hoped." He smiles faintly now. "The goddess...I was right to put my trust in her, then: that she would show mercy after all."

His words land hard. Their effect is unexpected. It feels as though I've been hit in the stomach.

Mercy, he says.

My father is gratified; pleased to think he did the right thing by giving me up. He thinks this is his reward. Memories, snippets I do not wish to revisit, pass behind my eyes. The way he struggled to meet my eyes that day. How, unlike Dimitra, he did not look back—could not look back—when the king's carriage bore them all away. How he begged me, when I reached the Underworld, to ask my mother to forgive him.

I close my eyes briefly.

He had another daughter to protect. A good soldier does not throw living men after the dead, but accepts the sacrifices that must be made, in order to protect those still under his care.

And yet I was his favorite.

If he had resisted that day, perhaps he would be dead now; perhaps Dimitra too.

Or perhaps not.

Those other pasts, other futures: they are cards we can never turn over. Cards whose face perhaps even the oracles do not know.

But I must set him straight on the facts.

"It was not Aphrodite who relented," I say, taking my hands away. I step back, looking over my shoulder. Eros has stood quietly since we entered the room, letting me do the speaking: he knows what this reunion means to me. Usually his tall, cloaked form would be the first thing anyone would land on, but my father only seems to notice the strange figure now, and his brows knit in consternation. The tall, hooded shape is not a comforting sight. I remember exactly what I thought, that first night I saw it. I thought him my executioner.

My father clears his throat.

"Who—who is this?"

"The one who saved me," I say, my gaze on that dark hood, and in my mind's eye I see the face that burns beneath it, the golden hair, the lion-bright eyes. I hesitate.

"Father...perhaps you'd better sit down again."

*

"A—a *god*?" My father stares at Eros, who stands hooded and calm. I can't tell if the look is one of wonder or horror. "*Here*? In this room?"

His face shifts between fierce intensity and a strange, slack blankness, as though the truth is too much for him to digest in one sitting.

Dimitra's voice is taut when she speaks.

"We have seen his face, it is true."

"But..." My father looks from her to me, and then again to the cloaked form behind me.

"Is it so unthinkable?" Dimitra says, some challenge in her voice. And she is right—our family has already learned what it is to catch the eye of the gods, in the most luckless way. The great goddess Aphrodite was the first to turn our lives upside down.

"*Khaire,* Andros of Sikyon." Eros steps forward, and though he makes his voice gentle, it carries through the room. My father just stares, open-mouthed.

"I admit, it is not the usual way of things, between men and gods. We are known for dabbling in the lives of mortals, for pleasure or for vengeance, but it is rare that we bind ourselves to them." As Eros speaks, I feel his eyes turn toward me. "Yet when I saw your daughter, I knew what I wanted was not what most gods want."

I flush, and feel my sister's stare. If I was astounded to find my sister married to a king, how must she feel now, to see me married to an immortal?

My father levers himself from the divan, prostrating himself on the floor.

"My Lord. I am forever grateful for your favor. For your intervention. For your—your protection of my daughter."

Eros inclines his head, acknowledging. It does not give him the same discomfort as it gives me to see a mortal prostrating themselves. He is used to it.

"Remember, Father," Dimitra says tartly, "your daughter is not out of harm's way yet. It seems the goddess still wants her dead, perhaps now more ardently than before."

I notice how she says *your daughter,* as if to remind him, perhaps, that he has another.

Eros nods at her words.

"It is true. She would gladly visit her vengeance on Psyche, as on me. Psyche's amulet"—he gestures to the Shroud, and I see my father's eyes widen—"protects her from the gods' eyes, while I may choose to conceal my whereabouts at will. But if mortal tongues begin to wag…"

"Only we in this room may know Eros's true name," I say. "Only we may know who stands among us. Do you understand,

Father? If gossip spreads, it may kill us."

"All of us," Dimitra says, her voice tight.

My father, eyes wide, looks from one to the other of us, nods slowly.

"I won't breathe a word."

I glance again towards the door, where the king stands, a little back from our small group, watching.

I feel a quick pang of guilt. Dimitra is right: we have brought danger to their home. And yet, how could I not have come in search of them?

The king's eyes are narrow, assessing. Is he thinking about Dimitra's words: thinking of the risks we have brought with us? I could hardly blame him. And yet, I do not think that is what's on his mind.

Just then, a knock comes at the door.

"Your highness?" A girl's voice comes from the other side. "It is Irini, your highness, with the prince."

The prince. It takes my mind a split-second to arrange it all again. My sister's child. My nephew. It is hardly to be believed.

Across the room, Dimitra's glance finds mine. Beneath all the noise, we're still sisters.

"Enter, Irini," she calls, and I feel the emotion in her voice. She walks quickly to the door as a startled-looking nurse enters.

"Oh—my apologies—begging your pardon—" The nurse bows in a confused way to the room at large as Dimitra takes the small swaddled bundle from her arms. The bundle lets out a lusty cry. Not a cry of distress, though: it is as though he is showing off the power of his new, small lungs. My sister's eyes light up with something I've never seen before. Pride, I think, but it is more than that, something fiercer and more primal. Something passes between her and the child, something in her face that is for him alone. And then she raises her head, radiant and regal, and her eyes find mine.

"Psyche," she says. "Come and meet your nephew—the Prince of Atlantis."

*

His eyes are blue, resoundingly blue, and so big, so watchful. He is barely in this world—they should be vacant still, half-blind from the womb. And yet there is such intelligence in them. Perhaps it's just the fancy of a proud new aunt. But even so, the small hairs rise on the back of my neck. It is as though he already knows he is a prince. There is some great calm behind those bright eyes, and suddenly I picture him as a youth, standing tall, that same assurance in his stare.

I swallow, and glance up. Dimitra's watching me with a knowing look, as though she can tell what I've just experienced.

"He is a marvel," I nod. "Truly."

"He looks like you," the king says, startling me; I had almost forgotten he was there. A strange little smile is on his face, but it does not seem to me a happy expression. I don't know why he should be other than happy—a son, an heir, in thriving health. Perhaps it is our arrival that has cast the shadow.

I look at the baby's blue eyes, which are indeed a similar shade to mine.

"What's his name?" I ask.

Dimitra smiles.

"Nikos," she says. Nikos, meaning *victor*.

I cannot deny it is a handsome name, and a suitable name for a prince. And yet I cannot help but think of battles, of men fighting and dying, the fields of war. It all flashes through me, clear as a vision, and I have to close my eyes a moment to shake it off.

When I open them, two birds are circling outside the window: birds of prey, falcons. I see their sharp silhouettes against the blue, following each other in a downward spiral, hunting whatever flies below.

"Psyche?" Dimitra is frowning at me. Father clasps my hand.

"Such blessings," he says. "Such blessings for us all."

Skin prickles the back of my neck, but with my hand in his cold one, I cannot but agree.

Seven

The guest apartments are hastily made up for us, and Dimitra takes us there. The room is large and airy, every bit as grand as the rest of this palace has led me to expect. At the far end, behind a pale linen curtain, I glimpse a balcony with a view of the sea.

Eros nudges the curtain aside and walks out to take the air—or, as I strongly suspect, to allow my sister and me a moment together. But now that we have it, we seem, for a moment, to have come to the end of the words. We look at each other in silence. Dimitra reaches a hand out towards me, combs it through my hair. She winds a strand around her finger, as though studying its gold shade against her skin. Then she lets it fall, and her eyes return to mine.

"So—we are to harbor Aphrodite's enemy."

She is shrewd, my sister. She always has been.

"I think there is much you have not told me." Her black eyes seem larger now, in her hollow face. The ordeals of Nikos's birth seem more visible, when I see her up close. Beneath the regal bearing, the fine clothes, my sister is exhausted. She is also right in her assessment of me; of how much lies unsaid.

Behind her, the white linen curtain bats in the sea breeze.

"We need not stay here," I say. "It is not our intention to endanger anyone. We can leave again in the morning, or tonight, if you wish it."

Something flickers across Dimitra's face.

"Leave now? Father wouldn't hear of it," she says. Perhaps it is her way of saying *she* wants me to stay, or perhaps not. "Besides," she adds, "my husband wishes you to stay. And he is a man used to getting his way."

I look up at her.

"Your husband is not afraid of Aphrodite's wrath?"

Her jaw sets.

"He is not afraid of much."

I cannot tell what emotions lie behind those words. Anger, fear, pride—does she think him reckless? But perhaps that is what drew her to him.

She glances towards the balcony, where Eros's tall shape is just visible through the linen curtain.

"So," she says. "You won him over with your famous beauty." Her voice is not sarcastic, exactly, but neither is it warm. Then again, Dimitra has heard enough about my "famous beauty" to last a long time. When people in Sikyon started speaking of it was around the same time they ceased to comment on hers. My sister was, and is, a remarkably handsome woman, but she does not enjoy being overshadowed.

"He risked much by going against Aphrodite's decree," she comments. She turns back to me, frowning as she looks me over. "I can see why he wished to bed you, but to marry you? The gods don't offer mortals such favor."

I flush. What she says is the truth, and yet I can't help but feel insulted.

She has a way of making me feel small. As though I have come by something I don't deserve. I want to ask her about the king—how she came to marry him; if she loves him, if she trusts him. But my face is flushed, I cannot find the words.

"Be at ease," Dimitra sighs. "The maids will bring water and fresh robes. Someone will call you for dinner. I have shown you where my room is; come to me if you need anything."

She leaves, and the room is quiet. There is only the distant roar of the sea. I close the door gently after her. It's many, many moons that I've been longing to see the faces of my family. But somehow, I had thought the reunion would feel more peaceful.

*

I go and join Eros on the balcony. Sea and sky, a mirror of blue on blue, all the way back to the mainland where we came from. Below us and a little to the right is the shipyard. There are men there, small, busy figures, sawing and hammering, distant sounds on the breeze.

Distant enough that it feels safe for Eros to pull back his hood again. It's a relief to see his face. And yet there is an expression on it that feels remote—or perhaps it's just me.

"Is my sister right?" I ask him. "Are we putting them in danger, by staying here?"

She didn't say those words exactly, but she implied them. Even if their home had been a hut in a nearby village, our presence would have carried some danger with it—but I can't help feeling that it's all more prominent, riskier, now that I know who my sister and her husband are. How many eyes are on them, day and night.

"They will be safe," Eros says, "as long as they don't talk." His bright eyes lock on mine, but softer now, like a fire burning low. "They are the only ones who know my true name. All they need do is keep that to themselves."

I nod.

Eros looks back out to sea.

"Kings do not live long, in your world." He glances at me. "And it sounds like this one may have made himself an enemy or two, of late. I suspect your sister will have brought more risk to her life by marrying him, than by hosting you."

I'm not sure if that's supposed to comfort me. I lean on the balcony too, letting my eyes drift over the calm waters. They're calm on the surface—but who knows what dangers lie beneath?

"I was thinking," I blurt out, "that my father might have answers for me. About myself. Why I can do the things I can."

This is the story I didn't want to go into downstairs. The facts are…sensitive, one might say. Because the truth is, I have always been able to do things I shouldn't be able to do—or at least, my body has. It healed itself in a mere day or two, when I was trampled by a horse. When Dimitra shore all my hair off—at my request, in the hopes of appeasing Aphrodite—it grew back in just one night. When Aphrodite's scorpion stung me with its deadly poison, I *felt* my blood fight back. I felt it hold the poison at bay, just long enough for Eros to save me.

And there's more.

Back when Eros was imprisoned on Olympus, when I had to go in search of him…many strange things happened to me on that mountain. But one of the strangest was when I looked in a wolf-cub's eyes, and felt it speak to me. Yes, speak. Not in words, not exactly, but I heard its meaning in my mind nonetheless—crystal clear.

I thought at the time it was the nature of the mountain. The gods' magic. But the truth is, I've felt whispers of it since then, too. Not often—but enough to make me wonder. It was Eros himself who raised the possibility that there was something different in my blood. That I might have something in me that most mortals don't. Back in Sikyon, they called my mother a witch. I thought it was only cruelty, harsh words for an outsider, but perhaps it was more than that. Perhaps she was…*unusual*, too.

If anyone knows the truth of it—of whatever curse or blessing may have run in her blood, and therefore mine—surely that person is my father.

But when Eros looks at me, he's frowning.

"There've been no…incidents, recently, have there?"

I shake my head.

"It's always possible…" he speaks slowly. "That we may have…that *I* may have, misjudged it. When many coincidences fall together, such things are easily mistaken for something more."

I fold my arms.

"I didn't imagine it." Why is he drawing back now? Denying the very thing *he* put in my mind?

He looks back at me, eye to eye.

"I'm not saying you did. But I think you should be careful how you speak of these things. And to whom you speak them." His frown deepens; he looks back out over the sea.

"I know this is everything you wanted," he says. "Finding them. Being here with them."

I don't tell Eros that in fact, this doesn't feel like quite the homecoming I have dreamed of; that something seems amiss. I'm sure if we just give it a little time, things will be restored to what they were. Dimitra will warm up; my father will be in better health. We just need a little time.

"My mother's campaign against me grows more successful every day," Eros says quietly. "I can feel it. My god-strength is waning more and more." He gives a small, humorless laugh. Sunlight moves over the sea in a shimmering pattern, like some promise just out of reach.

"Before, I told you we should not use my powers for fear of drawing the gods' attention. That we should live as humans do. But now…now I am not sure I am much better than a human, anyway."

I touch his back, his folded wings invisible under his cloak.

"Could you fly, still? If you needed to?"

He shrugs, looks out to sea.

"It is humiliating, Psyche. It should not happen to a god."

He sounds angry. Angry at *me*. I tell myself that he's not; that the anger he feels is separate from us. But the harshness of his voice still rings, and he makes no attempt to soften it, or look my way.

"You cannot know Ares will take your side," I blurt. Perhaps it bothers me more than I admit, the way he speaks of being "not much better than a human"—as though to be human is to stoop so very low.

"Even if we leave here," I plough on. "Even if we find him—"

"*Even*?" He turns to me. "You may choose to end your journey here. But I *will* leave here, and I *will* find him."

I stare at him. Words dance in my head, though none of them can seem to fight their way out.

I go where you go, I want to say. *Do you doubt it?*

But that's the thing. Apparently, he *does* doubt it. And that makes me close my mouth again, and turn away.

Distantly, the sound of knocking floats our way. Someone's at the door to our room. They're calling us for dinner.

Eight

The dining room is sumptuous in every way—decorated in purple and gold, plush and glinting, mirrored and gilded. It's almost too much to take in. I've heard that this particular hue—Tyrian purple—is made from the juices of crushed sea-snails, harvested at dawn from rocky coasts. They say it takes ten thousand snails to obtain just a pinch of pigment.

"Your room is to your satisfaction?" The king's voice is all solicitousness, but still, I don't quite like it.

Eros inclines his head.

"All is perfectly comfortable."

"Very good." The king laughs a little. "I would hate to displease a god!" He looks at Dimitra, as if it is some great joke. "Wife, did you ever imagine we would feed the like at our table?"

Eros says nothing. He hears nothing in the king's words except admiration. But to me, there is a touch of something else there. Irony? Jealousy?

Beautiful girls with elaborately braided hair come to the table to wait on us. They are dressed in the thinnest of robes, sinuously woven around their bodies, and their eyes are made up so heavily, they look like exotic birds. I see the king's eyes travel over them—approving, enjoying—as they bow and lean, serving him one sweetmeat and then another. I think my sister sees it too, but she doesn't seem to mind. Perhaps I am seeing more than is really there. Father doesn't seem to notice anything. He thanks the women gently, and puts only a small amount of food on his plate. He gazes at me across the table, a faint smile of bewilderment as we sit down, as though he still can't quite fathom that I should have appeared this way—not dead, after all, and with a god in tow.

Eros, too, takes only a little on his plate—out of courtesy, chiefly. Even the feasts of kings are not much to tempt him. He does not need mortal food, any more than he needs our kind of sleep, and even the best foods here pale in comparison to what he eats in the realm of the gods. Meanwhile there is more food here than our small party of five could ever eat—whole stuffed quails, trays of honey-glazed duck, figs, artichokes, cheeses, and pomegranates...The girls keep appearing, serving water and wine, and tray after tray of delicacies, until the king waves a hand, dismissing them. I am almost sorry to see them go—there is a sudden, silent intimacy in the room they leave behind.

Dimitra sips from her wine glass, turns towards Eros.

"So, my lord..." Her voice is cautious but determined. My husband intimidates her, but even intimidated, Dimitra does not stay silent.

"You tell us you are a fallen god. What does that mean, exactly?"

"It means that, for the time being, my powers are greatly reduced."

Her eyes widen.

"By Zeus's decree? Can he do that?"

Eros folds his hands in front of him on the table—those broad, bronze hands. I can tell he does not enjoy such a topic.

"Not by Zeus's decree," he replies. "At my mother's behest, many of my old followers have ceased to worship or make offerings to me. In this way, a god's power can quickly be diluted. Worship, prayer—these are what keep are powers strong."

Dimitra and her husband look at each other. It was a surprise to me too, when I first heard it: that it is we mortals, in a sense, who give the gods their powers.

"I have some followers, still," Eros says. "But they have gone underground, and are few."

"And when your powers were at their height..." the king pauses his chewing to speak. "What use did you make of them, if I may ask? I mean no offense. But I hear the gods are much like us. That they prefer to eat and drink and make merry—they do not spend all their time moving mountains, I think?"

I hold my breath a little at that, unsure how Eros will receive it. He is proud of the gods, proud to be among them. And I am not sure I have ever before met a mortal who seemed so nonchalant about them. But if anything, I think he is amused. Or at least, I hear no anger in his response.

"The difference," he says mildly, "is that when they want to move mountains, they can."

"Yes, or throw thunderbolts," the king nods. "Or wage wars. But I suppose you were not a wager of wars, my lord? That was not *your* role?"

Is he trying to needle? I can't tell. But if he is, Eros seems deaf to it.

"It was not. Love and desire—those were my domain."

The king frowns, pensive.

"And is there *less* love and desire, now, my lord, as your powers wane?"

For the first time, Eros's voice hardens.

"For that, you will have to wait and see. Even the hearts of men do not wither in a day."

The king mops his mouth, thoughtful.

"But if you regained your worship, you would regain your powers?"

Eros gives a brief nod.

"But it is not easily done. Aphrodite has forbidden it, and the people live in fear of my mother's wrath. I do not blame them."

The king chews thoughtfully, swallows. The candlelight catches his dark beard, the beads of wine glistening there where they dripped from his cup.

"And yet," he says slowly, "what if you were to be worshiped under a new name? A new guise, one your mother did not know." He pauses. "After all, new cults spring up all the time in these lands."

I glance at Eros, the hood low over his face, his face hidden. I cannot tell what he's thinking. But I'll admit, the king is right about the new cults. The great ones, the Olympians—these never go out of fashion, of course. But other, smaller gods may come and go. Like the god Serapis, imported from the land of Aigyptos, who I hear has gained much following here of late; or the new cult of the Orphics, who are said to believe in reincarnation. All sorts of things may come and go in these lands.

"It is a curious idea," Eros says, after a small hesitation.

It *is* curious. Though I am not sure how he would go about implementing such a thing.

"Just a thought, my lord," the king shrugs, smiles. There is something about the way he says *my lord* that I do not like. It should be respectful, humble, but somehow it doesn't feel that way. He tears the meat from a lamb-bone, throws the gnawed bone on the floor beside him.

"You will have heard, perhaps, that no gods are worshiped in Atlantis now. They say I am a godless king, Lord Eros, and yet it is not true." He pauses. "You see, I believe a man should stand on his own two feet. Make his own luck, take responsibility for his own failings. I have never chosen to petition the gods for any favors, nor to offer up my worship to them. I suppose that I can get along well enough without them, and certainly the gods can get along without me." He smirks, and steeples his hands.

"As for the priests, I disbanded them and sent them home to do some honest work. You see, I do not object in principle to my subjects casting their prayers where they may. But these priests were being paid quite excessively, and for nothing, in my view, except to sit around and drink from my wine stores." He sighs. "But I do not think the people of Atlantis have taken so readily to the new ways. Some men prefer to think for themselves; others prefer to act as sheep."

He looks at Eros with one eyebrow cocked, but Eros just shrugs.

"If you think you will offend me with your words, you are mistaken. We all must live with the choices we make. Your choices, and their consequences, are your own."

The king nods, and I see the hidden smile playing at his lips. As far as he's concerned, the "consequences" must look very healthy indeed. He is king of a storied island; he has a beautiful queen and a newborn heir. And all this without help from the gods. No wonder he feels no humility.

"And how did you spend your time, your highness, before you were king?" My voice sounds strangely bold in the large room. I'm only asking a similar question to the question he asked of Eros—but I admit, it might have a ring of impertinence. Still, the king, for all he looks surprised, only smiles at me.

"Well, little sister. You are not a shy one, I see. I suppose it is to be expected—neither is your sister." He throws a look at Dimitra, and then at my father.

"You have raised two bold daughters, Andros." He doesn't sound entirely approving, at least not to my ears. My father blinks, and bows his head briefly in acknowledgment, but I think the comment unsettles him, too.

The king turns back to me.

"I was the old king's *strategos*—the leader of his guard." He looks me straight in the eye. "You did not hear that detail?" His mouth twists a little, as though at an unpleasant memory.

"I had hoped to do my job well, but under such leadership, it was impossible. The men begged me to take control. To bring some order back to this kingdom, before it fell beyond repair."

The men. He must mean his fellow guards, the group who led the coup with him.

"Kostas offered him the chance to step down," Dimitra says. "But he refused."

Kostas shrugs.

"I will not pretend his death was any great tragedy. Leonides cared for nothing but his own amusement. He let the laws wither away, and kept no justice in the land. He was a weak man, and a weak king." He pauses. "No wonder, when his mother was some Kytheran whore."

I flush. It does not escape me how men—powerful men, especially—like to use "woman" and "whore" to mean the same thing. As for what the king says about the man whose throne he took, I suppose it is as likely to be true as not. I may not like this king, but that is not to say I would have liked the one before him any better. I'm not sure I've ever met a king I liked—certainly not the Sikyonian king. If he'd had his way, I'd be in Hades' realm by now.

But it unnerves me, all the same, to hear that this king was the last king's *strategos*. If you can't trust those meant to guard you, who can you trust?

Nine

My arms are cold in the breeze from the balcony. The night is here now, and the stars are out. But this is no time for stargazing. Eros stands next to me, his hood thrown back, his eyes glowing, his mouth frowning.

"I've been searching for him," he says. "Every night. I thought perhaps I sensed his presence, but…I cannot locate him."

He's talking about his father. You would not think the god of war could spawn a god of love, but so it is. Aphrodite's real husband is the great weapon-maker, the gods' blacksmith, Hephaestus. But it was her affair with Ares which gave her her three sons: first the twins, Phobos and Deimos, raised as war-gods at their father's side, and then her third-born, Eros, the one she kept close to her and raised in her own image.

Eros has explained to me that the gods have the power to locate each other, whether in this realm or another—*if* the god you're seeking wishes to be found. Of course Eros has hidden himself, for our protection, but I also know he scans the realms from time to time, checking on his brothers. Checking if they are safely distant on Olympus, or if they tread in the mortal realm—and if so, whether they walk too close to us. He doesn't speak of it often. I expect he does not want to remind me of how much there is to fear. But of course, I realize now, he has been searching for his father, too.

He sighs.

"My father has never liked his whereabouts known, and he has never spent much time in the halls of Olympus, not like my mother. He prefers adventure, and likes to keep his adventures secret. He likes his freedom more than almost anything."

I suppose he means freedom with women. Ares is a

philanderer, like most of the gods—and Aphrodite, I'm sure, doesn't take kindly to her lover playing elsewhere. I know all I need to know about how jealous the goddess can get.

I sigh. What is there to say? If Ares is not to be found, he is not to be found. I know Eros will keep looking.

There's a touch of something cold next to my heart: I'm still carrying my mother's knife under my robe, I've been carrying it all day. A good thing Eros managed to pass it to me last night; the guards were too bashful to search me properly. In the moonlight, I take it out, turn it over in my hands. I don't draw it from its sheath. It is a sharp thing, and dangerous. No, more than dangerous. Deadly. It gives me some comfort to hold, and yet, it is because of this knife that we are in so much trouble.

Yes, a blade with the power to kill a god should make the Olympians fear us. But fear makes a person dangerous, and the gods are not just worried, they are offended. Eros is only a lesser Olympian, not at the level of either of his parents, and I am nothing at all. And yet we are carrying a knife which could slay them, and which has already maimed Eros's brother Deimos for life—he has lost one of his wings thanks to this blade. Thanks to me. It's no wonder if the other Olympians want this knife out of our hands, and I don't know where they'll stop to get it.

Such power isn't ours alone, though.

Eros told me that, according to legend, three such blades were made, back in the time of the Titans. How one got into my mother's hands, no one can say. But another of them—the only other one that Eros knows of—is on Olympus. *That* blade is the one that killed Kronos, the one Zeus used to kill his father in the Great Uprising. And it is kept under lock and key by Zeus himself. If it is ever to be used, a Council of the Gods must be called, and the verdict given. I know that Eros's great fear is that one of these days, such a council will be called, and they will decide to unleash the blade and use it against us. But whatever about the other gods, I cannot suppose Ares, or even Aphrodite, have yet come to the point where they wish to see that blade used against their own son.

Sometimes I think Eros resents the blade we carry. How it

makes us enemies to the other gods. I suspect sometimes he has thoughts of throwing it away, into some deep ocean, off some great cliff. But we cannot risk it falling into the wrong hands. And besides—we can't get rid of it now. It's the only thing that gives us power.

"What if there's something to it?" Eros says abruptly. "What the king said: starting again with a new name, a new following?"

I look at him.

"Would it be safe?" I say. "Would word of you not reach your brothers' ears?"

He shrugs.

"There are many small gods in these islands, many myths the people worship. The Olympians do not bother themselves about such small entities, two-bit gods beneath their notice. As long as their following does not grow *too* strong…"

The idea makes me uncomfortable, but I can't say why. Perhaps it's just that the suggestion came from the king, and I don't like the man.

"I expect it would take many years to build," I glance at him. "If Ares takes your part—especially if he takes your part with Aphrodite—that will win you your power back, much quicker than you can do so with a new following." I shrug. "I suppose you will get word of him soon enough, one way or another." It cannot be otherwise, when my people are so often at war; when great battlefields so often present themselves. "Sparta, or Crete, or Athens: someone will surely invoke him before long."

It feels strange, to be saying such a thing. To be comforting my lover with talk of human bloodshed and death. I change the subject, though admittedly to something else that disquiets me.

"What do you make of him?" I say. "The king. What sort of man is he, do you think?"

Eros blinks, turns to me. His thoughts have been elsewhere, his gaze on the night sea.

"Ambitious," he says. "Arrogant, I suppose." He shrugs.

"A man."

A man like any other, is what he means. And for all I know there is some truth in that.

"Come," he says then. "The night is well advanced. You should get some rest."

Inside, I slip my mother's knife beneath the pillow, running my fingers once more over the carved hilt, its familiar ridges a comfort. Dimitra plans to show us the kingdom tomorrow, and no doubt it will be a full day. I would do well to rest—but something tells me I will not be able to sleep much tonight. I hesitate, feeling Eros beside me, the spark of warmth from his skin, the small flame that his touch can so easily kindle. I reach out a hand, run it down his arm.

"You will be tired in the morning, Psyche," is all he says. "If you do not sleep."

I think about what the king said earlier, the part about love and desire withering as Eros grows weaker. He meant the love and desire of mortals, in our world. But what if it's Eros's love that's withering; what if it's his desire for me that is slowly starting to ebb?

*

When I wake, the bed is cold beside me. A gust of wind drifts through the room, streaming from the balcony and making the linen curtain dance. I shiver, and reach for my chiton to wrap around myself.

"Eros?"

But he is not here. Where has he gone, and why did he leave me to wake alone in this strange and foreign place?

It is your family's home now, Psyche. Why should it be so strange and foreign? Why should I feel uneasy? And yet I do.

I roll onto my back, looking up at the gilded ceiling. And for some reason, I find myself thinking of that wolf-cub on Olympus. Of the voice I heard in my mind, clear as a bell. Eros told me yesterday that perhaps these instances were not all I have made them out to be. I have to admit, it's true: those strange occurrences have dwindled lately. These past few months, there has been nothing to remark on at all. No whispers, no voices; no strange recoveries from things that ought to have been fatal.

Perhaps, I think wryly, it's just that no one has tried to kill me of late.

A baby's cries abruptly pierce the air, pushing the questions from my mind.

I pin my chiton with a brooch, tidy my hair quickly, and open the door to the hallway. I suppose I had meant to go in search of Eros, or Dimitra, but the nursery door is ajar and the sound of my young nephew's lungs at work makes me pause in the doorway. The nurse looks up at me in surprise. It's the same girl who brought him to my sister yesterday—Irini was her name, I remember. The child's wailing stops; he's at her breast now, feeding hungrily. Of course, it's only proper that a queen should have a wet-nurse for her child. I had not meant to interrupt such an intimate scene.

"I'm intruding," I avert my eyes. "I'll come back later."

But Irini shakes her head.

"This palace is yours to roam, my lady; you are the queen's sister. Besides, a wet-nurse has no great modesty about such things."

I look at her face. She is young, and yet I wonder how many children she has nursed before this one. But I suppose it is a great honor, to be brought to the palace to nurse a prince.

"Come in, if you wish," she says, and I step inside, pull the door gently to behind me.

"My name is Psyche," I say. "Psycheandra of Sikyon."

"I know your name, my lady."

"And you are Irini, are you not?"

She nods, smiles a little, as if to say she is open to further conversation, but does not seek it. She gestures at the small footstool across from her, an invitation, and so I sit.

"You are from this island?" I ask. It is peaceful in here, after all, with only the soft, satisfied sounds my nephew makes. And since Irini is not shy, there is no reason for me to be.

She nods again.

"I have lived here my whole life, my lady."

It makes me wonder what she thinks of the new king, and his new order. She would have grown up under the old one—but perhaps none of that matters to her so very much. Perhaps for the everyday people of this island, one king is as good as another. Though if she dislikes the new ruler, I don't suppose she'll tell me.

I nod at the child in her arms.

"It was a difficult birth, I hear."

"Yes—they said it went on for many hours, and at great cost to the queen. They did not think that she would live." Irini shakes her head. "And is it any wonder? Look at the size of him! He must be twice the size of any newborn I've seen." She glances up at me. "He's a hungry one, too."

She transfers him to the other breast, and is winding him when my sister appears in the doorway.

"There you are." Dimitra's eyes flash. "I've been looking for you."

Ten

Dimitra gestures, and Irini obediently places the child in her arms. I watch my sister take in the sight of her son all over again, with a look that's almost hungry.

"Come, let us walk." Dimitra cradles Nikos in her arms. "The air is always freshest after the rain."

I suppose it rained in the night. I was sleeping too deeply to notice.

"Is Eros about the palace?" I ask her. "He was not there when I woke."

She blinks at me, and it feels as though I have been careless somehow, that I have misplaced my husband the way a woman might misplace a necklace.

"Perhaps he has gone to look about the citadel."

I nod. He has been restless; I should not have slept so late.

"What about Father, is he awake yet?"

Dimitra looks away.

"Father sleeps long hours, these days. And eats little." She pauses. "I thought that your return would revive him. But if *that* cannot, I am not sure what will."

"He is not so old," I object.

"No," Dimitra looks at me. "But the suffering has aged him."

Is she implying I'm the root of that suffering? I can't tell, but if she is, perhaps she's not wrong. He suffered enough in his youth—the war, his widowhood—but in the last year he lost me, then his livelihood and status, his home, his very identity.

The baby gurgles softly to himself as we move along the stately corridors, Dimitra nodding at the guards stationed here and there, who bow their heads as she passes. She carries herself well, and if I didn't know to look for it, I wouldn't have detected that stiffness in her walk that speaks of lingering pain. She has a little more color today, I think, and it is complemented well by her exquisite robes.

We go through a great sun-room, and out an arch onto a high, terraced garden, full of bright wind-flowers, anemones. The view is breathtaking. We are just below the battlements, almost as high as the watchtowers where the guards stood two nights ago, keeping watch for forbidden ships. And just like the guards, Dimitra and I have a view all the way out to sea—and, much closer, the fleet of triremes I saw from our bedroom window. They are large ships, and there are many of them. I remind myself that all kings have their war-ships; it does not mean they plan on war. At any rate, they are noble-looking ships. If I squint, I can make out the lettering on the hull of some of them: it seems each has a name. *Sosthenes. Artemion. Nereia.* Handsome names. I have not known a man to name his ships before. But then, I have never really known a king before.

Dimitra looks the other way, out towards the agora, and the citadel.

"I expect that's where your god-husband is now. Kostas will have found a suitable guard to go with him, and show him the city."

It still amazes me that she is here—*here,* in a palace, in such a situation. She cannot have met the king long after she arrived in Atlantis. It is a story I must hear. But it is my sister who speaks first.

"How can you do it, Psyche?" She shivers. "How can you share a bad with a man whose face is hidden from you?" There's a hint of disgust in her voice.

"He's not a man," I say simply.

Dimitra looks at me.

"When I saw his face, in the mirror…I believe I saw it clearly enough at the time, but once it was over…" She frowns. "I could not recall any features. Only a sort of bright whiteness, like a fire." She shakes her head. "A face that could destroy you. Does it not horrify you, the thought of that robe slipping; the thought of what one glimpse could do?"

I wish I could tell her the truth. But then again, even I

don't know what the truth is. I don't know why I can look on my husband's face, when other mortals can't.

"He will not destroy me," I say.

"So you say." She looks at me, frowns.

"He has saved me already," I remind her. "More than once."

She nods.

"Saved you, yes. While he let your hometown burn to ash."

I look away. The reminder is painful, even now.

"We found out too late what happened to Sikyon. We didn't know. There was no warning."

"No," Dimitra agrees, her voice tight. "There was no warning."

I know what she's thinking. *For all those people—the dead, the destitute. For them, there was no warning*. She looks back at me.

"And yet here you are, alive." She looks down at the waving anemones, their dark centers and pale heads.

"I almost died two nights ago, you know. Anyone who tells you that is not exaggerating. I saw the darkness. The doorway to Hades' realm."

She glances up at me.

"The world looks different, doesn't it, when one has dipped one foot in the River Styx."

I know what she means. There were many moments in the past year, when I was sure I was going to die. More than once, I was sure it was my time to pass into that other realm. But when I met death, I was thrown back, as if by a fisherman who didn't know his own desires.

Living feels different, once you've been through that. But I wonder if it feels the same kind of different for Dimitra as for me.

I follow my sister around the corner of the terraces. More flowers line the pathway. *A garden in the sky*, I think. From here the view reaches out over the township, beyond the citadel walls, and to the unrolling lands behind. Villages are dotted here and there, and in the distance is that singularly shaped mountain I noticed our first night.

"That's the Red Mountain," Dimitra points, noticing my gaze.

"Why red?" Its slopes are a rich green, like all the fields and pastures around it.

"It is a fire-mountain," she shrugs.

I have heard of those, but never seen one.

"Not to worry." Her smile is tart, sardonic. "It has run dry many lifetimes ago. But some say that is the reason for Atlantis's rich earth—they say the fire-water that spews from a volcano makes fertile soil in the years that follow."

"After is has destroyed everything," I point out.

"After it has destroyed everything," she acknowledges.

Total devastation in return for future fertility. It does not seem like a very good bargain, but I suppose the people of Atlantis are glad of it now.

The baby lets out a cry then—not the typical mewling of an infant, but a big, lusty cry that seems to speak of neither hunger nor pain. Perhaps it's my imagination, but it sounds to me as if he is calling out to the wind, testing the power of his voice against the wild gusts.

"Do you ever think back?" Dimitra says, after a pause. "Do you ever think about life in Sikyon?"

"Sometimes," I nod. The truth is, I try not to. It makes my thoughts ache.

We are quiet another moment.

"Back then," Dimitra says, "you were engaged to marry another."

"Yes."

I look away. Whatever fancy I once had for Yiannis Demou is long gone, and yet it's true that I think of him sometimes: I do not know whether the rock slide that killed so many in Sikyon killed him, too.

"Do you know anything of what befell the Demous?" I risk a glance at my sister's face. "If they are dead or living?"

She shakes her head, her expression softening for a second.

"I know nothing of any of them. Our banishment came before the earthquake: Father and I were gone by then, and whichever way the refugees came, none crossed our path."

I absorb her words, letting them settle in the place where I keep my last memories of Sikyon.

"Hektor is dead," I blurt. "Little Hektor, who rode alongside me in the pageant."

Dimitra meets my eyes. She is a mother now. She understands the death of a child in a different way than before. But she does not wince, and the dart of shock that flashes over her face is soon covered up with something stonier. I remember how as a child she would cry if an animal were ever hurt. But I don't think I have ever seen her cry for a human. She looks away, her face tight. Sometimes I think Dimitra tries to kill her own tenderness, for fear of what it may do to her.

"Human life is cheap," she says at last. "That is what I have come to see. Precious few have the luck they need."

Abruptly she bends over the infant in her arms.

"Isn't that right, my love?" she says. "Only a few are blessed."

Grim words, to be spoken like a lullaby. But perhaps she considers us the blessed ones. After all, here we all are, still alive.

For now.

"And what do you do with your days here?" I say. "How do you spend the hours?"

She glances at me.

"There is always something to be done. In the mornings, I sit in the throne room, with Kostas. The island should see that we are united; that the king's wife supports him in all things." Her mouth twists. "Besides, I like to know what's going on in these lands. What the disputes are, what the news is. The visits from the peasants and the petitioners is how I stay abreast of it all. It is the people of Atlantis who come to the throne room every day, to hear justice be done, and to see the king's face. I want them to see mine too. I want them to know who their queen is."

"Even yesterday, you were there," I say. "Though you

had been close to death the night before."

She says nothing for a moment, then smiles a little.

"I do not trust the king's advisors, Psyche. They jockey for position among themselves. They are jealous, miserly types, and they do not like me." She pauses. "You see, the king chose me because of a prophecy. Perhaps it is for this reason that some of them distrust me."

I look at her. I had not expected that.

"This prophecy—do you know what it said?"

She shrugs.

"That I was lucky; that I would bring him luck." Her dark eyes meet mine again. "But I think many of his councilors would turn the king against me if they could. They do not want to share their influence over him, certainly not with a woman. So it seems prudent for me to keep my seat by his at all times, and for the people to see me upon it." Her forehead creases, then smooths.

"My handmaidens had to help me to the throne yesterday, and every step was like walking on nails. But it was worth it," she says, with some satisfaction. "To see Dareios's face, and all those other men's, when I came into the throne room."

She looks up. "You should come and see. You can sit in the audience. Everyone likes to witness justice being done."

Justice: a bold claim indeed.

The baby wails into the sky again, puncturing my thoughts. His little hand waves in the air.

"It's a strong voice," I say.

"He will be a strong child," Dimitra answers. I am struck by how she says it. Not just proud, but as though she is stating a fact; as though she can already see his future. She has never lacked confidence, my sister, but something about this seems different.

"Have you brought him to the oracle?" I guess. But Dimitra shakes her head.

"I don't need to," she says.

I look at her sidelong.

"What do you mean? What do you know?"

But she just shakes her head.

I look into my nephew's eyes again, clear and fathomless. *Who is this child? Who will he be?*

The wind roars. The anemones throw their heads wildly in the breeze.

Eleven

Dimitra offers to have someone bring me to the auditorium, so I can be there for the morning's justice session. But before that, I go to call on Father.

"Come in," he calls, and I walk into a room lit with soft morning light. A table full of papers lies before the window. Has my father, the soldier, become a scholar in his advanced years? He looks up at me, his eyes bright. Something there that is too cautious to be called joy; relief, more like.

I understand—it all felt a little unreal to me, too, this morning. As though this extraordinary reunion might have been a dream in the night.

"I struggle to believe it still." He smiles, or tries to, but it's a little pained, a little lost. "I keep asking myself, you know—" He gestures around us, taking in the room, the palatial quarters, Atlantis; all of it.

"Why this? Why us?" He shakes his head. "I suppose many fathers like to imagine that their children are destined for great things." He looks at me. "But I never dreamed those things for you—either of you. And yet...look at you now. Your sister, married to a king, and you..."

He doesn't need to finish.

"The worlds of the gods are closer to ours than we realized, Father. And I did not marry him for glory, you know."

He nods, slowly. It occurs to me that if I *had* hoped for glory—for the poets to sing songs of us, for people to know my name—our current position, mine and Eros's, would be ironic indeed. Fame is the last thing we seek now. The last thing we can afford.

We are silent for a while then.

"Atlantis," I offer. "Has it changed much—since you were here last?"

It is many moons since he came here as a soldier. That was when he met and wooed my mother, and brought her home with him to Sikyon when the war was through.

He glances at me, a small, sad smile.

"Yes—or I have changed, perhaps. I came here then to fight a war—to free the Atlanteans from the shackles of the Cretan king. There was no time to admire the beauty of the land. It was all ships and swords and bloodshed." He glances toward the window. "And then, when it was over, there was your mother. The most enchanting creature I had ever seen. She would have liked to stay here, I think, in her home place—but there was Dimitra at home, motherless, waiting for my return." He stops. "But after all, the legends were right—this island is beautiful enough to be touched by the gods."

His hands tap softly against the table. He does not speak often of my mother. His first wife was an arranged union, but with my mother it was a love-match. And then her death—on the day she birthed me—left him alone with two little daughters. It is a sad story, a burden on us both. Perhaps that is why we have so rarely spoken of it. And yet I have more reason now than ever before to know the truth of it all. To understand who and what my mother may have been.

"My mother," I say slowly—this is difficult territory, for both of us.

"People said she was a witch. Why did they say such things?"

He looks at me more seriously.

"I know people spoke rumors about your mother. I should have expected you would have heard some of them too, as a child. I'm sure it caused you pain. I am sorry we did not speak of it then." He pauses. "As to why: I suppose they called your mother a witch because she had earth-knowledge that they did not. And because she liked her own company, and kept to herself, and that offended them. And because an Atlantean in Sikyon was considered a foreigner." He looks at me. "She was a good woman. She did nothing to deserve such judgment."

I look at him carefully.

"And was there anything…more than that?"

He frowns.

"More?"

"Any…" I feel my cheeks growing warm. "Anything she could do? Any…powers? Anything unusual?"

He blinks at me, and the warmth in my cheeks grows stronger.

"She was not a witch, Psyche. She had no magic powers. She was an ordinary woman. Beautiful, to be sure. But an ordinary woman, underneath it all."

There is some bafflement in his voice, and sympathy. He thinks I am a heartsick child, searching for evidence that my mother was special; longing to make her into the stuff of legend. It's true, when I was a young child I craved such words. I wanted my mother to have been extraordinary, magical—anything to compensate for the fact that she was gone.

But no longer.

Today, I would gladly settle for ordinary. And yet, if my father is right—if my mother *was* "ordinary"—it leaves other questions unanswered.

Perhaps Eros is right. Strange events abound in this world. Perhaps I have been making too much of them; making them about myself, when I should just accept the good fortune where it falls. I sigh and let those thoughts settle.

Father's window has no view of the sea—instead, it looks out over the lands of Atlantis, and the Red Mountain Dimitra showed me earlier.

"What part of the island was she from?" I ask then. I do not think it is a very large island; perhaps I may see my mother's hometown while I am here.

Father nods, on surer ground now.

"She was from the village of Lykaria, to the northeast. But it was a small place, and her people are long gone, Psyche. There is little to see there, now."

Lykaria. I tuck it away, all the same. Father looks at me.

"And how long will you stay with us, Psyche?" There is some shrewdness in his glance. "I do not think you plan to be here indefinitely?"

Outside the window gulls are diving towards the sea; flying back up, only to dive again.

"No," I admit. "We cannot. My husband seeks his father. Ares may offer him protection against the other Olympians. Protection we sorely need."

My father raises his eyebrows.

"You seek the god of war?"

"Eros thought we would find him here," I explain. "Ares goes where there is violence and unrest. But we were caught for a long season in the winter passes; by the time we got close to Atlantis, the rebellion was over, and the new king, as we've seen, well-settled on his throne."

My father nods, taking this all in.

"Were you here for it—the rebellion?" I ask.

He nods.

"We had barely arrived. I came before the old king to plead for some livelihood. I had fought for Atlantis, after all." He shakes his head. "It was only here that I finally heard tell of what had befallen Sikyon. The earthquake. The king seemed to marvel at it. We must have been blessed by the gods, he said, to flee just in time." My father sighs.

"He gave us some land, as I had asked—although the next day we found out it was not spare land, but part of a farmer's livelihood. The king had forced him to give up the parcel to us, and he was not best pleased. He eyed your sister as though he would take payment some other way, and I told her to bolt the doors whenever I was not home." Father glances at me.

"Within a few days the king had come—the new king, I mean; Strategos Kostas, as he was then—to call on us. He said he wished to court Dimitra." Father shrugs. "I suppose he told her everything—at least, she did not seem shocked when the rebellion came. But she told me nothing of that. All she told me was the prophecy which Kostas had told her. Kostas had been there, of course, that day in the throne room, when we were telling our story. Our lucky escape. It seems it was then and there he'd realized, Dimitra was the one who he must claim as his bride."

So: he chose Dimitra because she was lucky. Because she already seemed touched by the gods, managing to flee Sikyon in the nick of time like she had. And it's true, it turned out to be luck in the end. But I wonder if he knew, then, that they did not flee Sikyon from instinct alone. That my father and Dimitra were cast out, banished by its king.

No matter, now.

"They say the old king was murdered in his bed," I prompt. "Is it true?"

Father shrugs.

"It might be. It would not be so unusual—after all, a coup is not the same as a war, Psyche. Coups, rebellions: these are not fought on battlefields with spears and shields and rallying-calls. They happen in dark and quiet rooms, where the only sound is a dagger slipping from its sheath."

"So you think he was right?" I eye him. "Kostas—he was right to kill the old king?"

"I didn't say that." My father sighs.

I frown, looking down at my fingers.

"And you and your husband?" my father says then. He knits his hands together, a gesture that he did not used to have. I am not sure what it says—criticism, perhaps, or worry.

"It is not the way of things, Psyche. Gods and mortals—they do not belong together, not like that." He looks at me. "And you have told us that you are already in danger. That other gods wish you ill. It is a perilous way to live."

I fold my arms, bite my tongue to keep back the words that spring to mind.

My life was perilous before I met him. Father cannot have forgotten *that* already. How I was sentenced to certain death. How Eros saved me from it. How my father didn't. Wouldn't, couldn't; I don't know. But I see it as if I were there, still, at the rock called Aphrodite's Pillow: my father, turning away from me as I stood chained to the stone. Allowing himself to be led away into the king's carriage. Though I believe he did the best he could, I know now that something between us broke that day.

I believe he can tell where my thoughts have traveled. He sags a little.

"Forgive me," he says in a low voice. "I would have rather the king took my life than yours. I would not have hesitated. But there was nothing I could do. The decree was given."

Nothing he could do. He seems to believe it, still, but I am not so sure. Aphrodite may be one thing. But a king is just a man.

The moment is short-lived; a knock comes at the door. A guard stands there: a woman, I see suddenly, and with surprise. At least, she is armored like a guard, and with a guard's robe. Nimbly built; slender but boyish. Her hair is cropped like a man's, her eyes quick and clever under fair brows. She reminds me of a hare, or a half-tame fox, quick and lean.

She dips her head in a curt bow. "I am Phylax Thais. Your sister sent me to fetch you, Lady Psyche." She gestures before her, down the corridor.

"Let us be on our way. The Great Hall awaits—and I do not think you wish to be late."

Twelve

Phylax is a warrior's term, an honorary title meaning sentinel, guardian. But *Thais* is certainly a woman's name.

"You are surprised to see a woman on the king's guard?" She smiles. "It is unusual, you are right—though not in all parts of the Greek lands. In Crete, in fact, it is quite common. Women are warriors there, just as much as the men."

"But we are not in Crete," I point out, and earn another smile, this one amused, with only a hint of sharpness.

"Indeed, my lady. We are not."

*

I see the throne room with different eyes this time. When Eros and I were summoned here as prisoners, all I could see was my sister's face. Shock made everything else recede into the shadows. But now I take it in with full force: the great dais with the two thrones—the king's and, a little lower, the queen's, both empty right now; and the high ceiling, the tall Ionic columns, the elaborate paintwork and gilding. The guards that line the edges of the room—I remember *them* well enough, and their leader, Dareios, his glowering face by the doorway. But mostly what I notice today is the crowd. There is a barricade halfway across the room, to keep them an appropriate distance from the throne. Evidently these morning justice sessions are popular with the people of Atlantis. The people jostle each other, cursing, treading on each other's toes. What is it they're so hungry for? A glimpse of the king as he enters; the prospect of justice or retribution?

"This is the only time of day that commoners are allowed into the throne room," Phylax Thais explains as she escorts me through the crowds. "Shall I find you a seat at the front?"

I shake my head. Back here, it's standing room only, but I'd prefer to stay somewhere unobtrusive, unnoticed. I see the flicker of understanding in her eyes.

"Well, if you're sure, my lady—" She gives a quick nod and prepares to leave.

"But perhaps," I say, before she has quite turned away, "you could tell me a little more about all this. I've only been here once before, and that was under rather different circumstances."

That hint of amusement crosses her face again.

"Quite so, my lady. What is it you wish to know?"

I nod my head toward a banner hanging behind the king's dais. It's blue and silver, and bears an image of a serpent curled around a sword.

"Is that the king's insignia?"

Thais frowns.

"In a sense. It's the symbol for justice used in this part of the world. The sword for fairness, and the serpent for wisdom."

I turn my head to the side.

"A sword and a serpent. Neither a particularly friendly sight, I think."

That twitch of a smile again.

"Perhaps not to you, my lady. For myself"—she runs a hand over the hilt of the blade hanging from her waist—"I have long considered the sword a friend."

"And who is he?" I point at the small, whiskery man who sits at a desk at the foot of the throne.

"The scribe. And there," she points at a space on the ground, a circle drawn in chalk on the stone floor. "Is where the accused must stand. See, they are bringing someone now."

As she speaks, two guards escort a nervous-looking man to the spot on the floor, and one of them gives him a shove towards the center of the circle. I hear the scribe's quill scratching in the moment of silence. And then the door at the back of the room opens, the guards stamp their feet in unison—a salute—and in walks the king, followed by my sister. The crowd hushes, and then starts murmuring again, a hum now. Dimitra and the king take their seats.

"Name?" the king calls out, eyeing the accused man in the chalk circle.

The man gives it, stammering a little, but it's lost in murmurs and catcalls.

"Silence!" the king calls down from his throne, and there is an excited hush.

"And who is the accuser?"

Another man, better dressed than the accused, comes forward then. He explains that the accused has the neighboring farm to his, and that the man keeps trespassing on his lands with his livestock.

"Great King, you have promised us a stricter justice than under King Le—I mean to say," he corrects himself quickly, "the Degenerate."

King Kostas has been quick to rename his predecessor, I see.

"You have promised us that our rights will be upheld," the man goes on, "not left to wither like fruit on the vine. I ask you to uphold my rights to my property."

Murmurs of curiosity and approval travel around the room, and then the accused is nudged forward and given his turn to speak.

"Gracious king," he says, and his bold voice falters. He is growing more nervous the longer he stands here. "My cows have always crossed his land to drink at the river. The path was trodden by my father's animals, and his father's before him. If I cannot use the path, it will take me all day to go around the border of his farm; I won't return to my own home until nightfall."

The king thumps a hand on the arm of his throne, silencing the crowd's renewed murmurs.

"Whether it is nightfall or otherwise is not my affair, man—unless you would have me tell the sun and moon to change their paths so as to accommodate you?"

There are titters, and the accused man looks down at his feet.

"No, my king. But—"

"But you are a trespasser on your neighbor's land," the king's voice rises. "Your old king may have let the rule of law slide away to nothing, but his ways are dead. I am here to uphold the rights of the people. To ensure that property is respected. That its owners are not abused. You will not trespass on your neighbor's land again, nor will your livestock. Any animal of yours that steps on his lands is forfeit, and he may take it from you as his own."

The man turns a shade paler.

"But I, but—"

"But what—you wish to argue with the king's justice? Go, now, before you rouse my temper."

I look towards my sister. Does this please her, or does it sting the way it stings for me? Her eyes are keen and alert. It is the look she wore as a child when our tutor spoke of foreign lands, or when Father would tell us old histories by the fire. She misses nothing, but whether she approves, I cannot tell.

The man is brought off, and another accused brought in. This one is older, and instead of another commoner stepping forward to accuse him, this time it is the leader of the king's guard.

"Dareios," the king greets him. "What case do you bring us?"

Dareios clears his throat.

"This man has defied your royal decree, sire: that one man from every household must volunteer himself to work on the king's mines, if there be one such between the ages of ten and forty."

I had not known there were mines on Atlantis. Nor that they were operated through conscription.

"And how many such men are there in his household?" the king asks now.

"One, sire. This man is fifty, but he has a son of ten. But he has lied to your councilors, sire, and sworn to them the boy was only eight."

"He is small for his age," the accused bursts out. "He is not strong—"

"Silence!" the king says. He doesn't look angry, exactly. I suppose this kind of disobedience is something he expects. But he leans forward in his throne, as though to show that no transgression, however petty, will pass unnoticed.

"Remember: these mines are for the good of Atlantis. I have promised each of you a share in them. It is yourself and your own family you sabotage, by flouting the decree."

The man shuffles uncomfortably.

"If you please, sire. I only wanted to give him a little time. To—to catch up with the other boys his age. They must lift and carry in the mines. Heavy weights. And he—"

"Your son will report to the mines tomorrow, as his peers do," the king says. "You cannot expect that your neighbors will follow my laws while you receive special dispensation."

"Sire." The man acquiesces, bowing his head.

"Now, Dareios: how long has my edict been in effect?" the king turns.

"Three months, sire."

"Indeed." The king turns back to the accused. "Your son will serve double time for three months, starting tomorrow. If he cannot, you will take his place. To make up for the three months which you have robbed your fellow citizens of."

"I…your grace..."

"Three months," the king says crisply. "Maybe you will be lucky. Maybe he will find you a nugget of gold."

I watch the man being marched off the stage, and another take his place. This one is accused of stealing medicine-herbs from a merchant, expensive ones. He says he could not afford the price the merchant asked, but needed it for the pain. He broke his back tiling a roof two years ago, he says, and it hasn't healed right.

The king asks Dareios to refresh his memory on the traditional punishment for thievery, though it's clear there is nothing wrong with his recall. It's a charade, that's all, something for the audience to enjoy. Someone in the crowd shouts out the answer before Dareios can.

"Losing a hand, sire! Chop off his hand!"

The king waves the voice down, his lip curling at the man's enthusiasm.

"I am a merciful king," he says, and I see the accused's face brighten with a moment's hope.

"So I will take two fingers only. You may choose which fingers. Take him away."

The king waves again, and the thief, ashen-faced, is escorted from the dock.

I think I've seen enough.

"Thank you," I whisper to Thais. "I would like to leave now. Can you help me find a way out?"

All around us the room is thick with people. I don't want to cause a commotion by leaving, nor draw the king's attention, and there are many men around me so tall that I can't even see the exits.

"Follow me," Thais says, and cuts a path through the room. A door emerges as we get nearer. She ushers me through, and in her glance before the curtain falls shut behind me, I think I see some understanding there. Perhaps she does not quite like the king's justice either.

Outside the throne room I can breathe easier. It is a relief to be out of that heaving mass of bodies. I climb the spiral stairs slowly, my hand against the cool stone wall. So this is the man my sister has taken for a husband. I wonder what she sees in him, besides power.

I wonder what else power can make us blind to.

But is it possible I am being naive? No king can afford chaos. Those men *did* break laws, and in such cases there must be consequences. There must be order. And yet…

Was it like this in Sikyon; was justice so harsh there, too? Perhaps it is only that we did not make such public spectacle of the king's laws. Probably they were just as cruel. I shake my head, trying to untangle this mess of feelings, thoughts. I'm almost at the door to my bedroom.

"Oh!"

The door is open; a woman is in there. A maid. She's making the bed, and her hands are on the pillow—the pillow beneath which my mother's dagger lies. My heart stutters in my chest.

"I'll do that." I step forward, my voice sharper than I meant for it to be.

"It's no trouble, my lady—"

"I said, I'll do it. I'm tired, and would like to rest now."

She traightens, looks at me with a hint of fear.

"I—I apologize, my lady. I'll leave you be."

One she's gone, I exhale, heart still battering. Gently, I take my mother's knife from under the pillow, and look around the room, seeking a better hiding place. A chest of spare linens, made of cedarwood, and heavy. That will do: I ease it up, and slide the knife underneath, between the base of the chest and the marble floor.

Watch out for us, Mother, I think.

Help us keep your secret.

Thirteen

An impatient knock comes at the door, startling me. I had fallen asleep, I think; an uneasy sleep, not quite a nightmare, but haunted somehow. The feeling doesn't quite leave me as I turn and move towards the door. But without waiting for my answer, Dimitra steps inside.

"*There* you are." She looks at me. "The carriage is waiting."

"What carriage?" I say. It passes through my head that they are getting rid of us after all.

"Didn't the maids tell you? Kostas has arranged for us to see some of the island today. Your husband"—a flicker of some emotion crosses her face—"is already waiting for us, below."

My husband. I feel a wave of relief, and some resentment mixed in with it. What were these explorations of his, that kept him from me all morning? I would have wished for him to be in that hall with me, to have witnessed what I witnessed. My head is still uneasy with memories of the king's "justice"; with much that I have seen and heard and wondered.

Dimitra looks to the window, where the noon sun is still high.

"And Father?" I ask, smoothing my hair. "Is he accompanying us?"

She shakes her head.

"He says those old bones of his rattle too hard."

"He did not used to talk of old bones," I observe.

"He did not. But he is not what he used to be, Psyche. I think perhaps…he is drawing closer to his gods."

Towards the end of one's life, it is said that people begin to live in the other realm bit by bit. They do not depart this mortal life in one great jump, but by installments. So I understand her words, but they sink my heart, nonetheless.

Dimitra and I descend the staircase, where two guards stand to attention as we pass. Two more bow their heads as we go down the great hall, through the heavy doors, into the sunlight. I remind myself that I am a guest here, not a prisoner; something about the line of guards as we descend the steps makes me feel strange.

Ahead of us, four horses snort and stomp gently, waiting for us to take our places in the litter. Such carriages are not typical in these lands, but perhaps it is a normal luxury for the king, or perhaps it reflects my sister's condition. I suppose she will not ride horseback for a while yet. The horses, shining and well-brushed, snorting softly, make me think of Ajax. I feel a pang all over again. Did we do the right thing, leaving him behind?

"Good morning." The hooded figure seems to step from nowhere, startling me: Eros, waiting for us, just as Dimitra said. I want to fall into his arms—and then again, I want to stamp my foot and accuse him of abandoning me. But his voice is cool and light, as though nothing in particular has happened. His hood is down, so I cannot see his face. But even if I could, it doesn't seem like I would find an apology there, or any awareness of how adrift it felt to find him gone this morning. A ripple of irritation goes through me.

"You were exploring, Dimitra said?"

He nods. "A page came to our rooms this morning. You were asleep. At the king's invitation, I've been out to view the citadel. It is a handsome town."

So he did not simply leave me of his own accord; he was summoned—though I doubt he thinks of it that way.

Perhaps his morning was better spent than mine. It sounds as though he's formed a more favorable impression of the town than I have of the king and his courtroom justice. I feel his warm touch on my back as he helps me into the carriage, and wish I could have a moment alone with him.

"My lady," another voice says, acknowledging me. I look up: Phylax Thais again. It seems she is riding with us, alongside the young lad holding the horses' reins. I return her nod, but it makes me wonder, and inside the carriage, I ask Dimitra: "Why does one of your guard come with us? Is it a dangerous drive?"

My sister's lips thin.

"It is no harm to have a practiced sword-hand with us. But don't worry. Any supporters of the old king are only to be found in small pockets, now. They are no real threat."

"I suppose most of the old supporters were eliminated after he took the throne," I say, and from the way Dimitra eyes me, some distaste must show on my face.

"Don't act squeamish, Psyche. You know as well as I do, it's the way of the world. Besides, the process was more peaceful than you might think. Plenty sought exile, and sailed from here in the night."

"Is that why the king is so keen to keep foreign ships away from here, then? Because he fears reprisals?"

Dimitra's nostrils flare slightly. She feels I am interrogating her; judging her, perhaps.

"Atlantis is a coveted land. Many of the neighboring kingdoms might think it a fine time to try and take it for their own. Power is like water, it takes a while to find its level."

I wonder where she heard that. From the king, presumably.

"He will re-open the borders when the time is right," she says.

I look at her, wondering what she really makes of her husband. If she supports his policies, believes him a just ruler. I cannot tell.

Her eyes narrow.

"You think he should be more optimistic, more trusting, more open?" She folds her hands in her lap, her eyes on mine. "If his measures seem severe to you, Psyche, ask yourself: what do you think an invader would do with me, or with our father, if they were to capture Atlantis?"

The old king's allies? They would slaughter her, and my father, and most likely the little prince too. They would do it easily, coolly, without mercy. *Whose side am I on?* is what Dimitra means. Perhaps she is right. I reach across the carriage and press her hand, to tell her I don't mean to argue further about this.

Not for now.

*

It is a beautiful hour of the day—indeed, I suspect most hours are beautiful in Atlantis. As we journey inland, the sea winking on the horizon grows fainter, eventually its bright beauty giving way to open fields and distant forests. In the distance, the Red Mountain rises from the earth like a great wave. It dominates the horizon easily, now that we are outside the citadel.

I have never seen a fire-mountain before, only heard of them in stories. I stare out at it, the great, grassy cone, and think again how strange it is that everyone should think of this place as a "blessed isle," while somewhere outside living memory, such devastation has occurred here. But even so, I must admit that to see it now, this island is like something the great poets might have invented. The wheat fields are bright and golden, the grass shimmers with green. Vines cascade down the mountains; olive trees make shady orchards by the roadside.

We reach a crossroads, and the entrance to what appears to be a small village. Figures in the distance, children playing. A dark swathe of pines opens up behind the town, and behind that, a blue streak of sea.

"That's Athiri," Dimitra says. "A fishing village. I'm told that's where Irini, the wet-nurse, is from. Fishermen's daughters provide the best milk—that's what Atlanteans say, at least." She makes a face, as though she doesn't think much of the island lore.

But as the sea comes into view again, my thoughts have wandered back to the rebellion. To ships that fled from here, and are barred from returning.

"It must be hard," I say, "to defend a whole island. There are so many places one might come ashore."

Dimitra shrugs as we ride on.

"Atlantis is well-formed in that respect. The only natural harbor is the one you have seen. Elsewhere, the cliffs are high and craggy with little room to anchor, and the waves are rough. Only a madman would try to land his boat in such waters."

The island defends itself, in other words. That is convenient, indeed.

"And the king's own fleet?" Eros asks. We had a view of the shipyard as the carriage rolled by. There were many men there, hammering and sawing, busy as ants.

"He is building a bigger one?"

Dimitra nods.

"Atlantis has no military strength anymore, he says. The old king had let it wither; let the island go undefended. Kostas is intent on building the island a proper fleet, so it can defend itself in wars to come."

Wars to come. I can't help wondering if the new king is looking forward to those days. Something tells me he is a man who likes a fight.

The carriage rattles on; the roads are growing rougher, stones catching under the wheels.

"Where is this carriage headed?" Eros asks, and Dimitra smiles, seeming pleased at his interest, although the smile is a little tight at the edges.

"Kostas thought you might like to see the mines. They are a new initiative of his." Is that pride I hear in her voice? I can't tell.

"The last king would not allow mining. He was a primitive, Kostas says. All sorts of fears about disturbing nymphs and wood-sprites, even though legends abound of the island's riches." She looks up at us. "Atlantis is rich enough above the earth—there seems to be no plant that won't grow in this soil, and its vines never miss a harvest! But they say beneath the earth it is richer still, with pockets of the most precious jewels and metals. You see," she explains, "many generations ago, there used to be mines. But then the old king shut it all down—had some sort of religious conversion, by the sounds of it. Didn't want to offend the gods of the earth by taking what was theirs. Though I suppose he already had all the gold he needed by then."

I frown out at the lush green grass, the forests and hills clad with rolling vines. They look so ancient, so at peace in this earth. I suppose I have some sympathy with the last king's views. But few mortals have been known to resist the lure of gold.

"What if the old kings emptied out the mines already? What if there's nothing left?"

Dimitra shrugs.

"People are tired of living this way. You can only get so far being a fisherman. Who would not exchange a ship's worth of trout for a thimble's worth of gold? A day's work could feed a family for months."

I look up.

"You mean, they get to keep what they find?"

"Some of it," she says. "The kingdom must take its tithe, of course."

Of course.

"I heard a case tried in the courtroom today," I say. Part of me hesitates to raise it; to sound critical again. And yet I want to know. "I gather it is not voluntary, for the men to work the mines."

Dimitra frowns.

"Conscription is nothing new, Psyche. Kings use it every day, readying their people for war. That is what the mines are for: to help Atlantis defend itself against outside forces."

"Not to decorate the king's palace?"

Dimitra purses her lips.

"Kostas's goal is for Atlantean self-sufficiency," she says, no longer looking at me but staring out the side of the carriage now, watching the green hills and fields go by.

"And for that we need copper, and iron, and bronze. In the past, Atlantis has traded for these things, mostly with a neighboring island, Kythera. But if we can mine it ourselves, Atlantis will gain true independence."

I let her words settle. I can feel Eros's gaze on me, from beneath his cloak. Does he think I am asking too many questions? No doubt he can hear the flicker of impatience in my sister's voice.

"I suppose the mines carry risks," I can't help saying. "I am told it can be dangerous work."

Dimitra looks at me.

"Life is risk, Psyche. Fishermen drown. Farmers are trampled." She shrugs. "I am not the king. If you wish to rebuke him for his policies, be my guest." She glances out the side of the carriage, and almost the same instant, we come to an abrupt stop.

"Come." She rises from her seat, tosses her dark hair over one shoulder. "We're here. Now you can see for yourself."

Fourteen

The mine is a great, gaping void where the earth should be. Sounds of labor carry up from its depths as we approach, and there are men at the top, too, stationed all around the pit—these are the ones who haul up the buckets. There's a group of women also, not working, just talking peaceably amongst themselves, gathered a little way back from the pit's rim. Some of them have children with them. These are the wives, I suppose. I wonder if the mines are such a novelty to them that they choose to come and visit.

At the sight of Dimitra, though, all the chattering goes quiet. The people recognize her—or at least, they recognize her robes, her diadem.

After a brief hesitation, one of the men steps forward. The foreman, from the way he speaks.

"Your majesty." He bows. "You have come to inspect our progress?"

"We have honored guests at the palace," Dimitra explains. "I wished to show them the king's most important project."

"Your majesty." The foreman bows again. "Shall I alert the men?" he says. "You would like to address them, perhaps?" He has a whistle strung around his neck.

Dimitra peers down into the pit, shakes her head.

"No need," she says. "They are working; it is not for me to interrupt their labor." She turns to me. "Have a look, Psyche. Be careful, it is a very great drop."

Peering down, I'm startled by the depth of it. It is wide as an amphitheater, tall as five or six such stacked on top of each other.

Men—and boys, too—stand at various depths, on stone walkways cut into the sides of the pit. They are bare-chested, their skin slicked with sweat. The air rings out with the sound of metal against stone. Abruptly, one of the men jumps back, shouting a warning, scattering the men working beneath him. They move fast, and it is a good thing: the falling rock smashes to the ground at the base of the mine, but no one is injured. One of the boys nearby begins sweeping up the shards, dumping them into one of the great buckets that lie at the foot of the pit, waiting to be filled and hauled back up again. I wonder if this is a common occurrence. The sun beats down; a water-boy goes around with a pitcher, then carries the empty jug back to the baskets to be lifted out and refilled.

I feel Eros's presence beside me, and sense his gaze out over the scene below us. I feel, too, the stares from the other side of the pit, from the children and many of the women. It is Eros they are staring at. How could they not stare? A stranger at the queen's side, tall and cloaked, his face hidden, his robes all in black. The sight of him takes all their attention; they barely glance at me.

Only two of the children seem oblivious to it all: a boy and a girl, playing their game of marbles at the women's feet.

"Stay back from the edge, children," their mother instructs, a tall woman with a long brown braid and a voice of calm authority. Her eyes meet mine for a moment, before she quickly drops her gaze. These people are no different than the people I grew up among. Our king rarely came through our streets, but when we saw him go by, on horseback or, on ceremonial days, in his palanquin, no one would dare to look openly at him, curious though we were. Why is it, I wonder, that respect and fear should look so much the same? Or do we only think they should; is it our fault, for so often confusing them?

I touch Dimitra's arm.

"Do you remember?" I nod towards the marbles.

In Sikyon, the boys would often play at marbles. Dimitra had wanted to join, when she was small—her aim was sharp, her arm strong—but the boys only laughed. She knew better than to take her campaign to our father, who would have reprimanded her for wanting to participate in a boy's game to begin with.

For a moment I see a hint of a smile cross my sister's face.

There's a wistful flicker, and then it's gone—as though an inner discipline has driven away the memory and whatever it brought with it. She moves away, peering closer into the mine, and in her wake Phylax Thais draws near. She nods at me, and then, respectfully, at Eros, whose strange black garb does not seem to intimidate her.

"Are you familiar with these, my lady?" She points towards the contraption the men at the pit's edge are using. They're not simply hauling up the buckets, as I first thought. That would hardly be possible: these buckets are enormous, with loads that must be two or three times a man's weight. Instead, the ropes are wrapped around some sort of mechanism, with the men tugging down from the other side.

"It is a *katarti*, a pulley," Thais says, with the pleasure of someone who enjoys new discoveries, and expects that we will, too.

"The wheel bears half the burden of the lift. Besides that, it allows the men to pull downward, instead of upward; it is much easier. A brilliant device, is it not?"

"The king has inventors, then?" Eros sounds curious.

But Thais shakes her head. "I believe he learned it from his time in Crete."

It occurs to me that if other kingdoms were to adopt a policy of isolation like Atlantis, such discoveries would never have been available for Kostas or his mines to benefit from. But I keep the thought to myself: Dimitra has had enough of my criticisms for today.

Below us, the men continue their work, undisturbed. I suppose Dimitra is right not to halt them, but something about watching them when they do not know of our presence makes me uneasy; it is as though they are ants or bees, their labor a curiosity to be studied. I wonder what will become of this labor—what armory will be built, what wars fought and won. There is an ore-cart a little ways behind the foreman. It doesn't look very full to me, but then I know little of these matters.

I hear giggles from the little group on the other side of the mine. The children have paused their game now, and are watching us. The small boy waves, catching Phylax Thais's eye as if he knows her. I look to see if she will acknowledge him, but she does not. When the boy's mother sees him waving, she smacks his hand away.

Dimitra turns to the foreman.

"These women—why are they here, with their children?" she asks. "Don't they have work to do in their own homes?"

The foreman looks flustered, calls out hastily: "Womenfolk, you have brought your husbands' provisions. They thank you. Now you may return to your homes, and make them comfortable for their return."

Whether they are surprised or not at his abruptness, the women take it in stride. Surely they know it has something to do with the presence of their queen and the cloaked stranger. Only the children, immersed again in their game of marbles, pay no heed.

"Didn't you hear?" The woman with the braid reprimands them. "Come, we are to leave now." She clasps the little girl's elbow, and the child stumbles a little, her foot knocking into the marbles on the ground, sending them towards the pit's edge.

The boy shouts, on his feet instantly, racing after them, but the marbles roll fast. In an instant they're at the lip of the mine, slipping over the edge like water over a cliff—but the boy doesn't understand, his legs carry him too fast, too young to grasp momentum. At the edge, he tries to pull back, but stumbles. I hear his frightened cry, his mother's scream, the calls of the women, as one foot skids over the side of the mine and his small body flails.

And then falls.

*

Beside me, Eros moves fast. His arm extends; there is the smallest motion of his hand.

And the boy's fall stops only an instant after it began. He descends now, falling not like a rock but like a feather, and the men working the pit's walls can only stare, open-mouthed, as the boy comes to earth before their eyes.

I don't miss the quick look Dimitra shoots our way. She saw at once what others may have missed, in the cacophony of shouts and screams. But I don't think she was the only one to notice the motion of Eros's hand.

At the bottom of the pit men are running to the boy. One of them—his father, maybe—scoops the child into his arms, and even from here I see how his eyes rove wildly, looking around at the pit walls as though waiting for them to close in.

"What is he?" I hear the women nearest us murmuring—the ones close enough to have seen the gesture Eros made, the way the wind responded to his command. "How is this possible?"

That's when I feel Dimitra's glance—almost as if we did this on purpose. As though we were responsible for the child falling to begin with. The men at the bottom of the pit are staring upwards now, as confused by the situation as the women. I suppose they can tell it's the queen up here, but if they can, they're too distracted to kneel.

Eros grabs my sister's arm.

"You must not tell them my name," he reminds her.

Dimitra wrests her arm away. She's not used to being instructed, especially now she's queen. The only thing keeping her from snapping back is her knowledge of who—and what—my husband is.

"And what would you have me tell them?"

"What you please. Just not my name."

Below, in the pit, the man has harnessed himself into one of the pulleys, the boy still tight in his arms, and the fellow at the top is turning the lever as fast as he can. The boy's mother waits at the pit's edge, clutching her other child against her legs. Meanwhile the other women are watching us, and I hear the murmur of incantations, see them touching the amulets at their necks. The murmurs grow louder, more accusing. This will not pass without explanation.

Dimitra seems to sense that too; she clears her throat.

"People of Atlantis. You have seen the miracle that just took place. The one responsible is he who stands beside me now. You must not fear him. He has great powers, god-gifts which he has used for our benefit. Out of humility, he does not wish to share his name, nor reveal his face. But today our friend has saved a son of Atlantis."

Her voice carries down into the mine, for the benefit of the men as well as their womenfolk up here. Some moments pass, and I find that I am holding my breath, waiting to see what they will accept. Then across from us, the boy's mother kneels.

"Good stranger: I thank you, with all that I have. Your powers are truly god-given." Her voice is sturdy; I feel her control the tremor in it. Slowly, the others kneel with her. The women at the pit's edge. The men at its base.

"Well," Dimitra says, her voice quiet now, for our ears only. Her low voice does not quite hide the hint of displeasure. "You said you sought worshipers. It seems today you have them."

Fifteen

The men all flock to the top of the pit, one by one, climbing their way up the rough-hewn ledges, or hauled up by the pulleys. They gather around the boy and his parents, and then, more timidly, around Eros. The women ask if they may kiss his hand. The men touch their thumbs against their foreheads, a gesture of awe and humility.

I don't miss the expression on Dimitra's face.

The boy's parents continue to shower Eros with their thanks.

"We have little to offer," the father, a stocky, bearded man, greying at the temples, says from where he kneels. "But whatever we have is yours."

"You must show the stranger some hospitality, Theron," his friend nudges.

The man called Theron bows lower.

"Indeed, good stranger. We would be honored to break bread with you. If it please you; if it please the queen."

His wife shoots him a look, some alarm sweeping through her face. Her husband seems to regret his words, but the offer has already been made.

"Why not," Dimitra says, crisply. She glances at me. "You came out here to meet the people, did you not?"

Which is how we end up on the dirt road to Athiri, Dimitra and Eros and me, and Phylax Thais, and the villagers.

Eros walks in the road with the boy's father; with Dimitra's nod of assent, it is arranged that the wife may sit in the carriage with us. I think the woman is embarrassed by this arrangement, but the invitation cannot be refused, so she rides with us, her boy clutched tight on her lap. The little girl is gone on ahead; I saw the woman bend low and whisper in her ear before we mounted, and the little one took off as fast as her legs would carry her, as though the wind itself were at her back. I wonder what it means; whether it is anything to do with the look of alarm that I saw earlier.

The carriage jogs down the earth road, and I ask the woman her name. She is fifteen or twenty years older than me—not so old, but something in her person commands respect.

She looks back at me, uncomfortable but not shy.

"Drusa Sideris, my lady," she answers in a clear voice. "And this is Xenon, my son."

The boy looks embarrassed, refusing to meet my eyes.

I turn and look back at the road behind us. It appears some of the villagers are walking with us, not wanting to miss out on any more curiosities of the day, not ready to let go of this extraordinary day, its mysterious stranger. A small crowd mills behind the carriage.

We come to a halt before a low cottage, not far from the tree-line—the forest of pines I spotted earlier from the road. Drusa's little daughter stands in wait outside, her feet scuffing the dirt. I see the questioning look that flashes between her and her mother, the small nod she gives. It is brief, subtle, but I'm sure I did not mistake it.

"Please." Drusa gestures us inside, bowing her head low as Dimitra sweeps by.

The home is simple: one large, low-roofed room with a great hearth in the center, and a sleeping corner to one side. Woven mats, strings of dry herbs hanging from the ceiling, a small shrine to Hestia in the corner. It is a well-kept home, the domain of an orderly soul. As we enter, Drusa bears down on the only dirty thing in the room, the bowls from today's morning meal still set out on the rough-hewn table. As she stacks them and moves them out of the way, I notice there are six of them.

"You have other children?" I say, coming to help.

She smiles, but it is not an easy smile.

"Yes. My eldest, now full-grown, left us some years back, to seek his fortune on the mainland. And the second, a boy of sixteen, fishes with the men now. He will be out on the boats till dusk. At least he can swim, which is more than my husband ever learned to do."

A fisherman who cannot swim. It seems strange, but I hear it's not unusual. Meanwhile, I can't help noticing that if this woman's eldest no longer lives on the island, that makes only five mouths to feed, not six, which makes one bowl too many. But that can be no business of mine.

"Some wine, lady." Drusa hands me a cup, and I drink from it.

As the villagers crowd in behind us, others milling on the street outside, the gathering soon acquires a festive air. Even the foreman is here. I watch Dimitra pull him aside, and her crisp voice is just within earshot.

"This celebrating is well and good for today—it serves morale, no doubt. But they had better be back at the mine tomorrow at dawn, or the king shall know the reason why."

As Drusa busies herself fetching water and wine, and Eros stands receiving thanks and praise, I am left alone. The villagers don't pay me too much heed: I am in the company of their queen, and the cloaked stranger with magic powers.

I drift over to a corner of the room, where the young daughter of the house has retreated to, playing by herself with a clay doll. She looks up, a furtive glance at the strangers assembled in her home, then back to her doll.

And then I feel something. Something I've felt before.

Feel it—or hear it? A voice, is how I describe it. But the truth is, it's not a voice at all. It's an intrusion, a nudge inside my mind. Feelings, words. *Thoughts.* And it's in my head now, sudden and unmistakable—the little girl's voice. Because I know without a doubt, it's hers.

Secret, it says, like a whisper in my ear.

The child strokes her doll's hair.

Secret.

I take a step back, leaning against the wall, my heart battering. I had half-persuaded myself this had all gone away, but it hasn't. Everything I thought I heard before, it was real—the wolf cub on Olympus, the scorpion in the woods. And other times since then, when I thought I heard some flicker of animal life—the thoughts of a bird flying by, or a dog with his bone.

But I have never before heard a human voice.

I stare at the child, her attention back on the doll now, oblivious. What does it all mean? Why can I hear her? But as quickly as the feeling came, it disappears. If the child is thinking anything now, I don't hear it.

I'm still standing against the wall, breathing shallowly, when Eros approaches.

I want to tell him what's just happened—he must see something strange in my eyes, he must guess—but this place is too public, and I am too unsettled. My thoughts feel louder than the milling crowd in this room.

"Psyche—are you all right?"

I nod, still trying to find the words. *Let's go outside,* I'm about to say, but Eros speaks first.

"I do not think your sister meant it when she spoke about worship, but she was right." He shakes his head. "The people do not know my name, but this—what they are giving me, what they are offering me, just in this room—I feel stronger already." There is something keen in his voice, hungry even. It takes me a moment to understand what he's talking about.

"This?" I gesture. The kissing of hands, the men kneeling, the homage paid. "Though they do not know you to be a god?"

"Even so," Eros agrees.

It has only been a half-hour, and they are not such a very big crowd. If this can have such an effect, how must a whole temple of worshipers feel?

Eros exhales. "I had almost forgotten, Psyche. I had almost forgotten how it feels, to recover a little of that power."

"You were powerful already," I point out. "You stopped that boy from dying."

Beneath the hood I feel the look he gives me.

"That was a parlor-trick, Psyche, compared to what I can do. What I *should* be able to do. You know what I am. What I was."

And you want to be that again.

It crosses my mind for a moment that perhaps I *don't* want that. That I don't want him to go back to being more like a god—more like his family—more powerful than I can fathom. But I can't say that to him. Not now.

Not ever.

*

The sun is dropping low in the sky as the palace looms up in front of us, a different perspective now than before, with the land in front of it and the sea behind. Thais says something to the young driver and together they laugh quietly; the horses snort and pull harder at their reins, sensing their journey is almost done.

I wish I'd had a chance to tell Eros about the girl, about the voice I heard. *Later,* I resolve. Tonight, when we retire alone to our room at last, I will tell him everything.

As we slow to cross the agora, pulling up before the palace and its great double doors, I startle to see the king himself standing there. He has come out to welcome us, with his retinue of guards around him, his purple silk cloak draped back over his shoulders. He is in good form, reaching for Dimitra's hand to help her down, planting a kiss on it as he does so. Then he does the same for me, although without the kiss, which I am glad of.

"Sister," he smirks instead, as he helps me to the ground. The word in his mouth feels unnatural. "How did you enjoy your tour of the island?"

I don't point out that we didn't tour *the island,* just his mines. I suppose we would have seen more of the place, had it not been for the incident.

"The legends are not exaggerated," Eros says courteously. "It is a beautiful isle."

Kostas looks dismissive.

"It is a *rich* isle. It is a sin, is it not, to have a gift and not to use it? To let it lie fallow? We are done with the old king's primitive ways now."

"There was an event at the pit," Dimitra tells him, and

proceeds to relate everything that happened: the boy, the fall, Eros's intervention, and what came after.

"Indeed? Word will spread fast." His gaze travels over us. "Come—dinner awaits us."

The table is laid as sumptuously as before, and the lithe young girls bring flagons of wine. The king's eyes seem quickened tonight, roving over us all, but lingering on Eros.

"The incident in Athiri—it was fortuitous, perhaps. Well-timed." He puts down his cup of wine.

"You see, I've been thinking. A king must think on behalf of his subjects, must he not, as well as himself? And I wonder…I wonder if there is not a way to make them happy, that would also make *you* happy, my lord." He licks his lips, as if in preparation. Preparing *us*, no doubt, for what he is about to say. Something he considers quite delicious.

"We spoke yesterday of starting over, did we not? Of what it would take, for a god to assume a new identity. To gain the worship you seek, but under a new name, a new guise." He pauses. "And my subjects…the Atlanteans are a naturally god-fearing people, you know. I do not think they like it much, that I have closed their temples. And I do *like* to be liked." He smiles a little, a smile that seems directed at me, and yet I cannot help thinking there is something wolfish in it.

"They crave something to bow down before," he continues with a shrug. "And I do think it might enhance my reputation, if I gave them what they wanted. Indeed, something *better* than what they want. A religion of their very own. So, my lord—how about it?" He looks at Eros over the top of his steepled fingers.

"How would you like to be God of Atlantis?"

Sixteen

"It would be of benefit to you, would it not?" The king smiles, lips wet with meat-juice. "It would be easily achieved. We will convene the people at the temple—two, three times a day if you wish it. They will delight in it—a patron god of Atlantis! A god of their very own!"

I glance at Eros, searching fruitlessly to read something of his thoughts behind the black cloth. Often I can read him well, even when he is cloaked this way. I know him, his slightest gestures. But since arriving here, it's not so easy. His thoughts, too, seem veiled to me: he is less himself. Or perhaps I am less myself.

If he is surprised—shocked, even, as I am—he does not show it. He merely waits a moment, letting it pass, and then inclines his head, as if better to consider the king's words.

"A curious thought." He pauses. "But you...What would you seek from such an arrangement? I am a son of Ares, but I am no war god; those kings who wish to build their empires by subduing their neighbors, must look to other gods than me."

The king speaks smoothly. "You misunderstand me. I seek a way to unite my people—and your favor on our lands. You are a god of fertility, are you not?"

My husband gives a slow nod.

"It is one of my attributes, among others."

"Then bring fertility to our earth. I do not mean," the king adds quickly, "wheat and barley and the like. I mean our mines. You could bless our efforts, could you not?"

I hear the frown in Eros's voice.

"It is the god Hades who makes the gems and minerals of the earth. I cannot act for him."

"Perhaps not," the king says smoothly. "But you could bring good fortune to our endeavors. Your blessings. You cannot procure for us what is not there, but I tell you, my lord, it *is* there. All we need is some good fortune."

I look at Eros. Is it my imagination, or do I sense some excitement in him that he's trying to conceal? I remember the elation in his voice earlier, in Athiri, speaking of that rush of strength. How much it meant to him. How much he desired more of it.

"You ask nothing that is against my nature," he says slowly. "In principle, I see no reason why I might not do it…" He glances at me, then back at the king. "But I must caution you, we cannot stay here forever. We have a journey to continue. I am to find my father, so that he may hear my appeal."

Across the table, the king shakes his head, seemingly amused.

"My lord! Of course. You will leave when it is time for you to leave. As soon as you wish it. But build a temple with us here, show yourself before my people…and come back to visit us from time to time, when you can. Then you will have their loyalty for life."

I watch Eros's hands on the table; he folds them now, one on top of the other. It is a gesture he makes when he is thinking. I glance cautiously at Dimitra, who's frowning, and then at my father, who's blinking fast. Certainly, there is much here to take in.

"But how can they worship him," I say, "when they do not know his name?" I fix my gaze on Eros, hoping he will see it in my eyes: I do not want him to agree to this. I do not want this for him, for us.

"Surely it's not possible. He cannot be other than who he is."

The king looks at me as though it had not occurred to him that I even had a voice.

"You would speak for your husband? For a god?" His eyebrows are raised, and though he sounds almost amused, I don't miss the other thing in his voice, the dangerous thing. He turns back to Eros.

"They may worship you as The Shadowed God," he says,

pleased with himself. He gestures at my husband's cloak, his hood. "That is apt, is it not? A good name. A name to build a cult around. You will see. When there is a king's decree behind it, anything can be built quickly."

Eros nods again, his face unreadable behind the hood. But he turns, ever so slightly, towards me.

"What do you say, Psyche—it is an interesting proposal, is it not?"

I freeze, but they're all looking at me, waiting. What reason can I give, against a proposal that seems so in our favor? Only that I do not like this man, the king—and no good can come of saying that. I force a small nod.

"Interesting," I say, "indeed."

The king turns briskly to Eros.

"You see? Why be merely our guest, my Lord, when you can be our god?" He seems to think it a neat joke.

"The people are a willing sort," he goes on. "Country folk. They will not have to be persuaded to pray, it comes naturally to them."

I dislike his patronizing tone—his implication that only the stupid, only the primitive, should lower themselves to prayer.

Eros inclines his head; the dark hood catches the dying light.

"As I told you, we have other destinations we must yet reach. As long as it does not offend you, or your people, when it comes time for us to leave. But if you wish it, I will be the island's god until then."

"Until then, and after," Kostas smiles, as though he knew the answer all along. "We will not strip your idols from your temples, my lord, after you depart. If you can undertake to visit now and then."

Eros bows his head.

"So," the king claps his palms, rubs them together. "It's settled, then? Good."

He takes up a golden kylix, the ceremonial drinking-cup, and fills it with wine. He takes a sip, then passes it to me—I'm sitting at his right hand.

"Drink, sister." He smiles, the glint of wine wet and rosy on his lips. "We must celebrate."

There is nothing I can do. I lower my face, tilt the cup. But over its brim I see my sister, the thin, sharp line of her mouth, and I know she is not happy.

Not happy at all.

But then, neither am I.

*

Up in our bedroom, Eros stares at me, uncomprehending, impatient.

"I don't understand. I thought you'd be pleased." He frowns, searching my face for some sign that I at least know how contradictory, how nonsensical, I'm being.

"It is for you that we came to this place. You have never ceased speaking of your family, of your wish to find them. Now we have, and have been offered to make this our home for as long as we wish—and with a way to restore my strength, to boot. What is there in that which displeases you?"

It is a fair question. I hardly know how to answer. I had wanted to speak to him about something else tonight—of what happened to me in Athiri, the voice I heard. But now that will have to wait.

I finger the Shroud around my neck. I do want to be here. I want to be with my family.

"I just don't like the thought of you serving him," I say aloud.

At that, Eros laughs.

"I do not serve him, Psyche."

I don't tell him that's what it looks like to me.

He sighs. "I am not blind to his flaws, Psyche. But there may be good and bad in any man, just as there may be in a god. And for now, our interests are aligned. He has asked nothing of me that I would not give: health and prosperity to this island, strong soldiers and fertile land. Any king would ask such things, and why should Atlantis not deserve them?"

Again, what he says is true.

"But what we heard, back on the mainland—"

Eros looks at me.

"I remember. But Psyche—do you imagine your Sikyonian king got his power through gentle means? Or the last dynasty of Atlantis, for that matter, the one Kostas overthrew—you think it was through kindness that they took the throne?" He shakes his head. "That is not what men are." He frowns. "It is not just for myself that I seek to regain my powers, you realize: we have enemies, Psyche, and I need to shield you from them. I cannot protect you while I am weak—not as I need to."

I bite my lip. He is right. Surely he is right. And yet…

"'The Shadowed One,'" I murmur. There is some bitterness in my voice when I speak it, and Eros looks at me again. His impatience has softened a little. Not gone, but tempered.

"You do not like the name?"

I shake my head.

"Not especially." I move to the window, and stand looking out. Empty sea, empty sky. Suddenly it all feels bleaker than before. "I think I have seen enough darkness already in my life."

I feel Eros behind me, considering.

"You should not think of shadows so harshly, Psyche. They are not the same as darkness." His voice is quiet, persuasive without trying. "You understand, the shadowed hour does not belong to the night; it is also the herald of the dawn. The shadowed hour alone makes a place for all creatures—for the owls and the foxes, as well as the songbirds and the leaping dear. Only in the shadows can both worlds meet."

He takes my hand, turns me around from the window, back towards the lamp-light, the warm room, his beautiful face.

"And," he continues, his eyes glinting, leading me by the hand, "it is well known to be the hour of love-making."

He leads me back towards the bed; his free hand trails the

skin below my jaw. What can I say? What can I do—his touch, as it always does, sends shivers through me. The dark feeling is still there inside, the sense of something looming on the horizon. But after all, it is only a feeling. And there is another, stronger feeling at work in me now.

The Shadowed One. He touches me again, and my eyes close.

It's true, what he says about the shadows, and more besides. Because Eros himself is not all light: there is darkness in him too. I have seen the effects of his arrows, the ones tipped with poison and the others, their infatuation strong enough to coax a man to his death. I have seen into the depths of this god, into the worlds behind his eyes, and I know it's true: he's a creature of dark and light together.

Perhaps the reason I dislike his new name isn't that it's inaccurate. Maybe it's the opposite.

But if there are shadows in him, there are shadows in me, too. Shadows hungry as wolves, that only his touch can tame.

I sigh, and lie back, and let his warm hands find them.

Seventeen

It's barely dawn when the knock comes at the door, startling us both. Grey ribbons are just turning mauve on the horizon. The servant is impatient; I'm still pulling my robe around me when the door opens, but thankfully Eros had time to conceal his face.

"Do not move so hastily," he snaps. "You will regret it, if you surprise me unprepared."

The page steps back and bows low, his eagerness abruptly withering.

"A—a thousand apologies, my lord. It is only—that is to say: there is a sculptor here for you. And a poet, my lord. The king says they are to begin work on a great monument, and a new ode."

"There is no great rush, surely?" I say. It seems only moments ago that I finally had my lover back in my arms.

The servant bows again, apologetic.

"The king has ordered them to begin at once, my lady."

The page leaves again, but I sense he is only hovering outside the door, giving us some privacy while Eros collects himself, makes ready to leave. I watch him don his sandals, find the new mask the king had made for him. I think of the blood-red stream running along the temple floor. Of the king's pleased face.

"It will not be like this every day, will it?"

Eros frowns.

"A cult is being built overnight. Some effort—from all of us—is required."

I don't miss the faint reproach in his *all of us*.

His fingers graze my cheek, and he's gone. I sit in the empty room, watching the dawn come in. Eros is puzzled by my feelings, my lack of enthusiasm, and perhaps I am a little puzzled, myself. Why should I feel anything but lucky right now? We need refuge, and we have it; I sought my family, and we've found them. On top of all this, Eros now has a means of regaining some needed strength. Is it mere jealousy, some ungenerous spirit in me, that does not wish him to avail of it?

I should have told him about that strange experience in Athiri, how I seemed to hear the young girl's voice as if by some strange magic. I *will* tell him. But how to explain such strangeness? Once spoken aloud, it is undeniable, *real*. And what is to say it will happen again?

I sigh. Dawn is well past by now, the morning already advancing. They will have missed me at breakfast—still, no page has come to the room, asking for me. Perhaps I *am* jealous. Perhaps it's the fuss being made over Eros while I pass without notice, that perturbs me. But there are advantages, too, to passing without notice.

By the time I emerge from our rooms, the morning rhythms of the palace are in motion. The day's "justice session" is taking place in the throne room, which means my sister and the king are fully occupied. The nursery is empty—one of the guards informs me that this is the hour that Irini usually takes her young charge to the gardens for some air. My father is sleeping, or unwilling to be disturbed—when I knock at his door, there is no answer. He never used to sleep so late before.

But it is all the license I need to do some exploring of my own. I have already mapped the upper floors of the palace—the royal apartments, the nursery and guest bedrooms. Below those, the great stone staircase spirals down to the throne room, the dining hall, and the suite of reception rooms. To think, I once thought our king in Sikyon a rich man! He lived like a pauper, compared to the Atlantean kings.

But the great staircase does not end there, with these palatial rooms. I suppose the guards know enough of me by now to let me pass without comment, as I descend one more floor. It is darker down here, with smaller windows. There's a smell of boiled barley, and loud voices drifting from one end of the corridor—a mess hall, I imagine. There are many other doors down here, but all of them are closed. They are not like the doors upstairs, ornamental and prettily carved. These are thick, heavy doors, designed for one purpose only: to keep what's in, in, and what's out, out.

I try a couple, but as I suspected, they're locked. But the stone staircase is still not finished. It curves around and down once more—a level sunken all the way beneath the earth.

"Lady Psycheandra."

I look up. It's Phylax Thais, walking down the corridor towards me, shoulder to shoulder with another guard, a man. They must have come from the mess hall.

"Are you lost, my lady?"

"Just looking around." I try to add a little authority to my voice. I don't want them questioning my right to be here. Thais dips her head courteously, though her companion frowns.

"The palace is a magnificent structure. If you wish to see inside the armory, though, perhaps you should ask your sister, my lady."

So that's what's down there.

"My sister has access to the armory?"

Thais inclines her head again.

"Indeed, my lady. It is she who carries the key."

Her companion looks at her, a sharp look, intended as a reminder.

"Lady Psycheandra," he says gruffly. "May we escort you upstairs? This is no place for guests."

There's nothing to be gained by resisting, but that doesn't mean I have to forego my explorations altogether.

"Of course," I say graciously. "Only, since it is such a fine day, I thought I might go out for a walk."

*

Up in our room, I find Eros's old cloak, the one with the deep hood, and cover myself with it. It's foolish, perhaps: I am not a famous face in Atlantis, people will not take much notice of me. And yet, I feel more comfortable at the thought of walking around behind the hood's protection.

It's not only my husband who can hide his face when he chooses.

The day is crisp, as though spring's warm advance has retreated by a step or two. We ventured out in the carriage only yesterday, but somehow, on foot, everything in the citadel seems louder, more bustling. The morning market is ending in the agora, but the streets outside the great square are still thronged: vendors shouting, women haggling, children running. In between the market stalls are men pushing carts of their wares, or women with poles strung across their shoulders, selling bundles of dried herbs or small trinkets knotted onto long strings. And then, under the hawking and haggling, is a different register of chatter, soft and secretive. Women shopping together, whispering in each other's ears. And the vendors, they talk to each other too—in knowing murmurs, in between shouting about their wares. As I pass by I hear all sorts of things.

"...pulley broke, and damn near broke his neck."

"...up in the new pit, mined a ruby and put it in his pocket before the overseer saw a thing."

"...tides are too high, mark my words. A bad omen—"

My head starts to rattle with it all, the shouts and whispers, and I turn onto one of the emptier streets, following its path as it winds away from the town center. I pass the smithy—at least, that's what I assume the hulking building is, from the pounding and clanking sounds within. There's the hot smell of molten metal, and below it, the sweet, smoky aroma of burning charcoal. I remember those sounds and smells from Sikyon: as children Dimitra and I would sometimes wander over to watch the forge at work, peering from around the corner before somebody spotted us and sent us home.

The path dwindles, growing narrower, and I realize it's leading me out of the citadel, towards where the houses start to thin out, and the forest starts to thicken. I hesitate. Perhaps I've come far enough for one day. Father must be up by now.

Then, as I stand there, I hear a rustling in the trees, and look up. A graceful form, antlers and soft brown eyes. This deer has ventured farther from the forest than I would expect, but now it seems to be feeling the error of its ways: when it sees me so close by, it freezes.

Human.

I hear the thought, clear as a bell. In that moment, I seem to know everything the deer is thinking: how it sees me, how it knows to fear me. I'm not imagining it, this is not empathy: I *know.*

I blink, meet the deer's brown, liquid eyes. One ear twitches. But then it turns and leaps back into the woods, and in another instant it's gone.

I stand there, breathing hard. I have to tell Eros about this—he has to know what's going on. How *strong* this feels. How certain I am. If this is a gift I have, then surely it is growing stronger.

But what that means, I can't say.

*

On my way back to the palace, I see much activity around the great building opposite the palace—the one that backs onto the water, whose purpose I had wondered at when we first arrived. But now I know for sure: it is a temple, and the king's men are getting it ready for tonight. The doors are open, the entrance guarded, men in uniform flowing in and out. I wonder what, exactly, they are preparing. I can't help it, my stomach sinks at the thought.

The Shadowed One.

Is the king really right? Can something like this—a brand new cult—be built so soon?

I spot Phylax Thais among the guards at the palace gate.

"My husband—is he in the temple?" I keep my voice low. I dislike how it sounds—a woman who cannot keep track of her husband. Even when that husband is a god.

She frowns.

"I am not sure, my lady. He has been busy with many preparations."

I find Father in his study—at his desk, surrounded by paper and stylus, and a few small metal contraptions I don't recognize. I am struck again by the change in him. Throughout my youth I remember him as always being the most commanding presence in the room, without even trying: his muscular build, his large presence, his resonating voice. But he is not that man anymore. Or perhaps he never was—perhaps it was only the effect of his features, his bearing, his voice. Perhaps this older, more inward version of him was always closer to the truth.

I gesture at the papers, the diagrams sketched in ink.

"What's all this?"

"Ah." He looks up at me, his grey eyes red-rimmed, but bright. "I have become something of an astrologer now, Psyche."

I sit down opposite him, eyeing the drawings.

"You map the movements of the stars?"

"I try."

"And what do they tell you?"

He shrugs.

"This and that."

"Could you predict my future?" I say. I suppose I am teasing, trying to lighten the dark mood I sense in him, and if I'm honest, in myself, too. But he looks gravely at me.

"I am not sure that would be wise. There are some things we ought not seek to know."

There is some wisdom to that, I'll admit. But his sober tone does nothing to lift my spirits. I pull one of his drawings towards me, but I can make nothing of it.

"I heard the king frequents oracles," I say instead. "Dimitra told me that's why he chose her. Because the oracle selected her."

My father drums his fingers gently on the papyrus, then looks away.

"What?" I say.

He sighs.

"Prophecies have been known to lead men—even good men, great men—astray."

Yes: I know as well as any, the trouble the gods can bring. I glance out the window to the grand temple across the agora.

"They are preparing for the ceremony, it seems. Meanwhile, I have not seen Eros all day."

Father looks at me, then spares a glance out the window too.

"I hear the message has gone out across Atlantis. People are being summoned from every corner. Your husband will have the worship he seeks."

I feel an urge to defend Eros—to tell my father that the god who is my husband is not a vain god; that he does not want worship for worship's sake. That he will have a good reason for being absent all day. But my tongue is contrary, and will not do my bidding.

The door bursts open.

"Father?" It's Dimitra. She checks herself, seeing me. "Oh—you're here, too. Just as well. We will eat soon, then go to the temple afterward." She looks at me. "You'll get to see your husband in all his new finery. I hear it is to be quite the spectacle."

There's something crisp in her voice, something that tells me to be wary.

My father waves a hand.

"Eat without me, daughters. I have no appetite tonight."

*

It seems the king is busy with his preparations, too, so Dimitra and I eat alone. Though we are not quite alone—one is never quite alone, in these rooms. There are always the ears of the servants. Still, Dimitra does not hold her tongue. I had expected we would talk about Eros, about tonight's service; about this new cult our husbands have devised. She was not happy about it last night, I am sure. But today, it seems it does not please her to speak of it.

"Father is different, isn't he?" she says instead. She glances at me over trays of grilled meats and lemon-wrapped *fagri*. "With his maps, his star-charts. Sometimes I think he forgets about us altogether, for hours at a time."

There is a tradition in our lands for some men to become philosophers in their old age: after a lifetime living in the world of men, head of their households, when they are old and bearded and their children in households of their own, they become hermits, seeking out caves and hovels in the mountains, giving up worldly things for a life of contemplation. I never thought my father to be such a man. But some such instinct seems to run through him, too.

"I fought for you," Dimitra says abruptly. "I fought for you harder than he did, Psyche. He gave you up—you know that." She looks past me, to the closed door.

"But when you were gone—when we thought you were gone for good—I thought at least he would hold a little tighter to me. Since I was all he had left. His only child." Her bottom lip curls. "But instead it seemed the opposite. His grip was looser than ever."

I don't know what to say to that. It seems to me his grip has loosened on me, too; has perhaps loosened on everything in this world.

Perhaps when one has experienced too much sorrow, too much uncertainty, too many whims of the gods, something in us is forced to retreat. Perhaps he is calmer this way, spending his days in a world where galaxies bloom and our tiny mortal affairs fade into insignificance.

There is a stir, and the king enters the room, dressed in finer robes even than before. Tonight must be special to him, I think, and the thought unnerves me.

"You're ready. Good. And your father?"

Dimitra excuses herself to check on Father and say good night to the little prince. Now it is just the king and me in the great dining hall.

He smiles. It does not show his teeth.

"Your god-husband will do well in our temple," he observes. His eyes linger on me, expecting a certain response; sparking a little when that response doesn't come. His voice becomes more pointed.

"An excellent arrangement, don't you agree, little sister?"

"A clever one," I say, "to be sure."

I do not miss the way he looks at me then. He smiles, glances at the ceiling, then back at me.

"Do you know why the people of Atlantis welcome my rule, little sister?"

I shake my head.

"Because they know where their advantage lies." He tilts his head; he speaks lightly. As though he hasn't planned every word he's about to say.

"Some people are...sentimental," he observes, and his eyes land on me again, boring into mine. "The old king, for example," he goes on. "*He* was sentimental. But I believe in being practical. Anything else, in the end, is foolishness." He smiles once more—and this time, shows his teeth.

"And it doesn't do to play the fool. Now does it, little sister?"

Eighteen

The night sky is the color of ash, clouded over too thick to see the stars.

The sound of the waves is gentle in the dusk. They splash against the fortified wall of the castle, against the side of the agora that drops off into the sea. They splash on the carved steps that emerge from the water and lead up into the great temple we're now approaching. But we're approaching from the land-side, my father and I, where we walk at a solemn pace behind Dimitra and her husband, the king and queen leading our little party in their full, glittering regalia.

I think about how this island must have been once, in more peaceful times. Boats docking gently at the bottom of the temple steps, day and night, for passing sailors and travelers to make their pilgrimage. But if I turn and look back now, I know I will see those soldiers standing guard on the castle walls, arrows at the ready, to make sure no strangers come to land here.

Townspeople with their heads bowed are moving hastily towards the temple doors, skirting us with a wide, respectful margin. No one would even think about crossing our path.

"They have brought offerings," my father notes, nodding to the vessels they all seem to be carrying with them. We made offerings, too, at the temple in Sikyon, but only on special occasions. Then again, what is this if not a special occasion?

As we get nearer the temple, the sound of water seems to get louder, and I notice there's a stream running through the ground here, on the axis of the temple itself. A path for it has been carved into the rock, so that a narrow aisle of water runs right through the doors of the temple, all the way inside. I suppose it must run right through the temple's floor, and out the other side, into the sea. A question strikes me, one I should have thought to ask before.

"Whose temple was this? Before it fell into disuse?"

My father looks around us, taking in the evening sky, the crowds, the painted stonework of the great edifice above us.

"Poseidon's," he says.

That unnerves me. I wonder how long it has been disused for. I'm not sure the sea-god would like it very much, to be evicted by my husband. We have no need to offend yet another of the Olympians.

The scent of incense is almost dizzying as Father escorts me through the huge bronze doors. No temple in Sikyon was anything like this; the ceilings must be the height of ten men together. This king may not believe in worshiping the gods, but obviously the old kings of Atlantis had a different story. We walk inside, keeping to the right of the corridor of water, which seems to babble all the louder in its bed of stone as it courses towards the raised dais at the far end of the temple, before disappearing into darkness.

Another waft of incense comes down the aisle, making my head swim. The carved pillars we pass are wider than five men could put their arms around; the whole place is cavernous. It looked imposing from outside, to be sure, but on the inside, it takes my breath away. Further up the aisle, some kind of construction hangs below the towering ceiling. Skeins of rope go back and forth like some kind of fishermen's net, crisscrossing the room from wall to wall, suspended above the heads of the crowd. And at the top of the aisle, a great dais. It must have a room behind it, some kind of *adyton,* an inner sanctum. Is that where Eros is right now? My stomach flips over. Are we ready for this? Is he?

But Eros was born ready for this. He is a god, and it is the nature of gods to be worshiped. The discomfort is mine alone.

The temple is already full. The king's guards fringe the edges of the great space, their uniforms pristine and gleaming. It seems wrong to see them there, as though this were a military spectacle, not a religious one. It occurs to me that the people who stand row upon row inside this enormous temple are perhaps not all here by choice: their attendance is enforced by these men carrying spears. They turn to stare as we pass. The children stare most openly, whispering with excitement, but the adults are wide-eyed too. No doubt the king's seat is at the very top of the aisle; it feels like a long walk, past all the staring faces. One of the great columns we pass shows a painted scene of Zeus splitting open Kronos's belly, releasing the Olympian gods. I shiver to see it: this is the most famous of the legends about adamantine. I wonder if the blade the gods keep in Olympus is the same one shown here. One of the king's guards waits at the top of the aisle, ready to guide us to our places. We are all here now. Anticipation fills the air. We are all here—except for Eros.

Dimitra and the king reach the top of the aisle, and Father and I are right behind them. But the king doesn't stop there. Instead, he hands Dimitra off, and keeps going. He walks up onto the dais. So he means to speak first. Of course he does.

His guards are everywhere: by our sides, by the sides of the councilmen, and all about the temple, lining the walls. The crowd's murmuring grows louder, and I wonder how much they have been told. I wonder if what happened in Athiri yesterday is common knowledge yet; if all these people are curious to see the god who saved the falling boy from his death.

The king stands tall, facing the crowd. I can feel some new energy rolling off him, as though just seeing the assembled masses here makes his blood sing. Of course it does. Men aren't so different from gods, after all. This power feeds them, too.

"Hear me, Atlanteans!" he calls out, and almost instantly, the temple grows quiet, silence rippling from the front to the very back.

"Hear me, as I have heard you." He looks out into the crowd. "When I took on the mantle of King of Atlantis, I swore to protect you. I know some of you think me a godless king, but this is untrue. I merely wish to break us from the old ways—the old, hollow ways. Ours is an isle of untold riches, an isle of which great songs are sung. It *deserves* protection of the highest order. And it will have that protection now."

He begins to move as he speaks, striding to one corner of the dais, looking out at the people with an unyielding gaze. My stomach sinks.

He's good at this.

"Athens tells us that Athena is their patron," he says, his voice rising now, the crowd a fire he's stoking.

"Sparta tries to claim Ares for their own. Yet what is this but wishful thinking, and fantasy? Athena has never walked the streets of Athens; Ares has never sat in the halls of Sparta, and addressed the Spartan people."

He pauses, surveying the crowds gathered before him.

"The gods' loyalties are spread wide. *We* are the ones who are loyal, but where does that get us? What do we get in return?" He paces the dais. Despite my dislike of him, I can see that he is a natural on the stage, charismatic. His voice is deep and sonorous, carrying all the way through this enormous place, and the hum of excitement in it is contagious, his confidence absolute.

"But tonight, Atlantis, you will meet a god who has chosen Atlantis as his own. He is called the Shadowed God—because he is draped in mysteries, great mysteries beyond the mortal imagination. He has undertaken to be our patron. To take on Atlantis as his protectorate; to bless our endeavors, and bring fertility to our mines. And you will see him…" The king pauses. "…*in the flesh*. What other kingdom can boast such a thing?" It's clear how much he's enjoying his speech.

"Under my rule, Atlanteans, you will see your great island reborn. They say the gods walked here once. Now," he raises a hand triumphantly in the air, "they shall walk here again!"

The crowd starts to murmur, louder and louder, and soon they're stamping their feet. It becomes a low drum roll, spreading from wall to wall. Dareios, fading into the shadows in his black tunic, moves behind the dais, lighting torches—and then I see there is indeed an inner sanctum, a deep recess where the torches now flicker, and it's out of this, into the thunder of stamping feet, that my husband walks. All the small hairs stand up on my skin. It's him, and yet not him. He wears a new cloak, not the dark one he once wore, nor the peasant cloak he disguised himself in. This one is a dark, shimmering silver, like the surface of a river at night. And above it, instead of a low-draped hood, he wears a mask, black as iron. He is a stranger, awe-inspiring and a little frightening. The mask reminds me of the theater, and I remind myself that that's all this is: theater. A tremendous piece of theater.

"*Khaire*, people of Atlantis," he hails them, and they fall silent.

Even his voice is different. There is something of the ocean in it, something of the wind: a stormy night, a falling tree. It is more than the voice of a man, and my ears ring with it. It makes me realize how much of himself he restrains for me; all that he does to help me forget what he really is.

The crowd are hushed now. Their eagerness and impatience has given way to something else. Like me, they can feel it in his voice, from his presence.

"Yours is indeed a bounteous and beautiful island. I am glad to give it my patronage. And I undertake to do what I can for its people."

They are all listening, spellbound. I feel their thoughts, pushing and beating against each other. I can't *hear* them—either that girl in Athiri was special, or my mind is too overcrowded, too full of noise—but I can feel them. Their hunger, awe, confusion, and doubt.

"The way of the Olympians is not my way. I do not live on a lofty mountain where no man may climb: I live here, among mortals, beside mortals. I do not set myself apart from you. I do not claim to be as powerful as some of those gods, but such power that I have, I will gladly use to your advantage, people of Atlantis, if you take me as your god. I ask that you give me your faith. I am an honest god. I will offer you the loyalty you offer me."

The murmuring intensifies.

"Your king," Eros continues after a pause, "has made a request of me."

There is more murmuring at that, more speculation. I look for the king. He has found his place beside Dimitra now, surrounded by his councilmen, and there is a pleased curl in his lip. How much he must be enjoying this, even that turn of phrase: Your king has made a request of me.

What a powerful king, the people must be thinking, *for a god to honor his requests.*

"He asked," Eros says, "that I show you my face."

People shuffle; their curiosity is palpable, hungry. But I don't understand. Eros knows this is something he cannot do. *Would* not do. There must be some trickery to it—like in the throne room, with the mirror.

Mirror.

I look up, and now I see it. That maze of ropes I saw earlier above our heads is no mere ornament. It is suspending something above us: a huge, polished plate of copper, burnished to a mirror's sheen.

"You must understand," Eros says now, "it is not in the nature of faith to see a god's face. To have faith is to put one's trust in the unseen. But you are the first followers of the Shadowed God, and tonight, for that, I will reward you."

The murmuring swells again. He holds up a hand. And then slowly he walks down from the dais, and as the king's councilmen shuffle back, pushing the crowd away, pushing even the king's guards away, clearing space. And as they all part I see what I missed before: a silver reflecting pool in the ground—where an altar would be, if the altar was made of water. Which makes sense, in a temple built for Poseidon.

I watch now as Eros kneels before the pool, and bends over it as if to inspect his own reflection. Slowly he loses the mask and moves it aside, and a great gasp goes up from the crowd; many of them fall to their knees. I hear children shouting, and some of the women are weeping quietly. His reflection stares back at us from the ceiling, doubly mirrored—first from the reflecting pool, and then bounced back a second time by the tremendous mirror overhead. Everyone in this vast chapel can see it. The blazing face of a god, made just bearable to the eye.

I wonder what they see—if it is the same for each of them, or different. And then it is over. The mask goes back on, and it is as if a light goes out. The temple feels plunged into darkness, as though the flaming torches all around the walls were nothing. Eros waves his hand, and the water in the tunnel churns faster, a small wave rises, coursing down towards where he stands, and breaking by his feet into the reflecting pool, as though to shatter any image of him that still remained.

There is an instant more of absolute silence, and then a burst of noise, all the voices clamoring at once. In the wild hubbub I see Eros slowly go back the way he came, back into the shadows, into the inner sanctum. And Dareios goes after him, quenching the torches behind the dais, so whatever lies behind stays shrouded in a deeper darkness. And the king takes the stage once more.

"Atlanteans!" he shouts. "You have seen the truth. Now it is time: make your offerings to our great god!"

And then comes a clamoring of a different kind. The crowd are jostling each other, pushing into each other, all moving and shoving as the king's words herd them towards the middle of the temple, towards the stream that now runs steady and calm again. They come with whatever vessels they have brought under their arms—jars and flagons and bottles and pitchers. And one by one, they empty these into the stream.

Their offering is wine. I would know it by the smell, rich and dizzying, that rises around me. But I see it, too, from how the wine becomes its own river; as offering after offering is upturned into the water.

One by one, until the silver stream has turned blood-red.

Nineteen

I walk along the dark corridor, towards the door that leads out to the high, terraced gardens. The palace hallways are empty; the king has already retired. He spirited Dimitra off to his chambers almost as soon as we came through the door. I could see the triumph in his eyes, the glow of self-satisfaction. He and Dimitra sleep in separate rooms—a normal enough custom—but she will sleep in his room tonight, it seems.

The nursery door is ajar, but not a sound comes from within, not even the softest mewling from the little prince, not the lightest breath of his nurse. Only the lit sconces in the hallway keep me company now.

I step out onto the terrace, into the scented night. I cannot see them, not with the ledge above me, but I know that above my head are guards, all with their bows and arrows at the ready, should some ship approach in the dark hours. I wonder whether the king has as many enemies as he seems to think. Is he a paranoid man, or is he right; is his grip on the crown so easily lost?

"Psyche."

I startle. It's my father. He's wearing a white night-robe, the breeze rustling the cotton fabric as he stands alone in the dark.

"Father! What are you doing out here?"

He smiles slightly.

"I might ask you the same." He shrugs, returns his gaze to the heavens. "I'm looking at the stars, daughter."

I think of his star-maps, his dials and sketches.

"For messages, you mean?"

He shrugs.

"Messages. Guidance. Companionship. The stars look different to me now than they did when I was a boy. I feel closer to them. Perhaps because I am moving their way."

I don't want to indulge that line of thinking. Perhaps he knows it; he turns his gaze back to earth, gestures across the agora towards the temple, lit by moonlight.

"This god of yours spoke well tonight," he observes. "The people were transported."

The night air moves about us, cool but not cold. The king told me Eros will stay behind tonight to select his priests and priestesses. And no doubt there will be a long line of willing applicants. But it is hard to stomach—that after spending all day without him today, I am to wait, still, into the small hours of the night to see him. That great being in the temple…he was not my husband. He belonged to the people, not to me. Or perhaps I mean that we belonged to him. Either way, it leaves me uneasy. I had not thought to look at him and see some majestic stranger in his place.

"Do you think it was wise?" I blurt. "Accepting the king's offer?"

My father widens his eyes at me.

"I offer no council. He is a god; his wisdom is beyond any of ours."

Perhaps. The gods exceed us in many things, but I am not sure wisdom is always one of them.

I look out at the black seas, the dark sweep of sky. Sooner or later, Aphrodite and her sons will track us down. A king's palace is too prominent a place to stay forever. I find myself fingering the amulet at my neck. Scant protection, it feels sometimes.

"I suppose you are no closer," my father frowns, "to finding the god Ares."

I shake my head, my gaze still on the water.

"Something in me fears staying here," I sigh. "But in equal amount, I fear leaving."

Father shrugs again.

"You have a husband now. You are his wife. You go where he goes."

It does not matter what you fear, what you feel. His words sting, but these are the rules my father grew up with, the only ones he knows. In Sikyon, on marriage-days, the bride is taken from her old home to her husband's in a great carriage, and the more she cries, the better people like it. Her distress is a sign that she is dutiful.

Had I a daughter, I could never wish such a thing on her.

"Are you so sure," my father asks then, "that the god Ares will support you?"

He thinks he is the first to ask that question, but I have wondered it myself. The truth is, I'm not sure of much at all.

"What if he cannot call the other gods off your backs, as you hope?" Father continues. "What if he, too, spurns you—or, worse, wants you harmed?"

These are dark thoughts. And yet in the end, I know we have to try. I turn to him, my voice firm.

"We cannot spend our whole lives running."

My father looks back at me, his gaze steady.

"And what," he says, "if you have no choice?"

*

I lie in bed, waiting. I see the flames still burning in the temple. I see the moon moving across the sky. My thoughts keep drifting back to the twilight rites: how Eros looked on that stage, bathed in the awe and adoration of so many. Did he even see me among the crowd? How can it be that a new name, some new robes, could make him seem so unfamiliar? So unreachable, so *distant*?

I hardly know who will walk in the door. My husband, or some other, more remote being I hardly feel I know? I can hardly understand my own nerves, or what I am afraid of.

But the fear, the dry mouth and fluttering stomach, give way to a different sort of agitation as the minutes, and then the hours, pass. My doubts seem to grow with the darkness. Where is he? What can be detaining him so long? My thoughts swirl and swirl, and sleep comes and goes, and finally I hear the creak of the door, and see shadows in the doorway.

"Psyche."

I startle awake.

At the sight of him something releases, fear giving way to a different, sharper emotion.

"Where were you? I waited hours!"

I would not admit it, but some small flicker of fear had begun to suggest the unspeakable. That he was not coming back. That a god—a god like the one I saw tonight—has no need of a wife after all.

He laughs softly.

"You were cold without me, were you? Yes, this bed is much too big for you alone."

He moves closer, slides into the bed next to me. He leans into me, pressing against the length of me. I feel his breath, his lips against my ear, against my neck. He's eager for me, I can feel it.

"There was much to be done," he says. "Dareios had recruited many candidates for the temple. I selected some for priests and priestesses." He seems to glow brighter, just thinking of it. "Once initiated, they purified themselves and offered sacrifices. They sang praise songs, and danced for me."

His eyes gleam.

"I had not expected it to feed me so well, nor so quickly. I had forgotten what it was, to feel this way." He shakes his head. "I am already stronger, stronger by far, than I was a day ago. Can you not see it?"

I can. He's glowing, as if lit from within by some new, more powerful flame. His skin is brighter, his eyes have new fire. The blood flows more fully through his cheeks and lips. I try not to picture the dancing priests and priestesses, praising him with their glistening bodies.

He sighs, a pleasurable sigh. "The people of Atlantis are few, compared to Athens or Sparta. But their prayer is powerful. Perhaps it is because they see me among them; perhaps their faith is stronger." He sighs, his warmth radiating beside me. I stare at him, his face too beautiful for words, his power bursting from him like fire. If one night of worship can do all this, what will weeks or months of it bring?

Perhaps one day the sight of him *will* blind me.

"Do not look so troubled, Psyche." He smiles at me, and lifts a hand to my throat. I want to lose myself in the brightness around him. I want to forget my fears, and this night's uncertainties and doubts. I want his touch to erase everything.

He murmurs my name, slides my elbows back down where I'd propped them up, easing me back on the pillow. His hand plays at my throat. He pulls my body into his. I feel the warmth of him, his skin, the blood rushing beneath—or perhaps it's my blood, rushing in response. His muscles, lean and taut. Every part of me responds to him. My skin tingles. My throat runs dry. But my mind and my body want different things. My mind wants to deny him what he wants. I have spent the day missing him; let him hunger for me, now. But my body—my body wants to tremble until all thoughts fall away, like apples fall from the tree. It wants to feel the fire running through me, the heat that promises to never leave.

And it's my body I can't help but listen to.

Twenty

When I wake, he's gone. As if he were a shadow that came in the night and then, satisfied, took its leave of me. I lie there, watching the thin linen curtain flutter in the breeze from the balcony. A week ago I was the whole of his life—just me and the mountains, no other face for miles. I had not thought to miss those days. I wonder if the king is doing it on purpose, keeping us apart like this. Filling Eros's day with tasks, and mine with enforced idleness.

Last night, before I fell asleep, I made myself tell Eros about the voices I've been hearing— the little girl in Athiri, the deer outside the citadel. I had not expected skepticism.

Are you sure? He frowned. *Are you sure it wasn't your imagination?*

When I said it wasn't, he counseled me to ignore it, which I had not expected, either.

We are taking every precaution we can—and while you wear the Shroud, the gods cannot search you out. But even so, the less attention we call to ourselves, the better.

I had thought, perhaps, he might offer some encouragement…I had even thought, perhaps, he might be pleased. But then again, I have not always had the best luck telling gifts from curses.

At the breakfast table, it is just Dimitra, the baby, and me. The king often breakfasts in his rooms, I gather, and Father is sleeping late. Dimitra must have stopped by the nursery early, and had a whim to take the child with her. She dandles him now on her knee, and looks up as I sit down. Two servants stand at the back of the room, eyes respectfully downcast, waiting for whatever request we might have.

"Well, sister? Last night was a success, it seems."

I suppose she is right. Objectively.

"The king seemed pleased," I concede.

Dimitra looks at me, then glances away.

"Kostas sees his advantage." Her tone is frank, almost careless.

"Not many can say a god is in their debt," she continues. "I suppose any man would like to buy the loyalty of a god whose power is at an ebb. Then, when it reaches high tide once more, perhaps he thinks still to command it."

I search her face for clues. Is she trying to help me? Warn me? What she says makes sense—it makes sense, at least, for a man like the king. From what I have glimpsed of him, he is not short on hubris.

"Eros does not take commands," I say.

"Nor does the king," says Dimitra. "Nor does any man, in his own mind. And yet I think all men, mortal or immortal, may be coaxed with fine enough words."

I don't know what to say to that.

"And how was your god-husband this morning?" Dimitra says. I don't think I'm imagining the smirk creeping into her tone at this change of subject.

"Lusty enough, I expect," she adds, "after a night of dancing priestesses."

I flush, and turn away from her, glad that the servants all hover at a discreet distance.

"It is how gods work," I point out. "Worship, praise, prayer—it fortifies them. He has been starved of his share too long."

She carves a pomegranate, places a piece into her mouth.

"He is like mortal men, then. Without praise, they die."

My sister has always had a good way with a barb.

"I cannot complain about what heals him," I say. "When he is face to face with his brothers once again, he will need to defend himself, and me."

Dimitra shakes her head.

"You put too much trust in him, Psyche."

I turn, my cheeks warm.

"Why do you say that?"

"It is easy to see. You do not bother to hide it. You are…quite devoted."

Her words should not embarrass me—devotion to one's husband is good, surely. And yet I feel humiliated.

"You are no fool, sister. Do not let your husband make one of you."

"He won't," I say, but I don't want to look her in the eyes.

"It's what men do." She pauses, looks down at the child in her arms. "My husband cares for me so long as it suits him," she says. "But when it no longer suits him, I must find my own way." She looks up. "And our father…he gave us his protection when he could afford it well enough. But when the cost became too high, what then?"

I do not argue with her about Father. I do not say: *he did only what he had to do*. Because even I cannot say how I feel, as to that. And my sister has every right to hold her pain in different places than I hold mine.

"They don't mean to betray us, Psyche, but they do," she goes on. She looks down at little Nikos again, gives him a finger to clasp.

"But men do not so easily betray their mothers. You see how fast he holds to me, Psyche?" She looks up.

"*His* loyalty, I may rely on." Her eyes are shining, dark as jet.

"I will teach it to him. I will ensure it."

And I cannot say why, but there is something in her voice that makes me shiver.

*

I find myself lingering in the nursery after Dimitra has headed to the throne room. I want to hear from Irini, the nurse, whether she was at the temple last night, and what she thought. She nods when I ask her about it, a little shyly.

"The king said I was to go. That we were all to go."

As I thought—the crowd's presence there wasn't entirely voluntary. Still, she seems full of praise and wonder, and to my ears it seems utterly sincere.

"It was a marvel above marvels, my lady. I never thought to see such a thing in all my days. Everyone thought the Shadowed God most wondrous—they say his presence here is a miracle indeed."

"They are happy he is here, then?" Perhaps, after all, if Eros can do so much for the people's spirits, in just one night…

Irini frowns a little at the word *happy*.

"They are honored, my lady."

There is a difference, to be sure. And yet I wonder if it would not be better for the people of Atlantis to feel happy, than honored.

"We visited Athiri yesterday," I say then. "I believe you are from there?"

She nods, shy again.

"My family lives there. I saw some of them last night."

Her family. I wonder what age her own child is, the one whose milk her breasts run full with. Who is taking care of it? Are there others? She is young—my age, perhaps—but village girls are married quickly.

"You must miss them," I say now, and she looks away.

"I miss the children."

Nikos starts fussing then, as if to remind us that *he* is here, even if Irini's children are not. She takes him up in her arms, jogs him lightly to soothe him.

"He's very big, isn't he?" There's a look in her face, almost of doubt. "He's not a week old, my lady, but look at him. My own boy was two months before he reached such a size."

I suppose it's true. All I can see is how small he is, how new—but she's right, if he stretched out his legs he would already be too long for the crib.

"And he's strong, too," she goes on. "I've never met a babe with a grip like that—not at his age."

"You are feeding him well, then." I smile, but she doesn't smile back.

"They say—" she says, but breaks off. I look at her.

"They say what?"

She shakes her head, looking skittish, almost afraid. Rumors—they abound in every kingdom, in every town. Some gossip she heard at the temple last night, perhaps. No use for me to press her on it.

I look down at Nikos, into the wide eyes that gaze up at us. His face hardly has the look of a newborn; Irini is right about that. His blue eyes stare back at me, open and deep, as though he can hear what we're saying. I suppose it is just the way infants have about them. That deep gaze makes them seem wise beyond their years. And yet he *does* seem…different.

I think about my mother then, as I often do when faced with a life so new as my little nephew's. I can't help it. By the time the midwife placed me on her belly, my mother's life was already trickling out of her. Did she sense it? I'm told she lived long enough to give me my name and nothing more.

"He has a look of you, Miss," Irini says, and I glance at her in surprise.

She nods. "Yes, you're very like. His coloring: the hair, the eyes. More like you than his own mother, I should say. Or"—she hesitates—"or the king."

"They said I was not very like my parents either," I shrug. "These things change, I suppose, as we get older. He'll grow into it."

"I suppose so," she says dubiously.

The babe's blue eyes follow me as she lays him in the cradle.

*

Dimitra and the king come in before the lunch hour. The king raises his eyebrows when he sees me there.

"Little sister."

I had thought to see him still glowing with self-satisfaction, as he was last night. But the triumph of it seems to have worn off already. I can tell he's not in a good mood.

Dimitra bends to look down into the crib at the sleeping prince. The king joins her, but his face does not wear the same look of pleasure, of pride. His brows draw tight. It's almost as though he's searching for something in the child's face.

"Wake him."

Dimitra looks up.

"Wake him? Why?"

"I want him to see me."

Dimitra purses her lips, annoyed by such a whim, but she does it all the same, tickling a finger against the baby's cheek until he stirs, groggy, and opens his eyes. The king moves closer, frowns again. I think I see something pass over his face, something almost like dislike, but it is too fleeting to say it was more than my imagination.

I have not seen many fathers with their newborns, but I think it is habitual for them to be lit with pride—especially their firstborn. Not so with the king, it seems. And yet the child is strong, and healthy, and promises well. It's hard to see what more the king could ask for. I do not envy this little prince his road ahead.

"Give him to me."

Dimitra puts the prince into his arms. The king frowns, looking him over. His eyes move back and forth over the small face, as if there's something in particular he's seeking.

"Unnerving child. You do not have the eyes of an infant."

It is said lightly—lightly enough that it might almost be a joke—but I see Dimitra's face darken.

And as if on cue, thrashing in his father's arms, Nikos begins to wail.

No: I do not envy the little prince his father at all.

*

When the dinner hour comes, Eros is not at the table. The king looks surprised that this surprises me.

"It is no small thing, to begin a new cult overnight. Surely you understand this."

I force a smile, but I can feel its tightness on my lips.

"We will go back to the temple after dinner, to attend

tonight's rites." The king forks a duck leg onto his plate, and a handful of dates.

"I do not think I will go tonight. I am tired." The truth is, I do not wish to see my husband in his strange new role, his strange new garb, his new name. And I do not wish to watch the king parade about like last night, nor to sit alongside him, once his parading is done.

But at my words, the king drops the serving-fork.

"Not attend?" He pauses. "You would not wish him to doubt your loyalty, I think?"

I look the king in the eye.

"My husband knows very well where my loyalty lies." *And that is not with you, sir.*

I think the king feels my meaning well enough.

He smiles impassively, but at the end of the meal, after Dimitra leaves the room, he grips my arm.

"Little sister." He does not speak harshly, but instead, in a honeyed voice. "I see I have not yet won your trust."

I drop my eyes.

"You have done nothing to dispel it, sir," I say, which is true enough.

His eyes pass over me, lingering where I would prefer them not to linger, and finally settling on my face with narrowed eyes. "I think you are more like your sister than you realize. You have an eye for power, and for alliances to your advantage."

My blood boils at that.

"I did not choose my husband based on his usefulness, sir."

"Didn't you?" He raises an eyebrow. "Just remember, little sister, whose hand it is that feeds you. Your husband may be an immortal, but he is also an outcast and a fugitive. So," he smiles a wolfish smile, "I believe for now, that hand is mine."

*

I watch from the garden terrace as the king and my sister and their phalanx of guards cross the agora. The temple on the far side is lit with many torches.

I cannot get the king's words out of my mind. He knew what he was saying, he knew *exactly* what he was saying—but what am I to make of it?

Time passes. How much, I can't say. But the service ends; the people flood out, everything humming with life. Soon I hear activity in the palace corridors—the king and my sister returning, my father, the entourage of guards—but even that dies down, and I'm still awake, still pacing the floor of our room.

Finally I hear him enter, and whip around.

"You are still awake," he observes. His tone is easy, rich with pleasure. I force myself not to think about the hours between the temple service and now. The comments Dimitra made about the *dancing priestesses*. No doubt he thinks I was waiting up for him for some other reason—eager to have him warm my bed.

"I need to talk to you."

He frowns. My voice is cold. I suppose it is very different from that of the fawning priestesses in the temple.

"Well then? What is it?"

"The king," I swallow. "He said something tonight." I try to repeat it, to convey it exactly as it sounded, but I must not be doing a good job. Eros frowns: he seems disapproving, but not troubled.

"It was an arrogant thing to say, I'll admit."

"It was more that..." I don't know how to describe it. How it seemed like...a threat.

"Do you really think we will be safe here?" I say.

Eros looks at me, his golden eyes studying me.

"We are not safe anywhere, Psyche. Not yet."

Yet. He thinks the longer we stay, the more he is worshiped, then the stronger he will be. He thinks that will be our best protection. But I am not so sure.

"I do not like him," I blurt out. "The king: I do not like him."

My husband's bright eyes roam over me, sparking with something else now, a less patient emotion.

"No," he says. "But it is not necessary that you like him. No one is asking you to marry him."

I turn away. It is a while since he spoke to me like this—as though I were a stubborn young girl. It feels like those days when I first knew him—back when I *was* a stubborn girl, and he was an arrogant god. We have changed since then. Or at least, I thought we had.

"If you spent any time here," I snap, "you'd see. The king rides roughshod over everyone in the palace, and he thinks he can do as he likes with me. You don't see it. You don't care to see it—"

"I don't *care*?" he fumes. "You say you are not happy here, and yet it is for you that we came here, for you that we stayed. Forgive me if I do not quite understand your *suffering*—you are reunited with your family, while mine is severed from me. You are tended to with every luxury, secure behind palace walls. And yet because I have not been at your side these past few days, tending to you; because I have been strengthening myself, for *us*—"

"Oh, I see. I have fallen short on gratitude, is that it?" I plant my hands on my hips. "Perhaps you can remedy it with some more cossetting from your lissome young handmaids. I'm sure they show you nothing but gratitude."

His nostrils flare.

"You begrudge me this—my restored strength? When my strength is what we must both rely on?"

"I am not so helpless," I snap. "Not such a weak little creature, though it pleases you to think it." I remember what he said about my voices; telling me to suppress whatever little gift I have, while he works to grow his every day.

"I suppose it suits you, the more helpless I am. Isn't it what your kind likes about mortals? That we must hang on your every word, and trust you, and never question you!"

His eyes spark with quiet fury.

"You think that's why I chose you, Psyche? Because you were *helpless*?"

"What else would you call it?" I retort. "Trussed up like

an offering by a mortal king; persecuted by your mother?"

"You blame me for her actions?" he snaps. "I do not confuse you with your family."

I glare at him. "You like to pretend you're so different from them, but are you?" I gesture out the window to the temple, the two torches still lit at its entrance. "Seeking out glory, collecting it as your due? It blinds you to everything else."

We stand across from each other, staring, simmering. His eyes glitter with anger, his skin is flushed, his top lip puckered with anger. For a moment something ripples through me, ripples through the room. Anger is so close to desire. For an instant I think he's going to storm across the room towards me, that we will find our way to the bed after all. For an instant, I might even want that. But the moment passes—and something harder, colder, stays behind.

Eros blinks. Inhales hard.

"Get some sleep," he says. "It's almost dawn."

And without another word, without a backward glance, he leaves the room.

Twenty-one

He's not there when I wake—but then, I hadn't expected him to be. Where did he go when he left me last night? Back to the temple? I let myself be angry at the thought. I would rather be angry than any of the other feelings I sense, waiting just below the surface.

Lusty enough, after a night of dancing priestesses. And is my sister wrong? Eros is the god of desire, after all. I was surely naive to think that desire would be for me alone.

I'm out in the corridors when a door opens—the door to the king's bedroom—and I see a girl coming out, fixing herself. One of the maids. But something about the way she readjusts her clothes, and the way the guards at the king's door avert their eyes, lets me know she wasn't in there to clean the room.

I walk on, pretending I've seen nothing. I don't think the guards or the maid even noticed me. But it stings, the humiliation I feel on my sister's behalf.

Should I tell her? Or…is it possible she already knows?

I know many in these lands consider it a simple truth: You cannot have both a noble marriage and a faithful husband. If a woman marries up in the world, her husband has given her enough already, she cannot claim his freedom too. They would point out that Dimitra has been given a crown, and a son born to the throne. To ask for the king's loyalty too would be laughable.

All men stray, they say, but the more powerful the man, the more it is expected of him.

Even, perhaps, encouraged.

*

The king and my father are both at the breakfast table today, so whatever I might like to discuss with Dimitra is of no consequence. We end up making petty conversation, mostly the king observing how well last night's service went: how enthralled the people of Atlantis are, how overcome with the idea of a god in their midst. His boastful tone would lead anyone to imagine *he* is the god. But when a break comes in the conversation, I clear my throat. I have an idea of my own for what I would like to do with my day.

"Father—you said that my mother's home place was a village named Lykaria. I should like to see it, while I am here." I turn to the king. "I do not need a carriage—but perhaps a horse could be borrowed from your stables?"

The king half-turns, a tight smile on his lips.

"It can be arranged, certainly. Only not today. My stable-hands run a tight schedule, one that is not to be interrupted at short notice. Besides, you would need a guide, and today there is no one to spare."

The citadel is to be the limit of my day's adventures for now, it seems. But the king's horses cannot be training every day, nor can his guards. I wonder if *guard* is what he really means by *guide*—and if he wants someone there to ensure my safety, or to curtail my freedom.

I stop outside the palace gates to witness a huge statue being rolled into the agora, men at the temple doors ready to hoist it into place. The carving of the Shadowed God.

"It is quite something, is it not, my lady?"

I turn. It's Phylax Thais, one of the handful of guards manning the palace gate. She bows slightly. I nod back.

"I was told a cult could be born overnight, but I suppose I didn't quite believe it."

"The king is most resourceful, my lady."

Resourceful. I'm sure he is.

Another thought comes to mind then.

"Tell me: the town of Lykaria, do you know it?"

She gives me a polite look, not quite a smile, not quite a frown.

"Yes, my lady."

"And is it easy to reach? Might I find my own way there,

with a horse?"

She hesitates briefly.

"Certainly. It is neither a hard road nor a long one."

"Good," I say. "Will you give me directions?"

She looks confused, but offers them all the same, and they are simple enough. I keep them in my mind, for later.

I do not take the path out to the smithy again, but stay in the town center, watching the people, listening. I browse the market in the agora, and even bargain for a trinket or two, just for the excuse of getting closer to the chatter, hearing what the gossip is today.

There is mention of Eros: they are pleased with their new god, it seems. They are dazzled by him, their access to him. They believe everything will go right, while they have a god at their side.

Or, almost everything.

"Work at the palace, do you?" one of them says to me, a shrewd-looking young fellow. "I saw you come out o' that gate, yonder." He looks me over. "You're no kitchen wench, I'll wager."

"I'm…a companion to the queen," I offer. There have been no announcements about me, about the fact that the queen's sister has come to Atlantis. Not that I'm complaining. The more anonymity we have, the better.

"Companion!" the stall-holder snorts. "Look who rode in on her high horse. You're a maidservant, is that it?" He cocks his head at me. "I suppose you've seen him, then—the queen's bastard. Be honest: What does he look like? Has he got any horns? A tail, maybe?" He snickers.

I stare back.

The queen's *bastard?* Where did he get such an idea? The child may not have the king's coloring, but sometimes that is the way of things.

"He don't mean nothing by it." The older man behind the stall nudges him. "Ignore him."

"The prince," I manage, "is no one's bastard. He is the king's son." But I'm so startled that I fear my voice hardly sounds convincing.

"Course he is," the older man nods, but like he's humoring me. "It's only—"

"Only what?"

He shrugs.

"Only, others say different, don't they?"

"Which others?" I say, but he just hedges, says he must have been mistaken, then goes off to help another woman shopping for his wares.

I walk back to the palace gritting my teeth. It was like this in Sikyon, too: people love to accuse a woman of loose morals. It happened back home, whenever a baby was born with an unexpected mark, or the "wrong" shade of hair. *Not his child.* Everyone's favorite rumor. Should I tell Dimitra of it? But what good would it do? It is only foolish talk. And besides, knowing how my sister reacts to any indignity, I would fear for these fools and their loose tongues.

*

I find Father in his rooms, immersed in his papers. He seems far away, in another world. It takes him a moment, I think, to come back to this one.

"Have you heard any talk," I ask him, "any strange talk, about the prince?"

He looks at me. "What do you mean?"

I shake my head. I should not be guilty, myself, of spreading idle rumor.

"Oh, I don't know." I force a smile. "The nurse seems to think he's some kind of prodigy; he's growing at a tremendous rate, she says."

Father glances out the window, frowning.

"He'll be a fine boy, no doubt."

I think of my sister, the conversation we had that first morning.

"Dimitra spoke with such certainty of his future. To hear her, I would have thought she had consulted an oracle, though she says not."

My father grimaces.

"Prophecies have their limits."

His voice is strained, as is his expression. Something about the subject, it seems, displeases him. What was it he said before? *Even good men have been led astray by prophecy.* We were speaking of the king's prophecy, the one that led to my sister becoming queen. I study my father's face.

"Did Dimitra tell you what it said?" I hazard. "The prophecy Kostas received?"

Father turns from the window, his face tight.

"She did."

I wait.

"It said a girl would be found upon the shores of Atlantis." He looks at me, his frown deepening. "She would be of the north, yet of no home."

Of the north, yet of no home. The description answers. Our family is of the north, but our home is destroyed now, no more than rubble.

"She would have cheated death before, and in time would cheat it again."

That makes sense, too. Dimitra and my father should have died in Sikyon's collapse. It is only by luck and happenstance that they avoided it. But I wonder what *cheat it again* refers to.

"She would be of humble roots," my father continues. "And yet she would attain great power." He looks steadily at me, and I can hear that something's coming, something more.

"And he who sits by her side," he says, "would remake the world."

Remake the world. A bold claim, even for a power-hungry king.

But Father's still looking at me, waiting for me to understand something. For a penny to drop. I go over his words again, repeating the strange prophecy in my mind. It takes a few moments for me to understand. And when I do, my heart sinks. This prophecy…the words match Dimitra very well. But there is someone else they match just as well.

Me.

Twenty-two

I stare out the window. My sister is too clever not to have realized all this, and likely quicker than I did. From the moment I arrived here it must have entered her mind. And what's more, it will have entered the king's mind. It could make my sister's position precarious, if he comes to believe that he has selected his wife under false pretenses. Or that she is not the path to victory he was promised.

My father sighs.

"The gods delight in making us their playthings. You see why I say prophecies have their limits."

I shake my head. I don't know what to think about any of this. I don't want to be the subject of a prophecy, either. And I don't want to put my sister at risk.

"She has made him a good wife," I say. "She has born him a son, an heir. He will not put her aside now."

My father looks away, sighs.

"Indeed. We must hope not."

*

On my way back I hear a yelp from the nursery. When I enter, I find Irini covering her breast with one hand, her eyes wide.

"He...he bit me," she stammers. "He bit me! He has a *tooth*."

The child has started crying now, probably in response to the nurse's shock. I make hushing noises, and tentatively I feel inside his mouth.

She's right. One tooth.

"He's not two weeks old!" Irini stares. "A *tooth*, my lady? It's not natural!"

Perhaps it is not so strange as all that? I think I remember hearing once of this—how now and then, a child comes out of the womb with a tooth or two already placed. But I doubt it's much consolation to Irini. She looks from the child to me; shakes her head.

"Surely you see it too, Miss. He's twice the size he ought to be. I've never seen a babe grow as quick. And his grip—the queen may boast of his strength, but it's unnatural, if you ask me. He could tear your hair out by the hank, easy as you please." She glances at me sidelong.

"I oughtn't to say it, Miss, but he…sometimes he frightens me a little."

Frightens? For a moment I think she's speaking of the king. But it's my small nephew, crying in his crib, that she's staring at. I look at Irini's face, her eyes wide and wary. She's still holding a hand to her breast.

"He's just a child," I remind her. "An infant."

"I suppose so," she frowns.

I wonder if Irini's the one who's been starting those rumors I heard in the agora, and the thought makes me less sympathetic. Little Nikos is nothing to be frightened of. But rumors, gossip, loose tongues?

Those are more dangerous than Irini can possibly imagine.

*

I go to the temple that night, with the others. I don't want to go, and yet something draws me, all the same. I have not seen Eros all day—not since those late-night hours of cruel, harsh words. Ill-judged words, perhaps. And yet they were said.

But I'm not quite prepared for the spectacle that the Shadow God's twilight worship has become. It has only been a few days. Still, this cult has grown into something real. I stare up at the priests and priestesses—young women with long braided hair, thick-painted eyes, and gauzy costumes so transparent as to hide almost nothing. Young men with bare chests, oiled and glowing, bright youthful faces. All of them beautiful, doe-eyed, alluring.

When the crowd finishes their song of praise, Eros sings back to them. I am told this is the reason people keep coming to the temple; why tonight the cavernous room is packed twice as full as it was that first night. It is reported that no two mortals hear quite the same melody when he sings. Some say it is the sound of the stars, others say it is the song that gems make beneath the earth. They say no one can be hungry or feel pain for hours after hearing it; some say the feeling is one of ecstasy.

As for me? To me it is a sad song. The sound of longing. The song of the outcast, of vanished things, of autumn leaves as they lose their last hold and come to earth. It makes my heart rise up with a strange, beautiful melancholy. I look around, wondering if no one else feels the ache.

But they're all smiling, beatific, sleepy with pleasure.

I close my eyes and wait for it to end.

*

Back upstairs, I blow out the oil lamp and urge myself to sleep. I suppose I doze a little, but when I hear him come in, it feels as though I've been lying in this wakeful, watchful silence all night long.

"Psyche?" He slides into bed beside me, his body warm, firm, his voice pulling at my core like a siren song. But he has not troubled himself to come back before dawn. The curtain leading to the balcony is thin, and light is crawling at the edges of the sky.

So I keep my eyes closed, my body turned away from him. It costs me something, but it would cost me more to turn to him, to let him caress me, to feel his touch. To yield.

Eventually, I fall into an unfeigned sleep. But when I wake to a cold and empty bed, my heart sinks a little lower. I look out towards the water, past the pale curtain that flutters at the opening to the balcony. Towards the lonely sea.

Not so long ago, Eros wasn't just the center of my world, he *was* my world. Up in those ice-clad mountains when it was just us, telling each other stories, keeping each other warm, waiting for the snows to melt.

But it never felt so cold in those snowy climes, as it does down here.

*

A few days pass in much the same manner. During the daylight hours there are a hundred claims on my husband's attention—to supervise some adjustment to the temple or to speak with his priests, or to travel around the island in a great carriage, bestowing his blessings. I hear that wherever he goes word has spread, and the people kneel before him, hailing his name. The crowds coming to the temple each night seem to get bigger as the days pass, and word spreads—I see them from the balcony, lining up at the temple doors as the light starts to fade, and the torches start to blaze. It seems to me that the more he is seen, the more I become invisible. As his worshipers grow in number, and his reputation spreads, and his health blooms…all the while I am shrinking, growing paler and smaller, until soon I will be nothing at all.

I watch the king and his men go across to the temple at twilight, and then I stand on the balcony, waiting. I count the stars, until it's too dark and cold to be outside any longer. And my shadow-husband comes to my bed in the small hours of night, and is gone by morning.

He never hid what he was from me—not quite. I have bound myself to a god, and I thought I knew what that meant. But these days, I can't stop thinking of what he really is. And of how he will never truly be mine, not the way a mortal man could be. He is a god who has lived a million lifetimes before me, and will live a million lifetimes after. Eternity is the water he swims in. His mind is full of things I will never see, never know. In the past I have been better able to put this from my mind. But these days…these days it seems to me he stands on one cliff and I on another, and there is a chasm between us deeper than the ocean.

Sometimes I hear the page calling for him, early in the morning. When I stir I hear the man's voice: *Let her sleep,* he urges, and Eros leaves the room in silence. Other times, I wake when he comes back from the temple, and I sense his radiance in the dark room, and hear him say my name. I wait, then, for more. For something in his tone—apology, contrition. I wait for him to say my name a second time. But he doesn't, and I don't turn. As his strength grows, the animal pull of him is stronger than ever, but I do not give in. I think thoughts of ice, willing them to cool the fire he stokes in me, and I keep my head turned from him, feigning sleep. Other times, I wonder if he even returns from the temple at all. I turn to him in the dark from force of habit, and find only cold and empty sheets.

I know we cannot go on like this. I know we are sliding towards something worse, something more dangerous. But though I want him, I will not beg for him. And I don't know how to stop this tide.

*

There is a small room near the stairs which is the king's council room. Even Dimitra does not venture there; inside, the king meets only with his men. One morning, the door is ajar, and I hear voices as I pass.

"Still nothing?" the king is saying; his tones are unmistakable. Despite myself, I slow down. Something in his voice, something pinched and taut, makes me linger.

"Nothing of what you seek, your highness," another voice says. Dareios, perhaps.

"It will come," the king says, grimly. "They must keep at it. It is here, it *will* be found."

I wonder if it's the mines he's speaking of. There was so little ore to be seen that day when we visited the pit, and I wonder if I was right after all—if the reason the old king stopped mining was nothing to do with religion, but because the bounty had simply dried up. Kostas's great initiative may come to nothing after all.

"Your highness..." the other voice hesitates. "There's something else."

"Well?" I can feel the king's temper. "Speak, then."

"We have heard...that is, there is some noise...they say the king of Corinth has his eye on Atlantis. That he is building up his fleet. That he may be readying to mount an attack."

"What do you mean?" the king's voice is pale with rage. "He cannot dare."

"Yes, your highness, but—"

"Haven't they heard? Have you not spread the word abroad as I asked you to—that Atlantis has a god all of its own? Would they oppose such a force?"

There is an uncomfortable silence.

"Sire..." the man speaks finally. "They are saying this new god of yours is only a ploy: a man dressed in fine robes, and some tricks and sleight of hand. They say you have made people believe there is a new god when no such god exists. They say to worship outside the Pantheon is sacrilege, and gives them one more reason to want you dead."

Dead. The word seems to go around the room like a lightning bolt. Even out here, I feel it.

"Fools!" the king snarls, after a beat. "Pretenders! They will not kill *me*."

I shift my weight, unthinkingly, but the floor is not quite even and my sandals scuff against stone. The king's voice shifts instantly.

"Did you hear that?"

I move away from the door, hurrying down the corridor. It would do no good to be found out here. But what I have overhead is not good either. I do not like that the king has been spreading word of Atlantis's new god far and wide.

And *he* will not like that they call this new god a charlatan.

I wonder how long it will take before his alliance with my husband loses its shine.

I wonder where that will leave us.

Twenty-three

"Psyche?"

I turn from the window. Dimitra stands in the doorway, somewhat to my surprise. She is in a good mood, flashing me a conspiratorial smile.

"Shall we go to the stables? I think today we might be able to find you what you need."

What I need. Once upon a time, I thought I knew what that was.

"There is a new stallion has just arrived, purchased from across the water, a beauty by all accounts. And if you cannot ride that one, you can certainly have my mare." She shrugs. "I do not see why they cannot get her ready for you now."

It feels as close to camaraderie as we have had since my arrival. And still, it seems there is a wall descending between my sister and me, just as there is with Eros, these days. I do not know how to speak to her of the things I've heard, the things I've seen. The marketplace chatter; the pretty handmaidens in her husband's rooms. She would not welcome what I have to share. And besides, she is never alone. If she's not in the throne room, she's in the nursery, and there is always someone else standing by—Irini, or a servant, or a guard.

When we get to the stables I follow Dimitra down a corridor of obedient, wide-eyed stable hands—and as she comes to a halt in front of one of the stalls, I have to stop myself from crying out in surprise.

Ajax. Our horse. The one we left behind when we stowed away on the boat—how many nights ago that suddenly seems.

"Isn't he marvelous?" Dimitra smiles at me, a happier, truer smile than I have seen in a while. She has always loved animals—loves them better than humans, I believe.

"One of the king's guard found this beauty in Glyfa—that

little town across the water. Evander has an eye for horses, I'm glad to say. Though what this handsome creature"—she looks admiringly at Ajax—"was doing in a fisherman's hands I cannot fathom."

"Indeed," I manage. But Ajax has seen me now, and his excitement matches mine. He stamps, rears up, lets out a deep bray. Dimitra glances at me, then back at him, frowning.

"That's strange. He was even-tempered, before."

I reach out, put my hand against Ajax's muzzle. I suppose I could tell Dimitra the truth, but I know, too, that anything I say could get back to the king in moments—whether through my sister's lips or, more likely, through the stable hands. And though I can't quite see how he'd use that against me, every instinct says to keep my secrets to myself in so far as I can. I rest my thumb against Ajax's jaw, those liquid eyes, and look into them with what I hope is an apology he'll understand. *If I were alone, my friend, I would greet you with greater abandon.*

"He likes you," Dimitra says, offhand. But then she pulls me by the arm to another stall.

"And here is my pretty mare. Isn't she a beauty?" She rests a hand against her belly, still a little swollen from carrying her son. "I trust it will not be long before I am able to take her out again. In the meantime, you must do so." She looks at me with satisfaction.

"I should like that very much." I glance back towards my old friend. "But perhaps…could I take the stallion, instead?"

Dimitra laughs.

"I had not thought you such an intrepid horsewoman, sister! I applaud you. You have learned to tame a wild beast or two after all." She shrugs. "But I am afraid not. The king may call for him today. Better take the mare. She is mine—he will not notice her empty stall."

I could ask her why the king is not to know. Why he's so set against me exploring on my own. But I doubt there is an answer she could give me, that I will like. With a reluctant glance Ajax's way, I nod my agreement.

"Evander!" my sister calls, and a young man hurries over.

"Saddle her for the road." She turns to me. "And we must find you a guide, for wherever this place is you wish to see."

I shake my head.

"I know exactly where I wish to go. Trust me. I will not get lost."

She frowns.

"It is unlikely. But it is better to be safe." She shrugs. "You cannot expect me to justify it to Father, should anything happen to you."

Whether it's for Father's sake, or hers, or the king's, I can't say, but it soon becomes clear that I will not be leaving here unaccompanied.

I settle for the young man she calls over, a floppy-haired, eager-looking boy, no more than fifteen; I do not think he will do much to stand against my wishes, once we are out on the road.

And my instincts prove right. Once we are out on the road, he rides a deferential few paces behind me, since it's clear I know where I am bound. The heat of the day is rising, even though it is still only spring. Preferring to stick to the tree-line where we can, I skirt the town center, and set out east on the road to Athiri, following Phylax Thais's instructions, and at the first crossroads turn Dimitra's mare towards the north. The landmarks Phylax Thais gave me are few but clear, and I find I'm following them readily enough. The Red Mountain looms to the southeast, a tall dark cone with the sun behind it.

"An impressive sight," I say to Evander. He looks surprised to be addressed, but bobs his head readily enough.

"They say Atlantis is more beautiful than all the other islands of these lands," he says, tripping over his words a little. "But I have never left it, so I do not know. What is your opinion, my lady?" He flushes then, as though second-guessing his right to ask the question.

"It is certainly very beautiful," I say. "But I am not so well-traveled as you might imagine. Perhaps there are others more beautiful still."

He shrugs.

"I think we are more beautiful than Kythera, at any rate."

"Kythera?" I ask. The mare snorts under me. She is not unlike my sister, I have decided: graceful, but argumentative.

The boy nods.

"Our nearest neighbor. The isle of Kythera lies southeast of here. Their people are always coming to Atlantis, looking for a better life. They say the land is better here, the soil richer, the waters better stocked." He looks at me, wide-eyed. "It is said that many, many moons ago, when the Red Mountain last ran with fire, the people of Kythera took in the refugees of Atlantis. There is no one who remembers it now, but according to legend, half our people were lost—died, or took to the seas. Kythera gave them refuge. So, in return, Atlantis has accepted their people for generations, during seasons of poverty and bad harvest."

"But not anymore?" I frown.

"Not anymore," he agrees. "The king says Atlantis must take care of itself now, and our neighbors must learn to do the same."

An easy lesson, when your harvest is fine. A much harsher one, when times are lean.

We ride on, and it's not long before we come to a marker I recognize from Thais's description. A boulder by the side of the road, half-covered in underbrush, which if you squint at it a bit, might be said to take the shape of a wolf's head. *Lykos:* wolf. Perhaps that's where the village gets its name.

A sharp, blue blaze shows through a gap in the trees. One is never far from the sea, here.

"That would wash the dust off our feet nicely," I remark. The day's heat is making itself felt, now. It seems like a long time since I've felt the cool of the sea, the gentle tug of shallow waves against my skin.

"No doubt, my lady. But it is harder to access than it looks. Atlantis is full of cliffs, not beaches."

Ah. Dimitra already told me this. *Natural defenses,* all to the king's benefit.

"Still, I should like to see around." I tug the mare to the left.

"Here, my lady?" Evander sounds doubtful. "It is only a small village. Are you sure you would not like to see somewhere more...impressive?"

"Here will do fine."

We ride alongside low, dry-stone walls—boundary dividers between open fields. We're at the outskirts to the village. A tavern up ahead looks big enough to seat no more than half a dozen men, and behind it, scattered homes and outbuildings grow to a thicker concentration. Meanwhile straight ahead, at the end of this path, runs a river, its burbling audible from here.

An idea strikes me.

"I should like to bathe a while: I will require some privacy. Here." I pull a few coins from my pocket. "No doubt the tavern will have something to offer you. I will not be very long."

Evander blinks back at me, flushes. The very mention of bathing has, I fear, conjured those flushed cheeks.

"But I—I'm not supposed to leave you, my lady."

I smile.

"No, but it would hardly be proper for you to stay, would it?

He swallows—the flush gets deeper—and shakes his head.

"But, my lady...are you sure it is wise? To bathe alone?"

His eyes are so earnest, I have to keep the hint of laughter from my voice. He is not so cumbersome a companion, really—but he is still the king's eyes, and I am bent on freeing myself from him a while.

"Unwise?" I smile. "I shall not drown, you needn't worry."

He looks at me gravely.

"Perhaps, my lady, you do not know the stories of Atlantis. They say that before it was an island of men, it was an island of gods—and that sometimes, gods may walk here still. And," he plows on, despite his red cheeks, "a pretty maid is all too apt to catch their fancy. There are stories, my lady, of maidens who have been ruined this way, by a god's lust. That is why women rarely walk alone here, at least not in remote places.

And why," he stammers, "why bathing in the open is riskier still. It may invite unwanted…attention."

I nod. He is only trying to protect me. To do his job. So I do not tell him that any "ruining" of women on this island was most surely done by men and not gods; that these legends are merely a way for Atlantis to protect their sons from blame. I have seen enough by now to know how quick our people are to proclaim a fallen woman, and how resourceful they are in erasing men from that story.

"Thank you for your warning," I say. "But you need not fear. Those are stories from another time. Only the Shadowed God walks Atlantis now."

The Shadowed God. This new name does not easily leave my lips, but it proves useful. The boy brightens, and after once more urging me to be careful, trots off for the tavern. I tie Dimitra's mare to an obliging tree, with enough length in the rope for her to do justice to the new, sweet grass growing around it.

"I will not be long," I tell her, patting her neck briefly, and set off on the path that skirts around the village, instead of straight through it.

It takes me out a ways, nearer to the clifftops Evander spoke of. The sea sparkles; the air brightens. But I am focused on the village to my right. Evander, parked at the tavern on the outskirts, will not venture this way. As the houses grow denser, I take a small, winding path that promises to lead me back into the village heart.

Orchards, goat pens, vineyards. More shrines. A well. Father told me there was little to see in this place, and I suppose he was right. It strikes me that the citadel may be in healthier shape than many of the towns and villages out here, in the countryside.

I get a few strange looks—a woman walking alone, and in too fine a cloak to be from some country village. But they leave me be, and as I wander I let my mind do the same. Which house was hers? Which paths did she most often tread? Was she well-liked here?

I stop at a covered well to drink a cup of water. It is a shady spot, with a great olive tree whose branches spread unusually wide, and a strangely shaped trunk, as if two trunks had intertwined themselves, twisted into one great column. A bell rings in the back of my head. I was told about this, I'm sure I was. My father mentioned a tree like this. He and my mother were married beneath it—a tradition in her village. The Tree of Two Souls, they called it.

"Thirsty day, is it not?"

I startle. I hadn't noticed the woman approach. She's old, a decade or two older than my father, at least. She looks as though she has spent a lifetime in the sun: her hair and eyes washed to a pale grey; her skin, on the other hand, layered brown with the years.

"You are admiring our tree?"

I nod.

"I think I heard about it once. People from your village were wed under it, weren't they?"

"Yes. Not so much, now." She eyes me, her curiosity piqued.

"I don't suppose—" I hesitate. "That is to say, I heard about it from a Sikyonian man. He married a woman from here—Ismene, daughter of Philemon."

The old woman raises her eyebrows. *You have surprised me,* they say, and yet she does not seem surprised. She has become used to surprises, I suppose, in her long life.

"Perhaps you knew her?" I venture. My heart flutters when she nods: a brief, brisk nod, but a nod all the same.

"I remember. She married the mercenary. Her parents wept."

Mercenary. I am not used to thinking of my father in such terms. But it's true, of course. He was a mercenary.

And my mother's parents wept?

"They did not like her choice of husband?" I ask.

The old woman shrugs.

"They said they would not see her again. And they were right. She was their only child."

A pang goes through me. I had not considered such a loss, before.

"And they are…gone, now?"

She nods.

"In Hades' realm, these many years."

I look away, down into the well-waters, a faint dark gleam. What must it have been like for my mother? Leaving everything behind. Her parents, her home. Did she, too, suspect it would be her last glimpse of them?

"She must have been very in love with him," I say.

The woman eyes me.

"Perhaps. But there's many a reason a young woman might want to leave this place."

"Leave Atlantis?" I say. This island of such famed bounty and beauty; harvests that are always rich, colors and vistas that delight the senses? I should not have imagined its people leaving by choice.

The woman smiles.

"You're not from around here, are you?"

"I'm…from the citadel."

Her eyes pass over me.

"Mm. You're loyal to him, then? The new king?"

"Not particularly," I hear myself saying. It might seem an unwise answer. But by the woman's tone, I think I can guess at her own loyalties.

"I'm an outsider," I explain. "A stowaway, you might say. I came to Atlantis from the mainland. I was not here for the uprising."

"Uprising?" She snorts. "That's what they're calling it, now? Be glad you weren't here for it, girl."

"Was it…was it so very bad?"

She looks at me.

"You just steer well clear of the palace, mark me. Don't let that man's shadow so much as touch you."

I'm surprised by the energy of her words.

"You think him a harsh ruler, then?"

"I think him a monster," she says, unhesitating. "Tell me,

what kind of cursed creature slits the throats of sleeping innocents?"

I frown.

"You mean the old king?"

"I mean," she says, "the children."

Twenty-four

She tells me the story as the sun beats down on the fields, and the leaves move innocently in the trees.

How the old king had three children. The eldest, a girl, only a little older than me. Then two boys, the princes. The young one had barely begun to grow a beard.

"And he killed them in their sleep," she says. A long life has left her used to sorrow, too, no doubt, and injustice. But it has not weathered her capacity for anger. For judging evil where she finds it. Her voice leaves no whit of doubt.

"Their mother too. The whole family." She pauses. "I do not say the old king was a great one. Perhaps we needed a new ruler. But not like this. Never like this."

"What were their names?" I ask at last. I don't know why. Some need to rescue them, maybe, in the only way I can. Keeping their memories from oblivion, from the death of being unspoken.

"The daughter was Nereia." The woman looks at me. "Sosthenes and Artemion were the boys."

A sickly feeling goes through me. I have heard those names before. The ships, the great war-ships I looked out on from our balcony.

Sosthenes. Artemion. Nereia.

I wondered then why the king had given them such names. Now I am left wondering whether they were named by the old king, after his beloved children—or, in some grotesque cruelty, by the man who ordered them dead?

*

I barely remember the ride back. Untying the mare, stopping for Evander. The sun, the horse's hoof-beats on the road. It seems to me I only come alive again as I reach the agora, and the great temple where a statue of my husband—a lying pretense of my husband—now stands.

The services of the Shadowed God are held only in the hour of the shadows, and I am much too early. But two women—priestesses—stand like sentinels on the steps outside the great carved door.

I push back my hood and meet their eyes.

"I wish to speak with the Shadowed God. It is important."

The one nearer me looks down, her lip curling with amusement. The other doesn't bother to look at all.

"You seek a private audience?" the first says, her words lingering to show the absurdity of it. "With our god?"

"I told you—it is important." I hesitate. "I am his wife."

They glance at each other, nothing but mischief and scorn in their eyes. They don't believe me.

"Regrettably," the first one says, "he is not here. He is across the island, offering his benedictions to one of the new mines. Come back at sunset, and you may see your *husband* then." She snickers at the last sentence, like it's a great joke.

I'm feeling too many other things to make room for anger, or indignation. I just turn and walk away.

*

Nereia. Sosthenes. Artemion. The names circle around in my head like a chant, a dirge.

We live in brutal times, among brutal men. Bloodshed is not rare in this world; nor is mutiny or rebellion, insurgency or war. Nor is poverty or famine. People die in the Greek lands every day. Not just the privileged sons and daughters of inept kings, but farmers and laborers, blacksmiths and peasants. Women, children. They die needlessly, shamefully.

But reminding myself of this does not banish the images that dance before my eyes.

My sister—does she know? Does my father?

I cannot stay in this place.

The thought pulses through my head. If we leave here, we leave my father, my sister, my nephew. My father is not in good health. If we stay away too long—or if we are not allowed back in—I may not see him again.

But the names are beating in my head. Not the first innocents to be murdered in the trading of kings and thrones. Certainly not the last. But how can I live under the roof where such a deed was done? Look into the eyes of the man who, I am certain, commanded it?

I swallow hard.

Will Eros see it as I do? He has seen a thousand mutinies in his time, a thousand coups, a thousand-thousand bloodied swords. *Do you think your Sikyonian king gained his throne by gentle means,* he asked, when I first complained of this king's reputation. Perhaps what I have learned today will not shock him. Perhaps he will say it is no more than humans being humans; that it is the way of things.

And it's the thought of hearing those words from him, that frightens me the most.

*

"Lady Psycheandra!"

I'm at the staircase when one of the guards hails me. I turn, watching him approach. Dareios, captain of the guards. I don't think I'm imagining the dislike in his eyes.

"The king would like to see you, my lady." His voice is clipped, and the *my lady* comes out stiffly.

"Follow me, I will take you to him."

It's not a request, and he doesn't bother to look over his shoulder to check if I'm coming. Part of me wants to scoff and turn my back, retreat upstairs. But deep down, I know it is wiser to play the game.

Dareios swings open the door to the council room. No councilors are here now, though—just the king, alone at his great table, his hands resting, steepled, against the polished olive-wood.

"Thank you, Dareios. You may leave us."

It's not that I enjoy Dareios's presence, but I'll admit, something in my stomach tightens when he leaves the room.

The king gestures to the seat across from him.

"Well, little sister. Sit, sit." He smiles a smile that does not reach his eyes.

I oblige him, and he leans back in his chair, looking at me. Is this about my excursion today? Will he upbraid me for leaving the palace without his authority? Well, I will not grovel with apologies for that. I try to summon all the scorn I have for him, but it's no good. The names of the dead king's children are still swimming in my head.

But then the king takes something from his lap, and places it on the table.

Something I recognize instantly.

Something I have to do everything in my power not to reach out and grab.

The king has found my mother's knife.

Twenty-five

I sit across the table. Watching him watching me.

"You recognize it, I see." His mouth tightens. "The maid who cleans your room came to me with a curious story today. She said you kept a fearsome blade up there. I did not believe her, of course. But then..." he shrugs, looking down at the knife.

"I had to wonder, little sister: what on earth could you want with such a weapon? One you're harboring inside my home, no less?" He looks at me, and though I see the burn of his eyes, he does his best to hide it. He is a fire-tempered man who wants me to believe he is ice.

The most dangerous kind of all.

I swallow. I have the sense we are playing a game, but one where the rules can change at any time. One where the only guarantee is that I will not be the one to win.

"Your highness," I begin. "I can see how such a thing might appear. But this little knife is not a weapon—it is a keepsake, that's all. It belonged to my mother—see the sheath, the jeweled handle? A pretty thing, is it not? It is all I have left of her, and I have carried it with me since I left Sikyon. My sister can tell you."

He eyes me closely then, his eyes traveling over me more slowly than any other man would dare. But he can do what he likes, he is the king.

"A motherless girl's keepsake." His mouth twists. "Yes, I see. All very touching. However, I am sure you see, dear sister, why such things cannot be left lying about in my home. I have a son to protect now, too. So alas, I must take this pretty little trinket from you."

A bolt of fear goes up my spine.

"But—but it's mine. It belongs to me."

He smiles again.

"Indeed. But alas, one never knows whose hands such an object might fall into. And I must be careful. While you are under my roof, little sister, this will go in the armory, where it belongs."

The blade disappears from the table again, removing any last thought I had of lunging for it. The king gestures towards the door.

"Please. Enjoy the remainder of the day. Dareios is waiting outside. I have some palace business I must return to."

*

I burst into the nursery. There is my sister, the baby in her arms, Irini the nurse hovering by the crib.

"Were you part of this?" I demand. Remembering her in my bedroom doorway this morning, suggesting I take that ride. I buried that knife at the bottom of a wooden chest. No maid would have found it—not unless she were acting on orders to search the room. Knowing she could search it thoroughly, taking her time, because my absence was guaranteed for the day.

Dimitra just stares at me.

"The knife," I storm. "My mother's knife! That your husband...*confiscated,*" I spit out the word. "Did you have me sent away on purpose?"

Dimitra's face closes over. She stands, hands the baby back to Irini without speaking a word, then grips my arm and propels me out of the room into the corridor.

"What are you babbling about?" she hisses, once we are out of earshot. "Who is supposed to have sent you away?"

I stare at her face. My sister has many skills, but acting is not one of them—she is too impatient to dissemble well. That's what makes me think she's telling the truth.

"My mother's knife," I say, collecting myself a little. "Don't you remember? Father kept it in his room. It has a jeweled handle."

Something dawns in her eyes.

"The king has taken it," I go on, "and locked it in his armory."

"Well, I should think that's the best place for it," Dimitra says, her voice growing crisp now. "It will be safe there, and will be yours again when you leave here." She shakes her head. "Think, Psyche. You may not mean any harm with it, but there is a reason we do not leave weapons lying about in our rooms." She drops her voice. "Not just the threat of accidents, but worse. Not everybody loves the king, Psyche. His guards are hand-picked, but as for the rest—we cannot be sure of anyone's loyalty."

"I'm not surprised," I snap.

Dimitra just blinks at me.

I fold my arms.

"The king he took the throne from—the king he *murdered.* Tell me honestly. Did you know of his family's fate?"

Dimitra's face closes over again.

"I don't know what you're talking about. He banished them. That's all."

I stare at her, refusing to drop my gaze.

"Oh? Banished them where?"

I see her hesitation. Her displeasure when she finds she has no answer.

"How should I know? Some other island—what does it matter?"

I keep my eyes locked on hers.

"Two sons? Two would-be kings, in line for the throne? He banished them to some neighboring kingdom, to grow up nice and strong? To build their armies and wait for their revenge? Come, sister." I glare. "You are too clever to believe that."

Her eyes shift.

"But he told me—"

"And you believed," I snap back, "because you wanted to. Because it was easier for you."

Dimitra takes a step back.

"And what good would it have done me to doubt him?" she retorts, but I see a fleeting pain behind her eyes. "What power do you think I have here? Do you think I can curtail the king, make him gentle? Curb his appetites? Do you think anyone in this place *listens* to me?" Her eyes flash. "You judge me. You *dare* judge me for marrying him. Tell me, what ought I to have done, sister? I was a castaway, homeless, an outcast. So was our father. Tell me, then, who was going to care for him? Certainly not you."

Her words land hard, the way she means them to. Because she's right.

I never meant for it to happen like that—for her and Father to be left alone, without protection, fending for themselves. I never meant for it to happen, but it did.

And look at where it led us all.

*

"The priestesses said you came for me."

I had all but given up hope of seeing Eros tonight. But here he is, in the doorway, his eyes on me.

"They said it was important."

I sit down on the bed, look him in the eyes. "It is. The king has taken my mother's knife."

I have never before seen the expression that flits across his face. Eros prides himself on his controlled emotions, but my words have ruptured it.

"*Taken*?" He stares. "How?"

"He searched our room. It could not have been by accident. He sent someone to root around in here, and found it. And now he has confiscated it—so he says. He means to keep it in the armory."

Eros sits down in the chair opposite me. His thoughts are elsewhere—calculating, calibrating. I'm half expecting him to repeat the things Dimitra said: that the knife will be safer in the armory; that it's still mine, that there's no harm done. But he does not.

Of course he does not. Unlike Dimitra, he knows what the knife really is.

The damage it can do.

"The king cannot guess its true nature," he says after a minute. "He must already sense that it is valuable—that is why he took it from you. But we cannot let him know *how* valuable."

I swallow.

"There's something else." And I tell Eros what I heard in Lykaria. He's silent while I speak. I think I see something spark in his eyes, but I can't be sure.

"A grim deed," he says. I wait for him to add *if it is true,* but he doesn't. He doesn't question me or my tale. He doesn't tell me that, though barbaric, such actions were inevitable. That kings must guarantee their rule; that eliminating one's enemies is provident, that any strategician would insist on it. Instead he turns his eyes on mine.

"I, too, heard something today."

My neck prickles. What else is there to add to this sorry list?

"At the mine, I spoke with the foreman." Eros pauses. "I passed some comment about gold or precious metals, and he gave a strange sort of smile. Said, *the king's not looking for any of those things, my lord.*"

I frown, not yet sure where this is going.

"So what's he looking for?"

"I asked the foreman that very question; he clammed right up."

A deep unease goes through me. I can't put my finger on why, but I feel it all the same.

Eros's mouth is set in a tight line.

"The king has dug those pits for some purpose of his own, Psyche. The mining is just a front. Whatever his true purpose is, he has lied to me. To us."

I consider that.

"Whatever it is he's seeking, I think he blames you for not finding it." And I tell Eros what I heard this morning, behind the closed door. How angry the king sounded, when Dareios reported the lack of progress. And then the other thing I learned.

At that, Eros's eyes sharpen.

"He has been sending word abroad? Of me?"

"Not by name," I concede. "But..."

Eros grimaces. "But it is enough. Enough to put you in danger."

My eye catches on the quiver of arrows that hangs on the hook by our bedroom door. *They* were not confiscated. Apparently, unlike my knife, the king doesn't consider them a danger—perhaps because he, like so many, believes my husband's arrows cast only spells of love. He does not know about the second kind.

"I am not so fragile," I murmur. "I can defend myself."

Eros looks at me.

"That is not the point."

I think of the scorpion bite. The time Ajax trampled me. The way I recovered, that should hardly have been possible. All the evidence my body has given me that it can do things others' can't.

"You said I was not like other mortals. Those were your words."

He looks at me.

"Your body is strong, yes, and perhaps it is special somehow, but you are no immortal being, Psyche. Do not forget: it is blood, not ichor, that runs through your veins." He sighs, and paces over to the window.

"I heard word at the temple. Murmurs, but I think they may be true. Sparta means to bring war to Crete."

War. I know what he's thinking.

Ares. If war is coming, that's where we'll find him.

"But...you would leave here?" I say. "The worship? Your temple?"

His back stiffens.

"I would have wished for more time. More strength. But I fear you are right, Psyche. This king—he is not to be trusted."

Leaving here. Back out on the road, and my family left behind—just as I left them once before. This is not what I wanted, either. But our secrets are too great, the risk of discovery too precarious, especially in the hands of a reckless, ruthless king. If the gods come to ruin us, they will ruin my family, too.

"But the knife," I say.

Eros doesn't turn from the window, just nods.

"We will tell the king tonight that we travel to Sparta. He cannot refuse to release it."

I wonder how that conversation will go.

"He may ask when we plan to return. He will expect you back soon." It seems we have two choices: lie, and risk his anger later, or suffer that anger now.

Eros looks at me. "Yes, it will injure his pride. Perhaps, even, his standing with his people. He will be much provoked." His eyes hold mine. "It may be hard for you to return here."

I know what he's telling me, and it stings. If we abandon our alliance with him, the king will hate us for it.

But the alternative? I feel it in my bones: there is a rot here, and the nature of rot is to spread. To stay would be to invite disaster—and not just on ourselves.

I nod.

"I'm ready."

*

At dinner, when Eros tells the king of our plan to travel, the king raises his eyebrows, but smiles pleasantly enough.

"A good plan, my lord. But why not leave Lady Psyche here, in comfort, while you are away? The journey may be rough, and surely you would not be gone long."

The hairs on my neck prickle.

"I travel with him."

The king raises his brows again.

"My, my. You are anxious to be gone, I think. Should we be offended, my queen?"

I glance at Dimitra. The look in her eyes is complicated. Perhaps some part of her is glad that we are going? But I think there is something wounded, too. I feel like a traitor. I hardly dare look at my father, but when I do, he does not look so surprised. Resigned, perhaps, but not surprised.

"Well," Dimitra says, "we hope it will not be long till your return."

Her voice is flat. *She sees through it,* I think. They all do. My sister, the king, my father. They sense it—that we have no plans to return and resume this game the king's been playing.

Or am I imagining it?

"We hope the same," I say, and drop my eyes. I feel like a liar, a cheat.

"You need not leave at first light, I hope?" the king says, all courtesy. "We will breakfast together. Oh yes—and I will retrieve that knife of yours." He turns to Eros. "You heard, perhaps, that I had to lock away your wife's trinket?" He looks back at me. "We shall send someone down for it first thing in the morning."

He calls for one of the handmaids, and has a large kylix brought—the same drinking cup we used before.

"We must toast to your safe travels," he says, and pours the wine, and smiles.

*

The curtain in front of the balcony flutters in the night breeze.

"Come." Eros smooths my hair away, folds me in his arms. "You must sleep. It will be all right."

In the morning we will leave this place.

I hardly know what to hope for. The words Eros spoke to me days ago are circling my brain. *You mortals have little talent at telling gifts from curses.* I'm starting to think he's right. I thought it such a heady miracle, to find my family here, alive and well, and living in such high state. But now I wish they had been peasants after all, living in some humble shack, beneath anybody's notice.

Should we have been more honest with them, at dinner? Was it wrong of me to imply we would return? But this king is not one to accept rejection. We would make an enemy of him either way. Better to make nice with him now, while he still has my mother's blade.

"You don't think…" I hesitate. "You don't think he means

to keep it from us? The knife?" He spoke of it so easily at the dinner table. A different tone than he took with me this afternoon.

"It is only a trinket to him," Eros says from behind me, his voice reassuring and cool against my ear. "He would not be so foolish. Remember, I am a much stronger god already, than I was when he met me."

All that is true, I suppose, and it must be some comfort, because sleep comes, after all—a soft grey fog creeping in, settling in my bones, lulling me to rest.

Until a siren pierces the air, and I wake to the sound of running feet.

Twenty-six

Two horns; three. They are echoing from all over the palace. Eros springs from the bed, throws me my robe, and swings open the door to the corridor. Servants are running, the sound of feet pounding on stone.

"What is it?" Eros grabs one of them by the shoulder. "What's happened?"

"My—my lord," the man stammers. "There was an assassin. An attempt on the king's life. He has been apprehended, but there may be more of them. Please: go to the throne room, my lord. We are bringing the family there for protection."

"My sister?" I stumble into the corridor, breathless. "Is my sister all right? And her son?"

"The Queen and the Prince are well, Madam," the servant says hurriedly. "But please: to the throne room, quickly. You will find them there."

"And what about the others?" I think of the innumerable faces I've passed inside these palace walls, most of them nameless to me. "The servants. Irini, the nurse?"

The guard just stares at me.

"The prince's nurse," I repeat. "She's all right?"

He shrugs.

"I cannot say. Madam, please: the throne room."

Eros puts an arm around my shoulders and leads me down the hall, moving somewhere between a walk and a run.

He has nothing to fear from a mortal blade, but an assassin's knife may pierce my skin as easily as it pierces a king's.

*

The flames shiver and dance in their sconces as we run down the corridors. Eros is behind me, his dark cloak billowing in the corner of my eye. If there is someone running loose in these halls who wants the king dead, would they want me dead too?

Five guards stand outside the entrance to the throne room, but when they see us they step forward in a hurry, pulling the heavy door wide. All the torches are lit, and the lamps too, and it is so much brighter in here that it takes me a moment to see them. My father . My sister. Dimitra's dark hair tumbles in a great tangle down her back, the way it used to as a child. In her flimsy nightgown I can see her still-swollen belly, usually so well hidden under her queen's finery. When she turns her face to me I see her eyes are red-rimmed. Instinctively, she holds out her arms to me, and I fall into them.

"I was so afraid," she says.

It is as close as we will come to *I love you*.

"So was I," I say, and hug her to me.

The prince is swaddled in his bedding. My father, in his nightgown, is comforting Irini, who is sobbing openly.

Eros stands behind me. I feel the weight of his hand, warm on my shoulder.

"What happened?" I draw back, studying Dimitra's face. "Where is the king?"

"Thais," Dimitra spits out the name. "That monster from Crete."

Thais? I stare. One of his own guards…

Dimitra shudders.

"To think I favored her!"

"What of the other guards?" I say.

Dimitra's nostrils quiver, as she attempts to calm her breath.

"She was on guard with Briseus," she says, more quietly. "Outside the king's door. She drugged him, and stole into the king's chamber. By some miracle, the king woke just in time." She shivers again. "He saw her standing over him, ready to strike. He managed to wrest the knife from her somehow, thank the gods."

It crosses my mind for a second to wonder why Thais *wasn't* successful. She's one of the king's best guards. Dimitra calls it a miracle that the king woke when he did. But miracles should not happen to men like him.

And another thing: she may have drugged the guard on duty with her, but she can hardly have hoped to have escaped the castle—escaped Atlantis—all by herself.

"Have they searched for a boat?" I say. "Some way of escape? If someone else was waiting for her…"

Dimitra shakes her head.

"They've found nothing. No means of escape, no accomplices. Though I daresay once she is questioned, that may change."

"She meant to fall on her sword once it was done, perhaps," Father observes.

A suicide mission? Perhaps. But why?

Noise from outside the room makes us turn. The door is ajar, and a phalanx of guards is advancing down the corridor, kicking a stumbling, shackled prisoner before them. It's Thais—without her armor now, bloody-knuckled and beaten. Behind them walks the king. I stare at Thais, and just for a moment I think I catch her eye. Would she have killed us all—Dimitra, the prince, my father, me? Or was her blade sharpened for one neck only?

And I look at that neck now, a tendon pulsing there; the king's ice-cold face above it.

"Take her down," he snarls at the guards. "I'll join you soon enough." And as the guards move on down the hall, he steps inside the room. He wears his armor now, and his eyes snap with fire, but whatever he feels is hidden behind a fixed sneer. He is not a cowardly man, I'll give him that.

"She will be locked in the dungeon." He approaches us, his voice grim. "We will interrogate her most…thoroughly." He seems to find some satisfaction in that.

"Dareios will supervise. When she has given us every last drop of information, she will be executed. Whatever's left of her."

I suppress a shudder, and feel Eros's arm encircling me, gripping me tighter. I look down at Dimitra's baby, his soft, sleeping face.

"Has she spoken of her plot, my king?" Dimitra asks. Her voice is tight. She is keeping her fear on a short leash. "Her intentions? Accomplices?"

"She will," the king answers.

"But there is no suggestion of…a conspiracy?" I see the way her eyes stray to the guards at the doorway, despite all her attempts at self-control. She doesn't know who to trust, now.

The king scowls.

"I hope my faith in my guards is not so ill-placed. But Dareios and a few others—those who have my most unshakable trust—are interrogating the guards one by one. If there is any poison among my men, it will be purged." He grimaces. "Most thoroughly."

Irini is crying again.

"Stop your wailing, woman," the king snaps. He turns to the rest of us. "If you wish to spend the night here, in the throne room, I'll have them bring in bedding for you. Otherwise, if you prefer to return to your rooms, there will be extra guards on every door."

With that, he's gone—down to the dungeon to deal with Thais, I expect.

Thais.

It shocks me that it was someone familiar to me. Someone whose face and name I knew. Was it only the king she meant to murder? Or were others among us meant to die tonight? Somehow I find I cannot think that of her. I do not know her, but I cannot see her as a wanton killer.

"Psyche." My sister's voice cuts through my thoughts. By her expression, it is not the first time she has said my name. What time is it? Surely it is morning by now?

"The king can say what he likes about more guards, but I know I shall not be easy after this unless I have a weapon in my own hands." She's holding little Nikos against her chest; I can see how tight her grip is from the pink-and-white flush of her fingers.

"I'm going to the armory. Are you coming? You may take that knife of yours you wanted."

Eros glances at me.

"I'll come with you."

I shake my head. I understand he does not want me walking these corridors, but someone should stay with Father. Besides, I want to speak with Dimitra. And we still need that knife.

"You stay with Father. Please."

"Psyche—"

"*Please,*" I say, and he falls silent, though I feel his displeasure.

"We will not be long." Dimitra calls the names of a few guards to accompany us—the ones she trusts most, I suppose—and they walk ahead of us and behind, but not too close. Not quite close enough to hear us speak.

Dimitra keeps her eyes to the front, her voice a low, hard murmur.

"So, sister: you still plan to leave us, even now?"

Such a prospect has never felt more like desertion.

"Yes." I look her in the eye. "We must leave. If not today, then soon. Dimitra—" I take a breath.

"I do not trust your husband. I do not trust what will happen to this island under his watch. Although my path with Eros may not be easy, at least we will be under a god's protection. Might you not come with us? You, and the boy, and Father?"

Dimitra laughs in my face.

"'Under a god's protection?' Yes, while other gods wish him dead. Fine protection!" She fixes me with a hot stare, and I look right back. My sister isn't one to back down.

"But do you trust him, Didi?" I say at last, feeling my voice soften. Her old childhood name; it has been many years since it passed my lips. "Do you trust the king to take care of you? To take care of the prince?"

Dimitra closes her eyes.

"Do you know *why* Thais didn't kill him?" she says finally.

So there was something. Something more than this "miracle."

I shake my head.

"He had a girl in his bed. I heard the guards whispering it. He had a girl there, and Thais must have thought he'd be alone. She got confused, I suppose. She hesitated."

The words sink through me.

"I'm not stupid," Dimitra says. "I knew about the girls, I expected them." She looks away for a moment, then back at me, the fire in her eyes rekindled.

"You ask if I trust him to take care of me: I don't. I don't trust anyone to take care of me. Not him, and not you, nor the god you call your husband." I can feel it, how much she means the words.

"I will take care of myself, as I always have." She stops, looks at me. "Psyche, what do you think would happen if I ran from him? If I left in the night, and took his heir? Do you think he would let it rest? Do you think he would not drag us all from our beds and cut our throats, and leave my son motherless? I assure you, he is not a man accustomed to mercy. You have seen that for yourself, I think."

I don't miss the look that passes over her face, quickly hidden.

"And is this what you want for your son?" I say quietly. We've reached the staircase; the guards in front of us start to march down. Below us is the armory.

And below *that*, the dungeons. Gods only know what's happening there now.

"Is this the man you want him to become? If Nikos stays here, he will learn to be the same kind of man. The same kind of king."

She glares at me.

"And you would have the king be gentler, I suppose, and let traitors live? Let them go back to their homes, to gain in strength and try again another day? Thais's punishment is…distasteful, I grant you. But without it, what does my son stand to inherit? A kingdom of unrest, which breeds assassins; fear always hanging like a sword above his head? I do not want *that* for him, either."

The soldiers march us down the corridor, all the way to the end, to the room whose locked door I tried once before. Dimitra looks at me, and I look back. I cannot argue further with her.

"Wait out here," she says, raising her voice imperiously.

The guards fall back, letting us walk in alone. Despite everything, I feel some relief as we enter the cool, dark room. *My knife*. Soon it will be safe in my hands again.

The walls of this cavernous space are lined with glinting metal of every size and shape: spears and short-swords tipped with iron or bronze or bone; shields hanging on hooks, their metal domes winking like great eyes in the rare shafts of sun that make it through the high windows. My little knife would look like nothing beside all this.

Dimitra marches straight to the wall, pulls down a gleaming *xiphos* sword, and turns to me.

"You might want one of these, too." She gestures to the sword in her hand. "But that little blade of yours is over here." She leads me towards the far wall, and then, seeing my face, shrugs. "I came with him when he took it down here."

So she *did* know about it.

I grit my teeth. No point in arguing that now. I follow my sister to the spot where she stands. I thought I would notice the knife at once, but my eye must be dulled by all the other gleaming blades about.

"I don't see it."

She looks up at me, and there's something in her eyes I'm not used to seeing there. Confusion. Uncertainty.

Even fear.

"It's not here," she says slowly. "Psyche…it's gone."

Twenty-seven

"I don't understand. Who would have taken it?"

A cold thought goes through me. *Somebody knows. Somebody knows what it is.*

Yet how could they? The blade bears little outward sign of its powers, except to a well-practiced eye. And who on this island could possibly recognize adamantine?

But if no one knows what it is, then why is it gone?

It is small, easy to slip under a tunic—easier than the other, bigger weapons in this room. Easier to smuggle out of the palace, to slip to a merchant on the street. One wouldn't need to know anything about adamantine to discern the fine workmanship, the jeweled hilt.

Petty thievery. My mother's blade swimming somewhere around the streets of the citadel. If that's the innocent explanation, I am not sure I like it much better than the other.

Dimitra's looking at me. She does not know why the knife matters, but she senses something is amiss, and it troubles her more than she cares to show.

If I were to tell her…

If she understood the true value, the true danger, she could raise the alarm, have everyone and every room in this palace searched, and searched again.

But if I tell her, that means telling the king. And the king cannot know the truth.

What are we to do?

"Thais must have taken it," Dimitra says. "It is the only thing that makes sense."

"She has her own sword. Why would she need this?"

My sister frowns.

"I'm not sure. To frame you, perhaps. Maybe she wanted you held responsible for the king's death."

Could my sister be right? It is not a stupid theory, and yet…

A strangled cry drifts faintly through the window, and we both turn.

"Was that..." I think of Thais, and of the dungeons one floor below us.

Dimitra follows my thoughts. But she shakes her head, looking uncomfortable. "The king sent his men out into the town. That cry came from the street."

We stop and listen. Voices drift in. More shouts, more wailing. Children have started crying.

"The traitor says she works for the people of Atlantis. She tells us you want the king and his heir dead. Is that what you want?"

The guards' voices get louder and more raucous, and the other voices, more pleading. There is the sound of hard things hitting soft things, the deep, fleshy *thwack* of harsh blows. Cries of pain. Screams. In the little bit of window we have, I see sandaled feet running.

"Who helped her? Who are her supporters? Who does she speak for?"

Thwack.

Another cry, and a body crumples to the ground in front of our window.

"Well? Speak! Who are her supporters? Show yourselves. We will weed you out!"

I turn to Dimitra. "You can't let them do this."

Her dark eyes are wide, hollow.

"You think I have the power to stop it?" She turns from the window. "He does not listen to me, Psyche. And he will not listen to you."

The armory seems to exhale a smell of iron. Shadows hug the walls, dark spaces behind the rows of shields and blades.

"Perhaps he will listen to a god," I say.

"He is not afraid of your husband," Dimitra wheels around, her eyes snapping. "Don't you understand, Psyche?" Her face looks pinched, the bones of her nose visible and pale.

"He has no fear, only contempt. That is the king who rules this island. That is the man I have married."

*

Upstairs, when I tell Eros of my discovery, he is silent for so long I think at first he has not heard me.

"The knife," I say. "It's—"

"Gone. Yes." He sits down on a chair, as though the very words have weakened him.

Suddenly the lack of sleep hits me like a great weight. We've been up most of the night. I have no idea what hour it is now.

Eros looks at me, as though to impress some urgency on my mind.

"I cannot leave here without it." He drops his voice, conscious of the guards in the room; of Father and Irini nearby.

"I cannot look my father in the eye and tell him I left a god-killing blade in the hands of mortals."

I do not point out that it has been in the hands of mortals before. That somehow, for an untold number of years, it was in my mother's hands, and who knows who else's before that. What he means, of course, is the *wrong* hands.

I see his mind cycling through the same problems as I was weighing before. We could mount a search, but to give the blade that kind of urgent attention, especially in light of what's just happened at the palace...what would that signal? We would expose to everyone just how valuable it is, and just how desperate we are to recover it.

"Come upstairs," Eros takes me by the arm. "We cannot discuss this so publicly."

Our bedroom looks dimmer than usual, even though the morning is well advanced by now, and it is surely nearing noon. It is as though a great pall has been cast over this place—or it was always there, and I am only now beginning to see it.

Nereia. Sosthenes. Artemion.

What have these four walls witnessed? What bloodshed

may have taken place on these very floors?

"Dimitra thinks Thais must have taken the knife," I say, and explain the theory she voiced to me already. Eros nods.

"It is certainly possible. Her rooms must be searched again."

I think that, after all, there may be no way to keep this from the king's ears. Not if he is to give the orders that we need.

"He will be in the dungeon now," I say. "With Thais." I hate to think of it; what's happening down there.

"And his men…they're out on the streets, attacking people." I tell Eros of the guards we heard from the armory. Up here, with our rooms overlooking the water, we are sheltered from city clamor. But I have little doubt that the guards' rough justice is still at play.

*

By the time a page knocks on our door, we have made little progress. I have a thought of talking to Thais, if I can get access to her; if the king will let me. It is surely not coincidence that the knife disappeared on the day of her attack; she must know something. Eros, meanwhile, plans to join Dareios's interviews of the other guards. Perhaps one of them will let something slip. Because we know one thing: just like the attempted assassination, the thievery has got to be an inside job.

The castle has been locked down all night. Whoever took the knife from the armory, I doubt they would have had time to move it from the castle.

Which means it's still here. Somewhere beneath our feet, right now.

"My lord. My lady." The page hovers at the door. He is young but looks hollow about the eyes. Perhaps he has been facing Dareios's interrogation already.

"The king has ordered some food to be prepared. Will you come down?"

Food. I had all but forgotten such a thing existed. I glance out the balcony window. The afternoon is slipping away to evening.

"Come," Eros gives me his hand to lift me from the bed. But the thought of going down there, sitting at that table, facing that vile, vile man—I cannot summon myself to do it.

"I don't want to go. I can't bear it. I can't bear to see his face."

Eros looks at me, drops to his knees beside the bed, so he can murmur out of earshot of the king's page.

"We must play the game, Psyche. A little longer."

I close my eyes.

"Make my excuses. Tell them I am unwell. Please? I can't face him tonight."

Eros sighs.

"Rest, then, if you wish it. I will come back to you after the meal is ended."

I watch his cloaked figure leave the room.

Exhaustion takes me over, and I let myself close my eyes. Just for a moment, I tell myself, but I must drift deeper than that. Later, from somewhere far away, I hear the sound of the door opening again, but it doesn't wake me. When I finally startle awake my head feels thick, as though many hours have passed.

The room is cold, and dark. A wind outside is blowing, and the white curtain to the balcony whips and billows.

"Eros?"

Is he out there? He must be. The bed is cold. I do not think he has laid down in it at all. He is troubled, as I am. No wonder if he cannot rest.

His quiver of arrows dangles on its nail by the door, their heads sharp and glinting. A lizard skitters past me in the grey half-light, then runs up the wall in a flurry. My skin prickles. What was it that woke me? Am I just imagining it, or was there some noise—the door closing, perhaps? But no, that was hours ago. I grab my *chiton* from the floor. I wind it around me as I step out onto the balcony.

"Eros?"

Behind me, a voice snarls.

"Not a step closer."

Twenty-eight

Shaking, I turn around. There stands the king—holding a knife to my lover's throat.

My knife. The adamantine blade. The only kind that can kill a god.

"What are you doing?" I whisper. This is madness. Unthinkable madness.

"I think you have an idea," the king smirks.

Eros just stands there, perfectly still, the knife at his throat. His eyes on mine.

Keep calm, Psyche.

I draw a sharp breath. That was his voice, Eros's voice—*inside my head.* And not like the child's voice in Athiri, either. I'm not just overhearing this. He was *speaking* to me.

I try to do as he says, and keep calm. Perhaps he has some plan, some idea of what to do. But if he does, I'm not hearing it. Is my panic getting in the way?

The king tugs something from his robe with his free hand, dangles it in front of Eros.

"Put this over your head. Now."

It's a piece of cloth; a hood. Ragged and dirty and stained. Of course: he can't afford to see Eros's face. He must have managed this by sneaking up on him from behind. But even now, I see how he awkwardly keeps his eyes away, even while holding the knife against my lover's throat.

"Over your head, I said. I don't want any tricks."

Don't put it on, I think.

But Eros takes it from the king's hand. His eyes don't leave mine as he puts it on. But then the dirty cloth falls over his eyes, over his face, and it's like a light goes out, leaving me all alone. I want to fall on the ground and scream; I want to throw myself upon the vile man who dares to do this to a god. But instead I stand frozen to the spot.

"Adamantine." The king nods to the blade, a note of satisfaction in his voice. It makes my skin crawl.

"You thought I wouldn't recognize it? I am curious, sister, how you came by such a thing. What a foolish story you gave me about it. Your mother's little heirloom!"

"You have no right to it," I say between clenched teeth. "It will do you no good."

"I beg to differ," he says smoothly. He looks at me. "You see, little sister, the real road to power lies in knowing what deals to make. Which bargains, which favors. The one I made with your husband has not been serving me well—not well at all. So it is time to make another."

The brown hood flutters a little against Eros's face. I wish I could see him. I wish I knew what he was feeling. But if he is trying to speak to me, my mind is too full to hear it.

"You have told me," the king says, "of his brothers. How very keen they are to locate him. Only think what they will offer me, if I return their sibling to them."

A cold feeling runs through my chest.

Eros's brothers—the twins, Deimos and Phobos. Thwarted and insulted, Deimos maimed for life thanks to me and this very blade. How they hate us.

"I will be sending a messenger to the mainland shortly," the king goes on, his voice smug with pleasure. "He will seek out their temples, and deliver the message."

"They will not thank you for it." Eros speaks from beneath the hood, but his voice is clear. "They will not be pleased with any mortal who dares insult a god. Even me."

"We will see," the king shrugs.

He thinks Eros is just trying to trick him. My heart beats fast. It doesn't matter what the twins do to the king—whether they throw him some small boon, or raze his palace to the ground. Kostas is right about one thing. They will be delighted to have Eros back. Their prisoner, once again.

The blade is so very close to Eros's neck. If he inhaled too deeply right now, the tendons would touch that sharp edge.

"This is madness," I say. "You cannot expect it to work. And what of my sister, my father? Do you expect them to condone this?"

"Let me worry about that," the king smiles, his teeth flashing, and it makes my blood run colder still.

"Now, sister." The smile drips with condescension. "We must all make our way downstairs—you and your husband will be joining Phylax Thais this evening. You will walk ahead of us. Some of my guards are waiting in the corridor. I will take the rear, along with your husband. We will walk carefully—won't we, my Lord? We wouldn't want to stumble, and accidentally die."

My thoughts tumble wildly. The dungeon? Surely this madness cannot work. How can he expect to hide us in the dungeon, without my sister's knowledge?

Unless she already knows.

I push the evil thought from my mind. Whatever bad blood may flow between Dimitra and me, she wouldn't sanction this. I *know* she wouldn't.

I try to clear my mind, to make room for anything Eros might be trying to tell me. But how can I dare resist anything the king says, while he holds that knife against my lover's neck?

"Come, sister. You would not like to test me on this, would you?" The king nudges the knife a little closer, and sees me wince. "That's right."

All of it feels unreal. The moonlight on my hands and arms; the blue shadow on the ground before me as I walk, slowly, back indoors to our bedroom.

The king follows behind, nudging Eros forward, the knife's blade flat against his neck as a reminder. Even that must be agony—the touch of adamantine itself is searing to a god. But Eros says nothing.

At least, not out loud.

It's as I'm reaching the door that I hear it. One word, clear as a flash of lightning in my mind. It's so strong that I stumble for a moment—but I'm not the only one. Behind me, Eros stumbles too. I turn around in time to see him steady himself, regain his balance. The king is quick-handed. He's moved the knife in time, but he curses loudly.

"No more of that, my Lord," he says then, his voice unpleasant. "You are lucky I did not nick you with the blade. Next time I do not think you will be so lucky. And I would hate to return you to your brothers as damaged goods."

"An accident," Eros says curtly. "I am not used to walking sightless."

But I do not think it was an accident at all.

My breathing takes a while to slow, after that. Eros was so very close to the knife's edge. It was a terrible risk, to pull the king's attention from me. But it worked.

It bought me the few seconds I needed.

*

Outside in the corridor two of the king's guard are waiting for us: Dareios and some other man. When they see me, they hoist their spears in unison. They flank me, leading me down the winding corridors, as the torches flicker and burn. The sound of our feet seems dampened by the night, our movement wordless except for Kostas's occasional hissed commands. I could cry out, rouse the household, but I don't dare. Not when I know how close that blade rides to Eros's skin.

We descend the stone steps, floor by floor. Past the armory. Down again. When we get to that shadowed opening in the wall, the guard in front of me marches to the door and unlocks it.

But how long can the king expect to hold us here? It will take time, before he can get his message to the twins. Days will pass, maybe many days. A guard must be changed many times during then, the adamantine blade passed from one tired hand to another. All Eros needs is one instant. In a moment, he can rip that foul hood from his face, and let the sight of him burn their minds to ash, turn them into blubbering fools.

Dareios pushes the door open.

"Your new chambers," he sneers.

The room is dank and dark. I cannot tell at first how large it is. There is only one torch in the corner, guttering in the draft from the door. I wish I could at least feel Eros behind me—the warmth of him, the steady presence. But behind me are guards and their spears.

A figure rises from the shadows in the corner. Her face is bloodied, and she's been stripped of her guard's armor and dressed in peasant rags. But I hear Phylax Thais stifle a gasp as the soldiers march me in, and then, behind me, Eros. I wonder if, under all their menace and bravado, the guards feel it too: that this is madness, that only a madman would dare try to imprison an immortal. These men were brought up to be god-fearing, and that habit is not so easily broken.

But, "Chain her," the king says, and the next instant there are cold shackles on my hands. They push me unceremoniously against the wall, and fasten the chains around the great hooks there. I don't fight them. Instead I steady my breathing and remind myself that they cannot shackle Eros.

That is, they *can,* but to what purpose, when he can break free of iron as if it were glass? I wonder if the king can even fully comprehend what a god *is*. Perhaps by walking among mortals like this, as if he were one of them, Eros has helped them forget. Well, their mistake will only be to our advantage.

But the king is smiling as he turns to Eros.

"You, my Lord," he says smoothly, "will step in here."

In the shadows I see it: a large iron cage. The bars are almost as tall as the ceiling. My heart pounds. What do they need it for, this monstrous cage?

The king nudges Eros forward, but Eros cannot see the cage as he steps through its opening. Only when Dareios closes the gate with a clang does he start at the noise, his instincts filling in the details. It doesn't matter, I tell myself. He is not a mere man. He will break those bars as easily as a child breaks clay.

But the king is watching with a look of satisfaction on his face.

"Reach out your hands, my Lord. Feel the bars of your

cage."

At first I think Eros will not move; that his pride, if nothing else, will prevent him. But he extends an arm—and then, the moment it touches one of the bars, he flinches.

I have seen that before. But not at the touch of iron.

Kostas is smiling at me.

"I thought you an expert, sister. Do you not recognize adamantine when you see it?"

A cold wave rolls over me. It cannot be. A whole cage…it's impossible. This metal is unknown in the mortal lands. It is the stuff of legend—it cannot just be mined for, like iron or gold. The wave of coldness catches in my stomach.

Mined for.

Is that what he's been doing, all along?

"I am not like the last king, you see, nor his father before him. I am not stupid enough to ignore my greatest advantage." He glances at his guards, at Thais, back at me.

"I know it's more than a rumor, you see. There *is* adamantine beneath the soil of Atlantis, and I will find out where. The old kings may have been too stupid or too afraid to see its worth, but they weren't completely useless. They kept just enough of it, locked away for generations, for me to make what you see here."

"You're lying," I breathe. He smiles.

"You don't believe me? Well, you soon will." The king turns his head. "You can take off your hood, now, my Lord."

Eros's voice is taut.

"You know what will happen if I do."

I wonder at his restraint. These men deserve the worst that could happen to them. Then again, should he lift the hood and drive them to madness, it may go worse for us, for there can be no reasoning with madmen.

But for some reason, Kostas is chuckling.

"Yes, my Lord. I believe I do know what will happen when you lift the hood. The question is, do you?" He glances around and gestures at Dareios, who moves to where Phylax Thais is shackled.

"We will perform a little experiment. You will drop your hood, and Phylax Thais will watch. Dareios will tell me if my theory is correct."

And Dareios, smirking, grips Thais's skull in his big hands. They form a vise, locking her head in place so that she cannot help but stare in the direction of the cage.

"I'll see it if you blink. You won't blink, will you, Thais? Of course not." Kostas chuckles again, as Dareios pinches the skin around her eyes, holding the lids open.

"You can't do this!" I shout. "You can't make her do this!"

But the king ignores me.

"Now, my Lord, the hood."

"I have taken a vow," Eros says. "I do not harm innocents."

"Ah, but she is no innocent," the king sneers. "Besides, if you don't do as I say, I'll have Dareios here to take his blade to your wife's neck."

Eros grows very still for a moment. Then he reaches out, finds the cage bars, wraps his fists around them. It must cost him some pain to do it. Then he pulls—I see his muscles heaving, trying to prize them apart. But they don't so much as quiver.

"You don't understand, do you, my Lord?" The king's satisfaction crawls from his throat. "*You cannot get out*. You cannot save her. Not unless you do as I say. Now: drop your hood."

I do not think I have ever seen Eros's hands shake before.

Now, slowly, he withdraws his hands from the bars, and lifts the hood.

Twenty-nine

My breath is locked in my chest. I can't take my eyes from Thais's face. What's going to happen to her? Eros has described it to me before, the horror of a mortal losing their senses from one instant to the next, but I have never seen the unholy sight.

It seems to me all of us in the room wait with bated breath. Thais has set her face against what is to come, choking down any desire she might feel to plead or beg for mercy. Hungrily, the king and his guards watch her face. But…nothing changes. There is fear in her eyes, but it is only the same fear as before. The seconds pass. What is happening? Is she immune somehow, just as I am? Even Thais looks disconcerted, waiting for the agony that does not arrive.

I glance at Eros's face, and feel a dart of shock. His face is still beautiful, but in a different way now, a more modest way. A *human* way. Before, there could be no mistaking it—but now, I would not have guessed that I was looking upon a god.

What have they done to him?

"You were right, your highness," the second guard says after a few more moments.

Smiling, the king raises his eyes at last to look on Eros. There is a sneer on his face as he looks Eros over, letting his eyes rove slowly, insolently.

"Adamantine." He shrugs. "The only thing stronger than the gods. All your strength, all your gifts and curses, bounce right off it. While you are in there, my Lord, you are hardly a god at all."

My stomach roils. How can it be? I did not imagine there was anything in the world that could compromise a god's powers.

But if this king has it…

His eyes land on me.

"And *you* thought," he laughs, "that I was mining for gold. What need have I for gold, or pretty gemstones? I am not a woman—I am a warrior." He taps the bar of the cage as though he could make it ring. It must please him, that he can touch it and feel nothing, and meanwhile it makes a god flinch.

"Still warm to the touch," he observes. "An extraordinary metal, indeed. The smithy finished with this a day ago. Yet still, it feels sun-warm. It has been no small thing, you know, developing a method to mold and weld the stuff. For years it was thought impossible—that no furnace would ever be quite hot enough. Still, we found a way."

"You think you did," I blurt. "You think you will succeed in this. You won't."

I have no reason to be so cocky, and he knows it. The king looks me over.

"I do wonder, little sister, what Ares's more violent sons will do with you. They don't like you very much, do they? But I think they may find some use for you all the same. For a while, at least." His eyes travel the length of my body. I can read it now, more plainly than before, the mixture of disgust and desire. I shudder.

"She is right about one thing," Eros says, and we all turn. Even now, so much less godlike than he was, there is authority in his voice.

"You will struggle to keep this a secret." He fixes his gaze on the king. "You do not think there will be any dissenters? You do not think your guards will flock to join Phylax Thais's cause, when they hear what you have done? To insult a god like this is to invite ill-omen. Your children's children will curse your name."

"On the contrary, they will be most grateful." The king glances around the room. "Your absence, you see, will be quite easy to explain. Tragically easy." He looks my way. "You asked about your sister."

"She will not let you do this. You will have to lock her up, too. And how will *that* look to your people?"

The king brushes my words aside. His voice is cold, smooth as poison.

"I shouldn't worry about that. The people will hate you for what you have done. And your sister will hate you most of all."

My heart beats faster. What we've *done*?

"But we haven't done anything."

There's a cruel look on the king's face, almost of enjoyment.

"Is that so? I doubt very much that's how it will look tomorrow, when you two have vanished from the palace, having abducted the young prince of Atlantis."

That's when my blood runs cold.

"But that's…that's absurd."

"It's a foul, heinous crime, that's what it is," the king shrugs. "No doubt it was your plan all along, to take the boy. You have always been jealous of your sister, they will say. You have always hated her, despite everything she did for you. Or perhaps they will attribute some other motive to you—a madwoman, and a rogue god. But to stoop so low, to take from a mother what she cherishes most. Only a wretched woman would destroy her sister's heart so."

"But…" my thoughts are racing. "The prince is here in the palace, safe. He is not missing. Dimitra knows that."

And yet why does my blood feel so cold?

The king sighs.

"Alas, by morning, the prince will have disappeared, never to be found again. Poor Irini. It will not go well for her, I think."

Disappeared?

My breath feels short. What is he talking about?

"Monster," comes a hiss in the darkness—Thais.

The king takes a stone from the ground and flings it at her.

"Shut your mouth, wretch."

Never to be found again? This is some madness speaking.

"You can't mean…" I shake my head. "Your own son—"

"He is not my son!" the king erupts, red-faced now. The transformation is instant, from cold to seething hot.

"Your sister," he turns on me, teeth bared, "thinks I do not know. That I am blind to her whoring ways." His eyes flash. "But a man can always tell. A man knows when he holds his son in his arms. And a man knows when he has been handed someone else's bastard." He spits. "Blue eyes! Your whore sister thinks me a fool." His nostrils flare as he glares at me.

"Perhaps you know who it was, hmm? Some muscular whelp she met in the town square? Perhaps one of my guards?" His eyes drift to the two men at his side, and I see them recoil.

"No matter," Kostas continues. "After this, I will see to it that she never strays again. You can be sure of that." He smiles at me. "And once she's born me a nice litter, I shall do with her what I like." Then he looks back to Dareios.

"The preparations are made?"

Dareios nods.

"You mean to kill him." My tongue is heavy with the horror of it. But when I glimpse Thais's face behind the king's, from her expression I know I have guessed right.

The king sighs. "Dareios will bring the little bastard to the highest slopes of the Red Mountain. Then, the gods may do as they please."

"If you leave him to die, you murder him as surely as if you had wrapped your hands around his throat yourself," I spit.

But the king's composure has returned, as though airing his heinous plans has brought him comfort.

"Now, now." The king's voice is crisp again; he is all composure. "I suggest you hold your tongue, sister. A loose tongue must be punished, and I am sure my men have some ideas about how that would be best achieved—although I don't think your Lord Eros would very much like to watch them."

Bile turns in my stomach. This murder cannot come to pass. He will not see my nephew die. He will not hand my husband over to eternal punishment. He will not make a slave of me. But if I have to look at his face for one minute longer, my tongue may indeed take me places I'll regret.

So I duck my head down, turning my eyes to the floor. I hear him chuckle, and feel him step closer.

"That's it," he breathes into my ear, his breath hot and dry. "Know when you're beaten, girl."

Then he moves, his hot breath shifts from my face, and I hear his tread back towards the entrance.

"Dareios will be standing guard outside the door. He'll come to check on you from time to time, just for...peace of mind," he says. He looks around the room, appraising its bare stone walls.

"It's only a shame we can't put you up somewhere a little more comfortable."

He disappears through the door and the second guard follows. Dareios lingers, looking pleased. Evidently he likes the role of jailer.

And murderer.

"Now, I don't want any trouble," he says. "Understood?" He turns to Eros.

"We're to hand *you* over to the gods undamaged, but no one said anything about the girl." He jerks a thumb at me. "So we don't need to be so nice to her, you see. I could cut her throat, or take my pleasure of her while you watch. All I need is for you to make trouble." He holds up the key to our cell, brandishing it like a prize.

"So be good."

And the door closes with a bang.

*

No one speaks at first. It seems like no one even breathes. I raise my head and find Eros's face across the room. I see then everything that he hid while the king was in the room. Then he was like a stone. Now I see the rage, the pain, the blade-sharp purpose in his eyes.

"Did you get it?" he says, his voice low.

I had all but forgotten. I glance at the door. Even if Dareios is right outside it, the cell door is thick as a tree-trunk.

"Did you get it, Psyche?" Eros asks again.

I nod. His eyes never break from mine, steady as twin flames.

"Good," he says softly. "Very good."

Up in our room, when he pretended to stumble, when he drew the king's eyes away from me, it was just one word he spoke. One word I heard in the silence, as though he'd murmured it from inside my own mind.

Arrow.

It was right as I passed the hook on the wall where his quiver hung. I just had time to pluck one, slide it beneath my chiton before the king turned back—as carefully as haste allowed, because I know all too well what that poison can do.

But it does not seem like very much now: an arrow without a bow, when my hands are chained to the wall.

"Courage, Psyche," Eros says from across the room. As if he knows my faith is flagging.

Thais looks from one of us to the other, squinting through her bruised eyes.

The arrow is under my robe, straight between my breasts, but my arms are pinned behind me and stretched tight against the wall: there is no way for me to pluck it out. I will have to try something else. So I contort myself as best I can, curling over like a wilted leaf, shrinking my torso, my ribs, until the arrow nudges out from the fabric. I know what that arrow-head is coated in. I know what it can do.

"Psyche-" Eros breathes. But there's no other way.

I clamp my teeth down, oh so carefully, gripping the shaft just below the arrow's tip. I'm breathing shallow little breaths; I feel the air moving cold against my teeth. I focus all of my efforts on not letting the arrow-head touch the roof of my mouth, or the flat of my tongue, or tap for one moment against the back of a tooth. It is as though I have a viper's head in my mouth. And slowly I pull up, lengthening my neck notch by notch, until the rest of the arrow slides free. I unclamp my teeth with a gasp, and the arrow drops to the floor.

Across the room, Eros crows, and I hear the jubilation in

his voice.

But that's when I notice: the arrow is made of birch wood.

Eros has two types of arrow in that quiver: death-arrows, made of cedar wood, and love-arrows, made of birch. And I've taken the wrong one.

Thirty

I close my eyes, my head banging dully.

"I took the wrong one." My voice cracks as I admit my mistake.

We'll never get out of here. The prince will die, and I will die, and Eros will suffer worse than either of us, because he will suffer for a whole, deathless eternity.

Breathe, Psyche.

His voice comes into my mind like a wave, startling my eyes open.

"I can use it." He looks at me from behind the bars. "I just need you to get it to me."

I stare at him. What use does he possibly think we can make of an arrow enchanted with a love-spell? And how could I even get it to him? A kick will send it skittering only a few feet, not far enough to reach him.

"Hook your foot under it." Thais speaks from the corner of the room. I had almost forgotten she was there. But she's right. If I can loop my foot under…

I have no fear of the arrow anymore, at least. If it pierces my skin, so be it: I will fall in love with Eros all over again. I worm my toes around the arrow's shaft, picking it up carefully from its place on the dusty stone, then balance it across my other foot.

Steady, Psyche.

Then I lower my foot just enough, and fling it. When it clangs against the bars of the cage, I could weep with relief.

Eros thrusts his hand through the bars, grimacing at the adamantine's touch. Eventually he touches the arrow with the tips of his fingers and gets it through the bars. I let out the breath I didn't know I was holding. Eros's face is pale, covered in a sheen of sweat. I have never seen him look so like a mortal.

"Well?" Thais says into the silence. "What is your plan, my Lord?"

"Simple enough," he says grimly. "Stab a man through the heart."

*

"Dareios! *Dareios*!"

Our jailer doesn't come on the first call, nor the second. Eros must have shouted a dozen times before the door shudders open and Dareios's head appears, his thick jaw and heavy jowls.

"What the hell's this racket?"

"My wife," Eros says, "needs to relieve herself."

When Dareios understands, he looks at me and sneers with derision. "Are you going to soil yourself, my lady?"

I say nothing, keeping my face down. My cheeks are burning—with rage, but hopefully Dareios thinks it's from shame. I don't dare utter a word. Let him think I'm cowed and docile.

"Well? Can you bring her to the privy?" Eros asks.

Dareios laughs.

"She's not going anywhere. None of you are."

"A chamber pot then?" I say, my eyes still fixed on the ground. "Please?"

"What's that?" he leans closer. "*Please,* was it?" He stands back, folds his arms. "Go on. Let's hear you beg."

I can feel Eros's rage from across the room. That's good, it will make it easier to pick a fight.

"You dare speak to her this way, you witless lackey? You'll be the one begging when I'm through with you."

Dareios takes the bait. He turns, a hiss in his throat.

"What did you say to me?"

Eros comes right to the front of the cage. His face is bright in the shadows.

"I said," he speaks the words deliberately, "you are the lowest scum of the earth, Dareios. A sewer-maggot, a festering pile of excrement."

Dareios turns and takes a step towards the cage. I see the pulse at the base of his neck, the rage running through him.

"Speak to me like that again," he says. "I dare you." He pulls something from under his cloak. "The king had an inkling you might be a rowdy prisoner. He gave me this in case you needed...disciplining."

But even the sight of my mother's knife doesn't stop Eros.

"The only thing it reminds me of," he smiles a smile designed to infuriate, "is that you are nothing but a human stain, the most putrid filth of your kind. You're less than a bucket in a latrine, and I wouldn't stoop low enough to piss on you."

The back of that flushed neck quivers; Dareios moves sharply across the room, his knife-hand raised—

And the moment he reaches the cage, Eros lunges, his hand darting through the bars. Dareios gasps. The knife clatters to the floor.

The arrow is buried in his chest; I see the shaft as he staggers back.

"*Demon*!" he chokes. "What did you—"

But his words die out even as he speaks. Something is changing in him.

"Lord Eros," he whispers. There is a different kind of tremor in his voice, now. "What have I done?"

His tone is reverent, pleading, like a child.

I hear the quick intake of breath from Thais. She's never seen these arrows at work before, but I have.

"My Lord," Dareios murmurs. He shakes his head, and I hear the distress in his voice. "I can't seem to remember, but I…I fear I have insulted you."

"You have," Eros says

Dareios lets out a wail of distress, so genuine, so heart-broken, that my skin turns cold.

"I could never—I never meant—it was a mistake, sweet Lord! Do not send me away! I crave only to be near you. To see you—to touch your hand…"

Eros nods. "I know. But first, you must help me. Mustn't you, Dareios?"

Dareios, on his hands and knees now, shuffles close.

"Of—of course. If there is anything I can do, only name it! I live only to serve you! Only for you!"

The plan is working. It's what we hoped for. And yet I feel sullied, just witnessing this unfold. I remind myself that Dareios is a brute, a vile corruption of a man...and yet, I have to harden my heart not to feel something at the sight of him groveling like this. I know full well Dareios would debase himself in any way my husband asked, or throw himself from the window if he were bade to. Surely the poison of these love-arrows is worse, far worse, than the simple poison of death.

"It is simple, Dareios," Eros says softly. "You must open this cage."

Let him have the key, I think. *Please let him have the key.*

"Yes, my Lord, of course. At once, my Lord."

In moments Dareios has unhooked the key from his waist and flung the cage door open. Now he stands there like a man bewitched, staring at Eros like his world is born anew.

"Stand aside, Dareios."

Dareios bows, flustered, and draws back from the cage, making room for my husband to step out. And then I realize what's about to happen.

"Thais!" I call out. "Close your eyes. *Now*!"

Eros walks free. But Dareios never takes his eyes from my husband's face.

I hear his squeal, like a pig scalded, as Eros leaves the cage. But still he doesn't look away. He stares at Eros, weaving on his feet like a drunk. He's panting, his hand to his throat as though something is lodged there. He staggers, totters. When he wails, it's the wail of a child. Not rage, not fury—just pure incomprehension. Eros's eyes meet mine, and there are a thousand things in that glance, before he feels for the hood and draws it over his face.

"Dareios?" he says, but Dareios only twitches at the sound, as though it's a name he used to know, but has since forgotten.

"Dareios?" I try, and now he turns, but his eyes are glazed

over. He looks at me, then around at the others. He shows no sign of recognition—only puzzlement, as though someone has played a joke on him and he's not sure what it was.

"Thais," Eros says. "You can open your eyes."

Dareios is murmuring something now, real words or nonsense words, like some strange incantation.

"What's the matter with him?" Thais swallows.

"He's a fool now," Eros says briskly. "His reason is gone. It is my curse."

So this is the curse my husband has long warned me of. It's a terrible thing to see. I understand now why Eros has always been loath to let it happen, even to our enemies.

And yet he let it happen to Dareios.

Because of me, I think. Because of the things Dareios said to me, the threats he made against me. That's why my Eros's face was so pitiless, before.

Love is a dangerous thing indeed.

Dareios is staring at his fingers, turning his hands over and back again with what seems a mix of awe and fear.

"Careful," he murmurs. "We must be careful..."

Eros ignores the babbling, pushing Dareios from his path as he makes his way to me. He snaps the shackles at my wrists as though they were no more than crusts of bread. I wish he would lift his hood, just for a moment, but I think perhaps he doesn't want me to see what's in his eyes.

Then he turns to Thais, and snaps her restraints too.

"Remember," he says: "My face is covered now, but even so, take good care. You must not look upon it."

She doesn't need the reminder. Her eyes are wide as she stumbles out of her chains, rubbing one wrist and then the other. She looks from Dareios to us.

"I don't understand," she says to me. "How are *you* able—"

"We don't know," I say shortly.

The knife is still lying on the floor where Dareios dropped it. I run to pick it up, then stop short.

"It's not her knife."

My stomach turns over. *It's not my mother's knife.* Dareios was bluffing. And that means the king still has it. Of course the king would not entrust a guard with something so precious.

Behind me, Dareios is still murmuring to himself, lost in a world of his own. I look into his face for a moment—open, now, and guileless. I wonder which madness is worse—this madness, or the love-madness that came before it? At least this one's an honest madness. Dareios belongs to himself again, though he no longer belongs to this world.

He turns, as though he knows I'm thinking of him, and cocks his head.

"You see it, don't you?" he says. "The end—it's coming."

Thais glances at me again.

"But what can we do with him? We can't let him wander about like this. They'll raise the alarm the second they see him."

It isn't hard to steer him, still babbling, into the adamantine cage. He doesn't seem to mind, not this new version of Dareios. He's telling some other story now, speaking of great battlefields and moonless nights, of murder and death. The last remnants of a mind that's gone for good. Then Eros closes the cage, and we bolt for the door.

Thirty-one

A few paces outside the door, Thais stops.

"Wait! It's right here—"

She's searching the floor with her fingers, feeling for something.

"Here. This one."

She's got Dareios's knife, and now she drives it into a crack between two stones and pushes down, levering the stone free. She drags it back, exposing a round copper ring beneath, a handle driven deep into the layer of stone below. Thais grabs it and tugs upward, but it won't give.

She turns to Eros, panting.

"I need your strength, my Lord."

He wraps his hand around the ring and gives it a tug. A thick square of stone swings upward, a trap-door, exposing rough-hewn steps down into a tunnel.

"It will bring us out past the castle walls," Thais says. "Near the stables. We can steal some horses, ride to Athiri."

Athiri? I shake my head. I cannot escape, not yet.

"We have to stop him. You heard what he's planning."

Thais locks her eyes on mine.

"Trying to stop him is how I ended up here. I fear it's too late for that, my lady—but we can save the boy another way. We will ensure the king's rider is followed, and that the child is rescued once his back is turned. It is the surer way."

I glance at Eros.

"Even if you were right—my sister, my father, I can't leave them in this place."

Thais's eyes are fervent.

"We will come back for them, my lady. Believe me, we will stand a much better chance if we go now, and come back prepared." She hesitates. "I am not the only one who wishes

King Kostas dead. You will see. All that can be done, will be done. But we can do nothing for your family if you let the king throw us back in a cell tonight." She takes my arm. "I am on your side, my lady. I only want to see Atlantis safe."

I shake my head.

"You go," I say to Thais. "We will join you later, if we can."

She may save Atlantis. But I must save my family.

Thais frowns, nods. She must know, too, there is no time to lose in further argument.

"Very well." She steps down into the passageway, then hesitates. "If you make it…if you have love for Atlantis, come to Athiri. To Drusa Sideris's house. I pray to see you there."

*

The torches flicker as we charge up the stairs, as though even they can sense that something dreadful is afoot.

The armory. Then up another floor. Then another.

We keep running: past my father's room, past the royal apartments. I hesitate for a moment. Dimitra; my father. I could go to them now, wake them, tell them everything.

But I can't afford to lose a minute.

There are noises coming from the end of the corridor—from the nursery. Men's voices. Eros's hand is on my shoulder.

"Stay here. I'll go."

But I can't let that happen. This is my sister's child. Besides, I can't let Eros go alone in there. The king still carries the adamantine knife.

"I'm coming."

I feel Eros's glance from under the hood. If he were to take it off…but we can't risk it. The child, the nurse—what happened to Dareios might happen to either of them.

"Psyche—" Eros tries again, but I shake my head.

"I have to."

He draws back. Nods. I follow him down the corridor.

The door to the nursery is open. Inside are the king and the other guard from downstairs, and—

I choke back a sound of horror. Irini. Her face is toward the wall, but there is no mistaking the line of red that seeps from her throat.

"I told you to drug her, not to kill her," the king is saying.

The guard shrugs.

"I did, sire. Poppy-water in her wine, just as you said. But she stirred as I entered, and I thought—"

"No matter," the king says briskly. "We'll say the witch did it when she stole the prince. Hush, before you wake the child." He sighs. "It *would* be much easier to put a knife through him, wouldn't it?"

"You will not touch him." Eros steps into the room, and the two men turn quickly.

The guard looks afraid, but not the king, who pulls a knife from his belt and flings it, quick as a thought. But Eros is faster. The knife—*my* knife—whistles past him, and jams into the stone wall behind, hilt quivering. Before I can think twice, I dash past it, over to the crib. My nephew's wide blue eyes are just starting to open; I gather him into my arms.

"Put him down, wench." The guard advances, his spear pointed in my face.

"Drop your weapon," Eros says calmly, and the guard looks back. Eros has the king by the throat, holding him a foot above the ground. The king's face is turning purple, but he shows no sign of fear—only rage.

"Kill her," he sputters to his guard. "Kill the girl."

"Stop!"

The familiar voice—my sister's voice—makes my heart rush, first with relief, and then with fear. If she's here, she's in danger too. But as Dimitra advances into the room I see she's pulled my mother's knife from the wall.

And she's pointing it at Eros.

"Dimitra! What are you doing? Put down the knife!"

Her eyes snap to me.

"What are *you* doing, Psyche? What are you doing with

my son?"

"They attacked me," the king gasps out. "Wife! Throw the dagger!"

"He's lying!" I shout. "Dimitra, he's—"

"Put down my son, Psyche." Dimitra's voice quivers, but there's no hesitation in it.

"You don't understand! He means to—"

"Put him down *now*, or I will bury this knife in your husband. You know my aim is true."

The guard, spear in hand, is three paces away. If I let the child go now…

"Dimitra—"

All I need is the time to explain. Just a few words…

But she raises the dagger higher. Outside, I hear guards charging down the hallway.

"*Now*, Psyche. Or you'll regret it."

Then a word rushes through my skull, fast and strong as an ocean wave.

Window.

I blink, and see Eros's hooded face across the room. I feel his stare, questioning if I've heard him. Panic surges in me. Instinctively, I clutch the child tighter.

"I warned you." Dimitra pulls back her arm.

But before she can release, Eros is across the room, a flurry of wings and air hurtling into me. His weight carries me bodily out the window, Nikos clutched in my arms, into empty space. Falling....

And then not falling, but rising. His arms around me, my arms around the child. Wings beating, air rushing. The baby howls against my chest. An answering howl comes from the window. Dimitra races to the opening, grips the stone as though she means to throw herself out of it, too. She screams my name into the wind, a howl of rage and loss. I see the castle window growing smaller, the figures inside just dark shadows shouting.

I've left my family in the hands of a madman.

*

Eros's black wings carve through the night, blacker than the sky. Somehow he knows where we are going; I lost my bearings long ago. I'm dazed, head spinning. All I can concentrate on is holding Nikos tight against me. I don't dare focus on anything else; I don't know what those thoughts might do to me.

"What have we done?" I hear myself murmur.

"What we had to," Eros says, into the night.

Is he right? I don't know what to believe. All I can think about is Dimitra's cry of despair, and of my father, sleeping soundly in his bed. What world will he wake to?

The night swirls around us. The child, for now, has stopped crying.

"Where are we going?" it finally occurs to me to say. I can tell Eros is flying with some purpose.

"South," he says, his voice short. It is many moons since he had the strength to fly. Perhaps the strain costs him something.

South. My breath hitches. I cannot go to Crete—not now.

"We must go to Athiri," I say. I'm remembering the words Thais spoke as she disappeared down that tunnel: *I am not the only one who wishes King Kostas dead.*

She knows something. Something that could help Atlantis. And my family's fate lies with the fate of this island now.

"We have to," I say, as my nephew starts to cry again. "We have no choice."

*

I feel a bare flicker of hope as the outline of the village comes into view. It all looks so different from above. But there is the crossroads, there are the small houses; there are the forests on its border, and the black water beyond. And there, like a great, gaping socket in the earth, is the mine. It seems to hold shadows in its depths, a sea darker than the night. I stare down at it and think of my father's old myths of Tartarus, the place where the gods of Olympus buried their foes.

We drop from the sky, and in moments my feet touch solid ground. A cat, prowling the open spaces, rushes off to slink against the low wall nearby. I do not blame him.

We walk down the eerie, quiet street. At least Nikos is not crying; better if we can pass unnoticed to the Sideris house. There is no moon tonight, but the lime-washed stone reflects what little starlight there is, turning the houses ghostly, the gaps of dark windows like eyes.

I recognize it as we approach, this house we have been to before. And suddenly I remember the children at the pit that day, how they giggled and waved at Thais. How I thought nothing of it then, but now I understand: they knew her. Yet what business does a king's guard—a would-be assassin—have with this family?

I glance at Eros, settle Nikos against my hip. Whatever the business, it is my business now.

I draw close to the door, steeling myself to give a quiet knock, but then Nikos begins to wail again, his small lungs tearing through the night.

"Hush," I jiggle him. "Hush, little one." But he won't hush—why should he? He is far from home, and motherless.

What have we done, I think once more.

I'm still thinking it when the door swings open.

Thirty-two

I hardly recognize the woman who opens the door. In the darkness her features look craggier, unwelcoming. She peers out through the narrow opening, too suspicious to open it wide.

"*Khaire,* Kiria Sideris." I bow my head. "Perhaps you remember us?"

She looks panicked as she registers my face, and the shadowed figure beside me.

"We've done nothing! Nothing at all!" Her husband appears in the background.

Eros steps forward.

"We're not here at the king's bidding."

I drop my voice. "Phylax Thais told us to come."

"*Thais*?" The woman puts a hand over her mouth; her husband's face hardens fast. I suppose they've heard wind of what happened to Thais: the assassination attempt, the imprisonment.

"What did she tell you?" The husband narrows his eyes; Theron, I remember his name was. But then Drusa puts a hand on his arm.

"Hush—listen!"

She's right. There are hoofbeats approaching, fast ones, pounding up the dust road. Drawing closer.

Drusa Sideris and her husband exchange glances.

It's only one horse. The king's guard travel in pairs.

It's a moonless night, and the stars don't offer much to see by. There's a whinny, and shadows, and a flurry of kicked-up dust. A slender body swinging down from a horse I recognize.

Ajax.

And Thais.

"Phylax Thais!" I see the relief on Drusa's face. She

hurries out in her night-shift, a blanket clutched around her. Theron follows.

"We thought you dead," he says, as we gather around the panting rider.

"We heard you were to be executed," Drusa adds. "She's been inconsolable. Bent on riding to the palace to fight the king herself."

She? What "she" do they speak of?

Thais has her hands on her knees, drawing down air, but at Drusa's words she straightens.

"You can't let her talk that way," she says. "Her life is more important than mine."

"I told her it was not what you would want," Drusa says. Her voice softens. "But now she will be spared the grief."

Thais glances our way then, and her eyes widen as she sees what I'm carrying.

"You took him."

Drusa frowns, as if just now noticing the bundle in my arms.

"Phylax Thais!"

It's Drusa's daughter, the little blonde girl, bursting from the doorway.

"Shh." Drusa glances around at the empty street. "Back inside, Helia."

But behind the child, in the doorway, stands someone else. A woman, still and silent.

I know it right away. This is the "she" they were talking about. This is the extra bowl at the table, and the little girl's whispered *"secret"*. This is what Drusa sent her daughter ahead of us to hide, that day at the mines.

She is striking: tall and dark-eyed, heavy brows, cheekbones like knives. But what I notice most are her clothes—clothes made for another way of life than a fisherman's cottage.

At the sight of her, Thais's face lights up. Even though her eyes are still blackened, her face still bruised, she looks healthier somehow; she all but glows. She crosses the space between them in moments and puts her arms around the woman, lays her head softly against the stranger's neck.

"Nereia," she breathes.

Nereia. I've heard that name before.

Theron clears his throat, glances at us.

"Enough of this. Inside, everybody. And be quick about it."

Indoors, the oil lamp is burning low, throwing wild, guttering shadows against the stone walls. On the far side of the room, in the sleeping nook, the other children are stirring, roused by the nighttime noises.

"Xenon!" Little Helia runs over, pulling on her brother's arm. "Look who has come!"

The older boy has roused himself too, and is frowning over at us. At Eros and me; at Thais…and at this stranger standing at Thais's side.

"I am Nereia," she turns toward me, and there is something lofty in the way she speaks, as though her name carries some great weight. And suddenly, I remember where I've heard that name before.

She looks me in the eye.

"Daughter of King Leonides."

*

My thoughts are spinning, and I doubt I'm the only one. I felt Eros's surprise in his quick, startled movement.

"King Leonides?" The one whose family the new king murdered.

"But how is it that you live? I was told you and your family..."

"Yes." She meets my eyes. "They are all dead but me."

It has taken practice for her to be able to deliver the words as she does: without rage, without despair. Without tears.

"I was in the dungeons when the attack began. Only they weren't dungeons back then; my father had held no prisoners for many years. My brothers and I would play there as children."

She blinks away the memory.

"There was a tunnel, burrowed from the very bottom of the palace, which led out beyond the castle walls, near the stable."

The tunnel Thais escaped through. That's how she knew about it.

"All my family knew of the tunnels," Nereia swallows. "But they had no chance to flee. They were slain in their beds." She pauses. "I heard screaming, and swords clashing. I went immediately to the tunnel, as my father had told us all to do, if ever…if ever such a thing occurred. I waited in the dark for my family to join me. But they never came." She blinks. "Eventually, before the dawn came, I fled."

I can feel it in her voice, the great burden she carries. She blames herself, perhaps, for running. For surviving. There was nothing she could have done—and yet I suspect she will never stop wondering.

"And the king," Eros says slowly. "He knows you are alive?"

The room grows more hushed as he speaks. They have not forgotten who—*what*—he is. How could they?

But Nereia's gaze is steady.

"Kostas's men are scared of him. They would rather lie and keep their heads, than tell him the truth and die. After they had hunted and hunted and found me nowhere, they told the king I had jumped from the tower, and was drowned in the sea."

She glances behind me. I turn and see that her eyes are on Thais now, as though drawing strength from her gaze.

"And…you have hidden here since?"

She nods as Nikos writhes in my arms, and starts to fret and cry.

"He's hungry," Drusa says. I think of Irini, that red line across her throat. The baby cries louder, but I feel too in need of comforting myself to think what to do.

I know, little one, I think. I know: it is a tragedy, and I helped make it.

Thais looks from the child, to Eros, to me. "He is safe, at

least. But what of your sister? Your father?"

I swallow hard.

"There was no time to rouse my father. And my sister…my sister did not believe me."

Nikos lets out a wail, and I jog him uselessly against me.

"Here, child." Drusa opens up her arms. She thinks me his mother, no doubt, and a feeble one at that.

Feeling guilty, I hand Nikos over. His wailing doesn't stop, but it eases a little.

"Kiria Sideris—"

"Drusa," she corrects me.

"Drusa," I say, "you must know. This baby is not ours. He—"

"I know who he is," she says quietly. She sighs, looks down at him, a somber expression in her eyes.

"Hush, little prince. It will be all right."

"God of all the lands!" Theron stares at us, wide-eyed. The word *prince* has left him slack-jawed.

"The king says he is a bastard," Thais interjects, "and sought to kill him. That's why they took him—and it's why I had to act, Theron, even though we were not ready. I'm sorry, but I had to."

I look from her to Theron. So Thais's attempt on the king—it was for the prince's sake? But not only for his sake, I think…

"You took the *prince*?" Drusa's other boy, the eldest, pipes up. "You stole the prince from the king's castle?" He looks to his father, his face bright with alarm.

"I only pray," Theron says, "our heads will not roll for it."

Thais sets her jaw.

"Not if the king's rolls first."

The others exchange glances.

"It will be difficult, now," Theron says. "More difficult, even, than before. You were our insider, Thais."

She bites her lip.

"But you don't mean to call it off?

"I cannot." He looks at her, then at the rest of us. "The

others are already on their way."

Others. Something in the way he says it makes my neck prickle. I think we're about to find out what Thais meant, when she told us she wasn't the only one who wanted the king dead.

"In fact—" Theron glances to the window, and I realize that, unlike his wife, he's not wearing night-clothing, but fully dressed and shod.

"It is already past time for me to go and meet them."

*

The night is cool. We walk as quietly as we can, through dust-paths amid olive trees and scrub grass. The houses thin out, then disappear altogether, and the salt smell of the sea stings my nostrils.

I suspect Theron would have preferred to leave some of us at home, but there was no way Thais would have brooked the suggestion. And Nereia, once she heard what was to come, insisted on joining, too—in borrowed clothes, of course. She stands out too much already.

As for me, it seems I am committed to this now, whatever it is. If it carries a chance of overthrowing the king, I must be for it. Drusa persuaded me to leave Nikos in the house with her and the children. I was not keen to let him out of my sight, but if stealth is of the essence, it would not do to have him waking the whole village. Drusa had some goat's milk she was heating by the hearth for him when we left.

Thais and Nereia walk side by side behind us. Ahead, Theron leads the way, his steps confident despite the dark night. My arms feel empty without Nikos in them, and I keep picturing Dimitra—how she raced to the window as we dropped away from her; that agonized cry.

"We should not have run like that," I say.

Eros looks at me.

"We just *left* them." I think of my father, sleeping only a few doors away. Was it my sister's screams that woke him? The shouts of guards, telling him what I had done?

What lies will the king tell my sister, now that I am not there to defend myself? What will she believe?

"We had to," Eros says, but I shake my head.

We could have stayed; we could have fought. The accusations tumble over themselves inside me, fomenting in the pit of my stomach. Disappearing like that was Eros's idea. He lunged for me, for the window, and there was nothing I could do but hold Nikos tighter than my own life. None of it was my idea; I was trying to reason with Dimitra. And if I had just had a little more time…

Easy for Eros to leave them behind. He has little love for my sister, I know. But what matters is that he made *me* leave them behind. He made a traitor out of me.

Or perhaps I was one to begin with.

The sea comes into sight, and I stop short. There's a clifftop, and a gathering of men, maybe a dozen or two. Their dark shapes are clear against the fires they have lit. They seem busy, milling around, fetching and moving things. As we draw closer I make out coils of rope, boxes, saddlebags.

"What are they doing?"

"Preparing," Theron says. He wears a shell like a medal around his neck; he touches it now, as though for luck. And then I see what he's looking at. Out to sea, in the inky water, it takes a moment to discern the shapes. But straining my eyes in the thin starlight, I can just about make them out, and once I do, they're all I can see.

Boats.

Thirty-three

They are tiny black shapes, shadows on the colorless water. More of them than I can easily count.

"Who are they?" I murmur.

"Allies." Theron turns; one side of his mouth lifts. "From Kythera."

Kythera. I know that name. I heard it from the stable-hand: they are Atlantis's nearest neighbor. They took in the Atlanteans, many moons ago when the Red Mountain erupted. But now the Kytherans' lands do poorly, and they are the ones who became refugees.

Until the new king put a stop to it.

I stare out at the bobbing crafts.

"But I thought these cliffs were too rocky for any boat to land."

"They are." Thais comes to stand beside us. "Look."

She points into the water, further in. Black shapes like seals, bobbing in the rough water. The more I look, the more of them I see. And then I see the black shapes slipping over the side of the boats, into the water. The boats aren't trying to land. They're just coming in close enough for the men to slip overboard—all except the few rowers who stay aboard—and then they turn, and forge back the way they came.

"We had to plan it for a moonless night, all the same," Theron says. "And have them take the long way around the island—out of sight of the citadel walls."

"But..." I stare down at the black waves, the froth of white bursting against the cliffs below. "How are they to get up here? The men?"

"Don't you recognize these?" Theron says, some pleasure in his voice. I look where she's pointing. Those strange mechanical objects by the cliff's edge. I *have* seen them before—at the mines. The men used them to haul dirt and rocks up to the surface—great big baskets the weight of three or four men, yet it only took one man to lift them.

"The pulleys," Eros nods.

I understand why Theron sounded pleased. There must be some satisfaction in seeing the king's tools being used against him.

So these are the friends Thais spoke of.

"How many are coming?" I try to count the dark heads bobbing in the water, but I cannot. And there are more slipping over the side of new boats even now.

"Enough," Theron says. "I hope."

I watch them as they cut through the waves, those distant shapes coming ever closer to the cliffs, their movements sharp and determined. Kythera must want the king defeated very much indeed.

Theron seems to sense my thoughts.

"Their people are dying, my lady. Kythera is Atlantis's younger sister, and her soil is poor where Atlantis's is rich. We do not know why the gods made it so, but so it is. We have an ancient obligation to them, but the new king has forgotten it. What's more, since he has forbidden all trade with them, they cannot trade for food as they used to. They are skilled metal-workers and silk-crafters, but fine robes and shiny bracelets will not feed their children."

It is not so long before we hear a cry: the first of the swimmers has reached the bottom of the rock. Then men at the top shout their instructions. The harness is fastened, the ascent begins. They make good time. It seems less than a minute until he's clambering over the top of the cliff, and they're stripping the harness from him, ready to bring up the next one. Meanwhile the other pulleys are hard at work—there are eight in all—and soon more men are emerging over the top.

"Shield your eyes, my lady," Theron coughs, apologetic. The glistening, dripping figures are all entirely naked. "Apologies, your highness," he says to Nereia.

Thais smirks; Nereia frowns. But by now the men are

emerging over the cliffs almost as fast as I can count.

"And how are they to fight?" she says. "With what weapons, what armor?"

Theron looks pleased at the question. "The arms are coming now, your highness."

I step closer to the cliff, feeling the wind, the salt stinging my face. It reminds me of when I stood on such a clifftop once before. The darkest dawn of my life.

I touch the Shroud around my neck.

"But how?" I stare down at the waves.

"In lobster pots," Theron grins. "We'll have all the arrow-heads and blades we need. They can whittle shafts and the like in the woods. In a few days, we will be ready to strike."

Eros nods.

"And until then?"

"They camp in the woods," Theron says. "Our boys will show them where, and bring them food and wine."

More glistening bodies continue to clamber up and over, amid shouts and instructions and warnings and jokes.

"And what of the Atlanteans?" I ask. "Do they not wish for change as your Kytheran friends do?"

Theron glances at me.

"The Atlanteans, my lady, have more to lose."

"There are many who share our cause," Thais chimes in. "But the king has ears everywhere. We cannot easily unite. But there are pockets, like these"—she gestures at the men on the clifftop—"all over the island. Men who not only hate the king, but are brave enough to do something about it." The glow in her eyes fades for a moment. "Although I do not think they will be glad when they hear what has happened to their palace insider. I had my one chance, and squandered it."

"You did not squander it." Nereia takes her hand. "You could not take an innocent life. You should be proud of that."

Thais shakes her head, looks away.

"She woke just as I drew my blade. I saw the scream in her eyes, ready to burst out. I had a single instant to decide: slit her throat, or let her live, and suffer the consequences."

"It was mercy, not cowardice, that stayed your hand," Eros says, his voice grave. "Not all mortals know the difference. Be glad you do."

Thais bows her head, acknowledging his words. But still, she has not forgiven herself.

"Perhaps," she says, "if it had been some nameless face. But Irini's face, I knew too well. She looked so young, sleeping—just a girl."

I start.

"*Irini*? Irini was the one in the king's bed?"

Thais frowns.

"Surely you do not blame her? If she caught the king's eye, I expect she had little choice in the matter."

My stomach tightens, seeing again that thin red line across a dead girl's throat.

"It's not that."

Nereia eyes me. Thais senses something too, her eyes darting from Eros to me.

"What? You know something."

Eros is the one to speak.

"The nurse is dead," he says flatly.

"They killed her," I blurt. The image of death still hovers; my heart beats faster. "They killed her to get to the prince."

Thais stares at me, her face slackening.

"I spared her life for *this*?" she chokes. "Better she had died by my hand, than butchered by those animals. I let that tyrant live so that she might keep her life—and now she is dead, and he lives! I should have cut his throat when I had the chance!"

"It wouldn't have brought the change you seek," Eros says. His voice is quiet, but heads turn his way.

"Even if you had succeeded, even if the king had died. He has surrounded himself with his cronies: councilmen who would easily take his place and be no better than him."

Nereia and Thais look at each other. Eros is right.

And yet, if the king has dodged death once, when an assassin stood knife in hand by his bed…how much harder will it be to defeat him now?

*

Theron breaks the news once the men are all assembled, and have found clothes and wine to warm them after the cold waters. But once they understand what has happened with Thais's arrest and escape, the shouting begins.

"We were supposed to have an inside man! *Now* what do we do?"

"The king will be on his guard, now. He'll be *expecting* an attack..."

"How do we know she didn't blab? For all we know, she's already told him everything!"

Thais steps forward.

"I told the king nothing. He and his men tortured me, but I did not breathe a word. He thinks I acted alone."

The angry murmurs continue. Theron steps in.

"We will proceed as planned," he says. "Having an insider behind the palace walls was to be an asset, but it is hardly a necessity. Come, brothers! We are here to fight." He looks around, his fierce eyes seeking to kindle the same feeling in those assembled around him.

"On the first of the month, the king collects his tithe. This means many of his guards will be out in the towns and villages, making the rounds. We will strike on a half-empty palace, whose defenses are at their lowest." He glances at Thais. "We need only wait five days. Until then, you can hide in these woods—we have brought provisions—only do not leave the forest. We fear that the king's guards may come patrolling soon, on the hunt for their escaped prisoner."

Eyes turn again to Thais, but she does not flush, or try to escape their gaze. The men move their feet in the sandy earth, shuffling and glancing. The wind rustles.

"And what of the king's son?" one of the men pipes up. "The *true* king's son. You said we would meet him here. You said he survived."

Theron shakes his head.

"You *did*. You said—"

"The old king's *heir*. I did not say 'son.'"

Nereia steps forward before Theron's words have time to settle.

"*Khaire,* men of Kythera and of Atlantis. I am Nereia, daughter of King Leonides—my father's firstborn, and the only surviving member of his line."

"A *girl*?" someone says, as another lets out a low whistle.

"If a woman may be a soldier," Theron says quietly, glancing at Thais, "then why not a king? She has the spirit for it."

"Aye, but it's the other parts she's missing," one of the men scoffs.

"I'll not take orders from a woman," calls another.

"Aye, Simos. You get enough of that at home, I hear."

There's chortling, and then a new voice breaks in.

"She's alive, ain't she? The only one who survived. That ought to mean something. The gods must favor her!"

"She has the blood-rights!" another calls.

"And what of these blood-rights?" someone else interrupts. "Just because she has her father's name, why should she have the throne? Why should Theron not have the throne, or Belos, or…or me?"

At that, jeering breaks out.

"Or *you*? Pull the other one."

"*Ooh, me, pick me,*" another mocks.

"Gentlemen!" Nereia raises her voice. It is a stronger voice than I had imagined. She speaks the same way she carries herself—with the authority of someone whose birthright it is to be heard. The men quieten, one by one. She clears her throat.

"I do not seek to claim the throne by tyranny. If you do not wish me for your leader, elect one of your choosing. But you must make your election before we wage war on the thief who sits on my father's throne, and you must abide by it after. We must be united, and we must not let ambition divide us."

There's a moment's silence after that, not so skeptical as

before.

"And if you were to be queen," one of the men calls out. "What would you do for us? For Kythera?"

Nereia bows her head.

"I would restore sea trade to our islands, as before. And in times of hardship, our gates will be open to you as yours have been to us."

"Oh, yes? And where will that charity come from?" Another voice rises up—one of the villagers this time, not the Kytheran crowd. "Will you carve out land for them from *our* homesteads, as your father did? Remind us of the gods' bounty, and command us to share all the grain we've harvested with our own sweat and blood?"

Nereia looks at him, unfazed.

"The crown's coffers shall pay for the refugees. Any family of Atlantis who wishes to host their Kytheran brethren shall be paid from our stores. They shall not be out of pocket for their good deeds."

"And the mines," another voice pipes up. "Will they stay open, or close?"

Nereia surveys the group.

"The people shall vote on it," she says. "If the mines stay open, a man may choose to work there if he pleases. He shall keep what he makes, save for the crown's tithe, which shall be in the same amount for all men—farmers, fishermen, traders. No one shall be conscripted to the mines against their will."

There is more hubbub after that. The men are all unsettled, still, but I notice no one is proposing other names—men's names—to take the throne, now.

"Don't matter, anyway. I still say we can't pull it off," one of men raises his voice. "Not now, not like this."

Theron glances in our direction, and when he speaks again, I see why.

"True, Milos, the king has a great force around him—but we, too, have a new ally in our midst."

At that, all the heads turn in our direction, following Theron's stare. When they see Eros, this tall, cloaked figure, some—the Atlanteans, the ones who understand—drop to their knees, or react in other ways.

"I know him," one says. "He's the Shadowed One. He's a *god*."

"Aye—the king's protector," another snarls. "We're dead men."

"The king and I are no longer allies," Eros says, silencing them even more effectively than Nereia did. He is letting a little bit of his power show—just a hint of it, but it rolls from his voice like distant thunder. I see the whites of the men's eyes in the darkness as they stare harder.

"You mean…you're on our side, Shadowed One? You will fight with us?"

Eros is silent for a moment; it seems to me he is weighing the words.

"I am not a war-god," he says. "And I have taken oaths not to cut down mortals. I will not strike the killing blow. But I will protect you; I will shield you as best I can."

There is more murmuring.

"My—my Lord." After a while, one of the men turns. "Is it true what Evander said, about the princess? That the gods have chosen her? That she has their favor?"

His question must strike a chord, as the men fall silent.

"The gods do not speak with one voice," Eros says. "And if the Fates have decreed something for the Princess Nereia, they have not shared their plan with me. But from what little I have seen of the princess, I say a man would do well to fight in her name."

"We'll put it to the vote," Theron says, speaking as loudly as he can over the many voices. "Now: all those in favor of the princess as our new ruler? Here, Kallias: you count."

We wait. The hands rise, slowly and by degrees. The man called Kallias counts them.

"All those against?"

Other hands rise. It seems to me they rise quicker, more decisively—but there are fewer of them. The count confirms it.

"That's settled, then. All right, lads." Theron motions, and some of the younger men—boys, really—come forward, pulling the mules behind them. The mules are piled high with saddlebags and sacks.

"Kytherans: we have prepared a clearing in the woods, and will make you as comfortable as we can there. Our boys will lead you to it." He glances back out to the sea, and the first grey wisps of dawn.

"Sun-up won't be far off, now. Best head before it's light."

The voices rise again, more animated than ever, but this time with new purpose. The Kytherans are dried off now, more or less, their borrowed clothes sticking to still-damp skin, their hair slicked back and dark. Nereia looks at them, then back to Thais.

"I will stay with them," she says.

Thais shakes her head. "Don't be a fool. You will sleep safely in Theron and Drusa's home, as before."

Nereia gives her a steely look, and I see, for the second time tonight, the makings of a true queen.

"A good general would not abandon his men," she says. "Or seek out a more comfortable accommodation, while they sleep in the dirt."

But her words have reached other ears besides ours: Theron, the one called Kallias, and a third, stocky Kytheran stand nearby, glancing at each other. Then Kallias steps forward, bows.

"If you please, Princess: gods willing, you will be our queen soon enough. But we will never have the chance to crown you if you are eaten by a bear first."

Nereia looks startled; Thais smirks.

"Get your rest, Princess—as much of it as you can. We will have need of your clear head soon enough. Now, men," he turns, raising a commanding hand in the air. "Onward!"

The boys with the mules advance, and the Kytherans gather in behind them, some talking and laughing, some grim and silent. *Five days*. There is much that may happen before then, and all of us know it. We watch the narrow phalanx wind its way upward into the tree-cover. One by one they vanish, seeming to merge with the dark forest, until the last boy turns, giving one last look out over the sea. For a moment it feels as though our eyes meet.

And then he turns back, and disappears into the shadows.

Thirty-four

I wake in the morning to the sound of clinking earthenware, and children chattering outside the window.

"*You* can be a god," little Helia's voice carries. "*I* want to play the princess."

There's little enough privacy to be had in this small home, but our hosts have found a linen sheet to hang between us and the rest of the house while we slept. It was best for everyone's safety, to keep them from any accidental glimpse of my husband's face while he slept.

Eros isn't sleeping now, though. His tall frame casts a shadow as he stands with his back to me, blocking out the slanted light from the window. Last night we lay next to each other barely touching, which is far from how we used to sleep. But whenever his warm limbs brushed mine, I felt a rush of something other than desire. Coldness; resentment. *My family,* I wanted to hiss at him. *You took me from them—again.* It was a decision he made for both of us, too fast for me to question or protest, a decision to run instead of stay and fight. So now my sister and father are stuck in that palace with a monster, with no one to watch out for them. What if they're punished for how we fled? Or what if they blame us; what if the king manages to convince them, somehow, that *we* killed Irini? Surely Dimitra would not believe that of me...but people may believe all sorts of things when they are desperate, and with her son stolen from her, I fear she will hardly be in her right mind. Will I see my father again; will he take his last breaths believing I abandoned him? And what about Nikos, what will *his* future be, if we do not manage to reunite him with his mother? Yet Eros shrugs it off as though we had no choice.

But there is always a choice. Perhaps just not a choice that's convenient for *him*.

Eros has never cared much about my family, only humoring me and my desire to find them, to be with them once more. I never expected him to care for them as I do, but it's more than that: it's his old arrogance, his old disdain for my people, *mortal* people. I thought being with me had changed all that, but perhaps he never really changed at all.

"You're awake." He turns from the window, glancing at me briefly, not meeting my eyes. He's restless, and it seems to me the glance reminds him only of where we are, and how far it is from where *he* wants to be.

With his father, no doubt. Re-establishing himself as a true god, not slumming it in some village encampment, dragged into a battle among petty mortals. Well, this isn't what *I* wanted, either.

He uncoils his fingers from his balled fists, and starts pacing the small square of room Drusa has draped off for us.

"Anything out there?" I nod towards the window.

He shakes his head, a curt movement.

"I wasn't looking at the view. I was seeking."

Of course he was.

"For Ares?"

He shakes his head again. He won't even look at me.

"For my brothers. But I cannot tell their whereabouts, either."

I frown. Phobos and Deimos are always a threat to us. In theory, they could track us down at any time. But…

"You don't think the king would still attempt to contact them?" Not after Eros and I have fled, and the king has lost his hostages. He has nothing to promise the twins anymore, nothing to gain. For all he knows, Eros and I have left Atlantis altogether.

Eros only shrugs, and keeps pacing the small space. He makes me think of Ajax when I first met him, how he would fidget and pace in his stall. We tried to send Ajax back to the citadel last night—getting rid of him went against all instinct, but his absence will be noted, and he is a distinctive horse—but he would not go. So we have painted over the white streak on his muzzle, and put him in the barn with the mule. Hopefully none of the neighbors pay much attention. The roads to Athiri are well-trodden, at least, and the days have been dry, so there will be no way for the king's guards to tell which way their prize horse went.

"Can't you be still for a moment?" I turn back to Eros. His restlessness is putting me on edge.

"I-" He stops.

"What is it?" Our sharp tones are covered, at least, by the sounds beyond the curtain, the household readying itself for the day.

Eros turns around, pushes back the hood so I can see his face. He turns his full, direct gaze on me.

"Psyche, I cannot help it if I am restless. I have much on my mind. And…" He wets his lips, strangely hesitant. *Hesitant* is not a word I've used for him before.

"I am the god of desire. *Desire,* Psyche, you understand? And I have pledged that desire to you alone. Despite your doubts, despite your accusations, despite my appetite, I keep myself for you alone. But these past many nights, you keep your body from mine." He meets my eyes. "Many are relying on me, now. I know this, and what lies ahead will not be easy. I try to keep my head clear, my mind sharp, but desire clouds my thoughts, my blood runs too hot." His voice turns crisp again. "So you must forgive me if I am a little *restless.*"

I flush. So that's what he's thinking about. Silly me, to imagine it was concern for Atlantis; for justice.

"You have no right to my body," I snap. "Your desire does not give you rights to it."

He flinches, then turns those burning eyes from me again.

He shakes his head. "You did not used to speak in terms of rights and licenses. You spoke to me in the language of desire—our language, that we shared. Do not claim that I have ever treated you like—like *property.*"

I scoff. I know the world I live in. A world where men treat women like property, and gods treat mortals the same.

Beyond the curtain I hear Nikos start to fuss, so I secure my chiton and tweak the curtain aside. I feel Eros's eyes on my back, but I don't turn. Perhaps I would prefer him to lie to me. To say he wasn't tempted by those handmaidens, by their soft, perfumed, willing bodies. But that's not why I'm angry, or not mostly. His family, my family, the fact that he is a god and I am a mortal…all of it lies like sediment inside me, one layer building upon the next.

Drusa showed me how to feed Nikos last night: a bowl of goat milk, a linen cloth soaked in it, then held to the child's mouth for him to suck on. It is slow and laborious, but it is working. We cannot find him a wet-nurse here—we could hardly explain an infant's sudden presence. And Nikos seems to be thriving as heartily as ever. I could swear he has grown another inch in the night. He bats his hands from where he lies in his little basket, near the warmth of the hearth, one fist rising up, waving in the air.

"Here." Drusa sees me awake, and holds out a clay mug. "The child's not the only one in need of breakfast."

The stone tiles are cool under foot, but by the hearth, it's warm. Eros is still behind the curtain, keeping to himself. Still scanning the worlds of the gods, I suppose. I gather the linen cloth and the bowl of milk, and as I begin to feed my nephew, I look around at the room this side of the sheet divider. Thais and Nereia are a few feet away, coiled in a nest of blankets, seemingly still asleep. But they're the only ones here.

"Where are the others?"

"Theron is at the mine. Cleon is doing his father's work with the fishing boats. The little ones are outside."

I look around, curious. Something strikes me.

"Is there no other room?" I look around. "When we came here before—with the queen, with Thais—where were you hiding the princess, then?"

Drusa nods her chin towards a spot on the other side of the eating-table.

"Under those sleeping-mats is a grain cellar. Poor Nereia, she can't abide it down there. But we've had to make use of it often enough."

I glance over at the two sleepers, Nereia's dark head,

Thais's pale one. A question returns to me, one I had wondered last night, and then forgotten.

"How did the princess know to come to this house? How did she know she would be safe?"

Drusa nods. She's been busy with some bread dough, which she now puts in a pan and slides into the hearth.

"I nursed her when she was a babe. She was but a year younger than my eldest." Drusa sighs, closes her eyes. "I nursed her brothers, too, may the Lord of the Next Realm tend gently to them. I remember them all."

So Drusa was the Irini of twenty years ago. At least she did not meet Irini's fate.

"I spent quite some time at the palace. Nereia was five when I left for good—old enough to know me, and love me a little. She came to Athiri once or twice after that, to visit. Until her mother forbade it." Drusa shakes her head. "Poor thing—she was not a happy child, I think. Her brothers were different—boisterous, like puppies—and it seemed to me they would grow to be like their mother, carefree and handsome, and a little contemptuous. But Nereia was different. So serious; always a little melancholy. It made her mother impatient, which only made things worse." Drusa sighs. "Why would a princess who had everything ever be melancholy? Now I think perhaps she sits closer to the Fates than we do. Perhaps some part of her sensed this all along."

If it smarts for me to be parted from my family this way, how much more unimaginable, how much more cruel, is Nereia's lot.

"She has suffered much."

Drusa sighs, glancing at Nereia's sleeping form.

"It has broken her, to be sure, and yet not weakened her. She is a more courageous creature than most."

"And you?" I hesitate. "Her presence here…it puts you in some danger, I think?" I speak in a low voice. Even if the words are true, and Nereia knows it as well as I do, it would be unkind for her to hear me say them.

Drusa glances towards the door.

"Some," she acknowledges. "But if anyone at the palace still remembers me, I suspect all they will remember is some half-forgotten, nameless face. We are not important there."

I think again of Irini, how she was nothing but a body to them—a body to nourish the little prince; a body for the king to take pleasure in. *Useful flesh*. My stomach turns.

"Besides," Drusa sighs. "You heard how it is with the king's guard. They risk their own heads, if they were ever to suggest that the princess still lives."

The baby is fussing louder now, and the sound seems to stir the other two. Thais stretches her lean arms and yawns widely.

This all seems unreal, in the bright light of morning. All the details of last night—did they really happen? I think of the men by the sea, the pulleys, the naked, gleaming flesh. The Kytherans in the forest now, whittling arrows and blade-handles. And according to Thais and Theron, the pockets of rebels all over this island, ready to rise up at the cost of their own lives. I feel cold despite the warmth from the hearth. How many will die before the king is defeated?

If the king is defeated.

Then a noise in the distance makes my ears prick up, and Drusa turns quickly, eyes sharp.

"Horses. You must hide—now."

Horses. More than one. I doubt many of the villagers have more than a shabby mule or two, and mules don't sound like that.

Eros, hood down, steps out from our sleeping-corner and strides towards us. I see Drusa start, as if she had forgotten him, or forgotten quite what an imposing presence he makes.

"I saw them from the window," he says, his voice low and urgent. "Two, on horseback."

Two.

If the king's guard knew we were here, surely they would have brought more. Two means a standard patrol, something more routine.

I hope.

Thais and Nereia are awake by now, Thais grim and alert, Nereia still flushed with sleep.

"The cellar," Drusa says. "Go. I will see to the children." Her voice is steady. If she is afraid, she does not show it.

I hurry to gather Nikos from the little nest of blankets by the hearth, but Drusa shakes her head.

"We cannot risk him starting to bawl down there. Leave him up here with me. The guards will think he's mine. I'll keep him to my chest, they will not even see his face."

She's right. I know she's right. But it feels like the worst betrayal yet, to turn away from him.

Eros lifts the mats and the plank of wood beneath. Thais jumps down first, and offers up a hand to help Nereia. I see the pain on the princess's face—what a horror it must have been, to spend hours on end in the dark crawl space—but she takes Thais's hand and jumps down. I follow, then Eros comes last, closing the door. I hear rapid steps, and the sound of the rug being dragged back over our heads.

And then we wait.

Thirty-five

It's dark down here, and there's barely enough room for the four of us. I crouch down, trying to give myself more breathing space. Somewhere much too close for my liking, I hear a soft, scurrying sound—a rat, most likely. The creature's voice comes to me, a flash inside my mind. It was searching for food, but now its plaintive hunger gives way to fear. *Humans,* it thinks, and scurries away.

It seems like a small eternity before the sound of knocking at the door. The knock is a fiction, a gesture only. I don't even hear Drusa's feet crossing the room before it's thrown open.

"We are on a mission for the king," a man's voice booms. I don't recognize it, though perhaps Thais does. Did she stand beside him once, on the battlements? Did she laugh at his jokes in the mess hall?

"There has been an attempt on the king's life—foiled, thank the gods, but the assassin has fled." He leaves a brief pause so that Drusa can make the appropriate sounds of consternation.

"We seek the traitor now. We know they are still on this island."

"But not in Athiri, sir, surely?" Drusa's voice sounds suitably shocked, disbelieving. She is a good actor. She no longer sounds like the authoritative type I know her to be, a woman who commands respect. She sounds like the type to let her children run wild, to fuss and hover helplessly as men set the world to rights.

"Perhaps in Athiri, perhaps in any of its neighboring towns," the guard answers, curt. "Have you seen a stranger in this town, woman?"

"No indeed, sir," Drusa says, breathless. "What did he look like?"

The guard hesitates.

"It was a woman. Slight of build. Yellow hair. She took a horse—a black stallion with a white streak."

"A woman? Goodness, sir! She must be a dangerous creature indeed."

This seems to anger him.

"She is a weak thing, and puny. She only escaped because..." The soldier hesitates again. I wonder if he knows all the details of Thais's escape, and ours. The king, perhaps, is not proud of the tale.

I wait for the guard to speak of us next—of what happened to the prince, and the outlaws who took him. But all I hear is the guard hacking and spitting on the floor. When he speaks again, it is offhand.

"Those are your children playing outside?"

"Yes, sir."

"They gawped like idiots at me. Could barely manage yes and no. Simple-minded, are they?" he sneers.

I pray silently for Drusa to hold her tongue. If anything were to rouse her, it would be an insult to her children.

"I couldn't say, sir. They are children, is all."

He grunts. "Pray this one grows up with a bit more sense."

He means Nikos. He hasn't recognized the child, at least. I exhale a little.

Another voice speaks now—the second guard—and he speaks in chillier tones than the first.

"You have no false loyalty towards your neighbors, do you, woman? If you have heard or seen anything amiss with them, you must tell us. Your allegiance is to no one but your king."

"We are a loyal family, sir," Drusa says, her voice feathery and flustered. It is not her real voice, but I wonder if she is not frightened all the same, underneath it.

"My husband labors in the mine here. He works hard for the king."

"It is the king who works hard for his people," the soldier

corrects her.

"Yes sir, of course."

There is the tread of heavy feet above us. I hope the floor does not feel different beneath their boots in this one spot, or creak strangely. I cannot remember.

I hear the screech of some furniture being moved—overturned?—and the rattle of earthenware. But it is a small house, only one large room. There are no hidden corners. Within moments the boots are trudging back overhead. They come to a halt right above us. Why does he stand there, in just that spot? Is there a smell in the air, women's perfume, perhaps? What clues have we left behind despite ourselves?

"Pass me that bread, woman."

"Sir?"

"The bread," he says impatiently. "Or would you deny the king's men a meal?"

"Sir! Of course not." I hear Drusa step his way, all apologies.

"With a cloth, woman! Or would you have me burn my fingers, too?"

She brings it to him, I suppose, because he is no longer above us then—his boots are moving towards the door, his business concluded. We hear them leave, both of them, and their horses. Still, it seems like a long time before Drusa pulls the plank of wood aside, and light floods in. I have to shield my eyes.

"They've gone."

Gone. Without a word about Eros or of me; without a word about the prince.

I wonder why.

*

Drusa gives us a task of winnowing two sacks of barley grain: since we can't leave the house, we might as well be of what little use we can. More than that, having a task helps take the mind off things.

A little, anyway.

Drusa points out that the soldiers are unlikely to return today, and even if they did, her children would serve as lookouts.

"Life is too quiet here for a pair of men on horseback to hide their approach. Besides, Helia has ears that could hear a mouse."

Still, I can't help thinking about them: the king's guard, and where they might be going next, and where they have already been. Why didn't they mention us? Why didn't they mention Nikos? The abduction of a prince—surely the king does not imagine that he can keep *that* a secret.

"He looks like you," Nereia comments now, as we winnow the grains slowly onto the earth floor, with Nikos in a basket near our feet. He stares at the princess while she speaks, his rosebud mouth gaping open, those too-knowing eyes Irini complained of quite focused.

The son of the man who slaughtered Nereia's family.

Or is he?

The child bears no responsibility for his father's deeds, whether his father is the king, or otherwise. But I can't help thinking again of the things I heard in the town square, and then later, from the king's own mouth. Was the king raving, paranoid? But I can't deny it—the child has none of the king's dark coloring, nor Dimitra's. Instead, pale hair, and sea-blue eyes.

"Phylax Thais—" I hesitate. Thais has taken on the task of sweeping the chaff from the floor.

"I suppose you had heard the rumors? That the boy is not the king's seed?"

She does not meet my eyes.

"I heard them."

"And do you…that is to say…"

But why would my sister risk it? I think of how she spoke of Nikos, that day in the gardens. Her high hopes for him. The greatness she foresaw for him. Surely she could not have been so confident—so foolish—as to say those things, if she were raising a bastard under the king's nose?

Dimitra is not afraid of risk, I know that. But those risks all tilt in one direction—towards ambition. She would not throw all that away for an affair.

At least, not the sister I knew. But perhaps I no longer know her very well.

Thais looks awkward.

"I could not say, my lady. I know your sister took more freedom than was customary. She liked to go out wandering, sometimes even without a maid. But I cannot say I witnessed anything untoward."

"And what of the adamantine?"

We all look up. Eros has been moving restlessly about the room, but now he stops and turns in Thais's direction, his movement as abrupt as his words.

"The adamantine we saw in the dungeon. The cage." Though I cannot see his face, I can hear the way his mouth twists, just saying the words. "Is there more of it?"

Thais pales a little, but shakes her head.

"Not to my knowledge, my lord. The king has been mining for it, but without success." She looks at Nereia.

"The only ore he has is what he found in the palace. Hidden by King Leonides, and the king before him."

Nereia looks down at her hands as our eyes shift to her.

"My great-grandfather…it was rumored that some adamantine was found in the mines, back in his day. It was only a rumor, though. All I know for certain is that he discontinued the mines. Sealed them up and forbade Atlanteans to plunder the earth from then on. Said its riches were Hades' domain, and that he had seen the errors of his ways in trying to trespass there." She glances up at us, then goes back to the barley-stalk in her hands.

"There have always been rumors. Legends. But then, this island is rich in legends. Who was to say adamantine wasn't just another one? My brothers and I played at finding it. We told ourselves our great-grandfather had hidden whatever ore he found—somewhere in the dungeons, perhaps, or in the armory—and we'd go looking for it." She pauses. "I remember my brother asked my father, once, if it was true. If there was adamantine in the soil of Atlantis, if our family had hidden some little trove of it. My father got very upset. Angry, in a way I had not seen before. He had us leave the room and spoke to Sosthenes alone—it was Sosthenes who would be king one day. Apparently my father told him he was too young to know the full truth, but that he would, in time. So I suppose…I suppose I knew there *was* a story. But then…" She sighs. "We grew up. Stopped playing hide and seek. My brothers began to chase girls, not old legends from our grandfather's day. I suppose I forgot."

"But Kostas knew," Eros says, his grim voice breaking the moment's silence.

He's right. King Kostas must have known. He was the old king's *strategos,* his right-hand man. If King Leonides would have trusted anyone with his knowledge of the adamantine, surely it was the leader of his guard.

And then the penny drops: it's *why* Nereia's father, and her family, were killed. For power, yes. But not just for the throne of Atlantis. For what their murderer believed he'd find beneath the earth.

And presumably it is true…after all, where did my mother's knife come from, if not from this island?

We sit silent, and another ugly thought spreads through me, finds its way to my tongue.

"The cage," I say. "The cage he built for you, Eros. That was not the work of a day."

The king made that cage while we were under his roof; while we were his guests. And he made it for one purpose only. Thais looks at me, seeing my thoughts.

"I don't know when the idea came to him to entrap you like that. Perhaps the offer of friendship was sincere at first, and he became disillusioned later."

Or perhaps, I think, it was the very moment he heard our story. The second he realized he could buy the favor of many gods, by betraying one.

I asked my father once if Kronos, the great god who fathered the Olympians, was really as terrible as the songs and legends made him out to be. Did he really deserve to be slain by Zeus, his own son, with an adamantine sword?

Father looked at me, ran his hand over my hair.

"The victor writes the stories, Psyche. The victor chooses which songs we sing."

I look down at little Nikos. Nikos, meaning victor. If his name is as auspicious as his mother hoped, perhaps great songs will be sung about him one day.

Perhaps not.

I do not think I would wish greatness on him. I would wish him a quiet life, without battles or conquests, if I had the choice. But I don't get to choose, and I fear there may be more battles in our future than even we can guess.

Thirty-six

The light turns from morning to afternoon. The men won't come home until after dark most likely, Drusa says. The barley is winnowed by now, and ground. Nereia and Thais have started a game of *petteia* by the hearth. I do not suppose their hearts are in it, but we must find distraction where we can. Little Helia and Xenon have come in from their play, and Drusa is busy chiding them and scrubbing their faces clean.

Thais moves a piece, but Nereia has seen through the move and on her next turn, it leaves the board. Thais clicks her tongue, annoyed at herself.

"Nereia always beats me," she says.

Women in our country rarely play *petteia*. It is not encouraged. I, certainly, was never taught, though just watching these two, I can understand a little of the strategy.

"Did your father teach you?" I ask Nereia, and then regret it. I didn't mean to remind her of her life in the palace, surrounded by her family, her siblings. But she doesn't flinch. Her dark eyes swivel to mine.

"He taught my brother. And I begged my brother to teach me." She moves her eyes back to the board. "Sosthenes was never much of a player, though. He was impatient with games like this."

Her voice is steady, but I see the tremor in her nimble fingers as she moves another piece across the board.

"He used to say real strategy happened between people, not bits of clay. And he was right, of course." Her voice catches. "He was a natural leader. He knew how to speak to people. To make them like him. He would have been a good king."

"As you will be," Thais says gently.

Nereia looks away. Abruptly she takes her hands from the board, clasps them in her lap. She looks from me to Eros, and then across the room to Drusa and the children.

"The men yesterday," she says sharply, "chose me because they thought I was lucky. That I would bring them luck. They say I am favored, because I was spared when my family was not."

I bow my head.

"I cannot think of a harsher kind of luck."

"It was not chance, of course," she says. "The only reason I was not in my bed that night—the only reason I was three floors below, close enough to reach the tunnels—was because of Thais." She looks at the other woman, who flushes. Of course. What other reason is there to leave one's bed for a secret room in the middle of the night, than a lover's tryst? It is there in every look between them, every soft touch; in the way Thais flung herself into Nereia's arms last night.

For women to love women in this way was frowned upon in Sikyon, but I hear in Crete it is quite as natural as the love between men. I don't know about Atlantis, but it clearly doesn't bother Drusa or Theron.

"King Leonides liked me well enough." Thais meets my eyes, acknowledging what I have understood. "But he would not have approved a simple soldier for his daughter."

"You were never a simple soldier," Nereia says, and Thais offers her a small smile.

Not a simple soldier, maybe. But she *was* a soldier.

I hesitate.

"Phylax Thais: You were with the princess the night King Kostas launched his coup. But you did not know of it beforehand?" The way I heard it, Kostas had the support of the other guards. That's how he managed it.

A wave of pain crosses her face.

"Only the senior guards, his closest allies, had his confidence. The rest of us knew nothing."

"And yet…you all stayed? To serve the new king?" I sense I am treading on delicate ground, now. Something fiery and defensive rears in Thais's face, then dies down. Nereia slides her hand across, covers Thais's with her own.

"We were tested," Thais says crisply. "Made to prove our loyalty. Some did not pass the test." She looks away for a moment, and memories ride over her face.

"I did. I had to." She glances at Nereia. "That night, as soon as I knew Nereia was in the tunnels, I ran upstairs to see that the king was safe, to—to do my job. But it was too late. Kostas's men outnumbered us, and the cruel work was already done. I thought on my feet. I knew the only way I could still help Nereia—the only way I could still serve her father—was to stay close to the man who had done this. To pretend I was an ally, until the time came for revenge."

We are silent after that. Thais's voice, clear and defiant, seems to hang in the air.

"You play well," Eros says, breaking the silence at last. He means on the *petteia* board, I suppose, but perhaps he also means Thais's strategy.

"I have not won against Nereia but once," Thais says, nodding at the board. "Her hands are quick, but her mind is quicker. If she's seen something once, she can do it."

Nereia smiles at that—not with her mouth, but with her eyes. I have not seen her mouth smile yet. Perhaps it did, once upon a time, but no longer.

"She wins every time," Thais goes on. "And I was the best player out of all the guards, though they hated to admit it."

Nereia shrugs.

"Once our tutor left, I rarely had anyone to play with. My brothers were off doing princely things, while I could not walk in the streets without a handmaid, which I disliked. So I spent most of my days roaming the castle. Sometimes I stood outside the mess hall, watching the men drink and talk and play *petteia* together. I stood in the shadows. They never saw me."

"*I* saw her," Thais smiles.

"I invited Phylax Thais to visit my chambers, and play a round with me there." A soft look crosses Nereia's face: one happy memory, among the sad ones. "My father could not object to that; it was not as though I had invited one of the men."

"I knew she must like me," Thais says, "because she kept

inviting me back, even though I was no match for her."

For the first time, Nereia smiles. A small, wistful sort of smile, like the sun behind a cloud.

"Thais is a good player. Impulsive, but fearless. She always does the unexpected thing. Which is, I think, its own advantage."

*

The sun is low outside the window when Cleon comes through the door. It seems to me his eyes are wary, even resentful, as he takes in the scene. Three new interlopers since yesterday, four if you count the baby.

"What did you catch?" Drusa takes the bag from him and looks inside. "Enough," she nods.

"Enough for five," Cleon murmurs. "Not for nine."

Drusa gives him a quelling look, and he drops his gaze.

He has been fishing all day—doing his father's job, now that his father is conscripted to the mines. Even before this house had extra mouths to feed, surely it weighed heavy on him that he is the one who must feed his family now.

"Where's Father?" Helia asks then.

"Late. As he tends to be." Drusa sighs. "Come, we will eat. Perhaps he will be home by the time the fish is ready."

But Theron is not home by the time the fish is ready, nor in the hour after that. Drusa puts the young children to bed, but not Cleon, who takes wine and bread in a bag, and heads for the woods. The Kytherans may need more supplies, he says. Likely, he just prefers their company to ours. But I wonder why Theron is not home yet. I cannot tell from Drusa's face if it means anything; if she is worried for him.

Nikos has just woken and begun to cry when Theron comes through the door. I see it immediately, that look in his eyes that is all foreboding. When Helia bolts from her bed and runs to him, clamoring to be lifted up, he hushes her sharply.

"An announcement was made." He looks around, his eyes sweeping over each of ours; holding his wife's the longest.

"Before we left the mines. One of the king's guard rode to bring it." He licks his lips. "We have been informed that the prince is dead."

I stare at him. Nikos's weight is warm in my arms.

"*Dead?* But…"

The soldiers who came earlier said nothing of the prince, nothing of his abduction at our hands. Instead this is the story they are spreading. That the crown prince is dead.

"Murdered," Theron continues.

Now it's Thais who lets out a gasp.

"Why would he say such a thing?" I close my eyes, trying to clear my head. This doesn't make sense. None of it makes sense. I feel Nikos squirming in my grasp, warm and soft and entirely alive.

Eros's hand is on my shoulder, but its weight brings little comfort.

"It suits the king just as well as if Dareios had taken him away to die. Think about it. All he wants is for the baby to be gone, for good. If he says the prince was taken, he will have to search for him. He will be expected to send armies of men, all in search of his rightful heir. But if he tells the people the child is dead…"

"But there was a guard in the room that night! And my sister." Could Dimitra be going along with this, for reasons of her own? But how could she? I shake my head. "They saw what happened. They know we took him. They *know* he's alive."

Thais looks at me, almost pitying. "Like as not, that guard breathed his last that night."

"What can we do?" I stare down at Nikos. His wide blue eyes stare up at me; his hand reaches up for me with a gurgle. "How can we show everyone he's lying?"

"We can't," Eros says, his voice clipped. "It would only bring danger on the child."

I look up and see Theron's face. Nausea stirs in my stomach. There's more. Something he hasn't told us yet.

Murdered.

"Are they saying we did it?"

Theron shakes his head.
"Murdered," he says, "by the queen."

Thirty-seven

My legs turn to water. *I have to sit down.* It's the only thing I can think. Theron's voice, the details, wash over me.

"No one will believe it." The words tumble out of me. "They can't. Dimitra would never..."

"They are saying," Theron continues, "that she looked upon the Shadowed God's face and was driven mad. That her madness is what made her kill the child. They say the god and his mortal consort have fled." Theron licks his lips. "The kingdom is to go into mourning. And the queen, mad though she be"—Theron speaks quietly, knowing he's delivering the death-blow—"is to stand trial for the crimes of infanticide, and regicide."

The world blurs.

"Help her to a chair," I hear Drusa say. When my vision clears, I look up at their faces.

"I—I'll go to the castle now. I'll bring Nikos. I'll show everyone this is a lie, I'll prove it!"

"You will not," Eros says. I glare at him.

"How could I expect *you* to understand?" He may be a god, with a heart of stone, but I am not.

"*Think*, Psyche," he says, and his voice is rough. "Calm your mind and think. Even if you brought the child back now, the king would say you're lying. Call him an imposter. He wants the child gone, and your sister with him."

I close my eyes. It's true; I wish it weren't, but I know it is.

"He knows you cannot prove his lie without coming forward. And if you do, he will kill you."

"I can't just stay here," I say, staring at Nikos, at his bright, trusting eyes. He coos at me, a jarring, happy sound, and my chest tightens. What have I done? This is a nightmare, a nightmare I can't seem to leave.

Eros turns to Theron.

"When is this to take place? The queen's trial?"

"Tomorrow morning." Theron's voice is grim.

I must get to her. I must free my sister. But I don't even know where the king is keeping her. In the dungeons? In the adamantine cage? Not even Eros can bend those bars.

"We must be at the trial." I look at Eros. It's the only way. The accused is always on display in such affairs, and I know how much this king likes his "justice" to be public.

"We'll go there, and rescue her. Somehow."

Thais and Theron look at each other. Thinking of *their* plan, no doubt. Which my actions seem bound to disrupt.

"I'm sorry," I say. "I have to do this." I look at Eros. "We have to."

He nods, a small motion behind the dark hood, just as Cleon bursts through the doors. His eyes rove over us, searching for his father.

"You must come at once," he pants. "Kallias summons us."

*

As we move uphill into the woods the trees thicken, and the path all but disappears. Theron ploughs through the gaps between branches, leading the way. Only the smallest traces of moonlight make it through the canopy of trees, picking out Thais's pale hair in front of me, and the flash of her hands as they push back twigs and foliage. Theron did not want the women to come, but he had little choice. Whatever this urgent matter is, if it affects my sister, I need to be part of it. Thais and Nereia are here, too. Only Drusa has stayed behind, with the children—with Nikos, although I was loathe to leave him.

"Psyche—" Eros puts a hand on my shoulder, but I shrug it off. My sister stands trial tomorrow, for a crime she didn't commit. And apparently, it's our actions that have enabled it.

A spear springs from behind a tree, and hovers by

Theron's throat. It gleams, silver in the moonlight.

"Peace," Theron holds up his hands. "It is Theron Sideris."

The spear is lowered. Other figures emerge from the brush. I think I recognize one or two of their faces. Men who were on the clifftop last night.

"Hail, Theron," one of them says.

"*Khaire*, Phaedon. *Khaire*, Belos."

"Princess." One of them spots Nereia, and bows. But the men don't look happy to see the contingent that Theron has brought with him.

"What news have you?" Theron says, his voice tight. "Cleon says it's urgent."

The men glance at each other.

"Come," they say.

*

The men are gathered in a great clearing: the Kytheran troops, and Athirian men in village clothes. And in the middle of the clearing sit two men tied back to back, hands and feet bound, both gagged.

Both wearing the armor of the king's guard.

Thais gasps. A cold chill runs through me.

A big man, curly-haired and ruddy-faced, strides forward. A leader, by the way he moves.

"Kallias?" Theron seems to know him. "What is this?"

"It could not be helped," Kallias says. "We had no warning, no time to hide. By the time they were upon us it was too late. We had no other option than to take them prisoner."

"The king's guard—in our woods?"

"Doubtless they are the soldiers who came patrolling this morning." Eros speaks in a low tone, but the men immediately quieten.

"Aye," Kallias says. "They were looking for the runaway assassin, so I'm told." He glances back to the two prisoners, who, seeing Thais, have begun to make noise from behind their gags.

"They recognize you, all right," he says grimly.

"I suppose you know what this means," one of the other men says. He's younger, sharp-featured, with darting green eyes.

"Aye," Theron says, his voice heavy. He knows. We all know.

"The king's guard will return two men short tonight—"

"And tomorrow, when their absence is noticed, more will come to investigate," Thais finishes.

"Athiri will be ransacked," Nereia murmurs. "What happened today…that will be nothing, compared to what they will do next."

"We should kill them," Belos glares. "They will only make trouble, and eat our food."

Kallias shakes his head.

"Do not speak in haste. They may yet prove useful."

"Well, *we* cannot be found here, like sitting ducks," the green-eyed man snaps. "We must disperse. Move east tonight, away from the citadel. We'll keep to the woods, disappear."

"And what of our attack, Belos?" another man asks, a pale youth of slight build. "If we move further east, we will put ourselves a day's march or more from striking the citadel."

Belos grimaces.

"So be it. The king's runaway"—he glares at Thais—"has put the palace on high alert. It is no time to strike."

"So you would go home, then? Default on promises to your kinsmen and ours?"

"We would not be the only ones to default on our promises," Belos shoots another look at Thais.

Kallias clears his throat.

"There's something else," he says.

All eyes turn, expectant.

"The king knows of the tunnel."

There is murmuring, a sound of foreboding moving through the men.

"These useless sacks"—he gestures at the two guards—"let it slip. Before we gagged them, that is," he adds wryly. "You see, they have not been entirely without service to us."

Theron glances at Thais, who looks at Nereia.

"The tunnel?" She turns back. "The tunnel I told you of?"

"The tunnel you used," the one called Belos snaps, "when you ran away, drawing the king's heat on the rest of us. A tunnel that now we can't use. You left it wide open, I'll wager."

"It was not left open," Eros says, and though his voice is mild enough, it puts a stop to Belos's tone.

"There were traces of disturbances, perhaps, from where the stones were lifted and replaced. The king is not a stupid man."

This time, the guards cannot lie to the king, or cover up Thais's disappearance by pretending she jumped from a window. This time, the king has proof: someone has escaped the castle without passing a single guard, and surely he would not have let his men rest until they uncovered how it was done. Eros is right. It would always have been risky, using that tunnel to re-enter the palace.

"Meanwhile, Theron," Eros continues. "You have news of your own, do you not?" His tone is mild, almost conversational, but my heart quickens. I had not seen it that way until now, but perhaps—perhaps the ill news of my sister's trial can be used to some advantage. Theron frowns. His gaze shifts, his mind working fast, considering. He glances at me.

"There is an alternative," he says slowly. "A way to take the king while he is outside his palace, where he is not defended by his own walls." He explains what is to happen tomorrow. The trial. How the king will be in attendance—he will be the accuser, no doubt, and the judge in one.

"It is to take place in the agora, and we have been required to attend," Theron goes on. "There will be a crowd. It will give us cover. And from the way I was greeted earlier"—he swings a look at the man who all but attacked him with the spear—"it seems to me your weapons are already in good order."

The one called Belos folds his arms.

"Kallias, we cannot be swayed by this nonsense. It is too soon for us to attack. We have no plan. And in such a public setting? The guards will be upon us in an instant."

"The guards cannot be everywhere at once," Thais says. "In a crowd, we will blend in. Besides, few of the guards have much love for the king. Most of them submit to him out of fear, nothing more. If we can take the king down quickly, most of his guard will run."

Nereia chimes in, her voice slow and measured.

"I suspect that if you do not take this chance, the next one may not come soon. The king knows he is not loved. He just survived an attempt on his life. Do you think he will not surround himself with a phalanx of bodyguards? From what I hear, he already hardly leaves his castle; now, he may hardly leave his chambers. But tomorrow he will be outdoors. He will show himself to the crowd. He will be there, right in front of you, on a stage. Ours for the plucking, if we can take him down."

Kallias frowns.

"We must remember, it is nothing to chop the head off a hydra, if it has ten more. We must secure our position, and fast. The king's death may cause the guards to fall back, or it may not." He looks at Theron, at Eros, at Nereia.

"Phaedon, here, is the best bowman we have." He nods at the slim youth who spoke earlier, pale-faced with lank blond hair; little more than a boy. "He nailed that tree-knot from one hundred paces." Kallias gestures at a nearby tree with a thick burl on its trunk, neatly bisected by a red-tipped arrow.

"How close might he expect to get? Will he even be within range of the king?"

They are not planning to take him prisoner, or to try him in a people's court. They—*we*—are planning to kill the king where he stands. I search my heart to see if any part of me balks from this…but I find no sorrow or guilt there.

Nereia clears her throat.

"The agora is long, but shallow enough. If the king wants to summon a large crowd—and by the sounds of it, he does—then he cannot keep them at a great distance."

Kallias raises an eyebrow, turns towards Phaedon.

Phaedon shrugs.

"You will have one shot, no more," Kallias warns, "before the king's men take up their bows."

"Who says Phaedon can even get close to him?" Belos scowls. "The agora will be thronged." He shakes his head. "What if the sun is in his eyes? What if the king does not appear?"

"He will be there," Eros says, and I know he's right, I feel it in my bones. The king won't pass up an opportunity to show his power. And he will enjoy watching the suffering he has caused. Yes, he'll be there.

The men are coming around, I can feel it. They believe us. They believe in Phaedon, and in Kallias. If those two think we have a shot, so do the rest of the men.

I only hope we aren't leading them astray.

"But the queen," I raise my voice, as the murmurs around us thicken. "You must not let harm come to her."

Kallias looks at me with raised brows.

"She is my sister," I insist. "And innocent."

"Innocent?" Belos sneers. "Who allied herself to such a man! Oh yes, they all weep once their fortune turns. She should die like the rest of them," he mutters. "With all the tyrant's lackeys."

"You will see to it that she does not," I round on him, as though *I* am his queen. "You will see to it that no hair on her head is harmed. You *will* protect her."

"Our men must concern themselves with the king's guard," Kallias rebukes me. "We will not seek to harm her ourselves, but nor can we mount a rescue party for the tyrant's wife."

"Psyche—" Eros puts his hand on my shoulder again, but Thais is already speaking.

"I will charge myself with her safety, Lady Psyche."

I look at her small frame, her light, wiry body. I remind myself that a soldier's worth is not only in their brawn.

"You are not more concerned with who sits on the

throne?" Belos challenges. "With *winning* the battle?"

Nereia steps forward.

"Phylax Thais is interested in protecting the lives of the innocent. As I would wish for any citizen of my kingdom to be."

Kallias tightens his jaw. For a moment his eyes catch mine, and they are full of the things he has seen; of the knowledge of death, of the trials ahead. The men are murmuring amongst themselves, louder now, and he must raise his voice to be heard.

"Men!" he calls. The murmuring stops. "It's settled."

He balls his fists.

"Tomorrow, we strike."

Thirty-eight

The men of Athiri return to their homes—not to sleep there, but to make their farewells. To murmur in their wives' ears while the rest of the house sleeps, that come dawn, they will be gone.

In some cases, gone for good.

Theron is among them. Nereia wants to stay in the woods to make camp with the soldiers, and Thais unwillingly agrees.

"You have no need to travel with the men tomorrow," Theron frowns. "Better if you are kept safe in Athiri. Forgive me, Princess, but you are no soldier."

"Neither are you, good Theron," Nereia says, her hand on his arm. "You are a fisherman. And yet your heart calls you to fight. You must allow my heart the same freedom."

As for me, I have found my own tree to sit under, a quiet patch of earth from where to watch and think. The men are busy: some whittling extra arrow-shafts for tomorrow, others doing some final training, sparring with each other or shooting arrows. But only part of me is watching it all. The rest of me is thinking about tomorrow, and what comes next—and what got us here to begin with.

Eros walks over to me, a tall, dark shadow in the night. I watch him approach, and remember once more that first night I saw him. I was so sure I was watching my own death come towards me. And in a way, I was. That old Psyche is dead now. Her life, her world, all the things she once thought certain—gone.

"Psyche." He comes to a halt in front of me, and beneath the dark hood I can feel the burn of his gaze reaching down towards me. I do not get to my feet; he does not sit.

"You must go back, with Theron," he says. I scowl at him.

"Phylax Thais and Nereia are staying."

He nods.

"Thais is a soldier. Nereia is queen to these men. You are none of those things—only the sister of a woman they hate."

A woman *he* hates; he might as well say it.

"They have no need of you tomorrow," he continues. "Go home. For Nikos."

"For *Nikos*!" I explode. "Don't you think it's him I'm thinking of? The child needs his mother, Eros! And I need my family—I need them to be alive! I need them to be safe."

"I understand," he says, but his voice is flat, emotionless. I interrupt before he can continue whatever demeaning argument is about to come next.

"We could have stayed!" I burst out. "We *should* have stayed!" It comes over me in a wave, the anger, and I know with sudden clarity what it's about.

"You are so used to being immortal," I blurt, "*untouchable,* that you could not bear the sight of one little knife! One little adamantine knife, and you tore us from the room. Before I could explain, before I could plead with my own sister. We could have defeated the king that night. We could have saved my sister, my father. But we didn't. We fled. *You* fled."

I'm trembling when I stop. There's something bitter in my stomach: disillusionment. I had thought my husband braver than most. But it turns out it was just his immortality, and the arrogance that comes with it. Take that away from him, and he's just another person bent on saving his own skin—no matter who gets left behind.

Eros pulls me abruptly to my feet, steers me into the woods, into a deeper darkness. With no men around, he lifts his hood. He looks at me, bright eyes steady, dazzling through golden lashes. When he speaks, his voice is sharp as steel.

"You think I hurried from that place because of your mother's blade?" He takes a step closer, his eyes boring into mine.

"Psyche, there was *one* such blade to hurt me with—but in the same room, how many blades that could have killed you? Your sister had a new sword at her belt. The king never walks unarmed. And his guards carry a spear, and a dagger on each hip. You do not have my reflexes, you do not have my speed. I do not say this out of arrogance: *I* am not the one over-estimating my abilities, and the sooner you realize it the better. There was one path to death for me in that room. There were five, ten times as many paths for you."

I shake my head. I resent the confusion I'm feeling now. I resent his even tone of voice, the restraint in his fiery eyes. He cannot argue away the coldness I know is in him.

"You don't understand," I say through clenched teeth. "They're my family. Although I suppose *you* shouldn't be expected to understand that."

He takes a step back from me now. When he speaks, his voice is low.

"You speak as though I do not understand such things. I had a family too, or have you forgotten?"

"Of course I haven't forgotten!" My voice rises. "How could I forget them? I wish I could!"

His eyes snap.

"You insist on blaming me for my mother's work—yet I do not confuse you with *your* family."

"*My* family hasn't tried to kill me!" I bite back.

"No," he folds his arms. "They did a good enough job of leaving you to die."

"It wasn't like that!" I say, even as deep down, his words strike old wounds. "They couldn't help it."

"Do you think it did not cut through me, too, to see my brother sliced apart like that, like a mere piece of flesh?" His eyes burn. "You have heard, perhaps, how the others gods spurn Hephaestus, all because he is lame. Imagine, then, a wingless god—no, worse, a *half*-winged god! A god who cannot fly! He can be no war-god now. The pain will be with him forever. For eternity. Do you think I did not feel that?"

Is he blaming me? I used my mother's blade for *him*.

"Deimos would have—"

"I know what he would have done. I know what he is. Do you not think I see?" Eros's nostrils flare.

"But I know his pain, too. Remember, I have known my brothers since before the memory of man, long before your people walked these lands. And yet for all you yell at me about family, you think mine should mean nothing to me. You think I can simply forget them? Sweep them from my memories, from who I am? Rip them out of me, as one pulls a creeper vine from a tree? Those we come of age with, those we share blood with, are not vines, Psyche. They are the very sap of the tree. They are with us whether we seek it or not." He pauses. "And if the rumors are true…if there are caves of adamantine on this island, if mortals find them…" He shakes his head. "What happened to me could happen to any one of my brethren, or worse. None of the gods are safe."

I turn away. I find it hard to care about the plight of the gods right now. What have they ever done to earn my sympathy?

"Perhaps it would not be such a bad thing for the gods to fear death. For them to feel what mortals do."

Eros looks at me, and I can feel the heat from his body sparking towards me, the anger he's keeping back.

"You would like that, would you? For the gods to be no more than mortals—for mortals to be able to kill a god with one blow?"

"And gods who kill mortals—they are not to be punished?" I retort. 'Why are your people *better* than mine?"

"Why are you allowed to feel for yours, and I am not?" he counters. "I have given up my world for you, Psyche. Everything I was, everything I knew. You still don't see that?"

I bristle. "So I have fallen short on gratitude again! I have not worshiped, not groveled sufficiently! What about *my* world? I did not even have the luxury of sacrifice—it was *taken* from me, piece by piece. My family banished, my village razed, all thanks to your mother."

"She barely considers herself my mother anymore. Not after what I did. After all the ways I defied her *for you*."

We stare at each other, breath coming fast from our sharp words.

"You think you know what loss is," I glare. "But you don't know. Maybe you got a taste of it, just for a moment, with an adamantine blade at your neck. But don't pretend you or your kind know the meaning of real loss."

He stares a little longer.

"You mean this?" he gestures behind us, back towards the clearing where the men are training. "That some of them will die tomorrow? What they are feeling, what their wives are feeling—you think I don't know?"

I plant my hands on my hips. "You *don't* know."

He pulls me by the arm, yanking me towards him so that our faces are suddenly a mere inch apart. His golden eyes in the night. His warm, scented breath. My skin tingles with anger, and with a different kind of warmth.

"You are blind, Psyche." His voice is rough, but I hear the emotion in it, and that startles me. I know his way of arguing—emotionless, dispassionate. But that is not how he is now.

"How do you not see it?" He stares into my eyes. "I have you. And I will lose you. The knowledge that someday, I *will* lose you—it is the only thing that is certain. And I will go the rest of my days without you. How can you imagine I do not understand mortality? That I do not understand loss?" His grip tightens on my shoulders; I almost think he will shake me.

"You are my world. Do you understand?" he continues. The night moves through me. The air seems to change around him—brighter, clearer. "Without thinking of the consequences, you are determined to risk everything. Risk *yourself,* without thinking what it means. What it would mean, for me."

His golden eyes bore into mine. "I have given up my old world and I would give it up again—a hundred times over; a thousand. But you forget what I have seen of *your* world. You insist on thinking that men are reasonable, that the gods are fair, that fate will be kind. You think somehow, that because of what you have already survived, you have some special luck or skill; that you will cheat death again and again?" And now he *does* shake me, but not roughly. I feel the warmth of his hands, the sparks running through them. Through me.

"Miracles happen, Psyche, but they are no mortal's birthright." He looks at me, those eyes like molten lakes, like galaxies.

"My father taught me fear was weakness. Something to be crushed. I am not scared of adamantine, Psyche. But I am scared of losing you."

I feel something welling up in me. The anger I've been carrying that wants to stay, but that I can't cling to anymore. I am shaking, and can't seem to stop.

Eros looks down at me, fire in his eyes now, but a different kind of fire. I bury my face against his chest. He touches my hair, then he lifts my face and holds it. And then all words are lost to the feel of his mouth on mine.

*

To make love to a god under the stars, in a dark forest, on the eve of war—it is something beyond any reckoning. I feel it all. The weight of him, the heat of him, the hunger in him. The breeze is cool and his touch is hot. Together they send my skin shivering, and it won't stop. I cling to him, gasping, feeling a tide roll through me, roll up and over me. My ears ring with it. When I stop panting at last, he brushes leaf and tree-bark from my hair and takes me in his arms.

I close my eyes, and for a moment I am back on that clifftop, the first night I saw him. The first night I felt his arms around me, and felt him lift me from the ground. I felt so close to death that night, and have felt close to death many nights since. The choices we each made—the choice to be together—have made life more fragile, more dangerous, than I ever dreamed it would be. *Death will continue to stalk me,* I think. Every day that I am with him, I will feel the wind of death at my back.

And yet, and yet.

I have never, in all my days, felt so alive.

*

It seems one can tell a lot about a man by the way he chooses to spend these last hours before a battle, when it is too dark to train, too dark to whittle, and there is nothing to do but wait. Assignments have been made for the watchmen, who as night goes on will stand guard, two by two. But for now some pray, quietly and alone, or in groups at makeshift altars. Others drink, swallowing down wine by the skinful, stumbling away to piss it out and then start again. Still others, sober-eyed and weary, move off a little ways in hopes of getting sleep. Everyone has their own way to see in the dawn.

I glance at the praying ones, then back at Eros.

"Should we ask them to pray to you?" I say, looking at the group of men who have gathered in quiet worship. "Your strength will benefit them tomorrow; if they can add to it tonight..."

But Eros shakes his head.

"Some of them will die tomorrow. Let them pray to whoever brings them comfort tonight."

I feel suddenly very small, in a world that is very big. How did it come to this? Only a few nights ago we slept within the palace walls. Tomorrow, we will seek to destroy it. Eros speaks about bloodshed like it's an inevitability. But…

"Can't you *make* them win? If you are on their side?"

He hesitates.

"Men must make their own justice, Psyche. I can strengthen their aim, steady their resolve, lend them strength. But the Fates will have their way. There will be a battle tomorrow, and no way out but through."

Wordlessly, I lean into his warmth, and bury my head in his chest. He hesitates only a moment, then puts his hand to the back of my head.

"I will let no harm come to you," he says. "I swear it."

I shake my head against his chest, my breath muffled.

"Do not swear it," I say. We both know it: Fate will have its way.

I take a breath and pull back, then in the darkness cup my

hands under his hood, so that I and I alone can see his face in the dark.

Eros waves a hand, a small gesture to the trees overhead, which slowly bend and begin to knot together, making a little den whose roof is wood and floor is moss. A place to rest—if there is any rest to be had, on a night such as this. Eros draws me into him, wrapping his chiton around us both.

"Can you sleep?" he says.

I am not sure that I even want to. Sleeping, I would miss out on all this: this moment, his linen chiton and his warm skin; the sound of his heartbeat mixing with mine, the night noises of the forest beyond.

Who knows when I will hear them again.

Thirty-nine

"Psyche." The voice comes as if on the wind, at that point between sleeping and waking.

"Psycheandra..."

Psycheandra. Few people call me that now. I open my eyes, and when I do, I am not in the forest at all, but by a great sweep of water. My toes are in the sand. It's dawn, a red sun coming over the water, reflections of fire everywhere. I marvel at it for a moment, almost forgetting the voice that called me here. Then it speaks again.

"Daughter," it says, and something runs through me, not a chill but something like it: fearful and sweet and painful and hopeful all at once.

I don't say her name. I can't.

"Where are you?" I whisper instead. "Are you real?"

I may be dreaming, but I have not left all my wits behind. I know the gods engage in trickery of the cruelest kind, and it is not beyond them to use other likenesses to deceive us and lead us astray. Who is to say that Aphrodite could not find me in dreams, and take whatever shape she likes?

"Look into the water," the voice says. It does not feel like trickery. The voice is the sound of truth; of memories from before I was born.

I step closer to the water. Even when I walk into it, it isn't cold. I stand there, immersed up to my calves, and then I see it—a woman's reflection. Soft brown hair, grey eyes. She does not have my coloring, and yet I think she looks like me, a little.

"What is this?" I say. "How have you come here?" I step closer, but the reflection recedes a step, as if to match me.

"All the dead live after death, Psyche. There is no magic in that."

"You speak to me from the Realm of Shades, then?" I

picture Hades' towering halls and great fields, all in a hazy half-light, like our myths and paintings and songs say.

"You will see it one day. Then you will know."

"And when I do..." I try to keep my heart from pounding too hard. I don't want to miss a word she says. "When I do, you will be there? To greet me?"

She smiles again.

"Not as a mortal may greet another mortal…but after a fashion, yes."

"Is it…is it a good place?" I blurt, unsure of what exactly I want to hear.

She is silent for a moment.

"Perhaps *place* is not the right word, Psyche. The place I am is everywhere."

I shake my head. I want to understand, I so badly want to understand.

"Was it you?" I blurt then. "When I didn't die on Mount Olympus—and then the scorpion, the poison that didn't kill me. And the other things. Was that you, protecting me?"

She shakes her head.

"I have no such powers."

"But you have *some* powers," I point out. "You are speaking to me right now. You have crossed the realms to visit me." I swallow. "Was it true, then—what they said about you? Is it"—I hesitate—"why *I* am different, too?"

She is not quick to answer.

"Your people wait on the eve of death," she says quietly. "Its presence is strong in the air around you tonight. I suspect you will not be the only one to receive a visit. The specter of death thins the boundary between your realm and this one."

"Do you mean that I…am to die tomorrow?" I manage.

She bows her head.

"Death is in the air—but not, I hope, for you. After all, a god fights on your side. But I am no witch, nor goddess, Psycheandra. I cannot augur such things."

"But you *are* special?" I persist. "'Something more than mortal,' that's what Eros said. He said you must be; that *I* must be. That whatever powers I have, I must have got them from you. Certainly they are not Father's gifts."

Her grey eyes hold mine, for what seems a long time.

"Andros was—is—a good man. But he is not everything you think him to be."

I stare back. Does she mean that *Father* is the one with the god-gifts? It cannot be.

The reflection starts to dim.

"Wait!" I take another step into the water, but it only serves to break up the image of her, making it shiver.

"Please," the words hurry out of me. "I don't understand. If you know the truth, then tell me. Tell me who I am."

"There is one who can tell you better than I." Her reflection shivers again, weakening. An expression in her eyes I can't read.

"I expect you will meet him some day." She sighs. "Andros…He is not your blood, Psycheandra."

The words bind me where I stand. I feel something fall inside me, and keep falling.

Not my blood.

She means—

"There is another one who sired you."

My chest is tight enough to burst, my mind a flurry. I sense the pain, somewhere inside, waiting for me. But for now, all I feel is this sensation of falling. The pain is behind a wall of ice. It will come later.

"Then who?" I say. *Who made me this way?*

"He wore many faces." Her expression grows opaque, feelings she refuses to show. "He never gave me his true name. But perhaps it does not matter." She looks at me. "Whatever gifts you may have, Psycheandra, they are not who you are."

The water is cold now. Everything, suddenly, feels cold. My mind fights through the wave of questions. *If this is true…*

"Does Father know?"

She closes her eyes for a moment. When she opens them, the grey eyes are bright, full of an emotion I can't name.

"I believe he chose not to see. Out of love, Psycheandra:

he chose not to see."

The words seem to hold me in their grasp, the last warm thing in a cold, cold place, and then I blink my eyes open into darkness.

I sit up from the mossy bed. Eros is standing, leaves rustling dark around him.

Dawn is breaking, grey and watery, in the east.

And out there in the men's encampment, someone is screaming.

*

I rush into the clearing, the dream and all its hope and pain still lingering in my head. The first thing I see is the flash of gold—the king's guards. But they're not roped together on the ground anymore. They're on horseback. They're on *Ajax*. And there's a dead man by their feet, blood pooling by his neck.

The others, roused now, are racing and stumbling towards the scene. Cleon, Theron's son, is already there, a knife in his hand. He raises it and charges, letting out another furious shriek. But he is easily disposed of. One of the guards draws his boot back and lands a kick square in the boy's jaw, sending him to the ground in an instant.

"Go! *Go*, you fool beast!" The guard in front kicks his heels into Ajax's flank. The one in back smacks the horse's rump. He darts a glance our way, flashes his teeth. They think they're escaping. But Ajax has other ideas.

He rears up, whinnying, onto his hind legs. He bucks, and rears again. The guards yell out in anger; the one in front loses his grip. And then an arrow whips through the air, so fast it barely whispers, and buries itself in the guard's back. Left side, just above the heart. He sags, and as he falls, his weight throws his companion to the ground along with him. The second guard scrambles to hands and knees, but it's too late. Belos, the angry Kytheran from last night, is already upon him, sword in hand. He drives it through the man's back. There is a choking sound, a retching of blood, and then it's over.

Three bodies piled together. One of ours and two of theirs. Blood spattered in a circle, red on Ajax's shins, on Belos's hands; on Cleon, still panting on the ground.

Phaedon comes forward, pulls his arrow from the guard's back, and begins to clean it. Kallias was right: he is a good shot.

"What happened here?" Kallias strides in. "Cleon? You and Simos were to take this watch together. How is it that the hostages got free?"

"I know well enough how it is," Belos spits. He takes Cleon by the ear, pulls him, yelping, from the ground. I see the look of panic, quickly masked, on the boy's face.

"Tell us what you did, you little bitch-whelp!"

Theron barges through the crowd of men.

"Belos! What's the meaning of this?"

"Your son," Belos spits, "let our hostages free. To run back to their king. To have us all slaughtered."

"Don't be—" Theron begins, but trails off as he looks at his son's face. "Cleon? Surely this isn't true?"

"And what if it is?" the boy snaps. His narrow jaw works angrily. His skinny limbs are still shaking.

"You're fools, all of you. Racing to your deaths, and for what? For *her*!" Spittle follows the words out of his mouth as he points at Nereia. "This—this *parasite*. She has done nothing but be born a king's daughter, the daughter of a man who killed our people through neglect! She ran away like a dog when the revolution came. She took shelter in our house, took the food from my brother's and sister's mouths, to be served first while we ate last, and she took it all because she thought it was her *due*."

"Cleon." Theron covers his face with his hands. My heart is like a stone, sinking to my stomach. That hatred on the boy's face—I glimpsed it yesterday, and yet I did not imagine it would lead to this. I glance at Eros, unreadable beneath his dark hood.

"Don't you know the king's guard will beat us in any standoff?" the boy shouts. "What chance do you think we have—an army of fishermen and peasants? You might as well be sheep, herded off a cliff!"

Theron stares. His voice cracks. "Cleon...you would betray her so? Our rightful queen—a guest in our own home?"

Cleon's chin juts out.

"You raised me to protect our family. To protect Athiri. And she is no rightful queen." He glances at Nereia. "Simos fell asleep. The men said the king would spare us; that once we surrendered the usurper, it would be all right. That they would tell the king what happened, and in return for my loyalty, our people would be spared."

"You stupid little pissant!" Belos bears down on him. "You thought you could bargain with them? You thought the king would reward *you*? That *you* would be our hero?"

"Simos's death is on your head, Cleon." Kallias looks at the dead man lying next to the two guards. "A needless death, earned by your arrogance and deceit. You will be the one to tell his wife and children what you have done."

"If we don't hang you as a traitor first," Belos fumes.

Nereia speaks up.

"You will serve no such ill justice. He's a child."

"I'm no child," Cleon spits.

"There you have it, from the boy's own mouth," Belos glares back at Nereia. "He thinks he's a man, we'll punish him like a man."

Nereia steps forward.

"And *I* say you will not hurt him. If I am your queen then you will respect my rule of law." Her voice is shaking, but not with nerves.

"And *are* you our queen, my lady?" Belos's lip curls; he turns towards the men. "I say we vote on it this moment."

Kallias frowns, but the words are spreading through the crowd of men.

"It would be wise," Eros murmurs in Kallias's ear. "For the men's sake."

Kallias sighs. "Very good. Phaedon, come and count with me."

The young archer weaves a path through the men, back to his leader's side.

"All in favor," Kallias calls out. Some hands rise at once; others, more slowly. Phaedon murmurs as he counts.

"All against?" Belos speaks through clenched teeth. His jaw clamps tighter still, when the hands rise. There are too few of them—we all know the verdict, before Phaedon begins his count.

"It is settled, then," Kallias says. "And let us hear no more of it."

They tie Cleon's hands. He must come with us—there is no time to do anything else, and we cannot leave him tied up in the woods, though I suspect a few of the men would be happy enough to make bear-food of him.

"You'll walk beside me, boy," Belos snarls. "And if you try any nonsense again, my sword will be the last thing you feel."

We can't stop to bury the men, nor build a funeral pyre, but we throw some wood across them in the quickest of makeshift shelters, to keep the bodies from being scavenged by birds. Belos says we shouldn't bother with the guards, only Simos, but Kallias says we must not bring ill-will on ourselves, this morning of all mornings.

Three deaths already: a poor omen. But three is few, compared with what may come before the day is out.

"All right, men." Kallias raises a hand. "Forward!"

The men swing into motion. I take a breath, Eros by my side.

Forward.

What other way is there to go?

Forty

The roads are busy. The king has exempted even the miners from their work today. Farmers, fieldhands, fisherman, and their families: everyone has been summoned, just like everyone was summoned to the temple to see the Shadowed God.

I glance at Eros beside me, wearing the patched, rough cape of a commoner. But it's not just that: somehow he draws the eye less, his presence not so imposing. He even seems an inch or two less tall. All the gods have this trick, so I'm told: they can mask what they are, helping them pass as mortals, as insignificant. It's how they seduce many mortal women, if legends are to be believed.

I have my own borrowed cloak too, just like Eros. Meanwhile, Thais has rubbed mud into her face and her bright blonde hair, turning it dull and brown. She would pass for a farm-hand now, some scrappy lad used to working in the fields. As for Nereia, she, too, has cut off her hair, and wears a man's clothing.

We slip from the cover of the forest just outside the citadel, mixing with the other Atlanteans by the time we reach the wide dirt road. There are mules and donkeys on the path, too—there's always business to conduct in the citadel—so Ajax doesn't stand out so much as he might.

The walls of the great palace rise up ahead, blocking out the sea, but I can smell its sharp, clean brine. It brings me back to walking on the castle ramparts, the high garden below the guards' watch. My sister, her child in her arms. Flowers batting in the wind, and the great war-ships bobbing in the harbor.

Everything looked so different, only a few days ago.

Careful timing, or pure coincidence: I spot Drusa in the crowd behind us. Xenon and Helia are with her, and she's carrying a bundle in her arms. *Nikos.* My heart quickens. I had not thought she would bring him here. But then, how could she not? We've heard that attendance at this cruel trial is compulsory, and surely the king's guards would have made quick work of any woman who tried to stay behind in Athiri.

I comfort myself with the thought that to a stranger, one baby looks much like another. The king's guard were in Drusa's own home, close enough for Nikos to feel their breath, and they did not guess. Theron signals to his wife, and I tug at Eros's arm, slowing us down a little so that Drusa can draw nearer.

A young man falls into step on my other side: Phaedon, the prize shooter.

"I hear those are our allies from the east of the isle," he murmurs in an undertone, then nods to a group a little ahead of us in the crowd. "Some of them, at least. From Akreon and Erythra and Pharos." Phaedon glances at me. "Theron has been communicating with their leader, and with those from the south and southeast, too—just as he has with Kallias." Phaedon smiles. "The tyrant king may have outlawed boats, but he cannot outlaw messenger pigeons."

I look over the ranks of men Phaedon pointed out. We are many, it seems. But are we enough?

Drusa gets closer, and my chest tightens at the sight of Nikos in her arms. The others hang close about her, Helia clinging to her skirts. Xenon must have caught sight of Cleon up ahead, with his bruised and bloodied face; the young boy's eyes widen in fear. Nikos's chubby arm breaks free of the swaddling-cloth, reaching for me. Drusa's gaze meets mine, and I wonder if what she sees in my eyes is as stark and grim as what I see in hers.

Nikos coos, reaches again, and Drusa jogs him gently, then holds him out to me. I hesitate to take him—how can I be sure he will be safe with me? But how can I be sure of his safety anywhere? He is my family, and Drusa has her own to take care of.

"Where is Cleon?" She scans the faces nearest us. Theron frowns.

"He walks ahead, with Belos," he says, and takes her aside to speak of the rest.

As we pass into the citadel and get closer to the palace, the crowd swells. We thin out, becoming a divided party, but we keep track of each other; I can feel it in the glances, the awareness that crackles all around me. This near to the water, the sea-salt cuts through the softness of the air, stinging the back of my throat.

"Guards," Kallias says behind me. His voice is tight. The entrances to the agora are not usually guarded, but they are today; I see the shiny helmets of the guards at the entrance nearest us. Kallias glances around at our party. The men adjust their cloaks and capes, their movements subtle but anxious. If the guards are inspecting everyone for weapons, we will not last long. But surely it will not come to that. Not unless we make ourselves obvious.

Kallias turns to Eros and me.

"If they recognize you"—he looked between Eros and me—"then it will go ill for us all."

I hesitate. Then some people at the front pass through, and we move a few paces closer to the entrance. From here, I can see the faces of the guards on each side.

"I do not know them," I say. "Nor will they know me."

The men who guarded the king's rooms, patrolling the doors and corridors of the palace, were a different unit than the ones who kept order in the streets and alleys in the citadel and beyond. The palace guards would know my face, perhaps, even with my cloak, but not these men.

"Thais—" It's Nereia, behind us. I turn, and so do Kallias, Theron, and Phaedon.

Nereia has stopped short, her eyes on the two guards in the doorway.

"What is it?"

I see Nereia's hand tighten on Ajax's bridle.

"The one on the left—that's Gyras. He was my guard," she swallows. "My personal guard in the palace. He stood watch outside my room each night. He accompanied me on any journey I took. He has known me since I was a child."

And now he stands guard for the man who tried to murder her.

"Nereia." Thais puts an urgent hand on her arm. "You cannot risk it."

"But—" Nereia glances around at the rest of us. I know what she's thinking. If she is to be queen to these men, she cannot desert them now.

"You will put them in danger," Kallias says gruffly. "You will put us all in danger. Thais is right. You cannot risk it."

Nereia swallows hard. I see how she burns to come with us; to see justice done, alongside us. She would have protested, if it was just about her own safety. But Kallias's argument is one she can't dispute.

"Then I must stay with her," Thais says. "I am sorry, Kallias. I would wish to go in there with you. But I cannot leave the princess here alone."

He grimaces.

"I know you cannot," he says. "But I believe you will join us, if you see we have need of it. Till then—" he sighs. "Keep the cover of the woods. Bring Ajax with you."

"Sir." Thais bows her head. I see tears forming under Nereia's lashes.

The entrance to the great square draws closer, and I breathe deep, trying to ignore the sick feeling in my stomach, the ringing in my ears. But the guard only eyes us fleetingly as we walk through.

"All the way to the front," he growls. "Don't block the ones behind you. There's many coming to see the show today." His lip curls a little as he says it, and I want to lunge at him. But then I feel a steady hand on my back.

"Not yet, Psyche," Eros murmurs. "Do not give him reason to notice you."

We flood through with the next wave of the crowd.

A great platform has been erected, right by the palace entrance. *A stage,* I think, my blood running cold. A stage for this horrific piece of theater. But for now, it is empty. All I see is the thrashing sea behind it, and the bobbing masts of the king's war-ships. The battlements overhead aren't, though: I can see the guards posted there, waiting. Looking down at us. My stomach turns over again.

The sun is just eye-height now, pink rays streaming in from across the water. Underneath the brine, I smell the sweat of the crowds around me—the exertion of those that have walked many miles, and more than that, the acrid sweat of fear. No doubt there are plenty that will enjoy this spectacle—I remember the crowds in the king's justice sessions, practically baying for blood—but it seems to me that most of these people would rather be anywhere but here.

The children are different. Whatever tension hovers in the air, they take to be some sort of excitement. They are running in and out around their parents' legs, yelping and giggling. The sight gives me an ill feeling.

Our delay with Cleon and the hostages has made us late. We had thought to be among the first—those closest to the stage—but the king's summons has been effective. It seems half of Atlantis is already here.

Suddenly, an *aulos* pipes start up. A drum beats. A few of the king's councilmen step onto the platform, in their fine robes. And there is another man among them, not a councilman: my father.

He is dressed in fine robes but he walks between two guards, somewhere between a guest of honor and a prisoner.

Father.

I have not let myself think about the dream—a dream is what I have decided to call it—until now. It felt so real, but does that mean it *was* real? It chills me all over again to think of it.

If Father is not my blood-father…

If Dimitra is not my blood-sister….

It is too much to think about. Surely it is not true. And if it were…

If it were, it could not change my course. I am here to save them. *My family*. That is all I know. I stare up at the platform, at my father's empty face, those hollow eyes. I wish I could signal to him somehow—that I could whisper in his ear, *I am here. It will be all right*. But even I can't promise that.

The councilmen form a semi-circle at the back of the platform, and guards push my father into place along with them. More guards file out. The last two are dragging a woman between them, gripping her by the elbows—Dimitra.

My stomach turns.

She's not dressed in her finery any longer. She could pass for a peasant woman now—except for her haughty bearing, her fierce, fiery eyes. Around me, children jabber, the crowd swells, and a guard raises his voice. I feel dizzy. I stare up, my eyes locked on my sister's face. Her gaze bores into the crowd, more piercing than I've ever seen it, her eyes bright as a god's. It's rage that's making them shine, and the rage is for all of us: at the guards who dare to manhandle her; at the king who has betrayed her; at the crowd gathered before her, so insolently watching. And rage for herself. For letting anyone get the better of her.

But then the *aulos* pipe whines again, and the king walks onto the platform. At the sight of him, the crowd goes quiet, and so does my heart. Because he's not in his usual ceremonial robes. He's dressed in armor—in more armor, even, than his guards. He wears a full bronze breastplate and greaves, and a helmet in the Corinthian style, covering his face and neck. But I know it is him from his gait, and from the cloak pinned across the back of his shoulders, its swathe of Tyrian purple, the dye whose drops it would take a coffer of gold to afford. A heavy-looking *linthorax* covers him most everywhere else. The *linthorax* is fortified fabric, not metal, but according to my father's tales, strong enough to withstand all but the closest-range attacks.

The king knows, I realize. He has not forgotten about Eros, nor me. Not for a moment. Nor has he forgotten about Thais's attempt. He knows his people have no love for him. He knows there must be rebels in the crowd. And he has taken precautions.

"Gods' teeth!" Phaedon murmurs beside me. He looks from me to Eros now, those dark eyes grave and anxious. "An arrow won't pierce *that*."

"If he lifted the helmet…" I say. Phaedon gives me a grim

look.

"But how to make him do it?"

I stare at Eros. How, with the king swaddled in armor like this?

"Keep your calm," Eros murmurs to Phaedon. "Your advantage will come."

An arrow would not pierce the *linthorax,* not from this distance. A sword would, but how would any of us get that close?

Phaedon has started pushing through the crowd, trying to find his way nearer to the front of the stage. The agora is teeming; half of Atlantis must be here. I do my best to follow Phaedon through the seething crowd, Eros at my back. I hear Helia's bright voice somewhere behind us, asking her mother how long they will be here, how soon they can go home.

"People of Atlantis!" The king's voice rolls through the crowd.

"You gather today to grieve with your king," he booms. "And to quench that grief with justice."

I stare up at my sister's face, her near-black hair in the wind, her furious eyes. Her son's warm weight in my arms.

"My son, your future king, is dead. Killed at the hands of this woman, Dimitra of Sikyon, who in my grievous error I brought before you as your queen."

"He *is not dead*!" My sister struggles in the grip of the guards, furiously trying to tear herself free. "He is alive, you know he is alive!"

"Please, your Highness…"

My father steps forward from the line of councilmen, but his voice is the voice of one who knows he has already lost. He protests for the sake of his conscience, not because he believes he can change any of what is to come. He was like this, too, when he gave me up to the king of Sikyon: full of grief but no conviction.

"*Silence*!" the king roars, and one of the guards pushes my father back into line; another jabs the butt of his spear in my sister's side and she heaves for breath. I clutch Nikos against me.

"My subjects: this depraved creature speaks as a madwoman, for she has lost all sense and human feeling." The king looks out over the crowd. "For she looked upon the face of that treacherous creature—that monster whom I was persuaded to bring into our home, who claimed he was a god. This false queen, this—this *whore*, fell in love with the monster, and in her foolish passion she looked upon his face. And in punishment, was driven mad."

"*Lies*!" Dimitra thrashes, shoving at the guards who hold her, but she only receives another crack of the spear in return.

"It was her madness which drove her to do the unthinkable. To defile not only the laws of this land, but of all nature and all the gods! People of Atlantis: this woman before you, this most unnatural of mothers, has murdered her own child!"

Dimitra shrieks, throwing her full weight forward, but it is no use.

"Monster! *Snake!* You *let* him be taken from me. You sent no one to bring him back! If my son is dead now, it is by your hand!"

The king waves his hand, and one of the guards hits my sister in the mouth. I can almost feel the blow in my own teeth. I grab Eros's cloak.

"They're hurting her. We need to do something."

In front of me, Phaedon turns, and I see the look in his eyes. He has a gentler heart than Kallias or Belos. It pains him, too, to see an innocent woman so abused. But Eros puts his hand on my arm, radiating warmth, and speaks to me in a low voice.

"I will protect your sister. But to act too soon is to risk more lives than just hers."

My heart won't stop pounding. I hear again that crack as the man struck Dimitra's face.

"People of Atlantis," the king continues, but with a grotesque gentleness in his voice now, almost fatherly. "I hear your tender hearts. If she is mad, you say, then should we not show pity? Perhaps, you say, she does not deserve the same justice as if she had done the deed in sound mind?"

The crowd is murmuring. The king shakes his head, a pretense of sorrow. Then he steps forward, his voice growing louder, harsher.

"Yes, I feel your merciful hearts, my people. But it is my sworn duty to guard this kingdom and protect its subjects. Though a rabid dog may not deserve its death, for all our sakes, it must die." He looks over at my sister again.

"And so, Dimitra of Sikyon, by and on behalf of the people of Atlantis, you have been found guilty, and are sentenced to death."

The crowd erupts, whether in glee or horror or simple shock. I turn to Eros, Nikos tight in my arms.

"What are we going to do? Phaedon can do nothing while the king is armored head to foot!" He is invulnerable, invincible. Our archers could take out others of the king's guards, but where would that leave us?

Eros says nothing, but I can feel him watching the stage; I can feel his mind at work.

"If he takes off his helmet…" I say, and Eros nods. But before he can say a word, the king is shouting again.

"Guards!"

They move into action, surrounding Dimitra, spears at her throat and chest. But they do not attack. Instead they are pushing in on her, prodding with their spear-tips, forcing her to take one step back, and then another.

Now I understand. The edge of the platform—it juts out over the rocky shoal, the jagged stones where the sea begins. My stomach turns. They mean for her to die here and now. And just like the king's plan to leave Nikos out in the mountains to die of exposure, these men think they can escape the taint of murder if they kill by sleight of hand—if they can make my sister fall, instead of running her through with a blade. They think this way they can escape the gods' punishment. But I vow they shall not.

In each step I feel Dimitra's helpless fury, her struggle, but though she moves as slowly as she can, she has no choice. I hear seagulls in the distance, their screeching like the sound of my own heart.

"You have to do something!" I cry out.

Eros promised. He said he would protect her.

"Are you ready to meet your gods, woman?" the king says.

My sister opens her mouth.

"Great Poseidon!" she calls. "I appeal to you alone!"

The sudden piety of the doomed. But my sister will not be doomed. She *can't* be.

"Do something!" I cry again, tearing free from Eros, pushing desperately toward where my sister stands, on the very last edge of the high platform. From the corner of my eye I see Eros raise his hand. But as he does so, an arrow flies free. Not one of his. One of Phaedon's.

Forty-one

The crowd gasps. My sister, their queen, stands hovering in the air, a full step away from the platform she was thrust from, and yet not falling. And as she hovers there, one of the king's guards—one of those who held his spear to her throat—plummets downward instead, an arrow lodged in his chest. Screams rise up from the crowd.

Beside me, Phaedon notches another arrow and releases, his hands quicker than any bowman's I have seen.

"Assassins!" a man in front of us yells.

Phaedon releases another arrow, and another. Two more guards fall, and then a third. Phaedon has pressed the advantage while he had it, but now that the guards understand what is happening, they're rallying. On the platform, they get into formation around the king. Above, on the battlements, more are scurrying to the front. As for my sister, she has been set down like a doll by an invisible hand, but the men are too busy guarding the king now to pay her any mind.

"Too soon, fool!" I hear Kallias shout to Phaedon, even as I see him draw his own bow. Surprise was our advantage; now it's gone.

"They will rally to him now! We will not get another chance!" But still Kallias lets his arrow fly, and then another, and another.

I hear the captain on the battlements shouting instructions. And now the guardsmen raise their bows, all in unison, and pull back. My heart rocks forward in my chest.

Arrows—fifty, a hundred?—cut a sharp line through the sky, arcing from the battlements directly towards the crowd.

"Eros!"

I throw myself to the ground, covering Nikos's body with mine. But then something happens. The arrows that had been moving so ruthlessly towards us slow their arc, tremble in mid-flight. And then, as one, they fall to the ground. I exhale a gasp, and turn back to Eros. He stands braced and ready, hands outstretched, waiting for the next wave. I can almost feel the energy roaring off him. My heart shudders with a new, wild confidence.

How could we lose, with a god on our side? For a moment, I could almost laugh.

But whatever giddiness I'm feeling, the crowd is not. The people are still screaming, pushing, running in all directions. Perhaps some did not see the arrows drop from the sky, and those that did, can't understand it. But I'll wager the king does.

I look up, and though the king's mask keeps me from seeing his face, I don't doubt the rage that it must show. His guards' faces are a display of shock, and in many cases, fear. Meanwhile, the councilmen have run to safety. Only my father stays behind, with Dimitra at one end of the platform, and the king, surrounded by his phalanx of guards, at the other. The giddy feeling seeps out of my chest: my family are still up there. Still vulnerable. Eros is defending the crowd from the guards' arrows, but his attention cannot be everywhere at once.

"Again!" the king snarls, and I feel his rage. The guards notch more arrows, letting them fly. But again Eros curls his hand, and again, the arrows drop before they reach the crowd. But is it my imagination, or do they came closer this time? I hear scattered cries around the square, as though some arrows made it through Eros's defenses.

Our bowmen are still going strong. I see them all around the square, men from Athiri and others I've never seen, Theron's allies from villages across the island, exposed more clearly as the people around them crouch to earth or run for safety. The crowd pushes and swells. Mothers are screaming their children's names. Phaedon is not the only strong shot among the rebels. I see guards on the battlements go down, and even one or two in the king's phalanx. But when one manages to hit the king, he just plucks it out of his *linthorax* and tosses it to the ground.

I glance up at the battlements. Despite those our men

have taken down, there are still so many, and the guards are firing at will now, not in one unified wave but all at once. Eros has both hands raised before him, as if he were in some kind of trance.

"Eros?" I shout up to him. He flinches at my voice, as though it has broken a spell. His dark hood moves in my direction.

"I will hold them," he says, "for as long as I can."

So he cannot do this forever.

I glance behind me. Guards are standing at the exits, spears drawn, blocking the crowd's escape, forcing them back like sheep in a pen. By camouflaging ourselves among these people, we have endangered them.

If one of our men don't hit them by accident, one of the king's men will surely hit them on purpose. Despite Eros's help, the wall of archers on the battlements doesn't seem to be getting any thinner. And there are whimpers and shouts around the great square. Despite Eros's protection, I can hear the wounded—injured in the stampede, perhaps, if not by the arrows. I look up at the ranks of guards above us as yet another wave of arrows hails down. They seem to come closer and closer each time.

How many will die here today?

I push myself up from the ground and onto my knees, shielding Nikos's head with my arm.

"*Stop*!" I shout, at the top of my lungs, but surely no one can hear me. Still, I keep yelling.

"*Guards! Hold your fire! The prince lives*!"

They do not hold their fire, though I feel people fall silent around me.

"Psyche!" Eros says, beside me. "What are you doing?" His voice sounds effortful, as though, in the midst of keeping these hundreds of arrows at bay, he must drag his words from some deep, far place.

"What I must," I say. I look him in the eye—though I cannot see his face, I feel his gaze. "Can you cover us?"

I feel his eyes rake over us, the child and me. I can feel

him wanting to dissuade me, to pull me back.

"Protect us," I say. "Protect him."

A moment's more hesitation, and Eros nods. I don't stop to think about what this protection will cost him. What it may cost others, if the god protecting them must keep his sights on me instead of on the king's guards. I can't afford to. As the crowd draws back from us, I try again.

"The prince lives," I'm shouting so hard, it feels as though the back of my throat must tear open. *"Hold your fire!"* And I begin to walk forward. Towards the stage.

The crowd parts for me. Nikos is silent in my arms, when any other child would be wailing. I tighten my hands around his warm weight, shielding all the soft parts of him with all the hard parts of me.

"Guards, do not kill your own people. This crowd is innocent!" I turn my face up to the battlements, hurling my words as high as they will go. "The queen is telling the truth! I carry the king's son. Your rightful ruler! Hold your fire: *the prince lives!"*

I look up at the king's guard. They are hesitating now. They do not lower their bows but the rain of arrows dwindles as they look to their king for instruction.

And I look to my family. There, on the platform, my father, my sister. Dimitra is open-mouthed, entirely still. For the first time today I see fear on her face. Not for herself, nor for me.

Fear for the child in my arms.

And then the fear gives way to rage.

"*Psyche!* Get back, you fool! Get *away from here!*"

"Stay back, witch," the king says.

"Psyche." My father's face takes on still more pain, if such a thing is possible. "You returned."

"I'm here for you," I say, my voice trembling. "I'm here to save you and Dimitra."

My father closes his eyes. When he opens them, they are soft and sad.

"I do not think you will manage that, my child."

"Get *away* from here!" Dimitra screams.

I have you, Psyche. I hear Eros's voice then, somewhere inside my mind. Warmth, like strength, seems to course through me. *He is with me.* Protecting us.

The king takes a step forward, pushing aside his phalanx of guards.

"So, little sister. You thought you would surprise me? Well, I have a surprise for you, and your husband. You'll find out soon enough."

I hear the satisfaction in his voice. Satisfaction—as though he expected me to come here. As though all this was part of his plan. A new unease ripples through me. I curl my arms harder around Nikos, who by now, perhaps because of how tightly I'm holding him, starts to wail.

"Guards!" I call to the men above me. "This man has lied to you! The boy in my arms is your prince. The king slandered him as a bastard, and sought to have him killed—but we have brought him safely home. I come here before you now, an unarmed woman and an infant, for justice." I stare up at them—the phalanx guarding the king, and the rows of soldiers on the battlements. There is no jeering, no murmuring, only silence. I can feel their doubt, their hesitation. They can feel it in my voice—I am telling the truth.

I remember what Thais said, about how many of the king's guard only serve him from fear. They do not agree with his ways, with his claim to the throne or his cruel justice.

"Do not corrupt your own souls by bringing harm on us! If you put down your bows, so will the rebels. We do not seek your death."

A woman and a babe in arms. It takes a moment, but I watch one man lower his bow. And then another. I glance over my shoulder, looking for the others in the crowd—for Phaedon, for Kallias, for Drusa and her children. The rebels will not fire on those who surrender. Another guard lowers his bow, and another, and then a wave of them.

Not all, perhaps not even half of them, but enough to incense the king.

"She is *lying*," the king screams. "She is a scheming liar, sent to trick you! And that bastard she carries is *not my son*! Guards, if you value your lives, you will follow my word. Notch your new arrows, you hear me? Your new ones!" His masked face, that helmet of gold with slits for eyes, swivels back towards me.

"You are a coward, King Kostas," I say. "Your guards show their faces, yet you hide behind a golden mask. Perhaps you know they will recognize the face of a liar. Or perhaps you simply do not want them to see your fear. Take off your mask, king, and show them the truth. Show them who you really are."

The guards' perfect unison has turned to confusion now. Some, following the king's orders, have strung new arrows to their bows, and stand ready. But most are looking to their neighbors, to me, to the king, wondering what to believe, what to do now.

"Kill her!" the king screams, his voice growing higher with rage. He turns to the guard next to him, just a boy, smooth-skinned. "Do it! Do it now, unless you want to be convicted of treason, and skinned alive!"

The horror is starting to show on the other guards' faces, the same horror trickling through my blood. Hardly a single bow points my way now. But the boy the king has closed in on is staring at me, trembling. Somehow he manages to fit an arrow to his bow, his eyes never leaving mine, as though imploring me to stop this somehow.

I try to control the hammering of my heart. I can feel Eros behind me. He has stopped a hundred arrows in flight, I remind myself; he can stop this one.

"Not that one!" the king is screaming. The boy fumbles again. "Your *new* arrows, I said!"

A sudden, cold darkness rears up inside me, a clarity that turns my skin to ice. A dread that passes through me like a tremor.

New arrows. He said it with such vicious glee, such triumph.

Such lack of concern.

I think how smug he sounded, how satisfied, to find me

here. And suddenly I understand.

"Adamantine," I spin. Eros is ten steps behind me. "They have arrows of adamantine!"

But he knows already—I sense the dread in him, too. He understood it the same moment I did.

"I warned you, witch," the king sneers. I see my family on the platform, the whites of Dimitra's eyes, her terror for her son. My father's face, locked on mine. I see again the soft, sad look he gave me, the spark of pride and regret when he saw that I had come. And for what?

This is the end. I will die, and Eros will die trying to save me. My nephew will be prized from my cold arms. Everything, crushed. Gone.

Movement flickers in the corner of my eye, but I can't see straight, can't think straight. The king holds a sword to the young guard's throat.

"*Now*, boy, or I'll run you through."

I throw myself to the ground, covering Nikos as the guard's arm pulls back. I feel the current of air behind me—Eros, racing towards us. He throws his weight over us, covering his body with mine. But he doesn't cover my eyes. And up on the platform, there is a chaos of movement and sound, the whip of an arrow releasing. The young soldier is gone from view, blocked by a flurry of navy. A man in a dark robe has lunged in front of him—between me and the arrow's path. My heart stops. Time stops. It seems to me I hear every inch of air as the arrow whistles through it.

Father.

His face looks out towards me. Towards me, but not seeing me; his eyes are on the middle distance, staring at something I cannot see. He crumples. His robe blooms blackish-red, like a flower opening.

I scream, or Dimitra does. I cannot take my eyes from that dark-red mark. His eyes are still wide open. My sister falls to her knees. She moves towards the body, crawling, but the king is faster. He takes a quick step in my father's direction, pushes the body with his foot. Once, hard. And my father's lifeless body falls from the high platform, landing mere paces in front of me.

I free myself, scrambling from under Eros's protecting arms. I can see nothing, hear nothing, only the red flower on a grey chiton, the sound of my own heart. Something wild and desperate bursts inside me. I look up at the guards, the rows of them on the battlements, the ashen-faced boy at the king's side.

"He was an old man," I scream at them. Nikos howls in my arms. "He had done nothing wrong. *Nothing*. He was a soldier like you! He fought for Atlantis. For your people! For your freedom!"

On the platform, the king scoffs.

"Guards!" he calls. "Take down the rebel scum!"

But all that ripples through the guards now is a wave of fear and doubt; I can feel it. The king shouts again, but still no one complies.

But then a new arrow whistles through the air. Not from the guards this time. It comes from somewhere behind me, from the rebels. And it buries itself, neatly, in the chest of the boy whose arrow killed my father. That trembling lad who looked no older than Theron's son. Another arrow follows, then another. A cry comes from the battlements, a cry that ends in a terrible gurgle, and a guard's body falls plummeting to earth. And then it is a hail of arrows, all raining down on the king's guards.

Wait, I want to call. *Stop!* But it's too late, it's all much too late by now. The rebels' attack has stoked the guards to action better than the king's rage ever could. The guards take up their bows again. And this time the arrows fly fast and sure.

I see Eros trying to stop them, but it's useless. Just like the cage deadened his power, these adamantine arrows are immune to it. I hear the sounds of death all across the square, cries of horror and pain as the arrows bury themselves in our people's flesh. I feel numb, like a ghost myself. It is pure instinct that tightens my arms around my nephew's small body.

"Now, Shadowed One." The king snatches the quiver from the dead hands of his guard. "We'll see what you're really made of."

Eros.

Fear jolts my heart back to life. The king has set his sights on Eros. And this time, he has arrows that can kill him.

Those black wings burst free, and Eros rises from the ground as though he rides the wind itself. But the king's aim follows him, bow raised. He releases the arrow; Eros dodges it. Hardly a moment seems to pass before the king has notched another. Again he fires, again Eros swerves in the air, and I hear the whistle of the arrow as it misses him by a hair's breadth. The king's guards are firing on the rebels, and the rebels are firing back. There is death all around me, my father's body lies steps away, but I am rooted to the spot.

I knew death would come for us. I knew it would separate us in the end. But it was to be *my* death. Eros was to go on without me, alive forever, young forever. I thought that pain enough. But *this*—this pain, this fear, it turns out, is far, far worse.

Another arrow looses from the king's bow. This time it is so close that the king crows in triumph. I see Eros lose his balance for a moment. Only a moment, but in that same instant, the king fires again.

And Eros drops from the sky.

I run, hardly knowing what I'm screaming. I call his name as though I can stop time. As though his name can split the world in two.

He comes to earth, and I throw myself to the ground at his side. I know this: there is no life for me without him.

"Get back from me," he barks.

"But—"

"So long as I draw the king's arrows, you and the child will not. I said get back, Psyche!"

The words land somewhere below my ribcage. *He's doing this for us*. But the fall was no feint: I see the thin purple trickle against the black of his wing. *Ichor*, god's blood. Blood that was never meant to spill.

"You are hurt." Sounds echo around me as though I'm at the bottom of the well. The whistle of arrows, cries of pain, hoofbeats like a tremor in the earth. More arrows.

"Cover yourself!" Eros hisses. He pushes me down behind the bodies of two felled men, letting their bulk guard me from the whistling arrows. I barely flinch at taking refuge with the dead. I clutch Nikos to me.

"But—"

There is a guardsman's body, too, among the dead. I see Eros reach for it—no, not for the man. For his shield. The ichor glistens on his wing, but if he's in pain, he doesn't show it.

Hoofbeats pound somewhere behind me, a desperate gallop. The sound stirs something in my mind, something important, but it's all drowned out by what's happening in front of me: the arrows flying, Eros rising again into the air. He doesn't fly so high as before, though—no higher than the platform where the king stands, loosing one arrow after another from his bow. At least Eros has his borrowed shield this time. But it cannot shield all of him.

And then, as the king notches yet another arrow, Eros lunges, flinging the shield from him like a discus. The king topples, a great clanking of armor, and his metal mask skitters free from his face. I see all the hate written there, the cruelty and scorn.

His mask is off. Finally, the king is exposed—but where is Phaedon now? Dead, or alive? All around the square, the rebels are too busy defending themselves to notice.

"That's the best you can do?" the king wheezes, reaching for his mask. "A poor excuse for a god!"

The hoofbeats get louder.

"It is not my job to take your life," Eros answers. "And there are others with more claim on it than I."

The king coughs out a laugh, reaching for his quiver again, pushing against the ground to right himself. But I turn, and so I see what he doesn't: Ajax, thundering towards us—and on his back, Thais and Nereia. Thais's right hand holds a spear.

Others with more claim on it than I...

I clutch Nikos tight, my other hand shielding the warm dome of his head. And across the agora, Ajax gallops like the wind, and Thais's spear-arm draws back...

And then the spear releases, whirling through the sky, straight and true as if it had an intelligence of its own.

Right where the king's breastplate meets his bare, white throat.

Forty-two

Disbelief contorts his face as the blade finds home. His lips pull back from his teeth; he sways, stumbles, staggers a few paces. And then, at the edge of the platform, he falls. Tumbling to earth only a few feet from where my father's body lies. His body is inert, the blood pooling around him.

The king is dead.

But I feel no joy at the sight. No comfort, even.

Up in the battlements, soldiers are racing for safety. The jeers of the rebels follow them as they flee. The councilmen have taken shelter perhaps, or they are already dead. I do not know. I do not care.

The king is dead.

And so is my father.

I pull myself from the gruesome shelter of dead men's bodies.

"Cowards! Stay and fight!" one of the guard-captains is shouting. But they seem deaf to his cries. Meanwhile I hear murmurs drifting in the crowd.

The Lost Princess, they're saying. *Leonides' daughter*. They have recognized Nereia, it seems—but those are not the only cries. Other in the crowd have already begun to grieve their dead.

"Fire on the rebels!" the captain keeps shouting. "You are the king's guard! You will fight, or die at my hands. Cowards will be executed!"

He only stops when an arrow pierces his heart. Not a rebel arrow—this one was shot by one of his own.

I look for Eros. It's as though my thoughts are slowed, drunken, reeling. It takes me a moment to find him: no longer in the sky but earthbound again, coming towards me. He carries a shield once more, ready to protect me. My heart cracks a little at the sight of him, but I can't go to him. Not yet.

I need to get to my father.

Beside him at last, I crane over his body. His cheek is still warm, but his eyes are misted, their gaze lost, already staring at some other sun. I kneel over him. No air whistles from his lungs, not the smallest whisper. I can hear nothing but my own thudding heart.

It beats, and his does not. My throat is dry. No words, no sounds of sorrow come.

"Psyche—" Eros's voice sounds from right beside me. Time moves like water. Eros reaches for me, lifting something from my arms, and I realize I'm still carrying Nikos. I've got blood on Nikos's cheek: my father's blood. I let Eros take the child. My hands are shaking too much, anyway.

"The arrows are still flying," Eros says. "You should not linger here."

The king's guard may be fleeing, but they still want to save their own skin. Their arrows fly on the defensive now as they retreat. But we're probably more likely to get in the crossfire of one of the rebels giving chase.

I place my hand back on my father's chest.

Still warm.

I did nothing as the arrow pierced him. I did nothing as he fell. I know the moment will play in my dreams forever. That moment right before he came to earth, like Icarus.

I look down at his face now, those eyes still open to the world though the light has left them. I see the sky reflected there.

"You did this!"

Dimitra stands before me, trembling, her voice raw and wild.

"First you took my son, and now—now—" She chokes, and I can feel the wail inside her, a howl she can't let out. I lift my eyes to meet her burning ones.

"You wouldn't listen! You had to be the hero! You had to have the glory. He loved you and you killed him!" Her sobs break into gasps, dry and heaving, as though there's no air left in this world for her.

Can I deny it? My father's dead, and he died saving me. Was there another way? Another world in which the king dies, but my father lives? Then I have kept us from it.

I feel Eros's warm hand on my back. Theron's approaching too, sword in hand, glaring. His men are gathering behind them. To them, my sister is still an enemy, but they know better than to come between us now.

"All I wanted was to save you," I say quietly. "I came here for you."

Her eyes are brimming with tears that won't fall, but beneath them lies rage, harder than steel.

She's upon me then like the wind, her hair and her arms lashing. I turn my face aside as she lunges. I think she will tear my robe from me, or my hair from my head, but it's the leather thong around my neck that her hands land on. Eros steps towards her; Theron and Thais do the same. But it's too late: before anyone can stop her, the leather string has snapped. The amulet is in her fist. Her eyes meet mine, and I feel the desperate thought dawning. I grasp for it, but it's too late.

She turns her head towards the skies and shouts.

"See this, gods? I call upon you! Aphrodite! Sons of Ares! Come and find your justice here!"

She stares at me then, panting, her eyes defiant as they were when we were children. She has no idea what she's done.

"Fool!" My voice is nothing but a whisper. "You'll kill us all." Dread weighs me down like sand. There's no going back now. It's too late: I can tell by the swirling air, by the darkness in the heavens, by the cold current that seems everywhere at once. The others don't understand, but Eros does. I feel the cold ache that goes through him. The knowledge of what is coming.

Dimitra spins toward Eros.

"Give me my son! Now!"

But Theron hauls her back, sword raised and ready. Dark air is funneling around us, a vortex of blackness. Nikos is squalling. People all around the square are calling out, running, while others stand open-mouthed and mesmerized. Our little group stays locked in place. Theron's eyes flick to mine, verifying what he already knows: something terrible is coming.

"Get behind me," Eros says. His voice is even, steady. "*Psyche!* Get behind me! Take the child."

There is no hiding now—the Shroud is broken, there is nowhere for me to go. Nowhere they could not find me. Nikos fusses in my arms, his little hands grasping restlessly. With every animal sense he has, he knows that something's wrong.

Two white specks in the dark sky, faster by far than any birds of prey. Eros's brothers. Not specks for long, they soon take on form, hurtling closer at unnatural speed. Two figures, one flying, the other astride a winged horse. Even Dimitra can only stare.

"You must go now—all of you." Eros raises his voice, addressing the rebels who still linger around us: Theron and his men; Thais and Nereia; Cleon, Drusa, and the children.

"Better they do not find you with us."

Nereia's eyes meet mine, clear and calm. She has no intention of moving. Theron stands his ground, but grips his wife by the arm.

"Take the children," he says. "*Now.*" The rope still binds Cleon's hands; Theron slices through it. But Drusa hesitates.

"The children," Theron repeats, and she nods, once, and takes the young ones' hands in hers.

"Go, boy," Theron hisses to his eldest. "*Go*! You must take care of your mother." He gives the boy a push, and Cleon stumbles, then finally turns to go. His backward glance sears into me: the anguish and fear and pain. And then I turn back, heart heavy, to what's before me.

The winged horse touches earth, gallops to a standstill. The other winged figure alights behind him. My blood runs thin and cold.

The twins are here.

Forty-three

"So, brother," Deimos slips from his horse's back. His one wing trembles, as though in memory of the last time we met: the wing I stole from him.

"You thought you would hide from us forever?"

His face is that of a god: golden, luminous, utterly beautiful. But it is also harsh and pitiless, his eyes cruel and narrow. These are the gods of fear and terror, built for the battlefield.

And this is our battlefield.

My chest is tight, my feet frozen to the ground. The urge to scream, to run, all swallowed by the moment.

I suppose, deep down, I knew they'd find us eventually.

There's panic everywhere around us now, more and more Atlanteans running for the exits. Phobos scoffs, and gestures with his hand. Somewhere behind me there is the sound of crashing stone, as though a pillar has come to earth.

"Get back here and worship your gods, mortals," he smirks. With another flick of his hand, more crashing stone. He's blocking the exits. I hold Nikos tighter, urging him to hush. Eros stands in front of us, trying to block us from view, at least a little longer. Without seeing it, I know the expression on his face. I can feel the determination and the pain. He will fight to the last breath, but there are two of them and only one of him.

Dimitra stands pale and wide-eyed, some inkling dawning of what she's done—but too late.

"So here you are, brother." Phobos glances at his twin, as though sharing a joke. His wings are bone-white, his teeth sharp as a hunting cat's. "In Atlantis, all this time. Who would have guessed it? And yet, I think we heard a whisper, did we not, Deimos? Some new god they had dredged up."

"The shadowed god," Deimos supplies, his eyes locked

on the cloaked shape in front of me.

"That's right," Phobos agrees. "*The Shadowed God*." He scoffs. "We thought it must be some jumped-up mountain sprite, giving himself airs. We should have come to investigate sooner, shouldn't we?"

They are mere paces away now, advancing slowly, surely.

"You're not in the shadows now, brother," Deimos sneers, and his eyes swerve over Eros's shoulder. "And neither is your little mortal. Lost your Shroud, have we, my lady?"

"You will not harm her." Eros adjusts his stance, trying once more to block me from view. The baby wails and squirms again. A wave of dread comes over me. What was I thinking? I should have had Dimitra take him when we had the chance. He should be in any other hands than mine.

The child wails again.

"What's this?" Phobos's voice hovers dangerously. He pushes past Eros, his narrow eyes gliding over mine with disgust, then fixing on Nikos. Dimitra pushes towards us, but Deimos holds her back.

"*Ektroma,*" Phobos hisses.

Ektroma. A word for something that shouldn't have been born: a monster, an abomination. Something against the natural order. My hands are trembling cold as I hold the child tighter.

"No," Dimitra pants, pushing against Deimos, trying to free herself.

"Deimos," Phobos calls. "Our brother has spawned a halfling."

Deimos's features twist in revulsion.

"You are mistaken—" Eros snaps.

"He's *mine*!" Dimitra shouts. "The child is mine! Ask anyone."

"It's true," I say. "He's a simple mortal, my sister's child." I'm trying hard not to shake. I don't want them to have the satisfaction of seeing me afraid.

"Fool," Deimos sneers. "You think you can lie to us? You think we cannot tell from its face which of you whelped the bastard?"

Cold seeps through me. *He has a look of you.* Nereia said it, Irini said it, even the king said it. Now I wish I could destroy those words.

"He's my sister's," I raise my voice, looking Eros's brothers in the eye. "Not mine."

"They speak the truth," Eros says, his voice still and calm, but with a danger underneath it.

"Filth," Deimos murmurs, turning to Eros. "You'd pollute your blood like this?" And before I can move, he's pulling Nikos from my arms.

"No!" I scream, along with my sister. "He's done nothing! He's not what you think!"

"You will not harm the child," Eros says. I feel the ground tremble beneath my feet; his voice seems to come from the earth itself.

"You will not harm any of these mortals. Any fight you have is with me. I'll go with you—I'll go willingly—as long as you leave them untouched."

"You should have left *her* untouched," Phobos sneers, eying me.

"*Give me my son*!" Dimitra shouts, over Nikos's wailing.

"Where's your magic knife now, little brother?" Deimos laughs. He tosses the child to Phobos. "You take this one; I'll take care of the girl."

Dimitra screams and throws herself at Phobos, but with the back of his hand he sends her flying to the ground. She moans, and goes still. My heart contracts. I race towards Phobos, but Eros is ahead of me.

"Now, now, brother." Deimos catches my arm, his grip like ice. "Are you sure you want to make me angry?"

"Let her go," Eros says. His voice full of a terrible calm.

"Or what?" Deimos hisses. "You'll take my other wing?"

Eros lunges for him but Deimos blocks it, and with his other hand, throws me to the ground. I scramble up but he pushes me back as if it were nothing, then waves a hand and the ground subsides beneath me, the stone crumbling. I'm in a crater, up past my waist, scrambling like a sinking swimmer.

Eros lands his blow this time, and Deimos grunts, staggers a little. Eros hauls back for another blow, but he doesn't see what I see: Phobos striding to the water's edge, the baby in his arms. He means to throw him to the waves.

"Eros!" I scream, and he turns, understands. He moves to race after Phobos, but now Deimos is back on his feet, grabbing his arm before he can break away.

"No you don't. That halfling filth must be disposed of."

This time it's Deimos who lands the punch. Eros gasps out a breath as his brother's fist collides with his chest. He hasn't had time to recover from the king's arrow.

Thais is running to help me out of the pit; Theron races towards Deimos. Deimos's blow sends him instantly to the ground, but gives Eros a moment to gather himself, and aim his fist straight for his brother's face. With Thais's help I get one hand free of the pit, but Deimos, staggering, brings his heel down on the other, blinding me with pain, and I lose my grip.

Nikos. We don't have much time.

I look back to where Phobos has almost reached the water's edge. And Dimitra—where's Dimitra? I didn't see her get up, but she's not sprawled where Phobos left her. Then suddenly my eyes land on her. I don't understand. She's crouched where the king fell, wrestling something from his body. What's she doing; what about Nikos?

Between them, Thais and Nereia wrench me from the pit. My arm shrieks with pain, but pain is meaningless now. Only Eros can save my nephew—but not while Deimos keeps him trapped here.

"With me!" Thais tosses me a sword from the ground: the sword of a dead man. She raises her own, and together we charge toward Deimos. We don't stand a chance—we can't defeat him. But just for a moment, we can distract him.

He swings for Eros again, but misses, and Eros, as though he's been conserving all his strength for this moment, hurls his brother bodily into the ground, slamming him against rock. In the moments it takes Deimos to rise again, Eros is racing towards Phobos and the child.

But Dimitra is already there. *Almost upon him.*

Phobos's back is towards her; if he hears her coming, he doesn't care, doesn't even bother to turn. But in a flash I understand. I know what she was rifling the king's body for. I remember the quiver of arrows. *Adamantine* arrows. The ones he was shooting at Eros.

I watch, breathless, as my sister charges at Phobos's back. I see him half-turn, and scoff. He sees only a stupid mortal woman, helpless before a god.

I watch Dimitra leap, fist raised, the arrow like a dagger in her grip. And she clings like a wild animal to Phobos's back, drives her adamantine arrow into his throat.

Time stops.

For a moment, the sun itself seems to blink out.

The sky swirls.

Before he falls, Dimitra wrests the child from him, then stands there as he crumples. *Ichor* rains purple from his throat.

There's a ringing in my ears.

Beside me, Deimos chokes out a breath of disbelief.

"Phobos? *Phobos!*" he calls, as though his twin will rise and wipe the blood from his throat. But the blood trickles from Phobos's throat to his chest, and the god lies still upon the earth.

The sky swirls like the world is ending. Deimos races across the stone, and falls to his brother's side.

"What vile illusion is this?"

"It is no illusion," Eros says. His voice is heavy; stunned. A god. *A god is dead.* I knew it could be done, I knew what those arrows were. And yet the finality of it, of seeing it happen, makes my head spin.

With a roar, Deimos rises from his brother's side.

He lunges for Dimitra, but before he can grasp her, Eros throws his weight on top of him. Together they fall to the ground, a swirl of wings and limbs stained with their brother's blood.

The sky darkens, the air shifts again. The ground trembles. It seems as if the earth itself understands that a god has died, and is rebelling at such an abomination. It is not the first time a god has died. They say when the god Kronos was killed by his son Zeus, the heavens rained for forty days and forty nights; that the earth ripped open and mountains sank beneath the sea. But this time, for the first time, a god has been slain by a mortal.

With Nikos in her arms, Dimitra walks shakily back towards us. Deimos and Eros are fighting as though they will never stop. One lands a blow, then the other; one stumbles to his feet, so does the other. Then another blow brings them both back to earth, locked in this pounding rhythm. The damage they do with their fists—fists that could break a mortal man's neck in an instant—is a reminder of what a god's immortality means; that they could battle until the end of time and neither would break a limb or even bruise.

It is only adamantine that has changed all that.

The earth shakes again—harder, this time. And then again, hard enough that I fall to my knees. I hear Nikos wailing, and look over. My sister is on her knees, too, Nikos clutched to her chest.

And then I see her eyes open wider, her mouth fall open. She's staring at something behind me as she raises a trembling finger and points.

"Psyche," she says. "Psyche, *look*."

I turn, and feel my throat close over.

Forty-four

The Red Mountain.

Smoke is spilling from its throat; a red-black syrup trickles out and down one side. I remember Evander the stable-hand, and his story.

When the mountain last ran red, half our people were lost.

Men and women are falling to their knees all around us. The exits are still blocked, but even if they weren't—where to run to, now?

I stare at the blood-colored streak. "How fast will it run?"

"I don't know." It's Nereia's voice, tight as a clenched fist. "There is nobody alive who remembers the last time. But the stories say it was a matter of hours, not days."

Thais looks at me.

"This is the gods' doing, isn't it?" She glances back toward the Red Mountain, her voice a mix of awe and horror. "Surely it is the work of the Fire-Wielder."

Hephaestus, blacksmith to the gods, fire-wielder: he's Aphrodite's consort. He would do anything she commands. And if any god can make a mountain spew molten rock, it is him.

"We must pray," Drusa says, pulling Theron down beside her, making the children get on their knees.

"Aphrodite, great goddess." Her voice shakes. "Please, in your grief, show us mercy."

But no answer comes on the wind. If anything, the molten river only spews harder, faster.

Drusa puts a hand across her face, muffling a sob.

"Eros!"

He does not hear me. His ears are ringing with his brother's blows.

"Eros!" I force his name from my throat, and from my mind, calling to him with all the strength I have.

Eros pants, pushing Deimos from him for a moment. In the glance he throws my way, I see him see it all. If we don't do something, it will be a massacre. We may not have much time. Already it may be too late.

"We need your help. Atlantis can't survive this."

Deimos has seen the mountain too. He takes a step back from his brawling, a cold look spreading across his face.

"Do you see this, mortals?" He raises his voice, letting it echo all over the great square. "It will cover this island, and you will burn, every last one of you, and as you burn, you will scream. Scream *his* name, then"—he points to Eros—"for *he* is your murderer."

Deimos lifts his brother's lifeless body from the ground, summons the winged horse, and lays Phobos gently over its back.

"Brother—" Eros tries, but Deimos turns to him with a hiss.

"I have no brother," he spits. "The only brother I had, you killed. You armed these demon-mortals, you set them on him like rats. Your brother, who should have lived forever!" His eyes are rimmed with red, his voice shakes. "He and I were born together. He pulled me into the world with him. And now he's dead."

I see the flash of grief across Eros's face. The word *dead* still so unfathomable.

Deimos climbs up on the horse's back, behind his brother's body. Then they're in the air, climbing. Leaving us all on a burning island. But some last, small motion makes me turn again, before they disappear into the sky. And suddenly I see a dark fleck is moving through the air, a dark fleck with a jet-black tip.

"Eros!" I scream, running towards him.

He moves, just in time. The arrow, its shaft still bloody, buries itself in the ground where he had stood. The arrow from Phobos's throat.

My heart turns over. Deimos and his horse disappear into the clouds.

Small groups are forming across the agora, people huddling, silent or weeping or praying. The old king's guard, those who still live, lie bound or hog-tied, the king's councilmen with them. The rebels—Theron's men, the Kytherans, the other Atlanteans—are re-forming, as though waiting for instruction. But who is to instruct them? What can swords and arrows do, against a mountain of fire?

"Is this Aphrodite's work?" I ask Eros. He says nothing for a moment. For the first time ever, perhaps, words have deserted him.

"Perhaps. But I do not think so," he manages. "A god is dead, and the bones of the earth know it. Nothing can undo it."

A god is dead.

And so is my father.

I can feel the spot where he lies, cold and still, behind me. Where are the mountains that melt in his name? Where are the skies that weep, the seas that tear themselves to shreds? The black-red stream is moving down the mountain, thicker now, cloaking the earth beneath it like blood.

"Do you know what you have done?" Eros grips Dimitra by the arm. "Do you understand what you summoned? My brother, a god, is dead. It is through grace alone that your child still lives; that you and your sister still live."

A brother who would have killed us both. And yet his brother, nonetheless. I will not judge his grief, but he must save it for another hour. We all must.

As for Dimitra, for once she has no words to say in her defense. Her dark eyes look vacant, almost lifeless. Even Nikos is quiet.

Eros looks at me, shakes his head.

"There is nothing I can do to stop it. Not even to slow it. They must evacuate the island. It is the only way." He glances at the mountain. The red river is swelling, moving faster and faster.

"The southeast is already lost. But if they hurry, they may save the rest."

Nereia comes forward, Thais on one side, Kallias on the other. "We must take to the water. The king's ships. He has been building a navy, has he not?"

Mutely, Dimitra nods.

Nereia turns to face us all, her voice louder than I've yet heard it, and commanding.

"The fleet is large. We'll board as many as we can onto ships, get them out of here until it's safe to return. We'll send messenger pigeons from the castle to alert our neighbors, and ask for refuge. We'll take stores from the palace, and load the boats." She casts a look around the square. Many of the island's people are already here, at the tyrant's summons. Theron judged it to be half the island, though I fear that was optimistic.

"We must send out riders to round up the people. Raid the king's stables for the fastest horses. The people must leave their homes, leave everything," Nereia continues. "Those with fishing boats may make their own way, and carry as many of their neighbors as they can. The rest must hasten here and board the king's fleet."

The men murmur among themselves. No one contests the plan. It is a flimsy enough one, but it is all we have. One by one, the riders claim their routes.

"I'll go east," Belos says.

"And I, south," another volunteers. A dozen more divide up villages, territories. It is a small island, at least. They may reach many, in little enough time. But for the easternmost part of the island…for those, it is surely already too late.

"What if they will not come?" Cleon turns to his father. His voice is thin and nervous—fearful of what's coming, and of the men's hatred for him.

"Gods help them," Thais says quietly. "If they survive the flood of fire, they will perish in the ash that follows."

"We'll be refugees," Cleon murmurs.

He's right. The Atlanteans—those who survive—will be homeless, and who knows for how long. This is the kingdom Nereia wanted to reclaim—and soon, there may be nothing left of it but ash, and a flotilla of refugees.

*

"We start at once," Nereia says. Eros has rolled the boulders from the exits, and two dozen of the rebels have set out on their mission, riding stolen horses of the king's. Thais was one of the volunteers, riding out on Ajax. But for those thousands of Atlanteans still gathered in the great square, there is no time to waste. Luckily, the access to the shipyard is easy, and the boats are moored close enough to land. But as we rally them to start boarding, Dimitra speaks up.

"The dead," she says. Her eyes go to the spot where Father lies. "We cannot leave them littered here like so much detritus, only to be coated in tar and ash. They need a burial."

"We have no time for that," Belos snaps.

"And you, woman, are no one's queen now," Kallias adds. "It is not for you to say what must be."

"So you would deny them their next life?" She lifts her eyes to the men. "They are your kin. Without proper rites, they will not make it to the Next Realm."

Theron sets his jaw.

"And what do you propose?"

"One boat," she says. "Just one. The rest for the living."

The idea is not popular with everyone.

"We need all the boats we can get," Belos snaps. "Or the living will *become* the dead."

But Dimitra is not alone in her thinking. The people are not sheep; they will not let us decide for them. And many are calling out in support. Sons and brothers, mothers and sisters, too many have died in the crossfire today. And so the first of the king's boats becomes the boat of the dead. We move as efficiently as we can, the strongest dividing into groups, bearing the bodies in and laying them down. The women move around the ship, placing coins on eyes, saying the parting words.

I see again the moment of my father's fall, the red stain blooming on his robe. I see Dimitra on her knees, her body thrust forward in a prayer, as if to stop the moment from being real. It was how she used to look when we were girls, when, after bathing, she'd kneel in the courtyard and fling her wet hair forward, letting the sun dry it.

How strange, to remember that now. Those memories belong to some other woman, some other life.

The coins are cold; Father's skin still warm. He would have wished to be buried in Sikyon, but Sikyon is no more—his home is already dead.

Godspeed to the next kingdom, Father.

They bear more bodies onto the boat, rebels and kingsmen and civilians alike. They make quick work of it. My sister and I take Father's hands, one each, and say our silent farewells.

"He loved you most," Dimitra says. "Always."

I say nothing. I do not think she is wrong, but the words can only cause pain to us both.

Out of love, he chose not to see.

I banish those dream-words from my mind. They make no sense, and I have no room for them now. I have no room even for grief. All of it must wait.

The boat is launched out to sea, and our archers shoots flame-arrows to set it alight.

And then we attend to the living.

*

"Move down!" I call as we load them in, family after family. "Make room!"

They shuffle down the boards of the great ships, packing in tighter. Theron and Drusa, Thais and Nereia are on the dock, trying to keep order. Eros and I are among those in the water, marshalling the people into the boats.

In the distance the seas are flat and calm, but here, around the island, they are choppy and dark, and seem to be getting worse every minute. The erupting mountain, the unnatural storm, all part of the same thing. The air itself seems charged with dread, and the distant, sunlit horizon hovers like some strange dream.

A dream the other side of a nightmare.

The mountain is a mass of molten red now, no longer a trickle. If there are homes near its base, they are long destroyed. Any who doubted Nereia's proposal to take to the seas must see now: there is no other way.

The riders have started to return, bringing villagers with them.

Nereia, on horseback, rides into the water, approaching Eros and me.

"I've sent men to gather food stores from the palace. Who knows how long we'll be at sea. The people must not starve."

She's right—and Atlantis has few friends these days. If its neighbors do not come to the people's aid, the supplies may need to last some time.

"I have sent Thais, and some men she trusts, to take the gold from the palace treasury." Nereia frowns, her face clouding over. "We must not weigh down the ships too much. And yet, if my people are to be refugees, better they be rich ones." She pauses. "We may need to buy some friendship, in days ahead."

I doubt there have been many monarchs of Atlantis who wished to divvy up the king's coffers between its citizens. But Nereia's words tell me something else.

"You don't believe we're coming back here, do you?"

She looks at Eros, his face shrouded behind the cape. But I think she can read him just as I can; she feels the words he does not want to say.

You will not see these shores again.

The waters are becoming stormier and stormier all the time. A wave seems to come out of nowhere, and I hold my breath for the ships already far from land. Meanwhile we pack the last family onto this ship and ready them for launch. A woman with two sons grips the rail, her fearful eyes on mine.

"Safe journey," I say, and she nods, trying to keep the fear at bay as Eros unmoors the boat.

"Rowers, ready your oars!" Eros calls.

As the ship leaves port he stays out in the water, knee-deep, his focus on the vessel as it moves off to join those already launched. But it's the ones out front we need to worry about—the swell seems at its worst there. I catch my breath as one lurches dangerously in a new blast of wind, but Eros puts out a hand, and the boat rights itself once more.

"This storm," I shout beside him to make myself heard. "It's not natural."

He shakes his head, his eyes still fixed on the ships at sea. He keeps his hand outstretched, guiding, steering.

"Deimos was right. The death of a god…it tears at the fabric of things."

"How long will it last?" Waves crash next to my ear, I can hardly hear my own voice.

"I cannot say."

He moves his hand, righting another ship which is rocking too hard. He cannot stop the storm, but this much, he can do.

Storm-rains have started to pelt down on us, but still in the distance, molten rock gushes from the mountain like a cauldron running over. Soon that pool of red rock will become a flood. It will engulf this place, destroying everything in its path.

I catch sight of Drusa and her children among the crowds. Soon it will be their turn to board. But there is someone I keep looking for, a face I can't find no matter how many times I scan the dock. Where is my sister? Where is Nikos? Surely they are in the line somewhere. Women and children are being given priority; surely, any moment, I will see their faces.

The water laps around my thighs. I stare down. How is it so high, all of a sudden? Before, it was barely to my knees. When I look back to the dock I see the water lapping at its edges, where before it had a foot of clearance.

"The water," I call out to Eros. "It's rising!"

He nods, grim.

Theron comes forward, hands little Helia into my arms, and hoists Xenon onto the boat. Drusa holds Cleon by the hand. Wild-eyed, his wet hair plastered to his head, I see him now for the child he still is. The rain splashes into our eyes, matting our hair to our foreheads.

Drusa shakes her head.

"What's happening?" she shouts through the rain. "How is it flooding like this?" The rain's heavy, but not *that* heavy.

Theron looks at her, and then at me.

"It's not," he says, his voice hard-edged with knowledge. "The island is sinking."

I stare at him.

"But islands float," Cleon protests. "They're *islands.*"

Theron looks out over the fields of molten red.

"*That* lay, until moments ago, in a cavern under the earth. Now the cavern is empty, and water runs in to fill it. As the water rushes in, the island grows heavier."

Drusa stares at him, as do I. I look at the red sea pouring forth from the volcano's mouth. Then at the water sloshing over the dock, already wetting the ankles of the crowd.

"How fast will it happen?

Theron sighs.

"Faster than we'd like."

"Then come on!" Cleon, boarded now, reaches a hand back down to his father. "Quickly!" The boat is almost full; soon it will be time to push off.

But Theron shakes his head, retreats a step.

"I can't."

Drusa stares, stricken.

"*Theron—*"

"Theron," I urge. "You've done enough. Get on the boat with your family."

He hesitates, his head low. Then he looks back at Drusa.

"I can't." He looks at Drusa. "Not yet."

Cleon stares at him, the boy's eyes red and disbelieving.

"But we need you. *We* need you, Father."

"I'll catch you up, you'll see." He puts a hand on Cleon's head, briefly. "Remember, we have a god on our side."

His words pinch my heart. The faith he has in us.

Drusa's face is like a ghost. Helia wails in her arms. Cleon glances my way, his eyes like two wounds, raw and bright with pain.

"Cast off!" Someone calls, and the mooring-line slips free; the boat begins to drift from shore. It bounces and shudders. Someone retches over the side of the hull.

"Godspeed," I murmur into the galing winds. I don't raise my glance to the passengers staring back at us. I don't want to see Drusa's eyes among them.

Forty-five

I can feel the crowd's anxiety, their doubt. Eros is keeping the boats afloat thus far, but it looks increasingly perilous, the worse these waves become. Back on land, the crowds waiting to board are growing harder and harder to manage. At first they were reluctant to board the ships, but now they are fighting each other to get to the front. And I see why. The riders have done a good job alerting the townships, getting the people to ride or run here. But though the crowd seems to show no sign of dwindling, our fleet is. The terrible truth creeps into my bones: there are not enough ships for all these people.

"Eros!" I wade out towards him. The wind buffets his cloak, and his golden hands are outstretched like a weaver's, the sea his loom.

"There aren't enough boats. What are we to do? We can't leave them behind." My voice hitches. It's all too much. Too many people lost already; others being lost, even now, on the eastern borders.

"Keep boarding them," Eros says, his voice far away, steady as a trance. "Just keep boarding the boats. When you reach the last one, come and get me. I will see to it. But for now, I must keep the vanguard safe."

His words give me some comfort, though not enough. At least what he's doing with the boats is working. It looks as though the first few have made it past the storm's limit, out into calm waters. A few are safe, at least—but there are so many left.

Nereia has come to join me in the water, now that Eros is fully occupied.

"You should board the next boat," I tell her. "The people will want to see that you are safe."

She glances at me.

"Soon."

The crowds are moving quickly now, having seen their friends and families board and leave them; no one wants to be left behind. A quick glance beyond shows the lava has spread further past the bottom of the mountain now, glistening in a red fury under these dark skies.

"Nereia!" Thais is wading into the water. "You have to board this one. Please!"

Nereia hoists a child onto one of the boats; both parents' arms are already full with other children.

"I will, when my people are safe."

Thais glares. "This is no time to be a martyr. You are their princess."

Nereia looks her in the eye.

"No: I am their queen. And I will see them to safety before I board any ship."

Thais closes her eyes. I see her pain, her fear. So does Nereia.

"Even for you, Thais," she says gently. "Even for you, I cannot."

I stare out at the creeping tide of molten earth. Soon, all too soon, it will become a tide of death. Meanwhile, the waters grow choppier all the time. If these waves get much higher, I don't know if these ships can even make it out of the harbor.

And then, through the jostling and the shouting, I see the face I've been looking for, the one I know like my own.

"Dimitra!" I turn to Nereia. "I will return. I must speak with my sister."

I wade in towards the shore. The water is up to my waist now, though I'm treading inland.

"Dimitra!"

She's not lining up to board with the rest. She's standing by herself, a little ways away. She's staring out at the water, but she does not look afraid. She turns as I approach. Her eyes look focused, but not on the scene at hand. I cannot understand it, this lack of urgency. She's still in shock, perhaps.

"Dimitra—you must get in line. Please! What are you doing out here?"

She looks at me, blinks.

"We won't be going that way."

A chill runs through me.

"What are you talking about? There is no other way."

"There is—for us. You'll see." She looks down at the child. "You don't yet understand, Psyche. You don't know what Nikos is."

I stare at her. Has she lost her senses? Has the horror of today driven her to this?

"Lady Psyche." Theron appears at my side. "The people are raising uproar. We know, and they know, there are not enough boats. I cannot think how such a miracle is to be achieved." He looks at me, something pleading in his eyes. "What of the god—can he help us?"

"He has promised to." I pull my eyes from Dimitra and the child, looking behind me to where Eros still stands in the rising water, guiding the boats that have already left the shore. We're making progress: almost half of them seem to have reached the calm beyond this unnatural storm. But the crowd on the dock is another story. They're shouting, pushing, fights breaking out all over. I fear someone will soon be trampled underfoot. Thais calls from the dock:

"People of Atlantis—we must keep our calm! Trust us!"

"They're lying to us! They're liars!" someone is shouting in the crowd.

"They said the god would save us, but he won't! We'll die here!"

"It's time to fetch Eros," I tell Theron. Those ships in the storm need him, too, but we can't stem this tide on our own.

*

"All those who fought today: bring me your spears, your swords, your arrows." Eros stands on the dock, his voice booming over the mutinous crowd. I see him steal a glance out to sea. Almost all the boats have reached the calm waters now. Only two have yet to breach it.

"Waste no time," he urges. "Bring the weapons of the dead if you have none of your own."

Faces all over the crowd stare up at him.

"Do as the Shadowed God says!" Kallias hollers, and tosses a spear at Eros's feet. Rain pelts down upon us all. Eros nods.

"Two more. Right here."

A couple more spears arrive. In an instant, he breaks the metal tips from the wood.

"Now: like this."

He shows them how the wooden shafts are to be arranged: in a triangle, the three spokes interlocking so that each supports the others. An infinity shape—no beginning, no end. Eros moves his hand across them, a coaxing gesture.

"Step back," he commands. The spears begin to rattle and shift. They branch little tendrils, as though their wood is no longer dead but still green and quick; tendrils become vines, and vines, in an instant, thick as roots, then thick as trunks.

I can feel the energy humming from Eros's body; his total focus.

Even the most defiant in the crowd start to hush. It's as though the wood itself holds some magic of its own—and perhaps it does, perhaps there is such magic in the heart of all things—as it stirs and shifts, reshaping itself, reaching towards the sky. It swells and twists and curves, forming the lines of a ship, hull gleaming with an otherworldly sheen.

It is a moment of awe, quickly interrupted by a shout from the crowd.

"The waves!"

Another gale comes off the sea, roaring so hard that it brings me to my knees. But through the rain, I see them—the last two ships to leave harbor. The only two still in the thick of this storm. Fools! They've put their sails up! They were supposed to row until they reached the calm. But they were too eager, and now they're harnessing more wind than any ship can bear, heeling dangerously in the ever-increasing winds. One tilts further, on the point of capsizing.

Theron lets out a strangled cry. And then I see the small, golden-haired figure on the stern, clutching the rigging, climbing it like she's trying to escape.

Helia.

I feel her screaming into the wind. Her cries are too distant to reach our ears, but in my mind I hear them all the same: *Papa!*

The boat tosses wildly, rearing like an animal.

Eros turns, cursing. The ship is so close to overturning now, I'm not sure if even he can reverse fate. His fingers shake; a tremor passes up his outstretched arms. I race down to the water's edge. Theron's in front of me, Nereia beside me. Somehow, against all laws of nature, Eros begins to tug the ship upright. But then a swell bounces the vessel's stern high, and the small, golden figure plunges from the rigging into the dark waves. My blood freezes. Theron lets out a strangled cry. He runs into the water, his thick limbs splashing wildly, senselessly. And I remember what Drusa told me: Theron can't swim.

"Theron!"

Nereia grips my hand, points. Out on the boat, another figure has pushed onto the top of the stern, standing above the waves. It's Cleon. Drusa's grasping at his robes, trying to hold him back, but he frees himself from her grip and dives into the black water.

He's trying to save her.

Beside me, Nereia doesn't hesitate. One shallow dive and she's under the water, carving out towards the boat.

Father always said I was a strong swimmer. I take a deep breath, and plunge.

Forty-six

The water is cold and dark. It rushes through me in a gasp. When I come to the surface, panting, waves rip past me and around me. I take another breath, and go under again.

The thrashing waves have kicked up grit, making it hard to see underwater. And above, the rain is pelting so hard, it's not easy to make out where I'm going. The boats in the distance seem farther than they did from shore. Back on the dock, others have pulled Theron back from the waves and are struggling to keep order, stemming the chaos that has broken out there. I hear Thais calling Nereia's name.

Psyche. I feel Eros's voice reach me, in my mind and all through me, reverberating in my ribcage. *Psyche, get out of the water.*

But I can't. I'm more than halfway to the ship now. I feel my way by instinct, by the sound and thrust of Nereia's kicking feet, by glimpses through the rain. Salt stings my eyes and throat and nostrils with every new wave; the water pulls at me hungrily. I plough through the cold, and as I near the boat I hear the keening of the women and shouting of the men, gesturing wildly to the spot where the children disappeared. But there is no sign of them now.

Nereia dives, surfaces, dives again. I try the same, breathless as I already feel. But the water is dark and empty, yielding nothing.

And then both of us glimpse it: a flash of golden hair, just a glimpse before the wave swallows her again.

"You get her," Nereia shouts. "I'll look for Cleon."

She's already beneath the water. I dive back through the waves, keeping my eyes on the spot where Helia flashed into view. The water sloshes up and over me. I have to focus. I cannot think of those other, unsaved lives today. I must think only of this one, only of Helia.

Papa. I hear the voice in my head again, but weakly now. *Papa, help!*

I swim towards it. The water bobs and flattens again and finally I see her. She's face down in the water. My heart quickens. I reach her in three more strokes. I swim under her, grab one dangling wrist, and tug from there until she spins onto her back, a limp weight floating.

Stay alive, I think, heart pounding. *Only stay alive.*

With her face clear of the water, I hook an arm around her little bird-chest, and start to haul us in the direction of the boat.

"Find a rope!" I scream up at them. "Find something!"

I scan the water for Nereia, for Cleon, but all I see are the heaving green-black waves without end.

When a rope lands in the water, I knot it around Helia's small torso, under her arms. She's not conscious yet, but I can feel her pulse. I slam hard against the hull of the boat, yelling against the wind.

"Lift!"

They begin to haul her up. And with a burst of hope, I see two more figures surface, gasping violently for breath. Nereia's found him—but he's struggling, thrashing.

"Cleon!" I hear her yell. "If you want to live, stop fighting me! You're going to drown us both!"

He claws at the water, at Nereia, his breath panicked and choking. She slaps at his face.

"Cleon! Listen to me!"

His breaths turn to sobs, but he's stopped fighting.

Only then do I see the mighty wave surging up behind us.

"Watch out!" I scream. My eyes close. I feel the crash, the jerking sensation as the water tugs me downward. I blink through the grit, and swim towards the light until I breach the surface.

There's yelling on the boat, shouts of relief. They've got Helia safe. Another rope is in the water, and Nereia somehow manages to knot it around the boy's waist. She pulls the knot tight, securing it, and tells him where to grip the rope.

"Hold this," she instructs him. "Brace your legs against the hull."

In moments, he's clear of the water. But before we can exhale I feel the surge, the pull and sweep of another wave coming.

Too hungry. Too fast.

For a split-second, Nereia meets my eyes. I see the fire in them: the animal fear that any animal must have, but also something greater than that, something human and proud and fierce. Something greater than the fear.

And then, before I have time to turn and see what's behind me, I feel it close over me.

I'm pulled under. Deeper than before, and faster, sucking the air from my lungs. The light disappears like a snuffed candle. When I open my eyes I can't see the surface—no light at all, just eddies of grey and black. The water tears at me, tosses me this way and that. I am nothing. No more than a pebble in its great, heaving maw.

There's no air left in me. My chest feels like it's going to explode. I cast around for light, for some sign of the surface. But I see none.

I cannot give up. My father gave his life for me today. I won't let this be what he died for.

I push out, hoping I've got it right; hoping I'm swimming towards the surface, and not closer to the bottom. In another stroke or two, perhaps, I'll see the light.

And then I feel strong arms lifting me, hauling me into the air. Black wings beating near my face.

Eros.

I shiver in his arms. Water streams from my limbs. His grip is fast. I hear his voice against my ear, but I don't hear what he says. I blink my eyes open, feeling the wind keen against them. Below us is the expanse of black water. The ship is behind us, the dock in front. And from the dock, I hear screaming.

"Nereia!" I remember. "Nereia—where is she?"

"She went under in the same wave that took you." His

voice is grim, flattened of emotion. A darkness washes over my heart.

"I will go back for her."

The men on the docks are holding Thais back; she struggles in their grip, trying to launch herself into the sea.

"Nereia!" she screams. "*Nereia*!"

"Phylax Thais," Kallias is urging. "Please. Come to higher ground."

The flooding is getting worse. As a wave rears up over the dock there are screams, people tugging each other back towards safety.

"*Nereia*!" Thais screams again, her voice cracking.

The second I'm on dry land, Eros turns and swoops back over the water, back to the spot where Nereia went under. The first time he goes under, I'm expecting to see him re-emerge with a figure in his arms. And then he goes under again.

This time, I think. But again he is empty-handed. He ducks and dives, over and over, and every time he rises from the waves, my stomach drops a little lower.

Thais has stopped screaming now. She's not weeping, either. She's perfectly silent, like someone who knows they'll never have need of a voice again.

Twenty breaths. Forty. One hundred.

Two hundred; three. I look over at Thais by the water's edge. I see it in her face, in her stance. She knows it in her heart, as I know it in mine: no one could survive under the waves this long.

When Eros finally lifts the limp body from the water, I feel it, the one-word song in Thais's mind.

Agony, it whispers, over and over.

*

Nereia's body has already been carried onto the last ship, held aloft by the men who fought for her this morning. Our final fleet—the one conjured from the soldiers' spears—is already on the waves, under Eros's guidance. Only this last ship remains,

The storm pelts down. The agora is mostly underwater now, well past my knees. Meanwhile, the red sea from that unholy mountain blazes farther and farther across the land, creeping ever closer to our gates. The air is full of fevered urgency as we board the very last of our people, and yet a great pall hangs over us, too. The new ships were boarded in near silence. Nereia's fate was one of many noble deaths today, but the sight cut through all who saw it. I have tried to pack the memory down inside me, confined alongside the last image of my father. I will take those memories out later, like bitter gemstones, to hold and touch and remember. While we linger on a doomed island, we do not have the luxury of grief.

I walk to where Thais stands by the water.

"We must board," I say. "The fire-lake approaches." We have already left it to the last minute.

"Strange, isn't it?" she murmurs. "Even a god cannot bring back the dead."

I think of that last glimpse I had of Nereia. I believe, now, that she knew what was coming. And yet she met it with those steady eyes, that steady soul. She was a queen indeed.

"She was not afraid," I say to Thais, who looks up at me, dry-eyed.

"And I shall never be afraid again," she says. "How could I be? I had only one thing to fear, and now it has happened."

My heart breaks for her.

"This is not the only kingdom," I remind her quietly. "You will see her face again."

She's silent then. Her eyes move away from the sea, over to the final ship, ready to push off. Eros stands by the boarding-planks, guiding the last passengers on.

Theron approaches. He looks ashen-faced, and I understand why. Nereia would not be dead, had Cleon not jumped from the boat. Cleon would not have jumped, but for Helia. Helia would not have fallen, if Theron had been there.

He gestures at the boat, all but ready to depart. He has come to herd us on.

"We board the last among us." His voice is hoarse. He

hesitates. "Phylax Thais…I have no words."

She closes her eyes.

"It was not your fault, Theron. You risked everything for her, and she knew it."

I excuse myself. The water is rising, the fire spreading, and there is one person that I, too, must gather.

I locate her on a rocky outcrop, dangerously close to the water's edge. Sea-foam is hurling high over the top, rough enough to blind us both, and making the stone slippery.

"Dimitra," I say nervously. "What are you doing? We must go—the last ship makes ready to launch."

She turns, and an eerie feeling takes root in my chest. The way she's standing so close to the edge. The strange look in her voice.

"Nikos could get hurt. Please. Step away from the edge."

She looks at me.

"Nikos won't get hurt, Psyche." She glances down at him, smooths a hand over his hair, then back at me. "His father will look after him."

I stare at her. These are words of madness.

"The king is dead—"

"Not the king," she scoffs, as though I am some kind of fool. I hear a rumble in the distance, from the direction of the Red Mountain. A sound that should terrify me, but all I can focus on now is Dimitra.

"Don't tell me you haven't heard the rumors," she says. "You don't *really* believe he was Kostas's son?"

I stare at her, at Nikos. I remember that strange, almost secretive satisfaction I saw so often, when she looked at him. As if she knew something the rest of us didn't. *He will be a great man,* she'd said. More than just a mother's pride. As if she knew it already. As though it had been foreordained.

"You are not the only one, sister," she smirks at me, "who can lay with a god. And I have lain with a more powerful god than yours."

My thoughts are spinning. Do I believe her? My nephew, a *god-child*? I shake my head. It doesn't matter what I believe, not now. Miracles or delusions are all the same. What matters is getting us all off this island.

"Call your father," I hear her say then, perfectly distinct, perfectly calm, like she's standing in the middle of an open field, and not in the middle of a raging storm.

"Call him and tell him to bring us home."

She holds Nikos out over the water. My stomach lurches.

"Dimitra!"

But Nikos claps his little hands together, and the sound feels more powerful than it ought, as though beyond the soft press of a baby's flesh there's something else echoing, resounding. Nikos burbles, and the sound carries too, even across the lashing waves. And then he lifts his little arms up in glee as a new wave rises in the distance.

A wave unlike the other waves. It follows no rhythm, no sequence as it rises, pushes towards us. It is sheer as a wall, glassy, an almost luminous green. The wave rises to the height of a man, two men, a house. Nikos laughs and claps again, and my sister laughs with him, takes another step closer to the edge.

"Dimitra," I whisper, then scream it. "*Dimitra*!"

It rushes closer, and closer still. The wave is all but upon us now. I charge towards Dimitra, but she pushes me back; my feet skid on wet stone.

"Goodbye, sister," she says, as the monstrous wave towers, crests…Am I imagining it? It *reaches* for them. Arcs over them, like a tunnel. And when the water clears, they're....

Gone.

I stare, dazed and slack-jawed. I don't know what I'm supposed to think; to feel.

Gone. How is this possible? Were her words madness…or truth?

Something dangles in my hand. The broken Shroud. She must have pushed it into my hand when she shoved me away.

I run towards the spot where she stood, but before I can get closer to the edge a firm arm grabs me and pulls me back. I slide on the wet ground; Eros steadies me, fastening me in place.

"You saw it?" I murmur, and I feel his nod.

"She said—she said there was a god," I manage. "She said a god would rescue them."

"Perhaps it is so," Eros says. His voice is grave. "The gods wear many faces."

I breathe out, still unable to tear my eyes from the spot where she vanished. Rescued…or drowned? A pulse beats behind my eyes, but no tears come.

Eros's hand is warm against my arm. The air, too, is warm. Smelling of fire, of molten earth. Of death.

"We must go, Psyche. It is time."

*

The dirge songs echo up to us from below, a ring of rebel men around the body of their queen. Phylax Thais does not join them. She stands alone at the prow of the ship, still as a wooden carving. Only her pale hair moves in the breeze.

They will wait to bury Nereia's body in their new home. They have the gold to pay for a great funeral there, one befitting a leader of men. It will take but a small fraction of what they carry: thanks to Nereia's forethought they will be rich refugees after all, and therefore more welcome than most.

We did not wait to watch Atlantis sink. I picture its lush hills and fields, its green pastures, slipping from view beneath the waves. Will it sink all the way to the sea floor, to join the deepest-swimming nymphs of Poseidon's kingdom? Or wait beneath the water's surface, its spires ready to graze the unsuspecting hull of some future vessel? Perhaps it will rise again someday. Eros says that, if man's memory was longer, we would have seen many islands rise and sink and rise again. Nothing lasts forever, he says. No state is permanent.

None except death.

I think of my father's soul, journeying on its new path to Hades' realm. Will he meet my mother there?

My eyes sting. *An unrepayable sacrifice*. The truth is, I had not thought my father such a brave man—not brave enough to fight a king. And yet he was brave enough to die. Without hesitation, without question. For me.

His eyes, that last look he gave me. It will haunt me forever.

I came to Atlantis to find my family—and here is my result. My father, lost to a king's bullet, my sister, a god-killer, swallowed by the sea. Found, only to be lost—more deeply, more irreversibly, than ever before.

"It was not your fault, Psyche." Eros's voice pulls me back. "None of it was your fault."

Wasn't it? I'm not so sure. I keep my eyes from his, looking down instead at the ship below us—Eros has made a high perch for us, coaxing the wood of the tallest masthead to bloom, budding into a little nest from where he may look out over the whole fleet.

The ships are bound for the isle of Naxos, now, or wherever else will take them in.

"We cannot stay with them, you know," Eros says, and this time, I turn. He is far from the men's gazes here and so his hood is down, his shining face exposed to the heavens. His eyes are sad, a mirror to mine.

I look at him.

"What do you mean?"

His mouth tightens. "We put them at risk, the longer we journey with them. Thais, Theron, Drusa—all of them."

A dark, creeping feeling moves in my stomach. What little family I had, I have lost. And now the few friends we made—we are to leave them, too. And yet once the words are said, I know he is right.

"It was not you or I who killed him," I can't help protesting. "Your brother's death was not our doing."

Eros fixes me with that somber gaze. My words hang in the air, hollow and foolish.

"To the Olympians, Psyche, the death of a god is something unspeakable. They will not, cannot, let it rest." He looks at me. "I fear there will be a gods-trial. They will sentence me; perhaps both of us."

I shiver. The broken Shroud is still in my hand; I turn it

over in my palm, over and over like a worry-stone. I have an urge to fling it out onto these waves, to watch it disappear into the blue. To call upon the gods as insolently as my sister did; to make them serve up their justice here and now, and let them speak it to my face.

The stone of the Shroud grows hot in my hand.

The blood debt must be paid.

The words tumble into my mind unbidden. The stone burns; I almost drop it.

"Psyche?" Eros looks at me, his hand closing over mine. "What is it?"

"I..." I turn the stone over. It's normal, cool, entirely as it was before. Perhaps this time, it really *was* just my imagination. After all I have seen today, who would not be haunted?

I shake my head. Eros takes the stone from my palm, knots the leather thong together where it snapped, and slides it over my head once more.

So, the Atlanteans are bound for Naxos—but we must hide elsewhere. I take a steadying breath.

"And what of your father? You do not think even Ares will defend us?"

Eros looks at me with his golden eyes.

"Phobos was his first-born. He fought at my father's right hand."

Clouds move fast across the dome of the sky. I watch them for a minute, envying them their sure path through the heavens. They know where they are bound, much more surely than we.

"Before," Eros says slowly, "I was seeking my father in hopes that he would champion my cause. *Our* cause. I thought he could help restore my strength, my standing among the gods. That hope is gone now. And perhaps—" he pauses. "Perhaps it was always the wrong one." He looks at me.

"I can give it up, Psyche. My god-strength, my powers. I *will* give it up, let it sink away. I won't complain any more about living like a mortal. We can make a quiet life for ourselves somewhere, without gods or kings. In the mountains, perhaps.

No one will know what we once were."

I look out toward that distant indigo ribbon, where the sky meets the sea. Imagine if such a thing were possible. The two of us, living a simple life, uninterrupted and untroubled, in harmony with the trees and the earth and the seasons.

Yet somehow, I don't think the Fates will let us.

"Before the wave swallowed her…" I hesitate. "My sister said something. She told me she had lain with a god; that Nikos was not the king's child, but a god's." I turn around. "One more powerful than you."

Eros frowns.

"It is possible. The gods wear many faces."

I think of Irini's words. The palace rumors. How quickly Nikos seemed to grow; the strength in his small fists that an infant ought not to have. And that wave…it did *look* as though, somehow, he had called it forth. Although perhaps that is just what I want to believe. Better he and my sister be taken by a god, than dead.

"And if he really is…what my sister claims?"

Eros looks at me.

"Then he must hope to find favor with the god who sired him. It may go ill for him, or well."

I'm silent again. There are thoughts I fear to speak aloud, and yet they have been fomenting in my mind too long now. The dream—no, *vision,* for it was no simple dream. The words my mother spoke. I clear my throat, and tell it all to Eros. How there was someone else who could tell me who I really was; someone I hadn't met yet.

"She said," I swallow, "that my father was not my blood. That there was another one who sired me."

The words fall like stones. Now they are spoken, they take on more reality. I feel a pang of regret. I should have kept them inside me, after all. I should not have let them out into the world.

"She said," I murmur, despite myself, "she said he wore many faces."

The same thing Eros said just now. *The gods wear many*

faces.

Eros holds my eyes. They are steady, watching me. There is infinite patience there, as he waits for me to find the truth, to say the words.

I stare into those eyes, the eyes that no ordinary mortal can see without losing their senses. *Yet I am different.* I always have been.

"Don't you know it yet, Psyche? Don't you know what you are?"

He's right. I do know, although I don't know how. The knowledge asks more than it answers, and the questions chill my blood.

I am what my nephew is. Born half-mortal and half…something else.

"But how? *Who…*"

"I don't know how," Eros says, his voice gentle. "It is a question for another day."

He pulls me closer. I shiver. He knows it as well as I do: the story isn't over yet. Gods and kings will rise and fall, will war and die, before our fate is through. But until then…

"The world is a very wide place," Eros says, observing the direction of my gaze. I tear my eyes from the horizon, from the mysteries I can't begin to fathom.

"Does it look wide to you, too?"

I would have thought this world small to him, though it is big for us mortals, just as mortal time shrinks to nothing through his lens. I lean into his warmth; it's cold up here, where the sea-winds meet. Across the water I see ships. A flag—is that the flag of Naxos, already?—beating in the wind.

If so, we cannot linger.

A great horn sounds across the waves. I take a breath.

Debts must be paid. Scores settled, sins accounted. All stories must have their endings. And ours will, in time. But until then…

Until then, life is for the living, be they gods or men.

And the world is a very wide place.

A letter from the author

Dear Readers,

I so hope you enjoyed *The Bride of Atlantis*!

I assume if you're reading this book, that means you've already read the first book in the series, *The Ruin of Eros.* It means a lot that you liked it enough to keep exploring this story with me, and continuing the journey alongside Psyche and Eros and their friends (and enemies…!).

I knew almost as soon as I began thinking about this story that I wanted to set it on Atlantis. Like so many people, I find the idea of a lost, undersea island totally enthralling, particularly the way myths tell of it as a "perfect" place. I think it ties into the idea so many cultures have of a "Paradise Lost" - a magical land from before where everything was harmonious. But I really wanted to experiment with an Atlantis that *wasn't* perfect - in fact, this Atlantis is quite the opposite. Just as people can wear masks, seeming to be approachable and friendly even when they have hostile intentions, so can places. I really enjoyed exploring the idea of a dystopian Atlantis with a tyrannical ruler, and unveiling little bits of that dystopia bit by bit. It also helped me explore some ideas around "justice", which is a big theme of the book - justice of the gods, justice among mortals, and so on. I'd love to know if those questions resonated for you.

Where *The Ruin of Eros* was more or less a re-telling of the ancient Psyche and Eros myth (though admittedly with some big departures), *The Bride of Atlantis* doesn't have any ancestors in traditional Greek mythology. It came about because of all the fascinating bits of lore that I wanted to keep writing about (like the adamantine knife, for example) and because I wanted to spend more time with these characters. It meant a lot to me to be able to continue with these people that I'd begun getting to know in *The Ruin of Eros,* and I learned so much about them by getting the opportunity to spend another book with them. It made me care for them more, and made it harder, too, to say goodbye to some of them.

I love stories about sisters (even though I don't have any!) and am always fascinated by the complex relationships there. I'd love to know what you thought of Dimitra. Did you like her? Did you hate her? Personally, she's my favorite antihero in the series!

Of course, I also needed to see what happened to Psyche and Eros after they ride off "into the sunset" in Book One. The first book was so much about their relationship coming together, but just because they're a couple now, doesn't mean their relationship has no speedbumps. That's part of what I wanted to explore in Book Two - what happens as a relationship matures, and two partners start to deal with having different priorities, different needs?

In *The Bride of Atlantis,* Eros is suffering from failing health and strength, as well as a loss of his former role and status. He feels humiliated, desperate to get back what he's lost, and doesn't know how to accept his new vulnerability. Even though the situation is a fantasy one, I bet a lot of us can relate to this dynamic in a relationship. Maybe we've been the one, like Eros, who lost something important to us. Or maybe, like Psyche, we've struggled in a relationship where a partner was suffering from physical or mental health issues, or a job loss or other blows to their career or ambition.

In *The Ruin of Eros,* Psyche and Eros built their relationship alone together, set apart from the rest of the world. But in *The Bride of Atlantis,* the rest of the world comes flooding in. Suddenly there are other people involved in their relationship, and Psyche finds herself looking at Eros with new eyes. This, too, brings its own baggage. What about when other people get inside your head, and maybe cause you to see your relationship differently? (For better *and* for worse?) Even though I loved writing the breathless love/hate courtship of those early days, part of me was even more interested to see how Psyche and Eros would make it through those kinds of "real life" pressures once their relationship is up and running. What happens when your trust in a partner gets shaken, and how do you find your way back? I hope you enjoyed watching Eros and Psyche grow and develop during these challenging times, too.

I really hope you liked *The Bride of Atlantis*, and I would love to hear what you think! Please feel free to reach out—it's a wonderful thing to hear from readers. And maybe we'll get to connect again in the final installment of the story, *The Reign of Olympus*!

Again, thank you: I really appreciate the time you have given to reading this book—I know you have a *lot* to choose from—and I want to make sure you know how grateful I am!

MG

Acknowledgments

Thanks again to my wonderful family: my mum and dad, Anne Anderson and Martin Wheeler, and to Frank Lowe and Manuel Dudli Bertran; and to my husband Pavol Roskovensky. You are the very best, and a constant source of self-belief, inspiration and gratitude. Thanks also to my amazing friends, who have been so supportive of my writing endeavors and so generous in always cheering me on. (Including those of you who have never been remotely interested in Greek myth and yet still went to to the trouble of getting a copy!) Thanks to you all, from the bottom of my heart.

www.ingramcontent.com/pod-product-compliance
Lightning Source LLC
Chambersburg PA
CBHW020606310726
48979CB00008B/1370/J

* 9 7 8 1 7 3 7 0 1 8 9 7 1 *